IT'S ALL IN YOUR HEAD

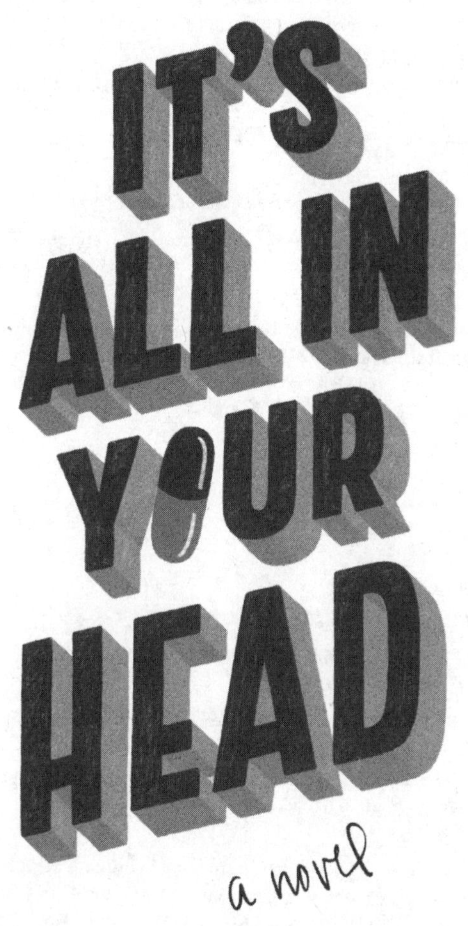

SABINA NORDQVIST

GCP
GRAND
CENTRAL
New York   Boston

Copyright © 2026 by Sabina Nordqvist
Reading group guide copyright © 2026 by Sabina Nordqvist and Hachette Book Group, Inc.

Cover design by Liz Connor
Cover title art © 2026 Lauren Hom
Cover copyright © 2026 by Hachette Book Group, Inc.

Grand Central Publishing
Hachette Book Group
1290 Avenue of the Americas, New York, NY 10104
grandcentralpublishing.com
@grandcentralpub

First Edition: February 2026

Grand Central Publishing is a division of Hachette Book Group, Inc. The Grand Central Publishing name and logo is a registered trademark of Hachette Book Group, Inc.

The publisher is not responsible for websites (or their content) that are not owned by the publisher.

The Hachette Speakers Bureau provides a wide range of authors for speaking events. To find out more, go to hachettespeakersbureau.com or email HachetteSpeakers@hbgusa.com.

Grand Central Publishing books may be purchased in bulk for business, educational, or promotional use. For information, please contact your local bookseller or the Hachette Book Group Special Markets Department at special.markets@hbgusa.com.

Print book interior design by Taylor Navis

Library of Congress Cataloging-in-Publication Data

Names: Nordqvist, Sabina author
Title: It's all in your head : a novel / Sabina Nordqvist.
Description: First edition. | New York : Grand Central Publishing, 2026.
Identifiers: LCCN 2025038128 | ISBN 9781538771570 trade paperback | ISBN 9781538771587 ebook
Subjects: LCSH: Romance fiction | LCGFT: Novels | Fiction
Classification: LCC PS3614.O7336 I87 2026
LC record available at https://lccn.loc.gov/2025038128

ISBN: 9781538771570 (trade paperback), 9781538771587 (ebook)

Printed in the United States of America

LSC-C

Printing 1, 2025

*For the incredible friends I've made online, the virtual spaces
that became my lifeline, and the vibrant disability community
that shows up for one another day after day.*

*And for my IIH support group. There isn't a day I don't wish for
all of us to have less pain, more answers, and the care we deserve.*

Author's Note

Dear Reader,

Thank you for picking up *It's All in Your Head*. While this is a romance novel filled with beloved tropes and a happily ever after, it is also a narrative that refuses to treat disability as an afterthought. The title comes from a phrase that people living with chronic pain hear all too often when their symptoms are dismissed. The truth is, not everyone has ideal pain management, supportive doctors, or families who truly understand. For a lot of us, support groups are the only place where we can speak openly about our experiences and receive validation, insight, and help.

In this novel, you'll encounter characters navigating chronic pain within the US healthcare system and facing systemic ableism. Some content may be triggering to readers sensitive to these topics, which are listed below for reference. While the narrative doesn't shy away from the tough realities many disabled people face, it also unapologetically calls out ableism and microaggressions toward our community.

Although I've done my best to accurately portray these characters' struggles with chronic illness and long-term pain, many of them drawn from my own lived experience, this remains a work of fiction and is not intended as medical advice or a one-size-fits-all depiction. Every individual's experience with disability is unique; even with the same diagnosis, no two people face identical challenges in severity, pain, or treatment. The medical details in this story, including surgical interventions and outpatient procedures, are not endorsements. The narrative also doesn't attempt to address every systemic issue disabled people face. While COVID-19 remains a serious and ongoing concern for our community, *It's All in Your Head* takes place in a world where COVID-19 is not a factor.

At its heart, this book is a love letter to online Spoonie friendships and the support of the disability community, acknowledging the care, resilience, and connection that sustain us. If chronic pain or illness has upended your life, I hope you'll hold on to the possibility of your own happy ending. Joy, romance, and belonging are not out of reach just because we are ill or disabled. We do not need to be cured or inspirational to find love, in whatever form it takes.

Thank you for joining these characters on their journey, and I hope something in this story makes you feel seen.

With love,
Sabina

Content Warning

This work contains medical trauma (including medical gaslighting, pain, side effects of medications, trauma responses to seeking emergency care, and medication rationing); on-page lumbar puncture; BMI weaponization and fatphobia from a medical professional; emotional, physical, and psychological struggles following a life-altering accident; online harassment (trolling) with ableist and threatening language; ableist commentary; conversations about forced psychiatric care; toxic relationships between disabled adults and nondisabled parents; ableist language in the context of unlearning ableism; discussions of parental abandonment; mentions of parenting struggles within the disability community; on-page sexual content; and a minor, single-vehicle car accident with no injuries.

1

Skylar

There's nothing like a notification from the hot guy in your support group to make you momentarily forget how miserable you are. I refresh the page, half-sure my painsomnia has reached a level of making me hallucinate. But it's still there.

Pike replied to your post.

I switch my cooling lavender compress from the left side of my face to my right and adjust the heat pack under my neck. It doesn't take away the feeling that invisible brain fingers are trying to pop my eyeballs out of their sockets, but it makes squinting at my phone through one eye more tolerable. Since I've come out of remission with my idiopathic intracranial hypertension, hanging out in my online chronic pain support group is the only thing that gets me through unbearable nights like this.

I click on my latest post.

Skylar King: Anyone else's champagne tonight electrolyte water? Their party hat a pillow? *gestures around in exhaustion* Can't wait for the holidays to be over.

There are a host of commiserating replies. Members who are looking forward to tonight's hangout. And now, Pike.

Pike: Couldn't have said it better myself.

I screenshot and jump into my private chat with Analia and Emy, my best friends and fellow group members.

Yes, it's a generic reply, I write. **Anyone could've said it. But the fact that it's *Pike* makes me want to squeal.**

ahh! Emy sends thirsty GIFs. **it says he's online too! welcome to late night with the ladies, sir!**

I laugh into my heat pack, the smell of stale rice making my nose wrinkle, then check the member list. There are 1,179 of us; right now, 77 are online. And Pike—no last name, no emojis—is one of them. I'm always online at night, and I've never seen Pike in the group past 10:00 p.m. He's probably a functioning adult, not a twenty-six-year-old with a parasympathetic system that makes her body think it's awake when it's supposed to be asleep (among my other great qualities).

Analia sends a wink. **Someone still has a crush on a profile picture.**

I reply with a heart. **He's online on New Year's Eve! Makes me like him even more.**

maybe he's joining the party, Emy says.

As a group admin, I host virtual hangouts for people like me who don't have supportive friends or family outside the group. Tonight, we're supposed to be watching the ball drop together, but I can't handle all the flashing lights. The only part of me ringing in the New Year is my tinnitus.

I enter the hangout room. At least ten others join in succession. Did they notice Pike come on and also want the chance to chat with him before anyone else? All it takes is one hot man joining your support group for grown-ass women to regress into middle school girls.

For the record, I noticed him first.

When he joined three months ago, it was his picture that caught my attention. Side profile. Pensive in front of a mountain peak. Muscular build. A bit too *I know I'm hot.* With a brush cut, sharp jaw, and a hint of scruff just a shade darker than his rich brown hair, it was hard not to take a second look.

Or a twentieth.

After all, I'm the admin who approved his request. All we require for membership is that either you or a loved one have chronic pain, are over the age of eighteen, live in Rochester, and promise to abide by all group rules. Some applicants give us essays on their diagnoses. Pike just answered *yes* to every question, so I didn't learn anything else about him.

Nope, I say. **He hasn't joined.**

Emy sends a detective emoji. **lost: mysterious sexy man we're dying to meet.**

I grin. **If found, please return him to my DMs.**

The thing about Pike is, he lurks. He rarely replies to anyone beyond offering a stray like. I get it. A lot of people in support groups lurk, overwhelmed by the plethora of knowledge and the number of different health conditions represented.

Pike has only ever posted four times.

First, an intro—common for new members: Hi, thanks for letting me join. Hope everyone is having a low-pain day. Not much to go off, pretty generic. He got a whopping 257 likes.

Second, a mobility aid question: Any suggestions for canes that work in the snow? What are your favorite models?

Unless he was Christmas shopping, the man uses a cane for something.

Then, the most interesting one: For those with visible disabilities, are people constantly asking if you can still have sex?

The answer is, yes, of course, everyone is a nosy fuck when it comes to disabilities, especially if it relates to our sex lives, so he might be more recently disabled.

And lastly: Is it okay to have a beer every once in a while with oxy? Just one. Special occasion.

I spent a night fantasizing about what his special occasion might be. If there was a special someone. Maybe someone asked him about his junk again and he finally told them, *Yes, I can still give you the best orgasm of your life.*

I've commented on his posts, but this is the first time he's interacted with me.

I drop a few replies in the hangout to show I'm around, but a part of me hopes he won't join. Not tonight. Being online is such a double-edged sword. I love talking to my friends, but it also hurts to look at screens when my cerebrospinal fluid pressure is skyrocketing, the way it is now from my IIH.

The base of my skull burns, so I reluctantly shuffle out of bed to switch out the compress for my ice hat. Every step feels like a plane roaring off the runway that wants to jerk me back into my seat. I grab a sip of water too. It doesn't help the tingling in the left side of my upper lip.

My fault for waiting until winter break to start my meds. I've spent the holidays stumbling around banging into random walls and gasping for air while I get re-accustomed to my meds. But I'd rather waste my uneventful break than take sick leave.

That gives me another two weeks to adjust to the many side effects of the pills meant to lower my intracranial pressure. Among them, the torturous zapping that's overtaken my fingers and face. People with my condition don't call this medication the devil's Tic Tacs for nothing.

Luckily, it's not fair season at work yet. But it's coming. I need to be more stable by then—both with my condition and the medicinal side effects—so I can safely drive and stand up all day without passing out.

My muddled mind goes back to Pike when I lie down again. **I'll like his comment but not engage. It's not like anything would come of it. Besides, if there's anything I've learned, it's men are always better admired from afar.**

So true, Analia says. Another client from work sent me a DM today asking if I'd give him a massage with a "happy ending." Still vomiting in my mouth a little.

Eww, I write. **That's so inappropriate.**

Sometimes I want to write ASEXUAL on my forehead so everyone will leave me alone. Maybe they won't even talk during their session.

i worry that'll make some of them see it as a challenge, Emy says. **better to report.**

Wait, Analia says. **Pike posted!?**

I scramble back into the group hangout. There's nothing from him there, thankfully, because I'd struggle to keep up with the constant moving text.

Pike's not even online anymore. I head to the discussion forum. And there it is.

A new post from Pike.

> "Write down what you're grateful for"
> Well, if you insist:
> I'm grateful for
> no longer holding myself
> to your toxic standards of positivity
> that have never touched
> the type of pain I feel
> or the loss I've had to overcome

Well, hello, Mr. Deep Dark Soul. Hot cane boy is a *poet.* And a salty one at that.

My ridiculous crush on a profile picture grows exponentially as I keep reading. There's a rawness to his words that leaves me feeling less alone. It's exactly what I wish I could tell my mom. If I were brave, I'd print it out and mail it to her.

Pike vents for a good page and a half. His vulnerability fascinates me. It's heart-wrenching and honest, with a lot of snow metaphors that go over my head, but the ending is simple.

No show and tell
I play hide and seek
but all that's left to find
is pain

By the time I'm done reading, I've missed the midnight ball drop, but I couldn't care less. His post already has fifteen hearts and four comments.

I click to expand the first one. A comment from Pike himself: Just writing out some vents. Thanks for reading.

Aw, he's polite too.

Second comment. **GinaB:** Needed this. Please write more!!

Third comment. **Laurie Durnam:** Brandon? It's your mom. This is very sad and alarming and I need to know you're all right. Please answer your phone.

I nearly choke. What's his mom doing in here!? Besides the fact that he's a full-blown *adult*, there's private messages for this sort of thing. He said he was venting. And beautifully, at that!

I check the timestamp. She replied one minute after Pike. Her screen probably didn't refresh in time to catch his comment. I cringe. He's going to be mortified.

Not his mom, Analia says. **Also, *Brandon*?**

I head back to the forum. Laurie Durnam posts another comment.

I'm calling, Brandon. Why aren't you answering?

Maybe he's not answering because he posted his poem and went to bed? Why can't she read the other comments and see how deeply everyone is relating? We understand how battered your heart becomes from fighting your body every day.

Soon there's a third plea. Brandon, if you don't answer your phone in the next five minutes, I'm going to call the police.

What the hell? We have protocols when people are suicidal, but that's not the case here.

Should I message her? I ask the girls. The other admins aren't on to confer with.

based on this interaction, Emy says, **i doubt his mom even knows how to check a DM. probably better not to do anything.**

Maybe I'm spurred on by a lifetime of my own parents misunderstanding everything I say, but I feel like I need to intervene.

I write, **I've seen horror stories in this group about disabled people who were forced into emergency psychiatric care. And doesn't he take oxycodone?**

Oh, yeah, Analia says. **They confiscate your meds. Isolate you. Forced psych treatment is super traumatizing.**

Analia would know. She's been through all kinds of psychiatric care.

good point. Emy sends a thinking emoji.

Pike was venting. An adult who vents in an online support group doesn't need family snooping around and making assumptions about what they post.

I'll tag her in one of the comments, I say. **She'll get a notification.**

But I don't know what to say besides: Hi **@LaurieDurnam**! Sending you a message about Brandon.

A message from her pops into my notifications after another minute. She's not *that* technologically challenged, after all. **Hello? Is he okay? What's happening?**

I type as fast as my medication-muddled fingers will let me, my thumbs slipping unevenly on my phone. **Hi, Laurie! I'm an admin. Brandon was just venting. If you scroll up, you'll see his comment. He's fine.**

A minute passes. **I know my son. He's never like this.**

It's a poem in a support group. We encourage creativity (and venting).

Something's wrong, she says. **There was suicidal ideation in that poem.**

My eyebrows shoot up. I scroll back through Pike's words. There's grief, but that's not the same thing.

I can see my own mother misinterpreting something I find cathartic as suicidal and further screwing up my life because I'm not "positive" the way she thinks I should be.

I send Pike a message. **Hi there. Bit of a situation with your mom, if you're on/invisible, could you please respond ASAP?**

Please be invisible, Pike. Please log back on.

He does not log back on.

I appreciate the "admin" help, Laurie writes, **but I'm going to call the police. If he's this depressed, he needs help.**

Wait! I type frantically. This is going to ruin Pike's New Year— his year *period*.

Just dissuade Laurie from calling the cops, Analia says, and Emy agrees. Of the three of us, Analia's the rational one who thinks things through. Emy is spontaneous, while I'm always ready to take charge. If they both think I should do something...

How?? I ask.

Don't you have his email as an admin? Analia says.

I look it up. A bunch of numbers. Probably fake. I email it any-way, then go back to the girls. **What if I say he's with me?**

She'll want to talk to him, Analia says.

say he accidentally got drunk married, Emy suggests. **she'll be so relieved tomorrow it's fake that she'll forget all about the poem.**

Spontaneous indeed. **How would I even know he got married?**

Emy sends another thirsty GIF. **u were the bride.**

He's so depressed after marrying me that he wrote a "suicidal" poem?? I can picture Analia and Emy laughing, but I go back to my chat with Laurie and write, **I'm pretty sure he's fine because...** I glance at my chat with the girls. Marriage seems a bit *too* fake, but...**I'm pretty sure he's fine because he's sleeping right next to**

me. My pulsatile tinnitus whooshes to the same tempo as my erratic heart rate. If I'm going to sell this, I need to commit. **I didn't want to say anything earlier because it's new and I'm guessing he didn't tell you yet. Sorry you were worried. I feel bad waking him up.**

I press send and hold my breath. Will she buy it? I send a screenshot to the girls.

WHAT DID YOU JUST DO. Analia is freaking out, but frankly, so am I. **DID YOU EVEN CHECK THAT HE'S SINGLE?**

"Fuck." I flip onto my elbows so my phone will stop falling on my face. **She wrote me back!** I open the message, my heart somersaulting, and skim. **I'm guessing he *doesn't* have a partner,** I report, **because his mom really wants to meet me!?** I keep reading. **She's buying it? She says she feels bad for worrying but this isn't like him and when can I come over for dinner?**

What are you going to say? Analia asks.

I pause. I have no idea.

Pike still hasn't responded to me. I google *Brandon Durnam*, and when that turns up nothing, I try *Pike Durnam*. I quick search his name with *Sutherland, Fairport, Webster Schroeder,* and other local high schools in case he grew up around Rochester. Nothing. *Brandon Pike* is a last-ditch effort, and when some Olympic athlete clogs the results, I groan and give up.

After eleven minutes, his mom writes me again. **Hello?**

She can see I read her message. I *hate* that feature.

~~Hi again, let me talk to Pike.~~ I delete that. ~~My relationship with Brandon is really new so I'll let him make that call.~~ No. Shit. How can I make this vague enough? **You should talk to Brandon. We're pretty new! Happy New Year!**

I send the message.

Then I screenshot the entire conversation and send it to Pike.

2

Skylar

Since pain won't let me sleep, I'm caught up on most of my admin duties by morning, from deleting buy links to reviewing the membership requests assigned to me. The sheer number of people who have joined in the last four years is overwhelming. But every newcomer reminds me that even if some of these tasks feel tedious, someone will appreciate this work when they're at their loneliest and saddest hour.

I've been there. When I first realized that most people couldn't handle me talking about my pain, it damn near killed me. There's no dagger to the heart like opening up to a loved one only to discover that your life is a little too inconvenient and sad (read: disabled) for them. I quickly joined a national support group for IIH.

But after attending a chronic pain retreat in Rochester, I wanted to be part of something smaller—something more than a Q&A forum. But it had to be online because in-person events drained too much energy. So I created this group with three women I met at the retreat.

I hoped we'd become friends, but our personalities never really meshed. Still, the group helps me cope emotionally with chronic pain. It gives me a community, a safe space to vent, and a place to share knowledge and lived experiences. Doctors tend to bristle when we bring in our own research, but patients know their conditions best. For many of us, support groups are the only way to find answers.

Every time I accept a new member, I feel like I'm paying it forward. Someone else no longer has to be completely isolated because they can virtually attend our movie nights or moderated discussions from their beds or preferred pain spots. As a bonus, I met Emy and Analia.

Pike has sent you a message.

I sit up so fast that black sparkles temporarily take over my vision. Once I can see again, I shake out my tingly hands. **He wrote me!!**

It's only ten, but Analia responds with a popcorn-eating GIF. **WHAT DID HE SAY**

I open Pike's message and cringe.

What the hell???

My pulsatile tinnitus whooshes louder and faster. Okay, okay. I expected him to be mad.

How does it even cross your mind to pretend to be a random dude's girlfriend?? To his MOM??

…But not this mad.

I'm sorry! She was going to call the cops!

Pike is typing pops up for so long that I turn on a rerun of *The Price Is Right*. I can't watch because of my eyes, but Bob Barker's voice is soothing in the background.

It has to be the worst-case scenario if he's typing this much. **If you already have a boyfriend/girlfriend,** I write, **I will totally call whoever and vouch for you.**

No girlfriend. But.

I wait. And wait. And wait.

She's already left me a dozen messages. She wants to meet you!

My thumbs pause. **I said our relationship is new.**

Yeah, thanks for that. Not.

Pike is typing. Good grief.

I haven't had a serious girlfriend…ever? I always told my mom the day I did, she'd be the first to know. Now she's not only

wondering if I'm suicidal but also why I didn't tell her about my new relationship. You said I was at your house, Skylar. Sleeping. Fucking. Over. Now I can't even pretend it's a casual fling like always.

My eyes narrow at our break in polite conversation. I copy everything over to Analia. **HOT CANE BOY IS A PLAYER.**

Not necessarily, she says. **You prefer casual flings.**

That's different, but Pike sends another message.

I don't need this bullshit. Not here. I'm reporting you to the admins for harassment.

I let out something between a gasp and a protest and almost swallow my cotton tongue in the process. **It's not harassment. I know the rules. I *am* an admin.**

Well, there's another one, he says. **Maria. We talk. Good thing you sent me a screenshot of your lies.**

My face flushes with a rush of irrational jealousy. Figures he'd talk to Maria. She's the prettiest admin and the most outgoing, the one everyone gravitates toward.

Oh shit, what if Maria also tells Tess and Adiba, the other two admins? My chest tightens unbearably. Pretending to be someone's girlfriend isn't against any rule, because who in their right mind thinks of doing that? No one, that's who. I'm not in my right mind, though. My brain is being squished. Surely that qualifies me for some leniency. But even in my panic, I don't want to use my disability as a shield. That's not why I helped him.

Analia's sent me about twenty messages, but I'm afraid to leave my chat with Pike. He might already be writing Maria.

Hear me out for two seconds, I plead. **I was trying to help. Your mom thought you were suicidal.**

That doesn't mean you pretend to be my girlfriend!

You're rgiht, I say, typing so fast I don't care about typos. **I messed up! I hvae family taht doesnt understand my chronic pain. I thoght yours was the same. I loved your poem! I'm rly sorry!!**

Pike is typing.

Note to self: Never engage with a hot profile picture again.

I had no idea my mom was even in this group, he says. **How the hell did that happen, admin?**

Let me check. I go to Laurie's profile. Adiba accepted her, so I pull up her application responses. I don't have chronic pain, but my son does. I want to learn.

We allow caregivers and loved ones, I say. **Her answers seem like she has a little kid. Usually that's why moms want to learn.**

I'm 27. There should be rules against parents joining without the consent of their ADULT children.

My neck throbs from holding the same position too long. I shove at my makeshift pillow throne and drop back against it, but my head still feels like it weighs a thousand pounds. **I fully support that!** I write. **I can look into changing those rules. Parents/partners could identify their loved one in the group and get permission? Either way, I'll remove your mom now.**

Wait. Don't remove her. Not yet. She'll worry even more.

I'm getting the impression this guy is more of a thinker than a slow typer. Maybe he hasn't messaged Maria yet.

I'll remove her when you give the word. Pike starts typing again, but I plow on. **Listen, now that she knows you're okay . . . can't you tell her I made it up?**

No.

Is she so horrible/ableist that there's no way you could explain why I stepped in?

Pike sends me a damn essay.

My mom isn't horrible. She cares a lot. But she's having trouble accepting my new disabilities. I can't open up to her about how I'm really feeling. I try to be positive and put any negative thoughts into my writing instead. Sometimes things are dark, but it's not because I want to die. I just need to get out the heavy, which my

mom's not ready for. Now—because of your interference—she sees an alternative to the depressing image she has of her disabled son. I have a girlfriend. Things must not be as bad as she imagines. I can still have the "normal" life she wants for me.

Ugh. He just had to pull on my heartstrings. And use em dashes in a chat.

You can still have a "normal" life while disabled! I say, but I get what he means. My parents haven't accepted my disabilities, either, and it's been five years. I didn't even bother telling them I went into remission for seven months. They don't understand that IIH is life-long, that remission isn't a cure but a temporary abatement of symptoms. And now it's back. Like I knew it would be but dared to hope it wouldn't.

I'll talk to Maria, Pike says. **This shouldn't happen in a group like this. Especially from an admin!**

I type a few words so it looks like I'm responding, then message Analia. **What should I do?**

Emy has entered the chat.

1) can't talk long because we're making pasta 2) this guy is an ungrateful mofo who should feel lucky u stepped in 3) u should meet his mom.

That'll make her seem like a stalker, Analia says.

no, meet his mom *with* him

I blink. **What.**

Log off, Skylar, Analia says. **He clearly doesn't appreciate what you did for him.**

He threatened to tell the other admins!

meet his mom, Emy insists. **pretend ur his gf for a day.**

He could be a serial killer, Analia says.

meet in a public place! is it bad i think u should suggest it simply because he's hot? She's obviously already forgotten that he's an ungrateful mofo.

I don't know what to do. I understand why he's uncomfortable. He might even leave the group. We're striving to be inclusive—a guy's perspective is rare.

And this group is my lifeline. I spend most of my evenings here. It's the only place I can truly be myself.

I won't allow anyone to threaten it.

What if I met your mom? I ask Pike.

Are you drunk?

Hear me out. You don't want your mom's ableist fantasies shattered. I would like to make up for putting you in a tough situation. So how about we pretend we're together? I'll make you look awesome so she'll stop hovering.

Pike is typing.

I proposed it, I tell the girls.

Analia calms down first. **I'll sit in my car with sunglasses while you're with him if necessary.**

i will bring my sharpest knitting needles, Emy says.

I love you guys, I say with sobbing emojis. We've never even met in person, but they have my back more than anyone I've known in real life.

I head back to Pike's latest message. The phone feels too bright now, and each new word stabs at my already aching eyes.

It's not the worst idea. But if you don't want me to talk to the other admins, we'll need to do this for at least two months. Having a "serious" girlfriend for only one day won't keep my mom off my back. And you and I will meet first because I'm a little creeped out by you, not gonna lie.

I'm screaming by the time I'm done reading.

You're creeped out by *me*? Read what you just wrote, buddy. You want me to date you for *two months*!

I don't want to date you. But you need to do this more than one time so I don't have to pay a random redhead to be "Skylar King."

I perk up a little. **Ooh, there's money involved?**

No! It was your idea!

two months with this broody hot poet? Emy sends eggplant emojis. **can *i* pretend to be skylar king?**

Ugh, go back to your pasta, I say, wishing I also had a family to cook with me.

Hello? Pike writes. **Don't leave me hanging, Skylar. You owe me.**

I glare at my screen. **I'm trying to be nice here, but let me be crystal clear. I don't owe you anything. You can't make me do anything.**

You're right, he says. **It's just—argh.** Argh? Another em dash? Is this guy for real? **All I want is to erase the part of my life where my mom read the most vulnerable thing I've ever written. But I can't. This is the next best thing. Please.**

What?? Now he's the one begging?

I said I would meet you. But two months? That's too long!

I've casually dated supermodels for longer than two months, sweetheart.

I rub my tired eyes. **Okay? I know I don't look like a supermodel, but...what does that have to do with anything?** I ask him, then tell the girls: **He told me he dates supermodels??**

if i looked like him, i would too. Emy is a beautiful Italian woman with raven hair straight out of a Pantene Pro-V commercial, so I'm not sure why she thinks she can't. But that's a conversation for another day.

I meant that they're pretty high maintenance, Pike says, **and they still tolerated me. It's not like we'd see each other every day.**

But there's still a problem. **If you date supermodels, your mom will never buy that we're together.**

Why not? You're pretty. I like pretty women.

So, he's shallow. Wait: **He said I'm pretty!?!?**

***SCREECHES* THAT'S BECAUSE U R,** Emy says.

Pike sends a raised eyebrow emoji. **Is this the part where you tell me your profile pic is fake?**

No. That's me.

I can work with that. So, you'll do it?

I hesitate. **I'll agree to meet to discuss details, and then we'll see. My job will be demanding soon, and I've just come out of remission with my neurological disorder. I'm really overwhelmed.**

He makes me wait an agonizing five minutes for a response.

Sorry to hear that. Sure, we can talk about the details when we meet.

And then you won't show our convo to anyone? I ask.

If your performance is satisfactory.

Tears unexpectedly prick my dry eyes. I'm absolutely terrible with parents. I haven't dated anyone in two years. With all my problems, there's no way I'm going to make a good impression.

No worries, I write. **I'll be the best fake girlfriend ever!**

3

Pike

Ignorant parents of kids who ski or snowboard are a pain in my ass. Half my job is wasted explaining why winter sports have value. But I'd rather deal with them than the people who recognize me. Element Ridge has been packed all week with both types of customers thanks to New Year's sales, and I'm spent.

The latest parent, a white man in a North Face fleece, fiddles with the skis I've told him to buy, like handling them long enough will magically make him understand what he's looking at. It won't. "You're sure these are good skis? I don't want my son to be a *Joey*." He waggles his eyebrows at me like we're in a secret club.

He's obviously googled ski slang, which I never encourage anyone to do. But that means he's trying, which is better than many parents, so I suppress an eye roll.

"They're all-mountain skis, so he'll be good for groomed and powder trails. Even moguls." I move on to a wooden rack still decorated with holiday lights. "Get these." I point to the Salomon boots. "Best of the season, marked down thirty percent."

"How do you know about this stuff anyway?" He gestures at my cane.

I smile with rehearsed pleasantry. I get this shit a lot. Back when my injuries were new, I wanted to throw my fame in their faces. Now it's the presumption that gets me. Dude with a cane can't ski, sure, sure. No such thing as adaptive sports.

"Been snowboarding since I was two."

I don't add that I have multiple X Games medals. Or two Olympic gold medals. Or that two years ago, I was once again the top contender for men's halfpipe at the Winter Olympics before I got injured. If his kid's as into freestyle as his dad says, he's probably heard of me.

"Huh." He clears his throat. "Did you have a bad fall or something?"

A fucking yard sale, sir. How's that for slang? "Let's focus on making sure your kid doesn't have one. You'll want a helmet."

I hand him the least expensive of the two we feature. I can't bring myself to promote the other brand. They pulled their sponsorship less than twenty-four hours after my accident. Only place their shit is going during my shift is in the trash.

"He thinks helmets aren't cool."

I pat him on the shoulder. "Concussions are pretty uncool too. Go see Jada for some hats when he's not on the slopes. She knows what teens like."

He trots over there, hands full, and Jada makes a funny face at me behind his back as she models hats over her shoulder-length box braids. Once he's at checkout, she comes over to me, her expression growing shyer. Like most boarding enthusiasts, she freaked out when I started working here.

"Hey, Pike," she says. "I finally nailed my frontside one-eighty."

"Yeah? That's awesome."

"You were right, I needed to focus more on landing with both feet at the same time to absorb the impact better."

"And the pop off your tail?"

"Working on it." She fiddles with the sleeve of her hoodie. "Do you think I could show you the recording sometime this week? It's not that good, obviously, but I really appreciate your tips."

"Sure," I say. "Don't worry so much about skill level. Everyone starts somewhere, and learning tricks is a whole new beast."

She beams. "Thanks!"

I sit on a fitting bench and check my phone. Three messages from Mom. I swipe them away without replying. Some weeks I can be the dutiful son, but this week, it's not happening.

Dad sent me a message too. **Happy New Year, kiddo. How are those legs doing? Could really use your support on this new venture I've developed. Different from the other stuff. I'll send you a brochure.**

Nope. One of my New Year's resolutions is to no longer be his piggy bank. Despite my better judgment, I've been bailing him out for most of my adult life.

An email tells me I still haven't responded to an invite for this year's Shred Awards. That's gotta be the third reminder already, and the season has barely started. This year it'll be in Whistler. My old home. *Delete.*

There's also a message from my best friend, Jax, who I've been avoiding almost as much as my dad. **Crew's all headed to Mammoth next week. Wanna come?**

Grace, another crew member, sent the same question right after Jax, but I don't know what to say to her either. *I'd rather shatter my pelvis again* seems melodramatic.

The last notification reads **12:00 on Saturday for lunch?**

I sit up straighter. So. After dodging my initial attempts to meet up, the elusive Skylar King is finally available.

I click on her profile picture, which says it all: black lashes that go on for days, loose red curls piled over one shoulder, and a smile like she knows she's got you by the balls just looking at her. I've stared at her picture so much, she might as well be my screen saver.

What kind of person pulls something like that? And with my *mom.* I joined a chronic pain support group, not a dating app, for fuck's sake.

Is Skylar a stalker? A snow bunny waiting for an in? I thought things had calmed down since I started ghosting media requests, but a fan *did* pretend to be my sister just so she could get into rehab to meet me. Pretending to be my girlfriend fits the pattern.

I scroll up through our messages, but my eyes keep returning to her picture. She'd look hot in board gear. And with that diamond septum piercing, she'd fit right in.

But Skylar did thwart my mother. She didn't mention my fame. She *seems* remorseful.

I may have reached a new level of desperation in agreeing to meet her. But she has Mom's info. She could say anything to get to me through her if that's her ultimate goal.

If I had the balls, I'd tell Mom the truth. Then demand she stay the hell out of my support group. Instead, I'll smooth this over like a blanket of fresh powder. I can't handle Mom sad anymore.

Brandon, if you don't answer your phone in the next five minutes, I'm going to call the police.

Sometimes I think she's waiting for me to kill myself. I'm learning that's what a lot of people would do if they became disabled, maybe even her. Strangers have actually said as much to my face: *You poor thing. I'd rather be dead.*

I go to swipe my bangs out of my eyes and stop. I can't kick the habit even though I cut them off a few months ago. Too many randos recognized me with my signature brown mop.

My hair's grown out a little, but I still keep it short. With a side view of my brush cut and a five-o'clock shadow in my profile pic, how did Skylar still recognize me?

She's in for a hell of a surprise if she's expecting Brandon Pike.

Brandon Pike is gone. Inside and out.

4

Pike

I sit on a bench by the parking lot in Schoen Place, sweating in my gray work hoodie. Everyone's walking and biking along the Erie Canal since it's randomly fifty degrees in January, which means sunglasses and short sleeves in Rochester.

When a Honda with an Uber decal pulls in and I spot a flash of red hair through the back window, I get to my feet. My palm sweats against my cane like I'm waiting for my prom date. Then there she is, swaggering out like a rock star in huge black shades, long locks blowing in the wind. And of course, *of course*, she just has to be cute in real life too.

Why can't her profile picture have been so heavily filtered that I barely recognize her? Skylar looks like she stepped right out of it, attitude and all, bringing gorgeous curves along with her. She has the kind of thick curls I'd love to run my hands through, which is an unwelcome thought considering the situation. I don't want to be attracted to the woman who upended my life.

At least pretending to be into her won't be hard.

After weeks of her canceling on me due to illness, I'm amazed at how put together she looks now. And shit, it's such an ableist thought. It's as bad as when people tell me I'm too young to use a cane.

I've had to check my thoughts a lot lately, trying not to lean on a lifetime of privilege when it comes to my body. When it comes to everything, really. Male, white, straight...now disabled. My life's been a shit show reality check since the accident. I've had a lot of learning to do, but even more unlearning.

"Pike slash Brandon?" she asks, sauntering up to me.

"Yeah," I say. "Everyone calls me Pike except my family."

She tilts her head, very obviously checking me out from head to toe. Sunlight beats down on her face, highlighting the contrast between her pale complexion and the freckles scattered across her forehead even more. I count them (nineteen) because I don't want her to catch me looking anywhere else. When her gaze finally meets mine again, her lips purse, their deep red color a shade darker than her coppery hair.

"Listen up, bucko," she says, arms crossed and eyebrows arched. "I know you're, like, huge"—she waves a hand vaguely in the direction of my chest—"and probably think you could take me in an altercation. But I have pepper spray. If you try to kidnap me, you'll lose."

She thinks *I'm* a threat? She's the one who slid into my mom's DMs!

But then I catch a glimpse of myself reflected in her oversized sunglasses. I'm towering over her, my expression set in what probably looks like a glare. I'm a big guy at six foot three, and while I've lost some of my muscle, it's obvious I work out. Even though I'm annoyed—she's the one who instigated all this—I get it. Meeting a stranger from the internet, even in public, isn't something most women can afford to take lightly.

I force my shoulders to drop and school my face into something friendlier. "If anyone's pulling off a kidnapping here, I figured it'd be you."

She raises her phone and snaps a picture of me without warning. "Sending this to my girls. You understand."

Yeah, I understand. You want them to see what Brandon Pike looks like now.

"If you take off running, I won't be able to catch you." I hold up my black cane. "Even a brisk walk would allow you to escape."

"Do you think a guy with a cane couldn't be a serial killer?"

"If you've ever seen a superhero movie, there should be no doubt. We're criminal masterminds. The supervillain you *never* saw coming."

"Are you attempting to endear me to you by citing ableist Hollywood stereotypes?" She considers me, hands on her wide hips. "Because it's kind of working."

With that, she spins on her heels and strides toward the Mediterranean restaurant she picked.

I follow her. Bad call. Now I know her ass looks amazing in tight jeans. I focus on the ground so I won't trip over myself. Loose gravel is already bad news for someone unsteady on his feet.

A middle-aged woman beams at me as I approach the restaurant stairs. "You're doing great, sweetie! Don't ever give up!"

I ignore her. Everyone needs to calm the fuck down when they see a disabled person. We're 25 percent of the population, not an endangered species at the zoo. The stares and intrusive comments are even worse when I use my wheelchair.

Skylar thankfully ignores me as I begin my painstakingly slow climb. By the time I reach the top, my legs are shaking so much that every part of me screams to just sink to the ground and never get up again.

At our table, Skylar orders "water, no lemon, no ice" and peruses the menu. Her shades stay on. I looked up *neurological disorders* after talking to Skylar and tried to guess hers. Turns out there are, like, a hundred. She said *remission*, so I was thinking cancer. Brain tumors can cause neurological issues.

But could it be TBI? After my concussion, my eyes hurt like hell. I needed shades for a while. The doctors said I was lucky everything returned to what they called "normal." My eyes, sure. The rest of me? Not so much.

I won't ask about her shades, though. I hate when people ask me about my cane. If I want to share, I will.

"Order whatever you like," I say. "It's on me."

Despite my offer, she only orders a small plate of hummus and pita. "So, Pike Durnam. Tell me about yourself." She pulls a banana out of her purse and leans forward on her elbows, staring at me while she eats it bite by little bite.

"Uh. I'm the assistant manager at Element Ridge. It's a ski and board shop in winter, mountain sports in summer…I'm sorry, what's with the banana?"

"What do you mean?"

I mean it's painting a vivid picture of what she can do with her mouth. "You didn't want more than an appetizer if you're that hungry?"

"My potassium's low."

Right. Next she'll say she's also low on Vitamin D. I've heard it all before.

"I'm avoiding my horse pill."

I blink. "What?"

She pulls out an orange prescription bottle and shows me a pill as thick as her pinkie. "The first one dissolved in my mouth before I could get it down. Threw up a little. Choked on the second one."

"Ohh," I say, startled. "My roommate takes those. They look… fun."

"The pins and needles in my extremities are off the charts. Paresthesia everywhere." She shakes her hands out. "On to business. I've made a three-step plan outlining an alternative to fake dating. Step one: You thank me for saving your ungrateful ass."

"Excuse me?" My eyes narrow.

"Step two: You tell your mom we broke up. Step three: That's it. You're welcome."

"I didn't need you to get involved."

"Are you unhappy you're not currently in forced psych?"

I shift, uncomfortable. I looked up the consequences of mental health checks and realized what Mom intended was dangerous—and not just because they would've found me knocked out on the painkillers I need to sleep. Turns out, once someone decides I'm a risk, they can strip away everything—my cane, my meds, my freedom. I'd be trapped, with no way out until a doctor I don't even know says otherwise.

"We've discussed my reaction to your choices," I say. "We're proceeding with the fake relationship."

Maybe. If she's not a stalker.

"Worth a shot," she mutters, then folds her hands in front of her. "Do you want to talk about your mom?"

"Only in relation to fake dating."

"But you're okay?" Lines bracket her mouth. "Safe? Is she still trying to force you into treatment?"

"She's not exactly trying to force me into treatment. It's more that she thinks I need it if I'm depressed."

"Sometimes those two things are the same if the parent has any say."

"I'm an adult."

"Yes, but you lose a lot of powers as a disabled adult if someone declares you incompetent."

"I know, but I think she's more...subtly ableist." If *subtly* means joining my support group in secret and freaking out over a poem I posted. "She just doesn't get it."

"Hmm." It's a small noise in the back of her throat like she doesn't believe me, but our food arrives, and I let it go.

While I dig in, her face goes a little green. I study the silver rings on her thumbs and forefingers while she picks at her pitas, unsure what to make of her. She called me Pike Durnam, and it didn't seem like a ploy to out me as Brandon Pike.

"You mentioned coming out of remission," I say. "How are you feeling today?"

It's a delicate question. I'm not even going to *imply* she doesn't look great. First, it's a great way to get slapped. Second, it'd be a lie. I'm annoyed by how effortlessly gorgeous she is.

"Have you ever woken up feeling like a sledgehammer's hitting your head?"

I nod over my souvlaki platter. I don't miss that feeling since I stopped drinking.

"Imagine that," she says, "plus a vise tightening around your head and a bowling ball hanging off your neck. Pain radiates from your skull to your back. Your ears ring and whoosh. Add dizziness, blurry vision, and extreme sensitivity to light. Then cheek and jaw pain, the sensation of a toothache and an ear infection, and finally, a band of pressure behind your eyes. Now you're getting closer to how I feel."

"Well, fuck," I breathe out. "You still came?"

"You threatened to report me for harassment."

Huh. I've been waiting for her to block and simultaneously drop me from the group. But something about the other admins finding out what she did stopped her. I wanted to use that if she pulled anything funny.

Now, I feel like the biggest asshole. My roommate, Luis, is chronically ill. Whenever he gets bad flares, he can barely leave his bed. I've forced her to do exactly that.

"I've felt this bad for months," she says. "It's how I knew it was time to start my meds again. Those little bastards are messing with me too. Today, it's muscle fatigue, air hunger, and this damn tingling. The potassium pills should help with the latter, once I can get them down."

Now that she's mentioned it, I do notice her heaving breaths. I thought she was nervous, but drug fuckery is something I'm unfortunately familiar with. I shift, and my cane crashes to the floor.

Skylar winces. "Really sensitive to loud noises too."

"Sorry. It falls all the time. No matter how I position it." To avoid another bang, I leave it down there.

"It's called idiopathic intracranial hypertension, by the way," she says. "You should know the name of my condition if we're going to pass for a real couple."

"Yeah, I'm gonna need you to write that down."

"IIH for short. An older, outdated name for it is 'pseudotumor cerebri.'"

"You can't throw Latin at me before I've properly eaten."

"Well, I'm not hungry, so you can have my food too." She pushes her pitas over. I can always eat more, so I dip one in the garlic hummus as she continues, "'Pseudotumor cerebri' means 'fake brain tumor.' Essentially, my brain acts like it has a tumor without a tumor present. It's caused by too much cerebrospinal fluid pressure. Think of the brain as a sink and the cerebrospinal fluid as the water level."

Never thought of a brain that way in my life, but sure. "Brain plumbing issues, got it."

She cracks a tiny smile, not quite the one from her profile pic, but it still makes me lean forward a little. "The faucet could drip too much or the drain could clog—or both—and you get a buildup of pressure from CSF that can't flow out properly. Besides the other symptoms I mentioned, it can lead to swelling of the optic nerves, so there's a big risk for vision problems and blindness."

"Shit," I say. "What's the cause?"

"'Idiopathic' means they don't know. They've discovered a lot of secondary causes, but it's still a rare disease with little research and no cure. High intracranial pressure also causes full-body problems you can look up when you're bored. I've written about it extensively in our group."

"I'll look it up tonight," I promise, though it's daunting to think about sorting through all her posts. A lot of the active members post every day.

"And remember, it's *pressure*, not 'a headache,'" she says. "Even if doctors often dismiss and reduce it to that. It's not a migraine, either, though it can trigger one alongside the pressure pain. The meds only lower cerebrospinal fluid production. They're not painkillers."

I pull out my phone. "Is there anything I should know that a boy-friend would take care of?"

Her eyebrows shoot up. "I can take care of myself."

"But a supportive boyfriend should be prepared."

"*Pretend* boyfriend. Real boyfriends don't want to hear about those issues."

Her voice is steady, but how detached and clinical she sounds catches me off guard. It makes me wonder what kind of men she's dating. Why wouldn't they care? Shouldn't her health be one of their top priorities?

"It seems important if it's as miserable as you described."

"That doesn't mean they want to know. I'll try to think of some things, I guess, but you're not allowed to complain that I'm high-maintenance."

"Cross my heart," I say, making the motion across my chest.

"What about you?"

"Oh, I'm very high-maintenance."

That gets me a laugh, and it feels good, like something I earned.

"Anything specific I should know about you?" she asks.

I spread out my legs. My sciatica's making my left foot tingle. "I need to know what I'm doing ahead of time so I can map things out."

Aside from my rigorous training, I went from a life where I could just go with the flow—ride hard, party harder, and not think twice—to being hyper-vigilant about every step I take. A sudden move the wrong way? Splintering pain. Spend too much time engaged in certain activities? Can't move the next day.

"Do you know anything about snowboarding?" This is when I find out the truth.

"No?" Her nose makes this cute crinkle. "Why?"

"I had a snowboarding accident. Messed up my back, shattered my pelvis, hurt my legs." There's a lot I'm leaving out, but when you're disabled, you learn to cut to the chase. I don't like seeming—how did Skylar put it?—*high-maintenance* either.

"A snowboarding accident?" She sits back. "I guessed injured biker."

"Was it the hair?"

"The hair and the mountain."

I reach for my former bangs, finding only barely there strands. "I cut it short recently. Still getting used to it."

"I like it." Her freckled cheeks bloom with a rosy hue. "It looks good."

Interesting. I've never had trouble getting attention from women, but I haven't tested the market since I cut it.

Skylar props her chin up with her fists. "Snowboarding's an expensive hobby, isn't it?"

"Depends."

"Am I into you because you're rich?"

"If you're meeting my mother, I really hope not."

"You said you dated *super*models. They don't usually hang around us regular-income folks."

I scan her, wary. "Ever seen the snowboarding events at the Olympics?"

"Like the snow pipe?"

"Halfpipe. You know how they do tricks in the air? I could do some of those tricks." To put it lightly. "Some women find that attractive. If they're supermodels . . . who am I to judge?"

"Oh, please. Stop smirking."

"Am I?" I bite down on my lip to come off less cocky, but internally, I'm brimming with relief. This isn't some desperate attempt to wriggle into my life. I could tell her who I am, but if she doesn't recognize the sport, she's not in that circle.

She gestures in the general vicinity of my torso. "Are most snowboarders this . . . ripped?"

"You should see my legs." It's a line, and it rolls off my tongue like a bad habit.

I sit up self-consciously as Skylar actually ducks down. It's not like she can see evidence of my surgeries through my jeans, but I'll never forget how my thigh looked when it atrophied after surgery. Took me eleven months to go from skin on bone to something resembling muscle.

Multiply that by six other body parts, and you've got my last year and a half.

"Snowboarders have strong glutes, quads, and calves," I clarify. "Lots of squatting. Lots of shifting from heel to toe."

"Strong legs are good," she murmurs. "In a very general sense."

"I'm still working on rehabbing mine. I've been more successful at building up my upper body. Also doing lots of core work." My abs will never again be where they were, but I won't complain as long as I never have to sleep with an SI belt again. Skylar's peering at me like I might unzip my hoodie and give her a show at any time, so I quickly add, "Other things to know: Don't assume I can't do something. Ask me. Don't walk close to me on the side I use my cane."

"Noted. Any other hobbies or interests I should know about?"

"Nothing interesting. I've only been done with rehab for six months. When I'm not working, I do physical therapy with my trainer, Ranielle. She hands me my ass three days a week, but she works with disabled athletes, so I trust her to know my limits." When Skylar only nods, I continue, "The most important thing to get across for my mom: I'm happy. I'm doing great."

"Are you?"

"What?"

"Happy. Great."

I squirm in my seat. "Can't complain."

"I read your poem, Pike."

"It was New Year's. I was drunk."

"Hmm." There's that disbelieving hum again.

And fine, I wasn't drunk, but I thought I'd remain a random name in a group. "What should I memorize about you beyond your IIH? What should I say about us?"

Skylar twists a curl around her finger, her gaze moving to an elderly couple at another table. She thinks for a while, and I like that she doesn't rush to fill the silence.

"I work as a regional college admissions recruiter," she says. "I spend half my time traveling around Ohio, PA, and upstate New York, mostly by car. The other half is at home, working from bed. As for what you should tell your mom about us…" She ticks off on her fingers. "We watch reruns of game shows like *The Price Is Right* together and you secretly love it. When we're not together, we chat online until at least midnight because we can't get enough of each other—"

"I go to bed at, like, nine thirty—"

"—and when we spend the night, you always bring me coffee in bed." Color creeps into her cheeks, but she barrels on. "But not too much. Caffeine can raise intracranial pressure. Sometimes you accompany me on road trips because work pays for the hotel. You get along great with my best friends, Analia and Emy. Have you seen them in the group?"

She pulls out her phone and shows me a picture, only to hastily swipe away a new notification, which, if I'm not mistaken, says, **IS HE BEHAVING!?** Do Not Disturb is switched on.

Then she shows me her friends. The first one, Analia, looks vaguely familiar. She sits at a desk in her profile picture, her hand running through her purple, angled bob while looking to the side, seemingly deep in thought. The other one, Emy, I'm sure I've seen post before. Long hair frames her tan face, but most memorably, she's blowing a kiss while winking at the camera. Skylar says she immigrated to the US from Italy when she was fifteen.

"You can say they helped you pick out the diamonds on this ring." She points to her septum piercing. "What else? You come to my doctor's appointments with me so I'm not alone. And we met snowboarding. How's that?"

I sit back, dragging a thumb over my lower lip. "We didn't meet snowboarding because I don't board anymore. And diamonds seem premature."

"Are you sure?" Her lips curl into a cute smirk. There's the woman from the profile pic who knows that look will get her anything she desires.

"They're too much if we're 'pretty new.'"

"But you've never had a serious girlfriend before. And if anyone deserves diamonds, it's me." When I stare at her, she laughs. "Just realized you can't see me batting my eyelashes at you."

"We should think of some flaws," I say. "Reasons we're not perfect for each other so my mom's not shocked when I tell her we broke up later."

"Flaws, right." The playfulness drops from her face. "That won't be hard. There's something I need to tell you anyway." She becomes fascinated with her nails.

I knew it. I fucking *knew* it. She's known who I am all along. "Let's hear it."

She grimaces. "I have…issues."

Yeah, you do, sweetheart.

5

Skylar

B etter if I find out now than later," Pike says.

But he looks like he's going to vomit. It's about time with how much I've overshared already. Any man on a real date would've run away screaming after I told him about choking on my horse pill.

Pike's taken it all in stride so far, even pretending he's interested in my complicated medical history. The next bit should send him packing.

"Well," I say, "my ideal temperature is low seventies. I can't go more than an hour without ChapStick or eye drops. I get motion sick in every moving thing because of dysautonomia, sometimes even just standing up. My medications have diuretic properties, so I guzzle water constantly, meaning I need to pee every forty-five minutes. You'll need to schedule bathroom breaks into any planned event. Bright lights and screens with strong contrast bother me. I need prescription sunscreen because my meds make my skin blister in the sun, and over-the-counter versions are useless. After any activity, I need to rest and recover my energy. Sometimes, I need to rest even if I haven't done anything. I take around twenty different over-the-counter medications for allergies, nutrition deficiencies, and sleep problems."

I exhale, hiding my trembling hands. Sometimes, when my pressure's intense, I also mix up words or even forget what I'm saying, but that's a cognitive vulnerability I don't like sharing. My words are already coming out slower than I want, since my mouth is struggling to sync with my brain these days.

Pike's forehead has become totally pinched. There we go. Now he'll want out of this for sure. If by some miracle it's not too much for him, it'll be too much for his mom. And while it's good for this fake-dating disaster, it still hurts to know.

"Is that it?" he asks.

I frown. He doesn't sound sarcastic.

"Um...I have two types of tinnitus. One ear screeches and rings, the other constantly whooshes with my heartbeat. You'd think I'd be used to it by now, but it can make me feel completely unhinged. I can't sleep without a sound machine, but...it's not like...I mean..." I gesture between us. "Don't get any ideas."

I've certainly gotten ideas during this lunch. The man is striking. It's a good thing I'm wearing sunglasses, or he'd definitely notice how much I'm checking him out.

He's broad. Jacked. Kind of rugged, with more stubble than in his picture, but I can tell he takes care to trim it. The way his mouth moves when he talks is delectable. His brown eyes are smoky and intense, but there's something guarded and sad in them. The whole broody vibe online wasn't off.

"I'm game to pretend about most things," I clarify, rubbing my tender cheek, "but not my health. I already do too much of that."

I still feel like a pressure cooker without a release valve. That haunting dread in my stomach won't go away—that this time, my meds won't work. I'll need to increase my dosage so much that the side effects will be unbearable, or I'll get metabolic acidosis, which causes fun stuff like organ failure and potential death.

Devil's Tic Tacs indeed.

Despite resting over break, I still had to cancel an entire week of work, so I'm behind and need to make up for missing an outreach program in Syracuse, which didn't sit well with my boss.

I sip my water, waiting for Pike's reconsideration, but his entire demeanor relaxes.

"I thought you were going to say you've been stalking me, or worse."

"What would you consider worse?"

"Something freaky. Like a clown fetish."

I choke on my water.

"What? I hate clowns." He makes a show of checking his watch and points in the direction of the bathroom. "I think forty-five minutes are almost up." His mouth hooks up at the corner.

He's *teasing* me. And seemingly not bothered by the laundry list of things I need him to be aware of if we're going to do this. What is going on?

I suppose I did tell him not to call me high-maintenance. And he's disabled too. But disability isn't a monolith. Sure, there are some things we all tend to relate to, but he experiences his physical disability very differently from the way I experience my rare illness.

"Nothing wrong with stating your needs," he says. "You mentioned dysautonomia. That's dysfunction of the autonomic nervous system, right? Like postural orthostatic tachycardia syndrome?"

"Yeah, I have POTS," I say, surprised and a little thrilled that he can recite the entire name. "It's frustrating because some of the treatments for POTS and IIH conflict with each other. Take salt. It often helps POTS, but with my IIH, salt wreaks havoc. I avoid as many salty things as I can to get rid of fluid rather than retain it. And my IIH meds? My cardiologist wants me off them, but that can't happen."

He pulls out his phone. "I say we pick a few dates to make an appearance together, and then in a couple months, I'll tell my mom we broke up. Are you free next Saturday night?"

"Hang on." I'm still trying to wrap my mind around the fact that

Pike still wants me to be his fake girlfriend. And that he's…nice? Considerate, even?

After our online talk and his brisk **When are we finally meeting?** texts, I thought he'd be more imposing. His physicality is. This is a man who can command a room. Still, he isn't in my face. The general annoyance that drips off him is laced with an unexpectedly calm demeanor.

It's not helping my mixed feelings about this whole debacle. I like men who are in control of their frustrations. Is he grumpy, serious, and closed off? Definitely. But he did think I was stalking him.

"I'll meet your mom twice," I concede. "We can space it out, but more than that is too much for me right now."

"Fair. Two dates it is."

"And I need to be able to reschedule last minute."

I don't plan things months out unless it's for my job: which schools I'll visit, which hotels I'll stay at, which conferences I'll attend. My personal future is cloudy because I can never predict how I'll feel. Mom says this type of thinking is negative; I think it's realistic. Whenever I make plans and have to cancel them, I always disappoint the other person.

I've lost a lot of friends because I'm not "reliable." It's certainly easier to be reliable when you're chronically well and don't require extensive rest, money, and accommodations.

"That's fine," he says, surprising me again.

I relax in my chair. "We can pencil in Saturday."

"How's five o'clock? She's out in Naples."

That explains why I couldn't find a Brandon Durnam in Rochester. Naples is an hour away. *Ample chances to be kidnapped*, Analia will say.

"We can't do something in Rochester?"

"Maybe for the second date? She wants you over for dinner. Sorry."

"In that case, I'll need a ride. I'm not driving at night until my eyes improve. What do you want me to wear?"

He glances up from his phone. His brown eyes drag over me in a way that sends an unexpected flame licking up my spine. It's a bit unnerving, his intensity. "Whatever you want."

"No, whatever I want might not be appropriate. What are you wearing?"

He shrugs. "Jeans and a button up? I don't know."

Figures. But I'm not showing up looking out of place. "Send me a picture of whatever you decide on. I'll coordinate." I gather my purse. "If that's all, I'm going back to bed."

"You're leaving already?"

"I've maxed out my cognitive load for today."

He grabs his cane. "I can drive you—"

"No, thanks." I drop twenty bucks on the table. "For the tip."

"Wait. What about PDA?"

I freeze. "What about it?"

"How do you feel about it?" He holds up his hands in placation. "All consensual, of course. Predetermined. Maybe some hand-holding? A touch on the back? I'm a physical guy."

He's a physical guy. Emy's going to lose her shit. "Don't kiss me on the mouth."

"Wouldn't dream of it."

"You should. I'm a fantastic kisser."

His eyes drop to my lips and linger. Pleasant shivers flit over my skin. I shouldn't have blurted that out, but he makes me feel completely off. And fuck it. I *am* a fantastic kisser. He should be so lucky.

"You may smile at me adorably, hold my hand, and, on occasion, give me a peck on the cheek," I say. "Anything else must be negotiated beforehand."

"Understood."

A part of me wishes he wanted to get more handsy. Pike's hands all over me sounds incredible in theory. But most hot men sound incredible in theory. Then you find out their true colors.

It's good we've established the scope of our agreement. I give him two fake dates. He doesn't report me to the other admins.

I swagger out of there, hiding my labored breathing, then collapse the second my Uber arrives.

Once I've had a nap, I sprawl out on my sectional in my ice hat, a thick stack of papers in front of me, and my chat with Analia and Emy open on my phone. I finally have time to go through the medical records I received this week, even if I don't really have the energy.

What's going on with your medication, Emy? I ask. **Any improvements?**

She's had a whirlwind of doctors the last few years trying to figure out why she has so much pain. The latest attempt is an antidepressant.

i think i prefer the steroids.

Oh, no, I say. **I'm so sorry.**

She blew up like a balloon with the steroids, and her thyroid numbers got wacky. Then her blood pressure skyrocketed, sending her to the hospital for two scary nights. That was almost three years ago now, right around when we became friends. Analia and I started talking first. I don't remember how Emy joined our conversations, but I do remember it was refreshing to hear the perspective of someone who didn't grow up with US healthcare.

I put my phone down while she types and dim the lights. My photophobia is off the charts tonight. This is why it's so much easier to hang out online. When someone's with me physically, I can't control my environment as much. I get fatigued easily and end up flared because it takes a lot of effort to vocalize my thoughts and maintain eye contact.

Online, no one's offended if I need a break from conversation. No one cares if I sit in the dark or haven't taken a shower.

i'm at a point where i'm ready to self-diagnose myself, Emy says. **all signs point to hEDS, except the lack of hypermobility in my wrists. i'm not an obvious case.**

Self-dx is valid! Analia says.

Definitely, I add. From what I've learned in the group, it's easy for doctors to miss Ehlers-Danlos syndrome. **I'm convinced you have it, for what it's worth.**

getting a dx would give me mental peace, Emy says. **it's like, why am i exhausted today? pain? family? dehydration? acute illness? all of the above?**

It's so hard to know, I say, sending a hug. **The doctors should be the ones figuring that out, but they only want to know what your weight and mental state is.**

trying to explain my symptoms to a doctor is like nervously asking a guy, "what are we?" Emy sends a crying GIF. **it's kind of humiliating, i end up sounding desperate, and they always hit me with, "i don't know, i'm not really looking for anything serious."**

Omg so true, I say. **Even if you pour your heart out, they still look bored and dismiss you by saying, "Let's just see where this goes." Like, sure, I'll just sit around in pain for the next three months until you bother to pencil me in again.**

This makes me even happier I'm not dating, Analia says, but she sends a bunch of hugs too.

sorry i'm such a wet mop lately, Emy says.

Are you kidding me? I say. **Vent as much as you like.**

We're here for you, Analia says. **It's been a long time since I was undiagnosed, but we've all been there. We've all had crappy doctors.**

Just look at mine, I say.

When my IIH came back in November, I requested a CT venogram to see whether I'd qualify for a less invasive type of brain surgery, stenting, that helps some IIH patients. My neuro-ophthalmologist, Dr. Wharton, point-blank refused. He claims stenting is "still experimental" and I should focus on weight loss. I want a second opinion, so I requested my records to speed up the process.

I go back to organizing them. My eyes land on a note from Dr. Wharton in my chart, and my heart rate skyrockets. I attempt deep breaths, but that's near impossible with my meds.

I type, **I think I just found out why I'm not able to get a new neurologist**, then post in the group.

Skylar King: Help! My neuro-ophthalmologist blames everything on BMI, so I'm trying to get a new one. Problem is, I have a rare disease, so the specialized clinics require all my records. He put a note in my chart that since I haven't lost weight, I'm not "complying with his treatment plan" and have "self-victimization mentality." How can I report this when I still need him to continue prescribing my medication until I get a new doctor?

I cross-post in my IIH group since it's illness specific and my situation isn't an outlier. Most of us have dealt with a toxic doctor. Or ten. The egotistical ones, who feel threatened if you know more about your body, are some of the worst. But getting blacklisted this way? That's new even for me. A note like this in my chart can keep me from getting future help.

Three people write, :sending hugs: and one person writes, Doctors always fat-shame us!

I refresh the page. *Come on, IIHers.*

The only post with any traction today is labeled NSFW.

Paola: I asked my neuro about sex and if it was okay to engage in breath play. Y'all should have seen his face!! He didn't know, so I'm asking those of you who are kinky like me.

I expand the thread, which already has seventy-six comments in the last hour.

Claribel: I get lightheaded after, but I'm never giving it up!

Mel: If you have a shunt, don't squeeze on the side where your tubing is.

Priya: It can be really dangerous, so you need to have proper discussions about safe words and limits first.

Tia: What is this sex that you speak of?

I snort so hard it shoots a bolt of pain to the back of my head.

A new message from Analia brings me back to our chat. **I have to go, sorry. Kalle just got back from Sweden and stopped over to say hi.**

Emy sends a magnifying glass. **this late? is he sleeping over?**

He might, Analia says. **He's drowsy (and adorable when jet-lagged ♥).**

I send a dozen exclamation points to Emy in a private chat. She replies with an eggplant and a wink.

Kalle and Analia have been best friends since childhood. They aren't going to do anything but sleep, but we can dream. That dream involves their marriage and Kalle taking Analia to Sweden with him someday, but we'd settle for just a trip. Kalle's in Sweden at least twice a year to visit his relatives, and Analia's never even made it to the Canadian side of Niagara Falls.

So just relaxing, then? I ask.

Catching up and maybe a movie. My fibro's flaring, so I don't have the spoons for much else, despite a full day of getting nothing accomplished.

u don't need to be productive when ur in pain, Emy says.

I know, but I got locked out of my apartment earlier because I forgot my keys and ended up waiting outside for my landlord. Messed up my whole day, and now I'm sunburned on top of it.

sunburned? Emy asks. **it's february.**

I know! I'm very annoyed at my Irish skin. Why couldn't I have inherited my grandmother's Mediterranean sun tolerance? But no, the only thing I got from my Catalan side is my hair and a lack of cute freckles. 😭

I start telling her she's cute either way, but I pause halfway through. My post has a new notification. From *Pike*.

Oh no. Is he going through all my posts after what I shared? He could find the most intimate and embarrassing things about me if he bothered searching my name.

Pike: What an asshole. Hope you can get him reported. Also? You looked gorgeous today. Followed by the blowing-kisses emoji.

I stare at that little yellow face for a solid minute. Is he flirting with me?

Wait. *Wait.*

His mom is in the group. He has to flirt with me.

But then he sends me a message. It's a *picture* of him, captioned, **How's this for dinner?**

I fan myself. He's wearing faded jeans and a black leather belt coupled with a navy shawl cardigan. Dark stubble lines his strong jaw, adding a rough, masculine edge to his appearance. He stands in front of a mirror, biting the side of his bottom lip, but there's no smugness in his expression, no teasing glint in his eyes—just this unassuming stance, like he's completely unaware of how hot he is.

He *has* to know.

Omg, I tell Emy as I send her the pic. **He went home and tried on outfits! Broody hot poet is also a model.**

She sends a sweating GIF. **i feel personally attacked by how attractive he is.**

She's right. I'll need to dress up to feel even remotely adequate next to him.

That works, I tell him, knowing I'm in way over my head.

Glad I'm approved, he says, but then he texts again a few minutes later. **What are you going to wear?**

Whatever I want, remember?

I don't get a preview?

My eyes widen. **You don't have picture privileges.**

Fair. I'm sure you'll look nice no matter what.

So I can show up in sweatpants?

If that's what you need to be comfortable.

I heart the reply. It's a good answer. Pike is different than what I expected.

Maybe this ruse won't be so terrible after all.

6

Pike

I turn off ESPN when a car pulls into the driveway. I told myself I'd only watch the US Grand Prix at Mammoth highlights later—and just to stay up-to-date for work on Monday.

But Skylar was running late. Jax and Grace were both competing. There were three newcomers under eighteen who effortlessly pulled off the tricks we once thought impossible. Tricks I invented.

I should be there with my crew. I should have a third Olympic gold to my name. Instead, I'm back in Rochester, pain riddling my body as I watch from my couch like everyone else.

I discreetly part the blinds to steal a glimpse of Skylar. I'm closer to Naples, so she told me not to pick her up. She shrugs into her thin coat as she gets out of the Uber. In the end, she chose a little black dress with long sleeves. Her towering boots climb high, but just above them, I catch a glimpse of stockings that stop right below her bare knees. The way the fabric of her dress sways pulls my gaze to the tempting flare of her hips.

Not that I'm tempted.

"What are we looking at?"

I jump. "Nothing."

My roommate, Luis, rolls around the corner.

"Are you feeling any better?" I ask.

He spent a couple days this week bedbound. His light brown skin is still paler than usual, but judging by his damp, dark brown waves and the faint scent of shampoo, he finally had the energy for a shower. "My PEM is better," he says. "I was finally able to get up and out of bed yesterday."

"That's great, man. Glad to see you moving around again."

Except he moves toward me, parks his blue wheelchair, and opens the blinds wide. It takes everything in me not to cover my face with my hands as Skylar spots us. I smile weakly and signal that I'll be out in a minute.

"Someone you know?"

So much for sneaking out. I considered telling Luis about this charade all week, but I doubt he'd be comfortable helping me lie. He'd tell me to talk to Mom about everything.

I'm not ready. I don't know if I'll ever be.

"My girlfriend," I mumble. "Skylar."

"You have a girlfriend!?"

I twist my face into something resembling joy.

"Who has a girlfriend? Pike?" Luis's boyfriend, Cyrus, strolls into the den, and I want to melt into the wall.

He tugs a strip of lavashak between his teeth, and I'm tempted to grab a couple for the road. His mother makes that Persian rolled-up fruit leather from scratch using a recipe his grandmother brought over from Iran. Since he always leaves us a stash, I'm now addicted to their sour kick.

"Have you ever even had a girlfriend for more than a week?" he asks.

"Ha ha." Anyone can read about my past online, but Luis always teases that I've become a monk since I started living with him. "She's—it's sort of new. Don't get too excited."

They both grin way too wide anyway. I sigh.

"You're dressed up too!" Cyrus says.

"Hard not to be compared to you two." They're both in sweats, the way I wish I was.

Cyrus has a beanie pulled low over his thick brown hair, a few strands escaping at the edges. He tugs at the edge of it absentmindedly as he dips his chin toward the window. "She's cute."

Yup. My fake girlfriend is a smoke show, and it's so fucking inconvenient. She has the kind of body Renaissance-era sculptors immortalized in their statues. Soft freckled skin, generous curves around the cinch in her waist, and a pretty face that makes you look twice. Her swagger only makes her more attractive. She walks like she owns the world—and every man along with it. This woman takes no prisoners.

"You guys joining us for Game Night?" Luis asks.

He hosts a gaming group on some weekends for his disabled friends at our house, which is accessible in ways I didn't even know were possible. Automatic doors, ramps, railings, seats in the shower, you name it. Wheelchair-friendly kitchen. One floor. Not a single stair anywhere. It's exactly what I've needed while I adjust to having more physical limitations.

Luis is also decent in every way. He's respectful and nice, and he doesn't force me to talk about my past. When Cyrus isn't around, we often unwind together after work with a funny show.

"No, sorry," I say. "Heading to Naples."

"She's already meeting Laurie? Wow! Happy for you, man. She good with your disabilities?"

"Yeah, she's disabled too. This brain thing called idiopathic intracranial hypertension."

"Damn," Cyrus exclaims. "IIH is such a life fucker."

"You've heard of it?"

"We see intracranial hypertension in the ME/CFS community too," Luis says, which surprises me. I'm more familiar with myalgic encephalomyelitis after living with him, but I don't think Skylar experiences post-exertional malaise like he does. "Does she have a shunt?"

"I . . . I don't think so."

Luis's thick brows rise. "You don't know if your girl had brain surgery?"

Skylar never mentioned having one in her posts, but she did talk about a friend who's had thirty-seven surgeries in nine years. IIH *does* seem like a life fucker. Besides what Skylar mentioned, I found research suggesting it can also cause memory and balance problems, stroke, rhinorrhea, exercise intolerance, and pituitary gland issues.

"It's brand-new," I clarify. "I should really get out there."

I make a beeline for the garage, but before I reach my car, Luis sticks his head out.

"Pike! You got condoms?"

For one pathetic moment, I think he's asking for himself. "No, sorry."

"No good." He chucks a foil wrapper at me.

I catch it out of reflex. It still takes me a good second to grasp what's happening.

"I know it's been a while," he says. "Happy for you, man!"

I wave in acknowledgment until he shuts the door, my mind racing to inappropriate scenarios. I fling the offending object onto the passenger seat like it's radioactive. Then I realize who's about to sit there and scramble to retrieve it.

This is the worst plan of my life.

I open the garage door for Skylar, but my eyes catch on my old board, still shelved in its bag. Untouched since my accident. It's a cannonball to the chest every time I see it, but I can't bring myself to get rid of it. My friend Kal says I should sell it and make bank. He doesn't get that used snowboards aren't like used guitars, and insists some superfan will want it. "Better do it now, while they still remember you."

Kal's usually a good guy, but I wanted to knock his teeth out after that comment.

"Can you come out here for a sec?" Skylar asks. "I need a pic for my girls with your license plate."

I bite back a sigh, my hand instinctively tightening around my cane. The thought of stepping into the driveway, now blanketed under a two-inch layer of fresh snow, isn't appealing. But if this small gesture makes her feel safer, I'll do it, no matter how inconvenient it might be.

"Hey." I kiss Skylar on the cheek.

"What are you doing?" Her fist shoots to my stomach, but I gently catch it and offer my best lovestruck smile.

"You said cheek kisses were okay." I lean down, blocking the guys' view of her. "My roommate's watching."

"I didn't say I'd pretend in front of anyone but your mom."

"You agreed to make her believe this. She sometimes talks to Luis."

"Is your mom involved in *every* aspect of your life?"

My jaw aches from smiling. "Take the pic or get in the car, *sweetheart*."

She eyes my Ford Explorer MXV conversion like it's a fire-breathing dragon. "That is massive. Are you carting around your kids or your ego? It looks like it costs fifty grand."

"To make it wheelchair accessible, just about."

She breathes out hard, the condensation fogging the air between us. "You use a wheelchair?"

"Keeps people guessing."

"Hmm. Smile, boyfriend." She lifts her phone. "Aw, one could *almost* guess you enjoy my company."

"Give it time," I mutter, then hand her a nondrowsy Dramamine tube. "For your motion sickness."

She stares at it, snowflakes gathering in her loose red curls. When she finally climbs into the car next to me, my cane is in the way. I almost stab her with my retractable ice tip as I rush to put it in the back.

"Sorry, shit."

Once we're both settled, I glance at her. "I presume Analia and Emy are following us?"

Her lips twitch up in the first semblance of a smile. "Nah, they just know where we're going."

"So, you're good? Ready?"

"Only if you relax your murder face."

I grab my mechanical hand controls. I know I can look intense when I'm serious, but I've never heard that before. Do I really have a murder face?

I frown at myself in the rearview mirror. Women usually love my face.

"I'm kidding, Pike." She leans back in her seat. "You drive with your hands?"

I show her where the lever system connects and how my spinner knob moves, then head toward Bristol Mountain, where I learned to board as a kid. We moved near Naples when I was nine so we didn't have to drive an hour from Rochester on weekends. Mom kept the house even after we started traveling for competitions, then eventually settled back here when I bought a place in Whistler.

Skylar huffs, making me glance over. She taps at her phone screen with rapid, annoyed jabs. "I missed drama in the group getting ready to meet you. My co-admin has been sending me all this stuff. Your buddy, Maria."

I snort. "Not my buddy."

"You said you chatted with her."

She messaged me once, and I swiftly deleted it. But the topic seems to irritate her, so I only wink. "'Buddy' is too platonic for those messages."

"I knew it with Maria. I *knew* it."

Knew what? That so many women in the group keep sliding into my DMs? It's not like I'm asking for it, and with my past, I have plenty of practice ignoring unsolicited messages. No one knows who I am, though, so the attention has been surprising. I figured people were just friendly. Supportive. Everyone's always commenting on my posts, too.

But it's interesting that Skylar has thought about anything related to me and Maria—really, anything related to me at all outside of fake dating.

"What's the drama in the group?" I ask quickly. Skylar's a bit too perceptive, and I need to pivot before she can dig any deeper into my nonexistent relationship with Maria.

"People are fighting over diets," she says. "There's always someone who thinks only natural approaches work for chronic pain. I'm glad that helps them, but I can literally go blind if I stop taking my medication. And since doctors push dieting on people like me who are overweight, it easily becomes a heated topic."

I've seen lots of women in the group get treated badly by doctors due to weight. Skylar's not thin, but I wouldn't have guessed she's "overweight" either. Even I know BMI is arbitrary, and it pissed me off when I read about her neuro-ophthalmologist badgering her about it.

"Is it hard keeping up with all those posts when you're sick?" I ask.

"Yes, but I built that community from nothing, so it's worth it. It gives me a sense of purpose even when things are shitty."

Just like when we met at lunch, I feel like a jerk for threatening to report her. She managed to pick up on a problematic comment from my mother out of a group with more than a thousand members.

When I thought she was a stalker, I flagged notifications on her activity, and it turns out she's just kind. Smart. Helpful. It's clear she cares by how often she jumps in to validate people.

I turn my wipers up a notch to keep up with the snowfall. The forecast says we'll get another foot by tomorrow. "How's your health this week? Do you still have…" I trail off. *A million symptoms.* "The same amount of pain?"

"My eyes aren't seeing double as much. I'll find out how they're doing at my follow-up on Monday."

My hand tightens on my spinner knob. "With the douche who wrote a bad comment in your chart?"

"Yes. But let's not talk about him. How are you?"

Lately, I've come to hate that question. But considering Skylar dumped all her symptoms on me, she's probably not expecting the usual *fine, thanks, you?*

"There was a time I thought eating only unprocessed organic food was the answer," I admit. "I take oxycodone for pain now. It's working pretty well. Doesn't matter what I eat."

"Is that your way of saying you're doing okay today?"

I huff out a laugh. "That's my way of saying I rely on opioids to function. Not addicted, just necessary."

"You've given this speech before."

"More times than I can count. But I have a pain management doctor," I add, even though Skylar's unlikely to be shitty about it.

"That's good."

"I mean, it's not. I'm always worried they'll change the rules, and I'll be left unable to function. Doctors have tried to take my meds away before."

Patients with chronic intractable pain are supposed to have access to opioids, but it's a witch hunt out there. I'm luckier than most, only having to piss in a cup once a month. But the results have delayed my prescription refill up to five days because of paperwork.

After going through that nightmare once, I forced myself to stay in bed with blackout-inducing pain in order to ration pills for future disruptions.

"Does weed help?" Skylar asks.

"It takes the edge off, but it gives me the spins." Eventually, I'd like to transition, but it takes a lot of trial and error to find the right strains, and I don't have the energy right now. "Does cannabis help you?"

"My university gets federal funding, and they're in an illegal state. Fail a drug test and you're out."

"That's so shitty."

"Tell me about it." Skylar picks up her phone again as we turn onto the first of many small roads that'll take us to Naples.

"What should our backstory be?" I ask. "How did we meet?"

"It's up to you. Whatever we say, she'll believe. No mother suspects her son is bringing home a fake girlfriend to impress her."

"It's not to impress her."

"Right, so she won't think you're depressed. I'll make sure to reiterate that your beautiful poem was a vent."

"You thought it was beautiful?"

"Honey." She puts a hand on my shoulder. "I think half the group got pregnant from your poem. Do you write a lot?"

I ignore the way every nerve ending awakens where she touches me. "I journal. Therapist's recommendation after my first surgery. She told me to chronicle how I felt. Pain levels. Moods. Med reactions. Wasn't my thing, but I started jotting down thoughts at night, especially during painsomnia." Now I write when everything feels impossible, too, but I don't need to elaborate. This past week was particularly rough, so I've filled up a lot of pages.

"I bet it wasn't easy to share," she says.

"I doubt I'll ever post again."

"Aww, Pike. No. We'll get your mom out of the group."

"It was a wish," I explain. "The poem. Being grateful for no longer—"

"—'holding myself to your toxic standards of positivity,'" Skylar recites.

"You memorized it?"

"That killer beginning? Of course I did."

It's hard not to feel a little honored. "Thanks, but I'm not there yet. It would've been more appropriate to write 'I'm hopeful for the day I'll no longer hold myself to…' Future tense." I clear my throat. "Need a bathroom break? This is the last gas station for a while."

She nods, then puts her phone in the cup holder while she zips her coat. A notification pops up, and I'm not looking at it, not exactly, more trying to avoid looking at the flash of skin below the hem of her dress. She's got great legs.

Emy: IT'LL BE FINE. HE'S PROBABLY . . .

Analia: Be over-polite.

I smile to myself. They're talking about me, but not because I have a murder face.

The notifications come in lightning succession.

Emy: just tell him ur shit with paren . . .

Analia: She might not be shit!

Skylar snaps up the phone. I drum my fingers on the steering wheel while she's in the bathroom. Emy thinks Skylar should tell me she's shit with parents. Awesome. Unless, of course, she's shit with parentheses, because that's the only other word I can think of that starts with *paren*.

Skylar comes back with a bottle of water.

"Be honest," I say. "Are you nervous about this? You seem totally fine."

"Why wouldn't I be fine?"

I can't push without admitting I saw her notifs, so I don't.

Way too soon, we arrive at my mom's house. I ease up the long driveway at a crawl, the pines sagging under fresh snow, my chest tightening with every lie I'll soon have to tell.

Skylar checks her appearance in the sun visor. "Well, this is as good as it's going to get."

At least I think that's what she says. Because I'm staring at the newest notifications on her phone as I park.

Emy: is his name BRANDON PIKE?

Emy: because i stalked brandon pike

Emy: AND OMG

Emy: there's something u should know

Her messages send my stomach plummeting. Shit. This is not the moment for Skylar to find out I'm a washed-up, B-list celebrity. C-list, even?

Analia: Is he a serial killer!

Analia deserves a medal for responding so quickly. Emy's message disappears.

"I was hoping for some reassurance, buddy," Skylar says.

"You look great," I say hastily, my mind racing. How can I buy more time? I'll tell her the truth on the way home. "Uh—my mom thinks checking your phone around company is rude. Could you keep it in your pocket?"

Miraculously, she obliges. "Honestly, my parents say that too."

I struggle to exit the car, bracing with my cane to find secure footing on the steep step down and the slippery, snow-covered driveway. Mom comes into view through the windows, and for one terrifying moment, I think I might throw up.

"Last chance to come clean," I say. "Is this really an elaborate prank? See how I'll react if caught on camera? If it is, I'd rather know now."

"It's—" Skylar starts, but I slip.

I flail, my free hand shooting out for balance while I desperately grip my cane, but Skylar's just come up next to me, and I . . .

I grab on to her boob.

Accidentally.

Only for a millisecond.

But it's there, full in my hand.

Skylar gasps and meets my gaze, her pretty hazel eyes unobscured by sunglasses for the first time, revealing a glint of green. "Pike!"

"Shit! Fuck!" I steady myself, turning to grasp my car instead. If any other damn thing messes with me tonight, I'm going to skid again, and with how things are going I'd probably land with my entire face in her chest. "I'm so sorry, shit."

She raises her hand, and I flinch, expecting a slap. Even *without* PDA rules, it's crossing a line. But instead, her touch is gentle, tracing a path along my cheek with a chilly yet soft thumb. I freeze in place.

"Calm down," she whispers.

"I didn't mean—"

"I know." Skylar shoots me a wink. "And it's not a prank. Smile, boyfriend."

By the time Mom bursts out of the house, and Skylar turns on the charm in greeting, I've cycled through more emotions than I usually feel in an entire week.

"Hi, Laurie! Gosh, I feel like we already know each other from our talks online!"

Talks? Has there been more than one?

Mom envelops Skylar in a big hug. "I am so excited to have you here."

Ollie, our old yet still hyperactive Yorkie, comes charging out the front door with her screech-yaps. She skids on the icy driveway, re-collects herself, and barrels at us, jumping at me first.

"Hey, Olls."

She gives my palm a few kisses before Mom scoops her up and

tucks her under her coat. "Come on, baby. You're going to get sick out here."

She rushes back inside, leaving Skylar and me to trudge up the driveway. Wet snow melts on my tongue, and a familiar lurch of anticipation pools in my stomach. There will be amazing powder tomorrow.

And I'll get none of it.

7

Skylar

The last time I met a guy's parents, I was still with Owen. I could never establish an easy rapport with them, but then again, I can't even establish one with my own. It's not that I'm shy. I talk to people all day at my job. But at work, they're mostly teens, and it's repetitive information. I don't do well around people who have time to figure out all my problems.

This is going to be a long dinner with a lot of personal questions, so I'll need all the help I can get. Analia said to be polite, smile a lot, and avoid arguments. Emy said to screw Pike in the bathroom during dinner. So, we're going with Analia.

We walk up to Laurie's timber-framed cottage with floor-to-ceiling windows. It's beautiful amid the snow, the type of home I'd expect to overlook Canandaigua Lake.

"So." Pike stops on the stoop, nibbling his bottom lip. It's almost as tempting as the photo he sent me.

I'm noticing things I shouldn't, especially regarding his mouth. The way it curves, the slight flush from the cold air, how his lips press together in thought before he gives a response. I need to prioritize self-preservation here and remind myself this is all a façade.

But the man planted a kiss on me the moment he saw me. That mouth would fluster anyone. And now he's touched my chest. It was an accident, and I shouldn't embarrass him about it, but it's taking everything in me not to melt into the snow right now.

"We got Ollie after my dad moved out," Pike says. "Like a consolation prize. Have a divorce, get a dog."

As much as I don't want to be here, I don't mind learning more about him. Pike's not bad company, in the end.

"Your dad won't be joining us?"

"Nope. Last I heard, he was living in Vegas."

"Well…" I pause, searching for the right words. "I'm glad you got Ollie, at least."

"Mom was lonely. Ollie was small enough to fit in a tote, so she could bring her along whenever we traveled. To snowboard," he adds.

"On bigger mountains?" I guess.

"Exactly. Bristol's fine for ski club or whatever, but you need better terrain for big air."

"Big…air?"

He laughs. Oh, boy. Have I even seen him smile full-out like this before? His half smile already has too much wattage.

"For tricks." Pike opens the door. "Big air means you get a lot of height off a jump."

"Is that how you got injured? Jumping?"

"Yeah. Didn't stick a landing."

"You haven't watched the footage?" Laurie comes back with two filled champagne flutes.

"I didn't want to relive that trauma with her," Pike says.

I didn't realize someone recorded his accident. "I'd rather not watch him hurt himself," I add. "I'd rather watch him…stick landings."

Pike stifles a laugh at my ineptitude with snowboarding, but he swiftly places a reassuring hand on my lower back. "Skylar isn't into snowboarding. She's familiar with the faces, of course, but that's different from, you know, following the sport."

"Speaking of faces," Laurie says, "did you catch Grace and Jax today?"

"No, I was busy." He shifts more weight onto his cane. "I'd rather not talk about snowboarding tonight. We're here so you can meet Skylar."

I smile with my teeth. "After our funny little encounter online."

"Yes, what an evening." Laurie winds her slender frame around her son, the champagne still precariously balanced in her hands. Her soft brown eyes, strikingly similar to Pike's, grow glassy. "I was so worried about you."

He withdraws after a quick pat to her back. "Can I get your coat, Sky?"

One of my curls gets caught in the zipper as he tries to help me with it. He gently nudges it free, warm fingertips brushing along my collarbone in the process. I fight to keep my eyes from fluttering shut at the touch.

Wait. Why should I fight it? I'm supposed to be into Pike.

I lean against his chest. "Thanks, boyfriend."

Laurie beams. "You guys are adorable! Come, let's start with appetizers." She passes me a flute.

"I actually don't drink alcohol." A few months back, I would've accepted the champagne. But mixing alcohol with my meds will make me puke.

"Aw, Brandon doesn't either." Laurie's accent sounds more typically Rochesterian, whereas Pike's tends to have a strangely Canadian lilt at times.

"How about a Coke, Sky?"

"Sure," I say, relieved I didn't get any awkward questions. As soon as his mom heads to the kitchen, I elbow him. "Don't call me Sky."

"Shouldn't we have nicknames?"

"Not Sky. That's what my mother calls me." I rub my eye in a futile attempt to soothe the pressure behind it.

Pike scrutinizes me, his gaze locking onto mine. Are those flecks of gold and amber in his irises? That shit isn't supposed to be real. "A term of endearment, then. Baby. Babe. Cutie. Honey—"

"Can we do something that sounds less contrived?"

"I did! You didn't like it, *Sky.*"

"How about something international? Emy said her first boyfriend called her 'little strawberry' in Italian."

"Little…strawberry?"

"Doesn't sound as good in English," I agree, as if I have any idea how to say it in Italian.

"Pumpkin," he tries, and I make a face. "Sugar. Darling."

"I'm going to go ahead and veto all of those."

"So what are we going with?"

"I'm partial to *goddess divine.*"

Pike pinches his eyes closed in annoyance.

"Anything but Sky," I concede.

"Fine. You do me now."

"Isn't 'Pike' enough of a nickname?"

"It's certainly better than 'boyfriend.'"

"It was a joke! She smiled!"

"Don't be weird," he begs.

I deflate. That's exactly what Owen used to say. *Don't be weird. Act normal.* Pike's not talking about my disabilities, though. I need to remind myself of that.

Laurie ushers us into her rustic-modern kitchen, where a sizable island dominates the space. I sip my Coke, content to stay silent, then gag and nearly spray it out.

"Is it flat?" Pike asks.

"The opposite. I forgot my medication makes carbonated beverages taste metallic. It's like drinking rust."

Pike grimaces as Laurie asks, "Medication? Are you sick?"

"I have a brain disease." It's easier to say this to people who (1) I'll never meet again and (2) are probably ableist. Laurie fits both criteria.

"Oh my goodness! Cancer?" Laurie is relatively young, perhaps early fifties, but she adopts a worried expression that ages her twenty years.

"It's a problem with cerebrospinal fluid in the brain," Pike explains. "Skylar manages it really well."

Normally, I'd be pissed someone is explaining my condition for me, but I don't want to explain it to Laurie, so why not?

"Are you on disability?" she asks.

Pike's fingers intertwine with mine. "Skylar travels for her position as a college admissions recruiter."

I elaborate, and Laurie's expression relaxes.

"That sounds like a great job. Your pain doesn't get in the way?"

"Nope," Pike says. "Despite it being called one of the worst headaches imaginable. She's amazing like that."

A part of me is touched. Sounds like he looked up IIH, something hardly anyone bothers to do. Still, I tighten my grip on his hand while maintaining a pleasant smile. "I'm not doing anything extraordinary by holding down a job."

I don't want to be lauded for working, like that's somehow inspirational. I wish I didn't have to work, because it makes my pain worse.

"I'm just doing what's necessary to pay the bills and have insurance," I say. "Some people with my condition work full-time, and some can't work at all. I chose this job because I can make my own schedule, so I have more flexibility for appointments and bad days. Fall and spring take a huge toll, but I get two months off in the summer."

Pike draws me to him. He's still only holding my hand, so technically it's not off-limits, but it presses me against his side. Our interlocked fingers are the only barrier preventing us from being entirely hip to hip.

"I still think you're amazing. Everything you do. It's a lot."

He doesn't have any idea what I do, but it is a lot. In a few weeks,

I'll practically be living out of a suitcase. But I can't think of another job where I wouldn't be confined to a strict nine-to-five and can work from bed half the year. And hardly any company allows more than two weeks of sick leave.

Finally, Pike slides into a bar stool, so I scoot next to him and accidentally knock over his cane. It falls two more times before we leave it on the floor.

Laurie starts on her second flute. "Travel sounds exciting!" She hands us artichoke dip and sliced baguette. "I'd like Brandon to branch out from his current job."

My pretend boyfriend stabs a piece of bread into the dip. A storm cloud gathers in his pretty eyes. "I'm happy where I am."

That's right. Pike is happy and great. That's the only perception that matters.

"It's a sales position, honey."

"He's an assistant manager," I say. "Soon he'll be running the place."

"He has so much potential, though. Even now."

Oof. I'm beginning to understand his hesitancy in speaking up. I place my hand on his back and rub, breaking my own PDA rules. But Pike said he was a physical guy, and this is a supportive gesture to make in front of his mom. I can't help admiring his back. It's wonderfully solid and defined. I've never paid much attention to shoulder blades before, but his are delightful.

"I had an idea." Laurie pulls out a tablet and shows us an article about adaptive snowboarding. "What if we contacted some people? Kids like this could look up to you. See that they don't need to give up. You'd have to get back on the mountain, though."

Pike puts his hand on my knee like he needs me to steady him. "Those kids were boarding long before I had my accident, and they'll keep boarding without me."

"You could start an organization."

My eyebrows knit. Honestly, why would anyone care? I guess

all moms think their sons are special. But hey, if it'll help disabled kids…maybe the money they clearly have could end up somewhere useful.

"I've been looking for my tablet," Pike says, pulling it away from her.

"Alternatively, they could do a piece on you for normal snowboarders. If you can do it, they can do it."

Oh, gross. Analia would advise me to smile and nod, but I can't. And what kind of pretend girlfriend would I be if I didn't support my boyfriend?

"Using disabled people for inspiration is ableist," I say. "So I don't love the idea. Also, referring to nondisabled people as 'normal'— well, it's also offensive."

Laurie blinks over her champagne flute. Shit. I overstepped. This is what I'd say to my parents. I'm supposed to be different here. But I'm not a puppet. Even though I hate my pain, I still have disability pride.

"I agree," Pike says gruffly. "Enough about snowboarding. Let's eat."

"Honey—"

"You made chicken scampi, right? I'm sure Skylar's going to love it as much as I do."

"Can I help with anything?" I ask.

"Oh no, you're our guest. Brandon can set the table."

But when we reach the dining room, he backs me into a corner. His cane clatters softly against the wall. Before I can say anything, he plants his hands over my head, bracketing me in. His hard body angles toward me, and he lowers his forehead until it's almost pressed to mine. My awareness narrows to him and him alone. His clean scent—crisp air and fresh water, like snow still lingers in his rich brown hair—settles between us and sends my pulse spiraling out of control.

"What are you doing?" I whisper.

"We need to talk without her overhearing. Is this okay?" He's not technically touching me, but his breath brushes my lips, teasingly close. My knees weaken, and I grip the wall behind me for balance.

"Y-Yes," I stammer.

This proximity is intoxicating. One slight movement, and I could taste him.

"Was the knee thing okay?" His deep voice is a soft murmur. "You were rubbing my back—it felt natural—I'm sorry."

"It was my fault." I have to look down. His smoldering eyes are too intense. But then my focus shifts to his lips. Worse. I fixate on the strong chest in front of me. "Let's…do what feels natural."

Did I really abandon my own PDA rule? This could get me into trouble.

"It's easier," I say. "No innuendo touches, though. No—no mouth kisses. Got it?"

"No problem."

"And I wasn't trying to offend your mom by talking back. I was…trying to give her flaws."

"Speaking up when someone's wrong isn't a flaw." He exhales a slow breath. "I'm sorry I was ableist about your job. I'm still learning."

I dare to look up at him. His gaze pins me to the wall.

"Learning is good." I swallow, feeling my neck and cheeks flush. "Pike?"

He edges closer.

"I need…"

"Yes?"

I'm one breath away from closing my eyes and inhaling deeply. "A little space."

"Oh. My bad." His hand brushes my waist as he backs away.

I press a hand to my heart. Does Pike have any idea how all-consuming his presence is? His eyes alone felt like a brand on my suddenly sensitive skin.

As I peel myself off the wall, Laurie returns with a knowing smile, and I have to look away, my face burning.

I don't have to make that much up. I lie about my family, though, and say we're close. People want a snapshot when they're meeting you, but only from the happy reels. I mostly focus on my nine-year-old niece, Jasmine.

"Has Pike met her?" Laurie asks.

"Not yet. You're our first family intro."

Pike shoots me a look like, *Good one.* Maybe I'm better at this than I thought.

"I still don't know how you met," she says. "Did you recognize him? He looks different now, doesn't he? Without his hair."

"We have mutual friends. Luis. The gaming group," Pike says quickly. "We'd seen each other there before."

I have no idea what he's talking about. I'm itching to check in with Analia and Emy.

"But we officially met at Element Ridge," he adds.

A subtle smirk graces Laurie's lips. "Were you starstruck?"

What now? Am I supposed to be starstruck? "Absolutely," I say. "Very starstruck." Maybe she meant starry-*eyed*?

"We hadn't gotten a chance to talk at Game Night," Pike says, "so it was exciting to run into each other at the shop." He sounds like he's lost all confidence.

Time to help him sell this. "I was too nervous to approach him. I never thought he'd be into me."

"Because he's famous?"

I choke on my water. *Famous? Excuse me?*

Pike's foot finds mine under the table. His eyes plead with me.

"Of…course," I say. "That's why I started dating him. I mean!

Not dating. The reason I first noticed him. Can't forget a famous face. At Game Night, no less. Why would a famous person be into me?"

"Nonsense." Pike's foot squashes mine. "I didn't think you'd be interested in *me*," he says, the liar. "I'm so glad we got to know each other through our support group."

Laurie is freaking *beaming*. "I bet you thought all those medals had gone to his head."

"Oh, they've gone to his head all right." I push his foot away.

Pike laughs so nervously I can't believe his mom doesn't catch on. But she laughs, too, like we're all in on the same joke.

"He's always been humble. I think it's hard to stay that way when you're one of the world's best—you should meet some of his friends—but I raised him not to take things for granted, like his father did."

"Mom—"

"Let me brag about you. This is the first girl I've met." She covers my hand with hers. "I don't mean all those women he was photographed with. Everyone always speculated, 'When will Brandon Pike finally settle down?' but I knew he just hadn't met the right person yet!"

"The right person. Absolutely." I don't even know what I'm saying. "Excuse me."

I run to my coat, grab my phone, and lock myself in the bathroom.

"Okay, Google," I whisper to my phone. "Search *famous Brandon Pike*."

And there he is.

The Olympian I ignored on default.

Brandon Tyler Pike is an American professional snowboarder known for creating many of the tricks now standard in halfpipe competitions. He is a two-time Olympic

gold medalist, four-time X Games gold medalist, multiple
World Cup medalist, and five-time ESPY Award winner.

I gape at my phone.

At twenty-five, Pike was considered the top contender for
another Olympic gold until an accident ended his career.
He was critically injured attempting a frontside triple
cork 1440 during qualifiers. Pike suffered compression
fractures in his spine, spondylolisthesis, a broken femur,
a shattered pelvis, a sacral fracture, multiple knee injuries, torn ligaments, and a broken wrist.

After critical care, he went to a private clinic in Cali-
fornia, then returned to his hometown, Rochester, NY, for
long-term rehabilitation. He has declined media requests
since his accident, but sources report that he works at a
local ski shop and is permanently disabled.

The article goes on, but I stop reading. My mind spins uncontrollably. This . . . this is not what I signed up for. I'm fake dating a guy in
my support group, not some . . . Olympic gold medalist?

"Skylar." Pike knocks, his voice hushed. "I can explain."

I ignore him. Analia and Emy have bombarded our chat with
over five hundred messages since I put my phone away.

HE'S FUCKING FAMOUS, I write.

"Skylar, please, can I come in for a sec?"

"I'll be out in a minute!"

Help! I write. **I'm hiding in the bathroom. I just found out.**

did u find out his net worth is 6 mil? Emy says.

I didn't even know snowboarders made money.

does he have a secret twin? Emy continues. **can he promote my
reels?**

Analia asks, **Are you having a good time?**

I slump against the sink. *A good time* may be stretching it, but I'm not having an awful time. **My pressure's bad. Almost ready to call it quits early. Laurie is way less ableist than my mom. Food is good. Pike keeps touching me.**

Do we like this? Analia asks.

I don't know what I think anymore. I tell them how I'm accidentally talking back to his mom and how his presence makes me nervous. **In a hot guy nervous way**, I clarify. **And now he's famous!? Why wouldn't he tell me?**

He did say you had to meet his expectations, Analia says. **Maybe he's keeping that in his pocket. If things go south, he could tell the paparazzi you're a stalker who was so desperate to date him, you pretended to be his girlfriend. Or something. IDK.**

Pike doesn't *seem* like that kind of asshole. But he didn't tell me who he was for a reason. **Could he get away with that? I have screenshots too.**

My heart races even as I type it. Famous people do have a better shot at controlling the narrative. If he decided to spin this story to the media, I'd be left to defend myself against a horde of strangers who might believe anything he said. I'd just be some nobody trying to take him down. An easy target.

Fame and money come with power, Analia says. **Tread carefully until you figure out his angle.**

from the articles we read, Emy says, **his sex life is busier than a hotel on spring break. u could use that to ur advantage.**

Emy, I warn.

what! apparently, he's more available than a 24-hour diner. look.

She sends a link: **Brandon Pike + women**.

My dry eyelids scrape like sandpaper as I skim the search results. Most include words like *scandal* and *heartbreak*, showing Pike with stunning women on his arm. There are ridiculous titles like **Snow Heartthrob's Lovemaking Is an Olympic Sport of Its Own**.

HOLY SHIT, I write. **This explains the supermodel comment.**

right? Emy says. **not necessarily a bad thing, tho. son probably has some skills.**

With the way he practically pinned me against the wall earlier, it's hard not to imagine some of those skills. My skin grows hot just thinking about it. But that fantasy quickly vanishes when I remember why I'm here. If he's been lying about who he is, I can't help but worry that he might use it against me somehow.

My performance has to be perfect until we're alone.

I go back to the photo of Brandon Pike the pro snowboarder. He has unruly long hair, wavy bangs that fall across his face, and an irresistible, cocky grin.

I barely recognize him.

"Okay," I say after I've skimmed another dozen articles. "You don't know anything about snowboarding anyway. It's fine. It's just dinner. Just one more date."

I take my evening dose of meds, fix my lipstick, and strut out of the bathroom.

I can do this.

8

Pike

S kylar okay, honey?”

Mom's setting out frozen cheesecake and more champagne. Thankfully, she doesn't have to drive tonight. Since my accident, her liquor cabinet's never been so stocked.

"She's doing something with her medication," I lie.

Ollie paws at my chest, wanting down. I don't want to stand either—my knee's killing me. But I need to intercept Skylar before she tells Mom it's fake.

I should've been honest with Skylar. There was no need to mention my career, though. Mom rarely talks about snowboarding anymore. She even put away the framed pictures of my awards, thinking I can't handle them.

I need to stall. "What were you doing in our support group that night?"

"Learning," she says.

Too innocently.

"At midnight?"

"I get notifications when you post."

"You're serious."

"What were *you* doing in the group so late?"

Getting support, I almost snap. "Skylar and I *have* chronic pain. We spend a lot of time in there."

Mom dips her spoon into her raspberry cheesecake slice. "Talking about being depressed?"

That's it. I'm taking up Skylar's offer to drop her from the group.

"I'm fine. How many times do I need to tell you that?"

"Your whole life changed in an instant. How can you be fine? I'm not." Tears prick her eyes, and my sternum burns. I put Ollie down and give Mom a quick hug.

"I thought I was going to lose you," she says. "Again."

I pat her back like I always do. She saw me crash. She's told me a hundred times she thought I was dead.

"It was creative writing," I say.

"It read like a cry for help."

I grit my teeth. It was *not* a cry for help. I know because I fucking *wrote* it. It was…well, I'm still working out exactly what it was, but I'm not suicidal. I can have complex thoughts about my situation. Why can't she see that?

"You don't have to worry about me."

"I always worry. You've been so withdrawn lately. I never thought I'd miss reading about you sleeping around, but at least then I knew you were enjoying yourself."

I barely contain my groan. Does she seriously think the number of women I sleep with determines how "normal" I am—as she calls it? That my disabilities make me incapable of bringing someone home?

I am. I have.

Maybe consider that I'm burned out from rehab. That this is the first couple months I've had a moment to breathe. Maybe I don't feel like constantly going out anymore because I actually need sleep. Maybe the majority of people piss me off because they're so damn ableist.

Maybe try *anything* else.

But we don't discuss the women. Ever. She knew what went down—hard not to when she was my manager for most of my career—but we left it unspoken. I'm not about to start explaining that area of my life to her now.

"But you're with Skylar," she reasons, scooping Ollie up. "Of course, you won't be around much. It's the first hope I've had in months."

I nod, realizing all I've done is confirm her flawed perspective by bringing Skylar around. I wish I could articulate that depression isn't cured by a relationship. Hell, I wish I could articulate my *depression*.

"I read that men who have pelvic operations sometimes sustain erectile dysfunction," she continues. "I wondered if everything was still working. Oh, don't look so upset. I'm not insinuating there's anything wrong with your lovemaking—"

"Mom!" I cover my bleeding ears. It's too disturbing to know she's one of those people who wonders about my sex life. "Skylar and I have a great . . . *romantic* . . . relationship."

Perfect. Now I'm inappropriately picturing sex with Skylar.

"I'm delighted to hear it."

"We're done talking about this."

She pats my hand. "Let me give you some womanly advice."

"Please don't."

"You've never been in a relationship before. Indulge me, Brandon."

"It better not be about sex."

"I know it's easy to get caught up in the physicality of a new relationship, but make sure you're paying attention to your girlfriend's emotional needs too."

Now I'm just insulted. "Why wouldn't I?"

"Sometimes men miss these details. Think of how much your father missed—"

"I'm not Dad."

"No," she agrees, "you're not."

"I care about other people besides myself." And I've always made my casual intentions clear. I never cheated on anyone. Never would.

"Of course you do, honey. But ask yourself, how 'fine' can your girlfriend be when she's online by herself while you're asleep next to her? That's a woman with a lot on her mind. Make sure you engage with her enough so she can shut off after a long day."

"I engage plenty. Skylar is a group moderator. She likes being online."

"All I'm saying is it's helpful to check in with your girlfriend often."

"Thanks, but Skylar's perfectly okay."

"She has an incurable brain disease. How can she ever be okay?"

"It's—" I struggle for the right words. "There are *nuances*—"

Ollie barks and tries to escape Mom's grip. I turn and see Skylar, half-obscured by the entryway.

"Hi," I say.

Skylar bites her lip. "Hi."

Sorry I didn't tell you, I mouth.

"To answer your question, Laurie…"

My stomach drops. Skylar heard us talking about her. I'm losing count of how many times Mom's been offensive.

"It's none of her business," I say. "You don't have to explain anything."

She acknowledges me with a nod, then slides her arms around my waist from behind, her fingers interlacing against my stomach. I freeze, then force myself to relax. A soft waft of caramel and something warm wraps around me just as firmly as her arms. It's grounding and dizzying all at once.

She peeks around me to face Mom, who has the audacity to look like the world's most sympathetic citizen.

"I remember asking myself that when I got diagnosed," Skylar says. "How could I ever be okay? But you get used to it, even if it's scary. You find people who help you through it."

"Like our group," I say.

"I do get sad about it," she says. "Sometimes because of the pain, sometimes because I'm angry, sometimes because my brain is literally getting squished, and that messes with emotions and hormones. But I don't have to be happy all the time. Pike understands that. It's one reason we work."

"One of many," I add.

She hugs me with her whole body, sending a startled jolt through me. Her closeness, her warmth against me…it feels too real. I try to remind myself what we're doing here. I wanted to give Mom the impression everything's peachy, but what Skylar said is better— closer to what I wish I could convey.

"There are pills for depression too," Mom says.

"Mother," I warn. I rest my hand on top of Skylar's in hopes she understands I've got her back. "That's none of your business."

She points at the cheesecake. "Come, eat. There's a weather advisory for Ontario and Monroe counties. You should spend the night."

Skylar freezes. "We should take dessert to go so we don't get stuck here." She emphasizes *stuck here* with two tight squeezes around my stomach. "I have something in the morning."

"And I'm meeting Kal," I add.

"We'll be careful, Laurie." Skylar lets go, and the sudden lack of her warmth jerks me back to reality. A few more minutes of acting, then we're done with the first half of our deal.

Mom gets up to hug Skylar. "It was lovely to meet you. I haven't seen my son smile so much in months. Thank you."

I'd be touched if I weren't annoyed. I smile a normal amount.

Outside, my car's covered in thick, wet snow. I clear it off with determined swipes of my cane instead of stepping up into my car to get my snow scraper. It bothers my knee and hips too much.

Mom must've driven me to a million appointments in this beast, with its all-terrain conversion and platform wheelchair lift. Now that I'm mostly using my cane, the lift still comes in handy when I want to bring my wheelchair along. The downside is when I'm not using the ramp, the step up is huge.

As soon as I back into the main road, Skylar turns on me.

"You're famous? What the hell, Pike? I can't believe you didn't tell me!"

I keep my eyes on the road. "There was no need."

"You must love being on your end of this power dynamic. If I didn't meet your expectations, what angle were you planning to use with the paparazzi? Gold digger? Stalker? I can already see the trolls coming for me on your behalf."

It takes every sore muscle in my body to keep me from turning to her and gaping. That's what she's been thinking since she found out? I'm about to mutter, *Okay, crazy*, and drop the subject, but Luis pops into my head.

When I first moved in with him, he sat me down after a couple weeks and asked me to stop using ableist language. I didn't even realize it had peppered my vocabulary most of my life. Now I know that words like *crazy* and *stupid* and *dumb* have been used to oppress disabled people throughout history. Some were even invented by eugenicists. It's been hard to erase them completely from my vocabulary, but I'm trying.

How to rephrase. Skylar's not crazy. She's being *unreasonable*. It's because she thinks I'll hold this over her. Potentially tell lies about her to the media. It's sobering when I think about it that way.

But I'm still insulted.

"Involving the paparazzi would be *great* for me." I can't keep the sarcasm out of my voice. "Pity party for Brandon Pike. If my own mother can't handle my sad poetry, imagine the world."

We pass the tiny shops and bed-and-breakfasts along Main Street, the remaining string lights making it look like a Christmas village. I slow down as we hit the winding turns. Nothing's shoveled or salted out here.

"I didn't think about it that way," Skylar says when I stop at a light. "I don't understand why you kept it a secret."

"You freaked me out, that's why. I thought you were an obsessed snow bunny."

"Snow bunny? Do I even want to know?"

"Snow bunnies are like groupies for skiing and boarding." I leave out the fact that they're also typically gorgeous.

"Oh, thank goodness. I was picturing something like a snow furry." Her laughter clears the stiff air between us.

"I didn't tell you because once I realized you didn't know, it was nice not to have that in the equation. And I'm not famous anymore," I clarify. "I *was* famous. I'm a different person now."

"You can disappear from the public eye, but you still hold the power. If you ever decided to throw me under the bus, who would believe me over you? They'd think I was after your money, fame, or dick."

Hearing that word out of her mouth momentarily throws me off-kilter. "I get why you're worried. But I would never do that, Skylar."

"So, you're a closet celebrity and a closet poet," she says after a moment. "Anything else in the closet?"

"That's it. Besides this relationship, I guess. Which...you're not going to tell anyone about, right? Now that you know who I am?"

We pass another streetlamp, and I see her turn to me out of the corner of my eye. "What are you going to give me for my silence?"

The only thing she could want is money. Which is—not crazy, no. It's extortion. But I'm not as loaded as she probably assumes. Most of my money has gone toward an exorbitant mortgage, my parents' retirement accounts, covering Mom's salary, funding training and travels, and bailing Dad out.

In just the past two years, I've burned through nearly $2 million on medical expenses. Top surgeons, critical care, elite rehab clinics, and my custom $23,000 wheelchair have eaten through my savings. Insurance barely scratches the surface. Only thirty physical therapy visits a year? It's a joke. I'm paying out of pocket for everything else: pain creams, braces, supplements, stim and ice machines, a decent bed, massages, dry needling, an ergonomic desk, even pre-cut food.

I know that makes me privileged, but without any sponsorship money coming in, there's no way I can maintain my previous lifestyle. I finally cut Dad off for good, but I'm still paying for Mom's livelihood, like I always have. She uprooted her entire life for me. That's why she's pushing me to do work that draws on my notoriety. I'm eventually going to need something when my savings runs out. And it will.

So if Skylar's counting on a big check, that's not going to happen.

"Trust me when I say you don't want them sniffing around because you're associated with me."

"Relax," she says. "I'm not going to tell anyone."

"Thank you." I force my muscles to unclench. "People don't understand why I won't do an interview. It's less that the media wants to talk to me. It's what they want to talk to me about. Before, it was the women, the lifestyle, the snowboarding. Now all they want to focus on is my accident and everything I lost."

"That's fair," she muses. "People are always commenting on disabled people's bodies anyway. It's worse when you're a public figure."

I nod and sit back. "Listen, I'm sorry you got ambushed at dinner. You did great, though. Next time will be easier."

"Next time?" Skylar groans.

She's gonna bail on our deal. I can feel it.

"Can we discuss your blackmailing—Pike! Look out!"

Bright headlights blaze in front of us. My heart slams against my chest. I'm on the correct side, but this motherfucker isn't. I ease off my brakes and swerve off-road, grinding up the snowbank. Skylar lets out a bloodcurdling scream. A second later, we're back on the road.

"Fuck." I'm shaking. "That was—"

The car spins. Full-circle, fifty-mile-an-hour spinning. My heart-beat floods my ears. We must've hit black ice.

I reach for Skylar. My arm barely crosses her body before we fly over the snowbank.

9

Skylar

I stop screaming when we fall into a ditch. My chest slams into the seat belt as we jerk to a halt, but the airbags don't deploy.

The car's headlights are buried in snow, and it's dark with only the dash lights visible. But the rhythmic *whack…whack…whack…* of the wipers slowly grounds me.

Pike's arm is across my chest, as if he planned to keep me from vaulting through the windshield himself. "Skylar, are you okay?"

I put my hand over his. "I'm okay. Are you?"

A beat. "Yes."

We stay there for an eternity, just breathing.

"I'm sorry," Pike says. "That guy wasn't in his lane. I don't—" He inhales deeply. Exhales again. "I'm just glad you're okay."

"Let's go back to your mom's." Twenty minutes ago, staying over seemed like the worst thing that could happen. Now, it's dying in a freak storm in Middle of Nowhere, New York.

"Agreed."

But we get no traction. The wheels spin and spin, and Pike lets out curse after curse.

"Can we call a tow truck now?" I ask.

"Let me take a look first."

"You don't think you can, like, lift us out, right?"

"I do not. But maybe something's stuck."

"The *front of your car* is stuck."

"She's a big girl. She can get out."

I peer into the dark void of his car. "Do you have a shovel back there?"

"Wouldn't you think I was a murderer if I did?"

He has a point. "What about a snow safety box?"

"The hell is that?"

"You know…it has an electric blanket, a flashlight, a foldable shovel, some sort of weapon…"

"Oh, a winter survival kit? I had one for backcountry boarding, but there's civilization around here. Hang on, why is there a weapon?"

"You never know who you'll meet while stranded."

His eyebrows draw together. "I have my cane."

"True, that ice tip is stabby."

"I'm going to check the situation outside," he says. "I can't shovel. My back."

I crawl around in the dark, finding my phone wedged between the seats. No service. Perfect.

I can't open my door, so I climb over Pike's seat and tumble out next to him. I hold up my phone to get closer to a tower, but it only gets my screen wet.

Pike is on his butt by the driver's side front wheel, scooping snow with his gloves. I suppress an annoyed noise. Maybe he knows what he's doing.

"Do you have service?" I ask.

"Nope. Never do out here."

Panic rushes down my spine. I had service before—spotty, but there. Is it the weather? I go back inside and toggle my phone's airplane mode until Pike eventually joins me.

"Is it fixed?" I ask, and his silence shifts me from panic to survival mode. "I'll go flag someone down."

"No, I'll go. You're not wearing pants."

"If I get cold, I'll come back. You keep digging or…whatever you were doing."

I sink all the way to my upper thigh as I climb up the bank. "Oh, wow, that's cold, aah."

There's smothered laughter behind me. I'm too busy half shrieking to yell at him.

My toes go numb under my mostly-for-cuteness-and-not-warmth boots. At least I wore my compression stockings underneath. The wind whips my hair into my face. I can't blame Pike for not having a snow safety box when I didn't wear a hat or gloves. We are both terrible Rochestarians.

Ten minutes later, I'm an icicle and Pike is trying to coax me back to the car. "We can take turns waiting," he says. "Please. You're going to get sick."

Reluctantly, I return to the car to warm up. But the heat feels like air-conditioning, and the engine keeps making this revving noise.

Pike comes back after a while, all grimaces.

"We're going to freeze to death," I say.

He mutters "no" like a mantra. "I've gotten caught on mountains before. There are ways. We'll turn the heat on and off intermittently. And there's always…" He trails off, his eyes flitting over me, then away. "Never mind. Just take my jacket and try to get dry."

I take it, enveloped in that same clean scent that's hung around him all night. Pike gives me his hat and gloves as well.

"We're going to be fine," he says, more to himself.

Now that I'm slightly less frozen, I can think more clearly. "We are," I announce, "because I'm going to get help."

Walking in a snowstorm is worse than staying in a car without heat, but at least I have a destination. There are restaurants, shops, and homes along the route. It's probably only a fifteen-minute walk to the closest inhabited building.

I've lost feeling in every part of my body except my face and thighs, which sting like fresh cuts. Pike keeps offering me his outerwear. I only let him lend me his hat for a few minutes at a time. I have my own coat, and he needs his gloves. His hand is always exposed with his cane.

I wanted him to stay in the car while I got help, but he wouldn't.

Now we're silent. Which is bad, I think. Everyone died in *Titanic* when things got silent.

I loop my arm through Pike's non-cane arm. "How are you doing?"

"Fine. Great."

Not this again. Everything about Pike's posture radiates pain: pinched forehead, lips in a permanent wince, and an increasingly pronounced limp.

"Interesting. I feel like letting the Abominable Snowman claim me, and I didn't even have surgery recently."

Pike shakes me off his arm. "Your pace is throwing me off-balance."

"I'm not asking because I think you're fragile. I'm asking because I'm worried."

"We're going to be fine." His voice muffles as he tucks his chin into his collar. "What else do you want me to say?"

"Something real."

He grunts. "I think my nuts are getting frostbite."

I laugh, which makes my head throb more, and I wonder if the blackness creeping in on my peripheral vision isn't the night around us but the pressure on my optic nerves.

"I won't be able to walk tomorrow," he continues. "Potentially not for a week. But we're almost in town. Look."

There are streetlamps ahead, and beyond them, *houses*. With lights.

I whip out my phone.

Nothing.

"I like when you laugh."

I look up at Pike. "What?"

"Something real," he says.

I fall behind him, a little stunned. I did force him to respond. I do that sometimes. Get pushy. He sounded genuine, though. Which— no. It's sweet, but the poor guy probably just wants me to shut up.

By the time we reach the heart of the village, I couldn't say anything even if I wanted. The devil's Tic Tacs have made breathing too laborious. It's Pike who pushes me to keep going past a dark flower shop and an empty café. He holds my hand, murmuring that we'll be warm in a few seconds.

When we finally reach a house, Pike bangs on the door. It cracks open, and a white man in his fifties leers at me from the shadows. My mind flashes to horror stories of people getting murdered in scenarios like this. I slink behind Pike's massive body as he details our troubles.

"Can we sit inside while a tow truck comes? We can pay," he adds.

"That won't be necessary." The man ushers us inside.

The warmth of his home makes my nose run. I sit on a bench, shivering, as Pike speaks to him, then announces, "David's offered to let us stay the night. He has a guest room upstairs."

David smiles at me from behind Pike, and my stomach churns with unease. He's probably nice, but I'm not trading warmth for being murdered.

"Let's c-call the tow truck and g-go—" I take a few breaths to steady my clattering teeth. "To your mom's."

Pike's snow-covered brows draw together, his expression tightening with worry. "We need to get warm. Rest. It'll be midnight before we can get anywhere in this mess."

"Your mom—"

"—was drinking. She can't drive."

David's still smiling at us. At me.

"Can I speak to you in private?" I hiss.

"Sorry, David, just a sec." Pike drags me into a hallway. "Skylar. Please. My body is on the brink of collapse. Now that I know we can rest, I can't keep going. I physically *can't*. We'll sort out the car tomorrow."

I knew his body was giving out. Mine has shut down as well. But I don't want to sleep here. "Maybe I can get an Uber. You stay, and I-I—"

"If you find a ride, I'll go with you. But first, we need to warm up if we don't want to end up in the hospital."

"I want to get warm, too, but how do we know it's *safe* to stay with him?"

Pike's brown eyes soften in understanding. "I'll make sure he only interacts with me." His voice drops to a whisper. "I'll keep you safe, I promise."

The next few minutes whir by numbly as Pike and David arrange things. I find David's Wi-Fi and update the girls about the tow truck situation.

everything's going to be okay, Emy writes. **we've got the address bookmarked.**

Hopefully this isn't weird, Analia says, **but here's my phone number. If you give me yours, I'll add you to my favorites so my phone will ring even when I'm asleep.**

Emy shoots hers off too.

Despite my icicled face, the corners of my eyes grow wet as I share my number. I'm so grateful for their friendship. **I still don't have service, though.**

Then we'll stay right here in the group until you're settled, Analia says.

We search for rideshares, but the closest one is in Canandaigua, and when they don't accept my request, I follow David up his rickety

Victorian stairs. Pike is in so much pain he has to scoot up backward. David leads us into a room with a paisley rug and an adjoining bathroom. At least I won't have to exit once inside.

There's only one bed, I report.

i want updates! Emy says. **ur spending the night with brandon fucking pike!!**

A different kind of apprehension shoots through me. But even if David offered two different rooms, I'd still stay here with Pike.

Time starts fading in and out. My ears are so plugged I might as well be cruising at thirty thousand feet. My head wants to split open. This is why I don't overexert myself or exercise. It raises my intracranial pressure.

"Skylar?" Pike asks. "Skylar?"

He takes my phone from me before I even know it's happening. "Hey!" I protest, but he turns on the video feature in my private chat with the girls. We've never used it, and another nervous surge twists my stomach.

Pike angles the camera at his face. Analia answers, adjusting her screen as her long bangs fall over her eyes, the purple highlights of her inverted bob catching in her camera light. In her pictures, she often wears dramatic makeup, but tonight her face looks soft and shiny, like she just completed her bedtime skincare routine.

"Oh," she says, her cheeks tinging red at the sight of Pike. "Hello."

Emy answers next. She's already in bed, her long raven hair swept into a high bun against her pillow.

"Evening, ladies," Pike says.

"Brandon Pike," Emy purrs. She waves with a flick of her fingers, showing off a flash of silver nail polish. "To what do we owe this pleasure? Everything okay with our girl?"

Emy has an *accent*. How did I not realize this? Only a slight one, but it's still there despite her fluency.

"Skylar?" Analia asks. "Are you there too?"

Huge black glasses accentuate her green eyes. I've only ever seen pictures of her without them, so maybe she only wears them at night. Which reminds me.

"I don't have my glasses," I whisper. My contacts need to come out when I sleep. What am I going to do? I can barely see a foot in front of me without them. I don't have my sleep meds either.

Pike moves the screen so they can see me.

Analia's expression fills with worry. She sits up straighter, the sleeve of her zip-up hoodie falling down her shoulder to reveal a bright plaid tank top. "Skylar, are you okay?"

"I think she's in shock from the cold." Pike tugs me closer to his side. "Just wanted you to meet me so she can have some reassurance. She's scared of being stuck in this house. Probably of me too."

"No," I murmur. "Pike's not scary."

"Well," he says, "at least now you know what's going on."

Emy smiles like the Cheshire cat. "That's very thoughtful of you."

"We really need to get out of these wet clothes and get warm. My only motive here is keeping the two of us safe."

"Stay on your side of the bed," Analia commands.

Emy tsks, her brown eyes still glinting. "Unless Skylar's cold."

Pike chuckles, but it sounds muted. Distant. The lights burn too brightly, and the video's making me dizzy. I'm watching the world through falling snow, every detail blurred and unreachable. I want to see the girls, but if I don't focus on anything, the spinning is less intense. My eyeballs drift to the walls to balance me out.

On bad days, I always wonder if the rest of my life will be like this. Muted. Never fully capable of experiencing everything as it is. A blank wall for a view.

"Have you ever taken NyQuil?" I ask.

"Huh?"

It dawns on me that Emy's winding down from a joke, and my eyes flicker to her animated face. The room tilts. I focus elsewhere.

"Or a sleeping pill?" I ask.

"Skylar, are you okay?" Analia repeats.

Am I ever? Will I ever be?

"I feel like I'm taking NyQuil. Like it's in my veins, dosing higher and higher until I can no longer stay upright. Except I'm not tired."

Silence fills the room.

Wrong moment to share. I interrupted Emy's joke, though I can't remember what it was. Fuck, the spinning.

Pike's freezing fingers come to my chin, forcing my eyes up and to the side. My entire body cascades over an imaginary ledge. I grip his jacket.

"Do you need to lie down?" he asks.

"I'm okay." Emy and Analia are on video. They're meeting *Pike*.

"Skylar," Analia starts, "are you sure—"

"I'm fine." I barely recognize my own croak of a voice. "I'm great." Oh gosh, I get why Pike says this kind of thing now. "We should get warm."

"Let me give you my cell just in case." Pike leans heavily on his cane as he recites his number. He stands on his left leg, the right lifted off the floor.

"Get warm, Skylar!" Analia calls.

"And have fun," Emy chirps.

And just like that, we're alone.

10
Skylar

I blink at my blank screen. "You can't just call my friends."

"Hi. Welcome back." There's concern etched on Pike's features as he hands me my phone.

"Welcome back?"

"You were standing in the corner like a statue. I was trying to get your attention."

I stare at him, thrown. Most people don't notice how often I have to zone out just to keep functioning. Or if they do, they don't want to address it. Chronic pain isn't something they can fix, and sitting with someone else's discomfort is hard. Digging deeper feels messy, even awkward. It's easier to move on. So they do.

But Pike noticed. Even more, he cared enough to do something about it. It feels strange, almost unsettling, to have someone push past the surface and actually see me. My whole life, outside the group, is masking how I really feel.

"David gave us towels." Pike points to the full bed, upon which there are, indeed, two folded navy towels. "Please get in the shower and warm up."

"Why don't you go first?"

"I promised I'd keep you safe. That includes hypothermia."

"But your clothes are wet too."

"I'll take them off while you shower. I doubt you'd appreciate me stripping in front of you."

I might appreciate that, honestly. Especially in a reality that doesn't involve all this fake dating, blackmailing, and freezing. This whole thing is already too surreal without adding thoughts of his naked body.

"Skylar. I don't want hypothermia either." His tight smile reflects the bone-deep exhaustion in his voice. If I don't get a move on, Pike can't either.

"I don't have anything to wear after showering."

He points to another small pile. "Pajamas."

I work my way over there, my body stiff, and inspect a pair of pants. "Um...these are never going to fit me."

"Hmm, yeah. David has tiny hips."

I grimace at the long-sleeved shirts. "And a tiny chest."

His gaze flicks to my chest for a fraction of a second, then back to the shirt. He coughs. "How wet are you?"

My cheeks heat. Everything is soaked minus my underwear, but I'm not telling him that.

"My T-shirt is mostly dry." He runs a hand over his neck. "You can wear that to sleep, if you'd be more comfortable."

"Okay." *Please let it fit. Please let it fit.*

"I don't think his clothes will fit me, either, though. I'm pretty broad," he says, like it's not obvious. "So...I'll just be in my boxers."

I swing my arms at my sides. "Better you than me."

Based on Emy's womanizer articles, I expect him to reach for the back neckline of his shirt and tug it over his head. A lot of men get cocky the second they're given permission to remove clothing. But he just stands there waiting.

I head to the bathroom.

I don't trust myself to stand, so I sit in the tub. It's only once I'm under the steaming hot water that I realize how numb I am. How numb Pike must be outside the door. A small, unlocked door that barely shuts.

Sometime tonight, though, Pike became a reassuring presence. This nervousness I feel, knowing he's out there taking off his clothes, and the bed that awaits us, is completely different. It only escalates when he knocks and sticks a hand in with his shirt.

I let the warm water soak the back of my neck. It's all cramped up like it usually is in the evening. The shower is as close to a heat pack as I'll get tonight.

I feel slightly more human afterward. I slink out of the bathroom in Pike's shirt, the towel wrapped around my legs like armor. Pike sits on the rug, his back against the wall, with his coat draped over his upper body. His sweater lies next to him, soaked on the bottom like my dress.

"That, um." His throat bobs. "That fits you well."

The fabric stretches snugly across my chest, hugging the curves of my hips before it flares out just enough to tease the tops of my thighs. I tug at the hem instinctively, like I might somehow coax it to cover more, but the motion just makes it pull tighter in all the wrong places, clinging in ways that make me far too aware of myself.

I throw him David's pants. "Good luck with these."

If his grimace is any indication, it costs him a lot to get back up. Once I hear the shower turn on, I triple-check that the bedroom door is locked before removing my towel. Pike's shirt barely covers my butt.

I feel like this could lead to some awkward, accidental spooning, I tell the girls as I slide into bed and squint with one eye. **There's a 90% chance this shirt will ride up while I sleep and wrap itself around my boobs.**

body heat is important in these dire situations. Oh, Emy.

He was sweet! Analia says. **And thoughtful to call us. I bet you'd have to initiate any spooning.**

He called you guys spontaneously. I hope it wasn't weird.

it was fun! Emy says. **now go play with ur fake boyfriend.**

I rest my eyes before responding. **Pike is used to dating super-models. Him being in boxers is more of a courtesy.**

Emy sends four flames. **but u'd hook up with him.**

In a different reality, yes. In this reality, I actually have to see the man more than once.

The truth is, I'm as much of a one-night stand type of person as Pike apparently is. Less frequently, of course. *Much* less frequently. Every once in a while, I go to a bar when I'm out of town for work. There's also this guy, Marcus, who I hook up with whenever I'm in Ithaca.

Occasionally, I wonder if I'm missing out on something. If I should give relationships another chance. But then I see all the depressing posts in the group, and it reminds me.

Relationships don't work when you're sick. If society hasn't already convinced you that you're a burden, a relationship will. Instead of practicing self-love, you change so they'll keep loving you. You convince yourself to play down your concerns, because it's more important to make the relationship work than to honor who you are.

I refuse to do that again. I know my worth. A hookup now and then is enough.

There's a small TV in the bedroom. I can't watch, but I need to do something besides lie here counting the spins with the seconds. And to avoid listening to Pike shower. Is he having a hard time balancing in there too? I wish all showers had seats.

I find the Game Show Network and close my eyes. *Who Wants to Be a Millionaire* comes on after the commercials. Which state has one bear to every twenty-one people?

"It's C, Alaska."

I startle at Pike's deep voice behind me and mute the program. "I think it's B, Wyom…" I trail off at the sight of him. Pike looks like he stepped out of a romance novel cover.

The flickering glow of the TV highlights the wide stretch of his shoulders and the muscular curves of his arms, emphasizing his impressive build. His defined chest still glistens from the shower, and the water catches the light in a way that accentuates every powerful line of his body.

And there are lines. Hard angles meet smooth planes as his stomach dips into a deep V-cut. My blood runs hot. That body is going to be next to mine all night.

"No more room in the bathroom with your stuff in there." He carries his clothes awkwardly in front of his crotch, where I'm absolutely, 100 percent not looking. My eyes are up on his pecs where, on the left, he has a tiny roman numeral tattoo that looks like it starts with *MMX*—

"Skylar?"

"Maybe hang them on the blinds?" I respectfully sneak another peek while he loops his jeans over the curtain rod. My mouth all but waters.

His back is a testament to hard-earned athleticism. It flexes with a natural ease that sends his surgery scars rippling. His black boxer briefs highlight the narrowness of his waist and the strength in his legs.

Damn. That is one deliciously muscular butt.

His right thigh is smaller than his left. Scars and stretch marks cover his right knee. There's black Kinesio tape on his legs in intricate lines that I bet Ranielle put on for him. I hope it helped him while we hiked through the snow.

A foil wrapper falls out of his jeans.

"You brought a condom!?"

"No!" He scrambles to pick it up. "I mean, yes, I brought it. Obviously. But only because Luis tossed me one. He thought it was a real date. Which it's not. Obviously."

I shrink back under the covers. "Obviously."

He tucks the condom back into his pants and stands there, shivering.

"Well, come on," I say. "Plenty of room in here." There isn't, but I'm going to ignore that.

The mattress dips as he climbs in. "I like this one. But *The Price Is Right* is better."

"You don't have to pretend you like it because I put that in our fake-relationship story."

He hits my feet with his feet and retracts like he's been burned. "The Game Show Network always played at rehab. I thought you were the one pretending."

"I have a lot of game show apps on my phone. I play them when I'm in waiting rooms because they don't require internet."

I think he nods, but I'm keeping my eyes glued on the vicinity of the screen. There's less than one inch between our bare legs, and that one inch electrifies the air around us. My eyes already sting, and now they all but water. The pillow is a brick against my head. Falling asleep is already hard at home, so it's going to be impossible here.

We let the show run for a few commercials. Pike is more enthusiastic than I expected—especially when it comes to arguing with me about the correct answer.

Ninety percent of the time, he's right.

"No fair," I say. "I practice all the time."

"Mad skills." He's all smug. "Hey, we should take a picture. I need some on my phone in case Mom comes snooping."

I tug self-consciously on the shirt he lent me. "Just lock your phone."

"She could ask to see more pics." When I remain silent, he juts his lip out in a pout. "Please?"

Does he actually expect me to resist that face? I sit up straighter and smile at the camera.

"Nah. We need to sell this." He closes the space between us until our hips are aligned, and raises one arm up for me to slide under. I hesitate, already burning from the way we're now connected. "That's it," he coaxes as I finally settle into his shoulder. He leans his head against mine. And oh, he's nice and warm. Body heat is good. Body heat is great. "Smile like you're into me."

"You first, buddy."

Pike laughs, showcasing another megawatt smile, but he settles on a sexy look with closed lips: comfy, sated, and sleepy. My toes curl. If he's able to turn on this level of magnetism when he feels like it, what Emy said about his reputation makes sense.

I nuzzle more into his shoulder, going for in love but shy. After all, it's still early in our supposed relationship. The flash goes off, and as I blink, he lets go of me.

"Let's see." His head settles back against mine as he shows me the picture. And there we are. In bed. Together. Between his naked shoulders and my tangled hair, it looks like we just had amazing sex.

"That's pretty good," I choke out.

"If I woke up hungover tomorrow without any recollection, I'd buy it." He winks at me, and my soul tries to leave my body.

I lean closer for another look. Really, I want him to stay where he is because the heat radiating off his body is glorious. "It's too intimate for your mom."

"You're right," he says on a sigh. "I guess we'll have to take more tomorrow when we're dressed."

"Pike," I say after the show ends. "In all seriousness, is something going on between you and Maria?"

An amused smile twists his lips. "No."

"Really? Because if I was, you know, sexting someone, I'd be hurt if he was in bed with another woman, regardless of intent."

He rolls to his side to face me, and the glorious heat disappears. Our knees touch, but he doesn't flinch back this time. "We're not sexting."

"Flirting?"

"Nope."

"But you said…if it's not platonic…you could tell your mom you're over me. Then I'm off the hook for the second date too."

"Nothing's happening with Maria. Sorry, you're stuck with me."

Getting stranded here isn't enough? Ugh.

He moves a curl off my face. "Are you warm enough?"

"Getting there."

"Any frostbite?"

Is he offering to look? "Don't think so. You?"

"My body is on fire. I'm waiting for my oxy to kick in."

"You had extra medicine?"

"I once got stuck in stopped traffic on I-90. Vowed never to get caught without my meds again. You don't have anything in your purse?"

"I only took what I needed for dinnertime. No idea how I'm going to fall asleep."

His eyes fill with concern. "I'm sorry I've caused you extra pain."

I grumble something incoherent. It's hard to be mad at him when he's looking at me like that.

"So you do like game shows," he says. "But the part about getting along with your family…that was a lie, wasn't it?"

"You caught me."

"You mentioned something about them sucking before. Why's that?"

I open my mouth to answer. Close it again. "You keep trying to pretend everything's great in your life. Why's that?"

This close to him, I see the spark of defiance in his pupils, like he can't believe I called him out on his bullshit. He swallows before he answers.

"Next question."

So it's going to be like that. "If I looked into your reputation with women, what would it tell me?"

"That I like to party. That I have a different bunny every night. That I'm a womanizer." He says it like he's reading from one of the articles Emy sent me.

"Are you?"

"If I was, I'm not anymore."

"Anything else you want to tell me before I google you thoroughly? Because I will."

He props his head up with his fist. "There was this one time I was on a masked singing show. I had to dress up like a polar bear, and the judges guessed who I was based on my voice, which is awful, so I got booted off first. It's pretty embarrassing."

Of all the things he could tell me. "That's it? You can't sing? No skeletons?"

"If you dig hard enough, you'll find shit on anyone. My crew rode hard and partied hard."

So far, he hasn't mentioned any of his friends besides his roommate. "What happened with your crew? After your accident?"

"They were there, in the beginning. We were a tight group. Pro snowboarding in general is like one big family. But our paths diverged. It might've been different if I hadn't come back here."

"For rehab?"

"To get help from my mom. I lived with her in the beginning while I got back on my feet."

My level of respect for Laurie goes up. Emy lives with her parents too. I asked mine if I could move back in with them when I lost my job after the first year of failed lumbar punctures and medication. They told me I was an adult now, and adults don't live with their parents. In hindsight, I'm relieved I'm not stuck there. I'd have an even worse power dynamic with them than I already do.

"Do you call your snowboarding friends to talk?" I ask.

"We'd usually get together to do something, like have a beer or board. It's weird now, living different lives, trying to start up regular phone calls."

"That's so sad. I'm sorry." I thought if something big and visible happened, your friends would be there for you. When I lost my friends, it was invisible and gradual.

"It's fine. I'm having lunch tomorrow with a childhood friend. If we ever get out of here." His breath tickles my neck. "Your turn. Do you really have a brother?"

"Yes. Devlin lives in New York City, and we talk, like, once a month, max. And by 'talk' I mean we essentially make sure the other person is still alive, then hang up. I do love my niece, Jasmine, though. Just hard with my head to be around a hyper child."

"And your parents?"

"We have a toxic relationship. They have different ideas about how I should treat my IIH. Since I don't agree with their approach, they think it can't really be that bad. They like to tell me I'm too negative."

"Ah." A grimace brackets his mouth. "No wonder you related to my poem."

"I was born relating. Even as a kid, my mom's favorite idiom was always 'Rise and shine!' She's into toxic positivity culture. It's only gotten worse with my IIH. If I'm sick, I'm not trying hard enough. If I improve, maybe I was faking all along. If I'm honest about how things are going, I have an attitude problem. So, yeah. Rise and fucking shine," I grumble.

"Is it worth keeping the relationship, then?"

"Being sick is difficult when you're alone. Sometimes I need someone to accompany me to an appointment, like if I have sedation, because hospitals don't let you take a cab. That person is usually Mom, so I need to preserve the limited relationship we have."

Pike's whole face scrunches up. "I guess that answers my original question. I'm sorry."

"It's fine." Oh no, I sound like Pike. "I mean. It's not. But I'm used to it."

"An observation. You don't seem negative."

"You told me to act like everything's great in front of your mom. I nixed most of the complaining about IIH."

"Complaining isn't the same as stating your reality. But that's not what I mean. You seem *good*. Not with pain. I understand IIH is awful. But it seems like you've figured out your life despite what it's thrown at you."

That's the first time anyone has said anything like that to me. "Things are tolerable because I carve out space for self-care and listen to my body. I don't have to answer to anyone but myself."

"That sounds independent. Maybe a little lonely too."

I bristle. I am alone, but that's different from being lonely. "I have my friends. The support group."

"I'm glad." Pike spreads out onto his back and tucks a hand under his pillow. A tingle rushes through me when his warm thigh settles against mine.

I keep my focus on the ceiling. "I'm sorry about your family too."

"My family's fine."

"Right, you can totally be yourself around your mom. That's why we're in this mess together."

"We're in this mess because of you."

"I—"

The TV goes out. We're plunged into blackness. A *thump* comes from downstairs. I throw myself at Pike.

"Is that David? Is he coming up here?"

My tinnitus ratchets up along with my pulse when the stairs creak under footsteps. Pike tenses.

"We're going to be okay," he whispers.

Three quick knocks on the door. "We lost power." Is it just me or does David sound suspiciously pleased? "There are extra blankets in the closet. I can show you."

I clap a hand over Pike's mouth. "If you open that door, this deal is off. I'm only wearing a thong under your shirt."

A strangled sound escapes his throat. He nods, and I remove my hand.

"We're good, thanks," he calls hoarsely.

David retreats. I wait, listening for the sound of his footsteps to fade completely. A tense silence settles over the room.

"Skylar?"

My attention snaps back to Pike. "Yes?"

"You're…" He hesitates, his breath warm on my face. "Close."

Heat rises to my cheeks as I become hyperaware of the proximity between us. Pike's legs have tangled with mine. My shirt has ridden up over my butt in the commotion. His hand is on my back. Mine are on his chest.

"Much as I'm enjoying the warmth…" There's an unmistakable edge to his voice.

I jolt back over to my side. "Sorry."

"Do you want me to get an extra blanket?"

"I can get one."

"In your thong?"

His rough tone kindles a flame in my stomach that should definitely not be there. Nope. This is fake, and he just asked me to move off him.

"Right. You go."

He retrieves the blankets, then settles back onto his side, no longer facing me. "Good night," he says.

I wish he weren't ready to go to sleep. It's only midnight. It's unbearably quiet. I have at least another two hours before I get tired enough to even think about sleeping. And that's with a sleeping pill, which I don't have. My phone's almost dead.

"Pike? If the power doesn't come back on...if it gets really cold while I'm asleep..." I swallow. "I might gravitate toward heat. Toward you. It's nothing...intentional."

He grunts softly. "I move while I sleep either way."

"Oh?" There may be unintentional spooning after all, then. That wouldn't be the worst development. "Understood."

I try to focus on the sound of his breathing. Anything to distract me from the screeching in my own ears. I wish I had anything related to my nighttime routine.

"Good night," I whisper.

11

Pike

I huddle closer to Skylar, bringing her back flush to my chest. My one hand is already draped over her waist, anyway, and she's holding the other to her face like a personal pillow. She's soft and smooth and warm, her delicious curves inviting.

Mmm. Good. It's way too early to get up.

But my brain won't shut off. Burning pain in my hips pierces through the morning fog, a recurring torment that often wakes me and forces a position change, even in the middle of the night.

I refuse to move now. My body can go fuck itself. Only way I'm moving is if Skylar turns over and makes this even more enticing.

As if sensing my thoughts, she shifts, pressing her ass against me. I groan, and she murmurs something, settling even closer. All thoughts of pain are replaced by the desire to wake her up properly with leisurely kisses along her neck.

It's been so long.

A sudden sharp awareness makes my eyes jolt open. I'm staring at the spray of freckles on her neck now, where one tiny mole sits at the cusp of her hairline. I glance between our bodies, but there's no space. Only heat. We're all attached and stacked up and shit. My traitorous body is delighted to go along with it.

Fuck. This is Skylar. The only position I have the right to be in is the fetal position.

I extricate myself as quickly as possible, but I can barely make it to the bathroom. Walking hurts. Holy shit, walking hurts. I miss not being hyperaware of my body. Now I feel every nerve, every moving joint, every pulse of blood. I've been tapering to take a smaller dose of meds in the morning, but today isn't going to be one of those days.

I stick my face under the faucet and gulp water, my mouth chalky from my oxy. Then I glare in the mirror and give myself two good slaps. So what if there's an attractive, half-naked woman in my bed? So what if I imagined the thong she was wearing under my shirt? We gravitated toward each other while we slept. For warmth. Nothing more.

Back in the bedroom, I pull my still-damp jeans up. The heat came back on at some point during the night, but they're stiff and threaten to yank off the corners of my already-peeling Kinesio tape.

I need my wheelchair. Ranielle is going to be pissed that I pushed myself so much. Overdoing it brings my progress to a grinding halt. At $300 per session, I might as well cancel PT for the rest of the week.

Skylar stirs as I shake out my sweater. "Pike?" She squints and reaches out her hand.

That's right. She said she wouldn't be able to see. I'm even more relieved we didn't accidentally do anything.

"It's me." I give her a quick squeeze, and her warm hand sends another wave of mixed signals between brain and body. "Do you need anything?"

"New eyes. Painkillers. A teleportation device to zap me home."

"How bad is your sight?" When I researched IIH, it said about 25 percent of people go blind.

"I see your shape. Can you ask David for Benadryl and Tylenol? And coffee."

"Coffee in bed, right."

I slip into my shoes with a wince. I have blisters all over my feet. Another strange development after not walking for so long. As if my feet didn't rub against board boots for eight hours a day most of my life.

"I'm going to call my mom to come get us." I reach in my pocket where I normally keep my phone, and find the damn condom instead.

"Ask her if she has any bananas."

I need to get out of this bedroom *now*.

I could use a coffee too. After my accident, I attempted to cut it out, thinking my body wouldn't need the kick since I slept for almost fourteen hours a day. But I quickly learned I have even less energy now than I did after a full day of shredding.

It's like my body is still figuring out how to stay alive.

When Kal finally pulls into Mom's driveway, my impatience to head back to Rochester has reached a breaking point. My car needs an engine repair that won't be ready until Wednesday, and my legs are screaming for relief I can only find back home in my bed.

"It was really decent of you to come get us," I say. "Thanks, man."

"No point in Laurie driving all the way to Rochester when I was planning to see you anyway."

The glaring sun makes his long blond hair look golden as it whips into his face, briefly concealing the goggle tan on his otherwise pasty skin. It's been two full years since I had a goggle tan, I realize, a thought I quickly push away.

"Reminds me of when we'd come here after Bristol," he says, nudging me. "Good times. Feels like forever ago."

That's because it was.

Kal and I first crossed paths at Bristol Mountain's terrain park. Sometimes I'd invite him over afterward. But as I progressed in snowboarding, I outgrew Bristol and Rochester, leaving both behind without a backward glance. Interactions with anyone from here became rare—mostly a like on social media or a competition meetup.

Everyone from Rochester became part of my past. But Kal and I reconnected a few summers ago randomly when we ran into each other in Italy. Since I moved back, he's been eager to hang out, though I cancel often due to my pain. Every time I plan something, my body craps out.

"How was your trip?" I ask. "Good vacation?"

"Christmas was slower this year because my grandma's having a hard time with mobility. But it was nice to see everyone."

Kal is either Danish or Swedish. Unfortunately, I've forgotten which, and now it comes up so many times in casual conversation that I feel like an asshole asking about it. He moved to Rochester as a kid, so English isn't his first language, and he still speaks whatever-ish.

Despite my inability to recall his specific brand of Scandinavian, I've always appreciated his worldly perspective. Most of my snowboarding crew wasn't American, and it's nice to be around someone again who doesn't think the US is the center of the universe.

"Is that Skylar?" Kal asks.

She's in the all-season room with Mom, drowning in an old pair of my sweats. She wanted out of her dress the moment we arrived, and now, with her hair tucked inside my Burton hoodie, I barely recognize her.

He lets out an amused chortle. "Never thought you'd need a fake girlfriend."

"Don't make me regret telling you."

When I called this morning to cancel, I didn't have the energy to lie. I wave to Mom, signaling that it's time to go. She guides Skylar by the arm, moving slowly over the icy driveway.

"She doesn't have her glasses and she's extremely nearsighted," I explain as Kal watches them approach. I gesture at my wheelchair. "I'm having enough trouble on the ice as is."

Her head still down, Skylar lets go of Mom's arm when she reaches the car.

Mom beams at Kal. "It's so nice to see you again!"

He offers her a hug, then turns to Skylar to introduce himself, all smiles, but she's already climbing into the back of his Subaru. She shuts the door without acknowledging him.

"Real sunshine, that one," he says to me.

"She's understandably in a bad mood. Pain."

He helps me take apart my wheelchair. "Why is she in pain?"

"She has a chronic condition. Last night made her flare, and she's also out of spoons." *Just like me.* "Spoons are a measure of quantifying energy and energy pacing when you're sick—"

"I know what spoons are, man."

"Oh," I say, surprised by his eye roll. I only learned about it recently.

People without a disability or chronic health condition usually wake up with enough spoons, or energy, to handle everything they need to do. They're like a brand-new phone that charges to 100 percent. Meanwhile, I'm an old phone that only charges to 40 percent, if it even charges at all. My spoons are limited from the start, no matter how much I rest. And then there's running out of spoons more quickly too. Even something as simple as a shower can drain me like a super-demanding app, leaving me stuck in bed for the rest of the day.

"Lennox gets grumpy when she's out of spoons too," Kal says.

Lennox, right. Never takes long before she comes up. According to Kal, they're best friends, but anyone who spends time with him can tell he's totally in love with her. They even reserve Sunday after-noons for each other like an old married couple.

"Skylar doesn't have the same thing, right?" he asks.

I pause, trying to remember Lennox's condition. Every health issue has an acronym these days. Something with her stomach. Maybe.

"Nope." I don't elaborate. Skylar can share if she wants to.

"That's good—not her pain, but that you don't have to worry about sex."

I struggle to maintain a neutral expression. "Are you sleeping with Lennox?"

Kal does an about-face. "What?"

"The sex...I thought you meant..."

"Sky*lar*," he enunciates. "Sex. Having it. Pain-free."

I smack his shoulder. "She's right inside the car."

"She can't hear me. I'm just saying, some chronic pain gets in the way of that."

Does Lennox have endometriosis? That doesn't sound right.

"Skylar and I aren't having sex. That's the whole point of fake."

Kal gasps dramatically. "Brandon Pike spent the night with a woman just *sleeping*? Alert the press."

I flip him off as he loads my chair. I wobble to the front seat, but Kal still manages to beat me. It shouldn't feel like a competition, but it does. We used to race each other at Bristol—him on skis, me on my board. I know I went on to win fucking *gold*, but the fact that I can't even keep up in a driveway anymore makes my soul shrivel up like a prune.

When Kal offers to drop Skylar off, she recites her South Wedge address without hesitation. It's about twenty minutes from my place.

"I'm going to be antisocial," she declares and leans against the window.

As soon as she succumbs to her exhaustion, I wish I could do the same. Kal starts telling me about his plans for cross-country skiing tomorrow. That sport is some next-level bullshit. I'll never forget my dad putting me on cross-country skis and shoving me down a hill. It's like running on an elliptical in the snow, but you end up on your ass with every tiny slope.

"When you're back on your feet full-time," Kal says, "you should come with me."

"My doctors say I'm already doing better than expected. So get used to me like this, yeah?"

"Oh, sure. Sorry. Do you want to join my beach volleyball team this summer? There's an amputee on one of the teams. He plays with crutches."

Beach volleyball sounds mildly entertaining, and Charlotte Beach, where they play, is pretty nice. But when I was in the hospital, my mom made me watch documentaries on injured athletes finding "a new purpose." A lot of them were amputees. At first, I looked up to them, thinking their stories could give me hope. But now I know that everyone with a disability is different from the next—even those with the same condition.

I'm also not big on team sports. The best part of snowboarding is the way adrenaline makes all the noise in your life disappear when you're flying down the mountain or nailing a massive trick. I don't have a way to clear my mind like that anymore.

"With my knees hurting just walking on pavement," I say, "I can't imagine they'd feel better on uneven sand. I definitely can't jump."

"You don't have to jump," he says graciously.

I stab at the floor with my cane. "Can you let it go?"

"Seriously," Skylar mumbles. "He obviously has no desire to participate."

Kal glances in the rearview mirror, then back over at me. "Sorry for pushing. You know I'd never make you do something you don't want to do, right? I'm just glad you're back." He claps my shoulder. "No pressure. We can meet for lunch and play video games for all I care."

"Thanks," I say. "Maybe I'll come check out volleyball sometime. As a spectator."

"Or come chill in the sauna after. It'll be good for your muscles." Skylar coughs. "What sauna?"

"He has a sauna in his house." I suppress a smile, imagining her eyebrows shooting up. She probably thinks we're a bunch of rich assholes.

"Saunas are pretty common for Scandinavians," he says, but damn it, he doesn't say which type. "You should stop by sometime with Pike."

"Ew, no way," she says, startling a laugh out of me.

Kal's confidence briefly falters, and in that moment, I think I could fall in love with Skylar King.

You know. If this were real.

"I know your relationship's fake," Kal says. "You can still come."

"Saunas are *disgusting*," she says. "I can't handle a lot of heat."

I think she means due to IIH, but she doesn't mention it. I feel bad for telling Kal she even had pain at all. But she explains that her dysautonomia affects body functions like breathing, digestion, and heart rate, and that heat makes her symptoms worse.

"My best friend doesn't like it either. She says sweating with someone is nasty." Kal smiles to himself.

By the time we reach Skylar's town house, the sting in my body is less consuming, and I'm drowsy as fuck. But as I watch Skylar trudge up the walkway, her shoulders hunched, I can't shake my guilt.

"Hang on."

I climb out of the car. It's too low to the ground, and with my unstable knee, I stumble a little. Kal's hand lands on my back.

"I'm fine." I'm not, but I don't have time to unpack my wheelchair.

Walking is excruciating. My patella won't track. My back muscles feel like they're cutting into the delicate wire of my spine.

Skylar pivots when she hears me.

"Listen," I say, "I'm sorry about how everything turned out. Can I take you to your appointment tomorrow?"

I imagine her squinting at me beneath her shades. "You can't get enough of me, can you, Brandon Pike?"

"I'll pick you up so you don't have to drive. It's the least I can do after not getting you home safely."

"You don't even have a car."

"So I'll call us a ride." I pull out my phone, but the screen swims. Between pain, dehydration, bad sleep, and the sedative effects of my oxy, I can barely see straight. "What time?"

She fiddles with the drawstring of my hoodie, pulling it snug around her frizzy hair before letting it go slack again. "Why do you want to come?"

"I go to all your doctor's appointments with you so you're not alone, remember?"

She cracks a smile.

"I read that sometimes women have better outcomes with doctors if a man is present. So why not use me?" Yikes. Sounded like a bad pickup line. "In all seriousness, Skylar, I appreciate that you came all the way out to Naples and helped me with my mom. You're different than I expected."

She cocks her head, considering me. "You know, so are you."

"See you tomorrow, then? If we both manage to drag ourselves out of bed somehow after all this?"

"Fine. Be here by nine. I'm leaving if you're even a minute late."

I smile to myself as I head back to the car. It's refreshing how she always says what she's thinking. I wish I could do that.

Kal gives me a shit-eating grin. "Looks like someone's caught feelings."

"What?" I bark.

"All right, all right. Just messing with you."

And because I don't know what to say, and I definitely can't board, I pull out my phone and jot down some words.

12
Skylar

You don't have to come inside. It's going to take, like, four hours." I put more lubricating gel in my dry eyes. Blink furiously. Adjust my glasses. "Unbelievable amounts of waiting between tests."

"I spend half my life in waiting rooms these days," Pike says. "I'm used to it."

After a long moment, I nod. "One thing, though. Dr. Wharton has a fragile ego. So even though your presence might help, you're not going to say anything bad, right?"

"If that's what you need."

We both sluggishly exit the car. While I check in, Pike unloads his wheelchair. I rearrange the furniture so he can sit next to me in the waiting room.

Mom sends me a text. **Saw this article on juicing for headaches. Ask Dr. Wharton!**

I drop a screenshot into the support group, knowing I'll come back to comments commiserating about unsolicited advice.

Pike puts on a pair of reading glasses and pulls out a Moleskine notebook. "Anything in particular we want to discuss?"

"I'd like to get a specific type of imaging that will show whether I qualify for a stent."

"That's the tubing that drains spinal fluid from your brain into your"—he squints at his notebook—"peritoneal cavity, right?"

"No, that's a shunt. Wait a minute!" I grab his notebook. "You have notes about IIH? Let me see that."

In messy, old-school cursive, there's a long list of IIH terms like *lumbar puncture (spinal tap)*, *shunt*, and *papilledema (swelling of the optic nerves)*.

"Can't be too helpful if I don't know what I'm talking about."

My heart warms, even if it's just a little research. It's the thoughtfulness that counts. My eyes snag on a note scrawled diagonally in the bottom right corner. "What's this?"

Pike rips the notebook out of my hands. "Nothing. Leftover notes from a writing session. Long time ago. Didn't have a blank page." He blacks out the words with strong streaks of his pen, but I catch the beginning anyway.

> She is,
> bright red paint splashed
> against a faded mural
> in desperate need of color

Pike's neck is scarlet, so I don't press him. I'm honored he looked up my condition.

"So, a stent is different from a shunt," I say. "Shunts are more commonly used nowadays when someone is losing their vision quickly or medication doesn't work. For many of us, it's more of a last resort when other treatments fail. Some people do well with them, but there's a huge failure rate because of malfunctions, infections, and the need for frequent revisions. I know some IIHers who have upwards of four surgeries a year."

A grimace overtakes Pike's handsome features. He scribbles a note.

"It's not a cure," I explain.

"But if it could help, why wouldn't you get one?"

"Because IIH isn't one-size-fits-all," I say. "Some cases are caused by venous sinus stenosis—narrowing in the veins that drain cerebrospinal fluid away from the brain. A shunt reroutes fluid, but it doesn't fix the stenosis. A stent would open the veins up."

Pike tilts his head. "So, you need imaging to see if that's the problem?"

I nod. "If my veins are narrowed enough, a stent could treat the possible cause. It's also a less invasive procedure than shunting." I check my face in my phone's camera. "How do I look? Honestly."

Pike puts down his pen. "What do you mean?"

"I feel like a wreck, my meds are giving me acne, my hair is thinning, and I've slept a collective five hours since Friday. I can't look sloppy or unmotivated, but I also can't be so put together that I seem like I'm not sick. It's a hard balance to strike. Doctors judge you."

I'm wearing the most slimming thing I own, a long-sleeved tunic over leggings, along with heeled shoes, even though trekking in my boots this weekend gave me blisters. The tunic cinches at the waist, flattering my wide hips and hiding the folds in my stomach when I sit.

Pike tilts his head as he inspects me, his smoky eyes dragging down to my legs, then back up to my face. Unlike me, he's relaxed in gray sweatpants and a black hoodie. He reaches for my unruly hair and smooths out a few strands with his fingertips.

"There we go," he murmurs, gently tucking a curl behind my ear. "Perfect."

His hand lingers for a beat longer than necessary, his thumb brushing against my cheek before he lets it fall away. His gaze flickers up to meet mine, quiet but intense. A shiver flits over my skin.

"Skylar?" a tech calls.

It begins. The long series of tests before I see the doctor. First, it's pictures of my optic nerves while I focus intently on an arrow. The second test is my least favorite: the visual fields. It involves staring into this infuriating machine while wearing an eye patch and clicking a button whenever I think I see a blinking light. Every time it's over, I think I've lost my mind.

Then it's a regular eye checkup, IOP check, and a bunch of tools that test depth and color perception. Due to my low-grade papilledema, I'll keep repeating this every two months until it's under control.

By the time we go into Dr. Wharton's room, Pike is squirming. "My hips are killing me."

"I'm sorry. I said it can take hours."

"Guess time flies when I'm dominating at *Wheel of Fortune*."

I can't hide my smile. Pike keeps winning, but I loved having another player to compete against in the app. For me, the waiting time flew by.

"This is why I tolerate my job," I say. "Any other job, I'd have to take off the whole day because there's no point in showing up to work for only two hours."

This year will be more complicated, though. There's no time for these long appointments during fair season. I'll have to talk to Dr. Wharton about a note. My boss'll love that. Probably as much as Dr. Wharton, who will argue that standing on my feet will help me lose weight. If only I could flip the bastard off. But that's not happening when most specialists who treat my condition have nine-month wait lists and Dr. Wharton's made damn sure I'll have trouble getting into any of them.

A tech gets me on a scale. When she inputs the number on the computer, a red arrow on the screen flashes upward. Next to it, in bold, it says I have an increase of 1 percent and my BMI is 27.8: OVERWEIGHT.

Dr. Wharton comes in after another twenty minutes. He's a thin white man in his fifties with an air of arrogance about him.

"Skylar. Nice to see you. And who's this fellow?"

"This is my boyfriend, Brandon." I give Pike a pointed look.

Dr. Wharton's polite as he checks my eyes and reviews my tests. "Your papilledema hasn't worsened. Are you keeping up with your medication?"

"Yes, but the pins and needles this time are almost unbearable. The ringing in my ears has also gotten worse." I fiddle with my necklace to hide the way my palms are sweating. "Could I try methazolamide instead?"

Dr. Wharton returns to his screen. "It's the same thing as acetazolamide."

My shoulders drop.

"If it's the same thing, what's the harm in trying it?" Pike asks. "I read that it can cause fewer side effects."

A single gray eyebrow lifts. I bet Dr. Wharton didn't expect him to do any research either.

"I don't prescribe that for pseudotumor cerebri." Dr. Wharton turns back to me. "I see you've gained weight in the last month."

I sit up straighter at his accusatory tone. "I just got my period."

"You're supposed to be losing weight. You're fourteen pounds away from being obese."

I look at my lap. It's bad enough on my own. I didn't consider how much worse I would feel with someone to witness this humiliation.

"Sorry." Pike holds up his phone. "What's your height, Skylar?"

"Five foot six," I mumble.

"Five foot six? I'm looking at a chart that says a quote 'normal' BMI for that height is under 24.9," he says. "If she's fourteen pounds from being obese, she's also only eighteen pounds away from not being 'overweight.' Seems arbitrary. Most Olympic athletes would be considered overweight, even obese, based on BMI alone. I'm technically overweight too. So BMI's not the whole picture."

BMI also has racist roots, but I know Dr. Wharton won't care.

"You are fit and don't have pseudotumor cerebri," he says. The fact that he won't even use the updated term for my condition shows his ignorance. "Most patients who lose weight are cured."

That's not true, though. Beyond the cure misinformation, while weight can contribute, most of the population would have IIH if that was the only cause.

"I haven't seen that cure research," Pike says, giving *cure* air quotes.

Dr. Wharton's lips curl into a thin, practiced smile, the corners barely lifting. It's one I recognize well, the kind that dismisses the conversation without saying a word. "That happens when you consult Dr. Google."

"I consulted Dr. PubMed, actually." He flips to another page in his notebook. "It looks like there can be other causes, like compression, hormonal imbalances, autoimmune disease, medication, and post-viral illnesses. And while weight loss *can* help, many of the studies seem totally unsustainable, don't you think? Where they make patients eat"—he squints—"only four hundred twenty-five calories of rice a day?"

I nearly squawk. Pike found that old study?

"There's scientific evidence that bariatric surgery helps pseudo-tumor."

"Come on, man." Pike scoffs. "Skylar doesn't qualify for that."

"Weight loss is better than getting a shunt."

"Weight loss is more *conservative*," I cut in. When Dr. Wharton goes back to typing, I draw a finger across my throat. If Pike keeps defending me, it'll get worse. "But I'm not eating much already," I say.

"Good. By next visit, I want to see the numbers. Two pounds per week. It's a necessary part of your treatment plan."

I curl my fists in my lap where he can't see them. "That's not feasible when exercising is near impossible with my pain."

"She has a hard time just getting through the day," Pike adds.

"How about a GLP-1 inhibitor?" I ask.

"Ask your primary doctor," he says, unblinking.

"She won't prescribe those if my BMI isn't 'obese.' But new research shows they reduce cerebrospinal fluid secretion, so you could prescribe it and maybe it would help both issues."

"It's calories in, calories out, Skylar. We could staple your mouth shut, if it'll help. How about that?"

It's a matter-of-fact statement, said mildly to his computer screen. I hold my hand up before Pike can say anything. His face is a vat of boiling water. I get it, but I barely feel anger anymore, only defeat.

I take a much-needed breath and disregard his awful comment. "In the meantime, I'd like to get the imaging I requested back in November. To look for possible stenosis. I've read more about it, and a lot of patients have success with stenting."

Dr. Wharton gets to his feet. "Lose the weight, then we can talk about other treatments. You're in your own way here." He smiles pleasantly. "See you in two months."

13

Pike

By the time Dr. Wharton leaves, I'm seeing red. If my crew were here, we'd slash his tires.

"Why are you still seeing this man?" I demand.

Skylar rubs her temples. "I need him for these tests. I need the meds."

"He's disgusting."

"Welcome to being an overweight woman with chronic pain. If you spend more time in the group, you'll see this is normal."

I have seen it. That's why I offered to come with her.

"You should've let me defend you. He said he'd *staple your mouth shut.*"

"I appreciate it, but I have to tread carefully. It's a lot like an abusive relationship, and I'm trapped. He already put that 'not compliant' note in my chart. I think that's why I can't get appointments with other neurologists."

I'm seething again. "They just won't take you?"

"The better clinics have a vetting process because of long waiting lists. You apply with all your paperwork, recent lumbar punctures, doctors' notes. If they don't accept you, you get a letter saying you didn't meet the requirements or the clinic reached capacity."

"So you're stuck with weight loss as the only option?"

"Well, there's the meds." She adjusts the cute round glasses she's wearing today. "When I was first diagnosed, I lost weight, but my

IIH actually got worse. I went into remission after I gained ten pounds back."

A tech comes in with discharge papers and points down a long hallway for checkout. I roll next to Skylar. She's more down than I've ever seen her.

"Want to get a late lunch?" Maybe it'll take her mind off things.

"I should get home. I have a conference call at four, and I feel crappy."

Why am I disappointed? I've just spent four hours with her. I roll past an open door and pause, a bad idea forming. A reckless one. But I roll backward and enter the room.

Skylar follows me as I lock my wheels and slowly rise to my feet. The accumulated pain from this weekend shoots through my legs, but I limp forward anyway.

"What are you doing?" she hisses. "We can't be in here."

It's a dimly lit supply closet full of promotional gimmicks for Dr. Wharton's practice. Pens, plastic cups, lanyards, and notepads galore are stacked on filing cabinets. I help myself to a few pens.

"Don't worry," I say. "Just setting up a little stand at work. Free advertising, you know? Gotta get the word out about him, and it'll only take a single Sharpie to write 'misogynistic dick' over his branding."

Skylar tries to hide her smile. "You'll get caught."

I shove a plastic-wrapped Post-it cube into my pocket. "People think wheelchair users are angels. You should get out of here, though."

Skylar reaches into a container. "I think fifteen hundred dollars per eye and verbal abuse warrant a few pens. They're meant to be given out, right?"

"Three grand a visit?" I hand her a pack of Post-its. "Someone's getting canceled."

There it is. Another small smile. Good.

"You're not really setting up a stand, right?" Skylar catches her lower lip between her teeth. Those supple lips are so inviting I have to force myself to look away, just like I forced myself to look away so many times when we were lying in bed together.

"Nope. Just stealing some shit so fewer people hear about him. It's keeping me from keying his car."

She laughs, and it warms my chest. "Thanks, Pike."

"Go check out. I'll be there in a sec."

Skylar heads for the door while I struggle to find space for all the items crammed into my pockets. Sitting on pens isn't a wise move. There's that movie where the guy lost a testicle and everything.

My thoughts scatter as Skylar races back to me, causing me to drop half my pens onto my seat cushion.

"Pike, someone's coming!"

"Damn," I mutter, scrambling to shove any incriminating evidence into the back pouch of my chair. "Get out of here."

"It's too late. A tech is heading down the hallway."

"They'll walk by us without noticing. If they do, I'll handle it."

"No, I'm not leaving you. Quick," she says. "Kiss me!"

I drop even more pens. "What?"

"You'll get caught! We have to pretend!"

"I—uh—" I bend too quickly, straining my back, but Skylar's request scrambles my brain. She wants to kiss me? I grab the last pen and dare my hand to tremble one more time. "You don't have to—"

Skylar reaches for my face, pulling me close until her lips hover just an inch from mine. My body perks up and pays attention.

"Please," she whispers.

I close the space between us with the faintest graze, careful at first, barely more than a question. But Skylar answers with a slide of her fingers in my hair and a sweep of her tongue into my mouth. That's all it takes for the kiss to shift. Then it's hotter and hungrier, with no more space left between us. A soft murmur of approval passes from her lips to mine, and I go all weak and funny in the knees.

Shit. It's good. Holy shit, it's good.

A part of my brain registers that the kiss should feel forced, but it doesn't. It's incredible. Intimate. There's an emotional tug connecting us, one I've rarely felt with anyone else. Skylar and I are launching off the peak of a jump, a blend of tension and release.

It must be the adrenaline. The way this is taking me by surprise. Still, my hands find her soft waist. I tug her closer, and a small gasp escapes her mouth. It's an addicting sound, a drug I didn't know I craved.

All the blood rushes away from my brain. Until another sensation hits.

Pain. Legs.

I sit down on my wheelchair and pull Skylar onto my lap, then twist her sideways so her legs dangle over my right wheel, putting her face level with mine. Better.

"Oh," she breathes, then fuses us together once more. She tastes sweet, with a hint of salted caramel and chocolate coating her lips.

A low rumble vibrates from my chest. I wrap an arm around her waist to hold her to me and slow us down, spurred on by the pleasurable hum in her throat and the clench of her thighs on top of me. Kissing Skylar feels like a privilege. It needs to be savored.

I slide my other hand around the thin material of her tunic. I want to drag my mouth over every inch of exposed skin. Make her forget her shitty doctor until there's nothing left on her mind but me.

Her nails scrape lightly down my neck, and I'm not sure which of us groans.

A high-pitched shriek scares the shit out of me. The lights flick on. "You can't be in here!"

"You were amazing," Skylar whispers, then climbs off me.

No, wait, what? What the fuck was that, and why was it so good?

I run my tongue along my bottom lip, and the caramel-chocolate flavor remains. Skylar remains. It's that ChapStick she's always applying. I want more of it. More of her. So much I have to discreetly adjust myself.

"Pike!" Skylar pushes her glasses back up her perfectly blushed cheeks. *Be charming*, she mouths.

It's the bucket of cold water I need.

"Sorry about that." I roll toward the tech, a middle-aged woman with suspicious blue eyes. "We got bad news at the appointment and got caught up comforting each other." I wink, which I've been told is one of my best weapons.

"You can't do that here," she says, though the scowl on her face softens.

"Absolutely. I understand."

She grabs my wheelchair handles, a gesture that always feels like a violation, but I let her do it to keep her agreeable. She pushes me to checkout, then squeezes my shoulder. "You keep your head up, okay? You can get through this. Stay positive, honey."

Whenever I use my wheelchair, complete strangers think it's appropriate to call me *dear*, *honey*, or *sweetie*, even when they aren't touching my chair or otherwise crossing boundaries. I keep smiling, though. Anything to make sure Skylar doesn't get in trouble.

When our ride comes, I stretch out my legs in the back. "We should talk about that kiss."

Skylar wrings her hands, confirming my suspicion. I made her uncomfortable.

"I'm sorry," I say. "I shouldn't have gone in the supply room. It put you in a compromising position."

"Oh…it's okay." She won't meet my eye. "I hope the kiss wasn't too bad for you."

I blink. "Bad?"

"I was nervous. I'm not usually so boring."

Boring? Of all things, Skylar's worried I was bored?

"No." I need to choose my words carefully. I don't want to make things weird. Even now, I wouldn't mind scooting closer to see if she'd like to give it a second shot without interruptions. "'Boring' is the last adjective I'd use."

She breathes out a sigh of relief. "Great. Because I know I said I was a fantastic kisser, and I'm usually more confident, but I have a headache, and everything happened so fast, and, well, you're Brandon Pike."

"What does that have to do with anything?"

"Come on." She laughs sardonically. "Mr. 'Twenty Hottest Tricks to Warm Up Your Man'?"

My stomach sours at the reminder of my *Cosmo* cover. I hated doing those publicity stunts, but my sponsors liked it. That edition was filled with the top Winter Olympics medalists, and readers chose me as the "Hottest Winter Athlete Under Thirty."

So Skylar did google me. She read that issue. The sex tips they told me to offer. I sounded like such a jackass in that article.

"It's not like that." Now I'm the one unable to look at her. "When I'm with a woman, I mean. I'm not thinking about that stuff. It was just a stupid interview." I catch myself. "Sorry, not stupid. It was..."

"Intimidating?"

"It was a good kiss, Skylar," I say, frustrated. "I can't do half the shit I mentioned in there anymore, simply because of disability, but that doesn't mean I can't still make it good."

"I can imagine," she says, her eyes dipping back to my mouth, and my brain immediately shuts down for maintenance. Has she... imagined?

"Just...forget about the article."

I look out the window. All this faking is messing with my mind. I see why Skylar wanted PDA rules in the first place.

14

Skylar

I squint through one eye at my phone tabs. I have three open on Pike, one for my chronic pain group, one for the girls, and one for my IIH group.

Screens are getting harder to look at again with the pressure behind my eyes. There was new dizziness and migraine this past week too. I should avoid screens altogether, but it's beyond boring lying around doing nothing. Since I drive so much for work, I can't bring myself to listen to audiobooks or podcasts in my downtime.

Chastity's name pops up in the forum. I send a quick message to see how they're doing since their Chiari decompression surgery. I'm organizing a few events they can participate in during recovery. Then I return to Pike's tabs.

After Emy and Analia found out he was famous, they sent an email titled **Pike!!** with a compilation of interviews and articles. I'm through most of them. I've watched the video of him singing in his polar bear outfit at least twenty times (he warbled through a funny version of "Call Me Maybe" by Carly Rae Jepsen—his voice really *is* awful) and countless interviews of him after a win (he won his first Olympic gold at *seventeen*). I can't get over how happy and carefree he used to be.

His snowboarding videos make me dizzy with all the air rotations, so I have to take breaks, but they're surprisingly soothing. The tricks are incredible, and Pike, well . . . the hype wasn't for nothing.

He gets bigger air, pulls extra rotations, invents his own moves. Who knew this sport could be so hot?

I still haven't watched his accident. If he wanted me to see it, he'd send it to me.

Analia is talking about her interstitial cystitis in our chat. **I'm lying here with a heat pack, waiting for my cannabis to kick in while OD'ing on aloe vera capsules.**

Make Kalle take care of you tomorrow, I write. From what I've heard, Kalle is incredibly attuned to Analia's needs. It must be nice to have someone who cares that much. Someone who doesn't dismiss you when you're flaring.

Kalle's actually here now, she says.

ciao kalle, Emy says. **is he sleeping over again?**

I open a private chat with Emy. **On Valentine's Day?!?!**

He made me dinner, Analia says.

but it's saturday! Emy says.

Since Analia is a homebody and Kalle is super social, their schedules don't mesh, so they usually hang out on Sunday afternoons.

Well...

I hold my breath while Analia types.

After a few minutes, Emy screams in our private chat. **DID THEY GET MARRIED AND NOT INVITE US!?**

I laugh, then have to put my phone down. Laughing, sneezing, and coughing all hurt—another reason I think my pressure's elevated.

Analia leaves a small paragraph. **I finally told him I'm on the ace spectrum, probably leaning more gray ace. I was like, shaking nervous because he, you know, has a lot of casual sex and is a super commitment phobe. I was worried he wouldn't understand and think I was weird, but he hugged me and said he had a feeling. I cried (in a good way).**

awwwww! Emy sends a ton of hearts. **i'm so happy he was sweet about it!**

And that you finally felt okay telling him, I add. **From every-thing you've said, I can tell he cares so much about you.**

Kalle said he felt like hanging out tonight, so we're watching a movie after dinner. But first, heat pack. He's doing the dishes right now.

She sends us a sneak picture. Kalle's standing in front of a dish-washer, hamming it up with a sponge in one hand and a soft smile for Analia. We've seen pictures of him before, but never this candid. Never full body.

He's wearing fitted sweats and a white shirt that says MALE MODEL, and yeah, he looks like one, with lean muscle, sharp cheekbones, and piercing blue eyes. His blond locks fall sexily around his face, a few inches shorter than Pike's old, wavy mop from his snowboarding days. But where Pike's thick hair always had a way of falling into his eyes, Kalle's is sun-lightened and has that effortless, windswept look of a surfer.

Emy shoots me another private message. **yummy. if analia doesn't want him, think she'd mind if i took him for a spin?** 😉

Based on the photo, I say, **I think he's just as in love with her as we think she is with him.**

i know, sweets. i would never.

Sorry to change plans, Analia says. **I'll still be available.**

Pike has sent you a message.

My heart plunges as if I've been caught looking at something naughty. I drop my phone on my face.

Pike's sent me a few messages this week to check on me. We've avoided talking about the kiss, which hopefully means he's forgotten my awkwardness.

"It was a good kiss," he said.

Good was too underwhelming for it. If that's how he kisses when it's fake, my thoughts and prayers are with all the women he kisses for real. Good luck resisting that broody, talented mouth. Try not falling under his spell. It's taken me days to break free.

I can't believe the only thing I told him afterward was my insecurities. But this man has kissed a lot of women. I didn't want to be the worst he's ever had. Not that it felt that way to me. His unfocused, lust-filled eyes even suggested otherwise.

I have something for you. Up for a quick visit?

Uhhh...

I feel bad putting attention back on Pike and me when Analia just came out to Kalle. **How quick? I'm with the girls.**

I wanted to drop something off. In the neighborhood.

He's nearby? **Why are you in the neighborhood?**

...to drop something off. For you.

I'm in my pajamas.

You've seen me in my boxers. I think I can handle some pjs.

What he doesn't get is my version of pajamas are panties and a cami. I throw on the nearest clean things I can find, deep purple leggings and a baggy, mustard-yellow sweater.

Brb Pike is here randomly sorry, I shoot off, then throw my hair in a scrunchie even though it hurts. It's too wild and frizzy to stay down without product. There hasn't been any product, let alone hair washing, in at least three days.

I yank the door open out of nerves, the motion making me double as dizzy.

And *oh.*

Pike stands in front of my door with red roses. "Hey." His lips quirk into a bashful smile. "I'm sorry I got us stuck in the snow and made you flare."

I'm so caught off-guard. A girl should not be surprised by her fake boyfriend. Especially when the last time that girl saw him, he was all hard muscle beneath her, hands gripping her shirt like he could rip it off, his five-o'clock shadow grazing her cheeks.

I subdue the lurch of need that slams into me.

"It's Valentine's Day," I say suspiciously.

"It is." His eyes drag over me. "You're so colorful."

I look down. My purple leggings scream at me. The sweater is one of my favorite comfy tops, but I usually wear jeans to balance out my hair. "I said I was in pajamas."

"I like it. My favorite Gnu was purple and yellow."

"What's a Gnu?"

A warm, amused smile blooms across his face. "A snowboard. Gnu's a brand."

"I look like your snowboard?"

"She was a good board. I won my first gold with her."

"Your boards have pronouns."

"I don't have them anymore. Besides the one. Never mind. You look good, is what I'm trying to say." He hands me the roses. "Can I come in?"

"Are you sure you want to? It's suck city in here."

He unzips his backpack. "This is probably unexciting, but I figure it's what a boyfriend would bring."

He gives me a Tupperware, still warm, with a note attached to it.

> Roses are red
> Violets are blue
> Here's some chicken soup
> Just for you

It's incredibly dorky...and undeniably precious.

"You know." He looks at his feet. "Keeping with the poem theme."

"You do realize we're *fake* dating, right? You don't need to bring me anything."

"I wanted to. Probably Emy and Analia already hooked you up, though." He glances around my apartment. "Can I meet them?"

"They're not here."

"I thought you were with them?"

"I was talking to them online."

"Ah." He follows me into my kitchen, taking in my apartment. This is the only room that hasn't been destroyed this week, mainly because I use paper plates. No cleanup involved.

He picks up one of the flameless votive candles I've placed every-where. "Romantic. Expecting someone?"

"No. Light sensitivity."

My vases are up on a shelf I can't reach without a stool, but Pike easily selects an elegant one and fills it up with water. I can't believe he came all the way out here.

"I was thinking we should take another picture. One I can send my mom. Being Valentine's Day and all."

Of course. His mom. "Right, right. What do you need? Me gush-ing over your romantic gesture?"

A line creases his brow. "Does that bother you?"

"Why would it bother me?"

"I don't know. You sounded sarcastic."

"Sorry," I say quickly. "Pain gives me a short temper."

"No worries." He comes to stand behind me. "Whenever I take prednisone, I get angry at everything."

His arms ease around me until I'm sandwiched between the countertop and his warm body. My muscles go liquid, remembering the way he pressed against me in bed. The way I pressed against him while we kissed on his wheelchair.

Shivers run over my skin. I fit perfectly against him. Like we really belong together.

"Is this okay?" He rests his chin on my head, then quickly moves. "Sorry, your head, right." He holds out the camera and presses his cheek to mine.

Pike smiles, unlike in our bed picture, where he looked sleepy and sated. I've fixated on that photo a hundred times. One thing I've learned about Pike from my stalking? He usually smirks when there's a woman on his arm. Now, he looks more relaxed, like he's happy he gets to take care of me.

The way Kalle smiles at Analia.

I've never had a man truly care about my pain. While many have made me feel good physically, they rarely held me tenderly like this. I slip out from his arms. I want him to look at me like that for real. If only because no one ever has.

He zooms in on the picture. "Do I look overly happy when you're not well?"

"No, you look sweet."

"What should I text? I'm not used to talking about women with her."

"Well, I'm not any woman, am I? I'm your girlfriend, so she'll expect different."

He shows me his phone. **Skylar felt up for a visit. Taking it easy tonight with chicken soup and a movie.**

"Good," I say.

"Should I add hearts?"

"No. You add hearts when you're texting *me*. I mean, your girlfriend."

He dips his head and sends the picture. Two seconds later, my phone pings, but it's not the girls wondering where I am.

It's Pike. He sent me the picture along with a bunch of hearts. "For all intents and purposes, you're my girlfriend, so if you say to add hearts, I'm adding hearts."

I reply to the text. **I say to wire me a million dollars.**

Pike bites his lip in an effort to hide a playful grin. **I knew you'd want money. Total gold digger.**

You're full of shit. I add a wink.

So, what movie are we watching?

I glance up. Pike's still trying—and failing—to suppress a smile.

"You want to watch a movie with me?"

"Why not? After everything, I'd say we're friends, yeah?"

Friends. It's true I'm more comfortable with him now, but it's a strange label for what we are. Besides, I don't bother with in-person friendships. Not anymore.

But Pike is different, isn't he? He's respectful. Kind. Even if he is blackmailing me.

"Unless you're heading to bed?"

He knows by now that it's too early for me to even consider sleeping. I circle a finger around my eyes. "My pressure makes screens hurt, especially with moving pictures." And because everyone always calls me out on what they believe are *inconsistencies*, I quickly add, "I know I said I was talking to the girls online—and I was—but with one eye open. To stave off utter boredom."

I wring my hands. The last time I told Mom my eyes bothered me, she said it was because I spent too much time on my phone.

"We can just hang out," he says. "I know it can be boring by yourself when you have pain."

Some of the tension drains from my shoulders. He isn't questioning me. "What would we do?"

He crosses one ankle over the other and leans back, getting more comfortable in my kitchen than any man ever has. "I can think of a few things."

Suddenly, I can, too, and I grab a mug so he won't see my thirsty expression. "L-Like what?" I cough to cover my nerves, then end up choking on my saliva. That's what I get for my mind going directly in the gutter.

He reaches around me for my electric kettle. His snug gray Henley shows the shape of his body beneath it precisely. Not that I need help remembering the shape of his body.

"When I was recovering from my surgeries, my eyes hurt." He holds out my tea rack until I pick my go-to, Dandelion Leaf & Root. "First from the concussion, then from the drugs. I wore blue-tinted glasses for a while. Did a little vision therapy. You know."

I do not. My doctors have never offered me any of that, despite my inquiries.

"When screens bothered me," he says, "I tried stuff like baking, crafts, listening to audiobooks, and playing board games. Does your pain allow you to do those things?"

I gawk at him. "You bake and do crafts?"

"I said *tried*. Mostly, I sulked and did PT. Though I can make a mean chocolate chip cookie. Everything else takes too much energy."

"I love chocolate chip cookies."

He drops the tea bag in my blue-and-lime-green IIH awareness ribbon mug. "Is that what you want to do? Bake?"

"All I feel like doing is resting. But we could, uh. Talk a little?" I wish Pike's surprise visit was enough to distract me from my pain, but I learned long ago that I can't be distracted from it. I can only make time pass more quickly.

He gives me a banana from my tiered fruit basket. I decline.

"No? Enough potassium for today?" he teases.

"No, I took my…my…" My brain trips over the word. "Thingies. That you swallow. Um. From the doctor."

"Pills?"

"Yes! My pills. I'm a mess today. I found a pair of clean spoons inside my microwave earlier."

"Well, at least they were clean."

He makes his way to my sectional, his walk slower than I remember. Is he still hurting from last weekend? He lowers himself onto the cushions and sprawls out, legs stretching like they own the space. My thoughts spiral, unbidden, to how he could use those strong thighs, what they'd feel like moving over me. A slow ache unfurls deep within me as I imagine the weight of him, the power in every flex, the way he could cage me in, hold me steady, make me beg for more. It'd be such a welcome change from all this pain.

"IIH has a lot of similarities to a TBI," I say quickly, trying to dislodge the image. "Probably because they can both involve cerebrospinal fluid pressure."

"I read that too."

"You…you did?"

"Headache, dizziness, confusion, ringing in the ears, mood changes, problems with focus, blurred vision, fatigue?"

I did mention most of those symptoms, but I'm stunned he remembers. *My heart.* He pays attention.

"Did you have any permanent damage from your concussion?"

"Nah, I was lucky. The first month was disorienting, but I also had massive amounts of painkillers and nonworking limbs, so that was disorienting all on its own."

"I never get pain meds," I say with a long sigh. "And I have pain every day. It's the level to which it's tolerable or not that determines how I function."

"And right now?"

"Right now, I'm at the tail end of a two-day migraine, and my pressure feels sky-high. But I haven't thrown up in six hours."

"Can you increase your dosage?"

"Not without knowing my opening pressure. My insurance doesn't allow early refills, so I can't experiment on my own."

He frowns. "I'm guessing Dr. Wharton won't give you more."

"Not without another lumbar puncture."

"Luis's boyfriend, Cyrus, said one of his friends needed a spinal tap. Apparently, they're awful."

"They can be."

He drags a hand over his scruffy jaw. "They really want to meet you. I feel bad at how genuinely happy they are that I have a girl-friend."

"Why don't you tell them it's fake?"

"At first it was because of Mom. Then Luis invited us to Game Night as his friends were showing up, so now even more people know."

Game Night is our supposed meet-cute. "It's at your house? Why aren't you hanging out with them?"

"I don't belong there."

"Why not?"

"Well, I'm a bit of a fraud, aren't I?" He lifts his cane like, *See?*

I don't. "Because…your cane is fake?" What else could he possi-bly mean?

He shakes his head. "Most of them have lifelong disabilities. Seri-ous health problems. Luis got Epstein-Barr in college and now has ME/CFS. He's lucky he can work at all. Meanwhile, me, I did this to myself, didn't I."

"You crashed on purpose?" The room feels crowded by this reve-lation.

"No. But I signed up to fly twenty feet in the air off a twenty-two-foot snow ramp. I knew I could get hurt. I've gotten hurt before. I still did it."

"People choose to throw themselves out of airplanes for fun. Most sports entail physical risk."

"I liked the adrenaline rush." His eyes travel to the floor. "I was always trying bigger tricks. The one that got me injured was going to be a showstopper."

"Kind of the point of an Olympic event."

He passes his cane from one hand to the other, back and forth. "Some of Luis's friends were bullied for being disabled. I missed a lot of school dynamics, even before getting homeschooled, because I was always boarding or doing gymnastics—"

"Excuse me? Gymnastics?"

The corner of his lip twitches. "I've never hung out with anyone who was so uninformed about my career. I did gymnastics to get more flexible. Learn how to flip and spin. Until I got a sponsor, at least."

I picture him in tight spandex, and my mind explodes. "What does that have to do with the group?"

"I was a privileged S.O.B., just into my sport. And then there's them. There's you." He gestures to me. "Fucking beautiful you, with a condition you didn't sign up for. How does my presence not rub salt in everyone's wounds?"

"You think I'm beautiful?"

"That's what you got out of that?" He rubs his eyebrow. "I said I did the first night we talked."

"You said *pretty*."

"Skylar, you're the kind of woman who could bring a man to his knees with a single look."

I snort out a laugh. "You're still sitting."

"My knees hurt."

I laugh again, but it kills my head. He moves my knitting needles aside and holds up a fuzzy throw blanket. Pike is too sweet. I bet it was hard for all those women when he inevitably walked away the following morning.

My gut tightens. It might be hard to walk away when our deal ends.

He tucks me in. "It's not just your looks, you know. It's your whole 'I don't give a fuck' attitude. That confidence that's always there. It's a turn-on." He shrugs. "You know. For a lot of guys."

"And you?"

He nudges my leg. "I think you look like my snowboard."

I drop my head back against the pillows with a resigned groan. "I do give a fuck, you know. A whole lot of fucks. So don't be mean to me unless it's a hot mean."

He shifts, intrigue passing over his face. "What would you consider hot mean?"

Oh my God.

"All right," he says with a laugh, his gaze catching on mine as I let out a slow, measured breath, the air between us thickening for a beat. "Understood." He tweaks my blanket-clad foot. "Can I get you anything?"

"My ice hat, please. It's in the freezer." Before he can get to his feet, I place a hand on his shoulder. "Pike, you're not rubbing salt in my wounds. No one can blame you for pursuing an Olympic sport. You shouldn't either."

His gaze stays detached. "I can afford a personal trainer."

"That doesn't make you less worthy of having friends. Especially disabled ones." I also became disabled in adulthood. It was a lonely, frustrating ride until I joined my support group. I can't imagine having only nondisabled friends.

Pike still looks unconvinced.

Sometimes people want to hear they're disabled *enough*. Like there's a special club of us who are only accepting members with certain qualities. We see that in our support group a lot, especially with people who have invisible illness. But Pike has claimed a disabled identity. The problem is he thinks he acquired his disability the wrong way.

"Distancing yourself from disabled people with less privilege won't do anyone any favors," I say. "It's only allowing you to avoid whatever uncomfortable feelings you have about that. And it's isolating you."

"You're probably right." He shoves a hand in his pocket. "I don't think Luis is inviting me just to be nice."

"I bet they'd be excited to have a celebrity in their midst." I tug on his pant leg playfully. "You'll break some hearts."

"I'm not that guy anymore."

"That's okay," I say. "I like who you are now."

When Pike heads to the kitchen, I marvel at how true that is. I *really* like who he is now.

15

Pike

I open up a private chat with Skylar. **Hey, you up?**

She responds immediately. **You did not just send me a booty call??**

Oh, shit. I waited until it got late to message her because she was hosting a virtual craft event. **No, sorry!**

I'm joking, Pike. What's up?

I start typing but get distracted by a notification. **Skylar King replied to a post.**

My stomach drops to the ground. Then I remember Skylar can't see that I've flagged notifications about her activity. She replied to a woman who's being treated horribly by her partner because of her pain.

Skylar King: I'm sorry he turned out to be a piece of shit. So much for "in sickness and in health." If he doesn't love all of you, leave him. You deserve better.

One thing I'm learning from this group? Men are trash.

I go back to our chat, but Skylar replies to another post.

Skylar King: Dismissing women as "anxious" or "depressed" is the new medical "hysteria." Don't let him push you around.

Before I'm even done reading the rest of the thread, Skylar's posted her own question in the forum.

Skylar King: Does anyone recommend a good endocrinologist? I need one for empty sella and abnormal levels of free testosterone.

I'm amazed she can keep so many conversations going at once.

Even though I've been thinking about what I want to say for a few days now, I'm still having trouble getting it out of my brain. But once I finally do, I can take my oxy, get some sleep, and stop thinking about this.

You know what you asked me? I write. **About all the women? About my rep?**

With how long you were typing, I thought you were drafting an essay admitting your secret clown fetish.

I stare at my phone.

Yes, I remember, she says.

I wanted to clarify some things.

You don't have to excuse an enthusiasm for sex.

I know, I say. **But if you read those articles about me, you probably think I'm a player. The thing is, I was always busy with my sport. That was 100% my focus. I enjoyed sex and didn't have any trouble getting it.** That probably makes me sound even more like a player. But Skylar's one of the few people in my life I'm not lying to, so I don't want to mince words. **A relationship was unthinkable. I traveled around a lot, and you know how that is, right? The strain that puts on a relationship?**

I don't do relationships either, so I don't know. I'm also not a pro athlete.

She doesn't do relationships? Not the answer I was expecting, and now I have my own questions. But I continue: **It wasn't every night like they wrote, but it was a big part: ride with my crew, party at night.**

And then you had your accident.

Exactly. And here's where I don't really know how to word what I want to tell her. **I mean, yeah, sex is great, but maybe I don't want it with just anyone anymore.** It's something I wasn't able to articulate before now, even though the major lack of sex in my life should've been my first clue. **I'm not sure anymore if people actually want to**

be with me, Brandon, or if it's the famous snowboarder thing, or if it's just a pity fuck. I didn't care before but now I do.

Pike. Go look in the mirror. I doubt anyone would consider you a pity fuck.

The last woman told me she was going to be my "rehab."

Skylar sends an upside-down smiley. Hopefully you got your ass out of bed before it went any further.

Actually, I stopped halfway through because of all the comments she kept making, but no way I'm telling Skylar that. Not my best moment.

After my accident, it was like everything I thought was good and important didn't matter anymore. Life became meaningless. Same with the sex. Not that it had much meaning before. But it was an easy way to relax after a long day.

Your life isn't meaningless, Pike.

I know. But . . . purposeless, I correct. All my goals, gone. I scrub a hand over my mouth. How do I explain this? After my accident, I started overthinking everything, even sex. Is she going to make annoying comments about my scars? Is she going to say I'm hot "despite" my disabilities? There's pain in my back, should I stop? What if I can't leave after, because I'm too tired? Will she read into it? Am I even enjoying myself or am I going through the motions because this is what I've always done? I used to use sex to disconnect, and now my brain won't shut off. I hate it.

When I click send, my palms are sweating. I reread my message. Why the hell is there no delete button? This is too much. Too personal.

It can be hard to adjust to a new normal. This is why we have the group. 🖤

I linger for too long on the heart she sent. It's not just the platform—it's her. Since she already knows my truth, I don't have to bullshit. It's easier telling you than an entire group, I say. While she initially freaked me out, she now puts me at ease. There's an assurance in her responses that I haven't felt in a long time.

There's no judgment here, she says. **But I'm glad you shared. Up until now, I thought you were disturbingly well-adjusted for a newly disabled person.**

There's no point dwelling on something I can't change.

But like … you're not grieving your old life? Nothing? (Besides the sex)

I lie back in bed. My therapist talked about this. *The stages of grief are denial, anger, bargaining, depression, and acceptance. Which stage do you think you're in?* I always bullshitted to end the session quickly. The stage I was in was *thinking about how to get better.* So, denial.

I'm weary, I admit. **So over everything. I should be grateful to be alive. I am. But I'm tired of being grateful for scraps, like all that's expected of me now is to be happy I'm not dead.**

My ringtone blares, and I drop my phone on my nose.

It's Skylar. Requesting a video call.

"Hey?"

She's lying on her side, cheek scrunched against the pillow, and for a moment, I'm fixated on the way her pretty curls fall over one eye. Damn, she's adorable.

"Why do you sound breathless?" She squints. "Are you naked?"

I glance down at my bare chest. "I'm wearing boxers. What are *you* doing, calling me?"

"You gave me a real answer. I thought it deserved more than a text."

I swallow the sudden surge of affection I feel toward her. "Don't your eyes hurt with moving screens?"

"So don't move."

I nod, realize I'm moving, and attempt to speak through closed lips. "Okay."

She lets out a cute snort. The hazel of her eyes is tinged with more shades of blue tonight. "I get what you're saying about the 'being grateful' thing. Mom's always telling me I'm not grateful enough. As if being grateful will make everything better."

"Being overly grateful is probably the sixth stage of the cycle of grief."

She laughs. Fuck, I love that laugh.

"You look cute," I say.

My phone alerts me to another call, and I start. It's Jax. I never texted him back about Mammoth. Every time I've tried to reach out to my crew lately, I've drafted and deleted each message multiple times before finally giving up.

"Hey, can you give me a minute? My buddy, Jax, is calling. I used to board with him."

"It's fine. Go ahead and talk to him."

"No, don't go anywhere. I want to keep talking to you."

I reach for the stress ball Ranielle gave me. "Jax," I say.

"Pike! What the fuck is up?" He laughs like I told the best joke, and I sit back with a smile. Even after all this time, he's still happy to talk to me.

"I've got a girl waiting on the other line. Everything good?"

He whistles. "Won't keep you. Just checking if you're coming for the awards."

"Don't think I'm going to make it."

"Aw, come on. We miss you."

"How about I call you tomorrow?"

"Will you really?" His tone is friendly, but his words still make me feel like shit.

"Yeah," I say, trying to keep it light. "I need to hear if Trevor's going to propose already."

"I wish. We broke up a month ago. I'm already on my rebound, but it's hard. She's not Trevor. No one is."

"Shit. I'm sorry, man, that's rough. You'll have to tell me what happened tomorrow."

"I'll hold you to that. Now don't keep your girl up too late." He laughs again. "Or maybe do. Wouldn't want to hear about your rep suffering."

Skylar's squinting at the screen when I click our video.

"Sorry about that," I say.

"Oh. Hi. I'm looking Jax up. 'Jacques "Jax" Rochat,'" she reads, "'is a twenty-six-year-old Swiss Canadian snowboarder with two X Games bronze medals,' blah blah blah, okay, there's his picture. Ooh." She grins. "Hello, Jax Rochat. Is everyone in your crew hot?"

I smirk. "You tell me."

"Couldn't say. You're the focus of the videos I've watched."

Something warm lodges itself in my sternum. She's been watching me.

"So what did Jax want?"

I shrug. "The Shred Awards for snowboarding are in Whistler in a few weeks. He wanted to see if I'm going. I'm not."

"Why not?"

"It's a lot, you know? Seeing everyone but not boarding. Explaining my situation a million times. Not being negative. Facing the press. All of it."

"That makes sense."

"It's not that I don't want to see my friends. But the idea of going this year when I've just started rebuilding my life makes me want to throw up."

"Don't go if you're not ready. You can't force that."

"I won't." I drag a hand down my face. "There's something else I wanted to share earlier. About how my perspective's changed."

Skylar waits.

"It's not just about disability when it comes to sex," I say. "I had a lot of time to reflect while I was in rehab. I did some doomscrolling and read articles about my past with women."

"Hard to resist a good doomscroll when you're already wallowing, I imagine."

"Right?" I laugh, then quickly look away. Even Jax brought up my rep. "There are women who got hurt because of me. They thought they had a chance long term when I thought it was obviously a one-night stand. I didn't think twice about whether they'd be heartbroken after. But looking back, reading all that stuff from a different perspective…it gave me clarity on what can happen when you're careless about who you sleep with."

"Hmm," Skylar says. "Maybe it's less about carelessness and more about making sure both people are on the same page. When I hook up with someone, I tell them right away it's not going anywhere."

"I intend to be more direct about that going forward." I rake my fingers back through my hair. "You said you don't do relationships?"

"Nope. I prefer being alone." Doesn't sound like the full story, but Skylar says, "Oh! You'll never guess what happened at work today. I got in trouble because my skirt was too short."

I angle the camera closer. "I'll need to see this skirt to get a complete picture of the situation."

"I'll wear it for our next date. See if your mom objects."

"Trust me, she wouldn't care. So, what happened?"

I get comfortable. I don't care what we talk about. I'm just flattered she's choosing to spend her evening with me.

16

Pike

My phone vibrates as I lug in all the food I bought from Simply Crêpes for dinner. After canceling multiple times, Skylar's finally able to do the second date.

Hey kiddo, Dad writes. **Your mother said you've got yourself a nice girl. Let's talk soon. Did you get the info I sent you?**

I grimace as I thumb back, **Super busy, sorry.**

Luis comes around the corner, a headset around his neck. He's been so busy with meetings all weekend that he hasn't even had Cyrus over, but he's joining us for dinner. I hand him a plastic Rite Aid bag filled with the prescriptions he asked me to pick up.

"Thanks," he says, then surveys the food. "Wow. I didn't know you were capable of this much effort."

"Ha ha," I say flatly, pulling out the containers and avoiding his too-perceptive gaze. "It's dinner, not a national emergency."

"The guy who once said, 'I don't do second dates,' is now showing up with crêpes for fifteen people. All so his girlfriend can get to know his mom better."

"I wanted to surprise her and didn't know which crêpes she'd like," I force out, the oversharing eroding my core. "So I got some of everything."

His grin only widens.

"Go away," I say, "or you'll get *no* crêpes."

While I wait for Skylar, I pace around the front porch despite my pain. My legs hurt if I stand, but my back hurts if I sit. I'm antsy. Weirdly agitated.

This is it. The last half of our act. We get through this, and we're done fake dating.

Technically, we don't ever have to see each other again after tonight. The thought is disconcerting. Would Skylar consider hanging out with me outside of our agreement? I watch a guy in a parka walking around our cul-de-sac, and I wonder what she'd say.

When she arrives, it's hard to think about telling Mom we broke up. One look at Skylar, and I get that weak feeling in my knees again. She's in a short black skirt and a tight long-sleeved shirt, with big boots to mid-thigh.

"Is this the infamous skirt?" I say, delighted.

She twirls in the driveway. "You like?"

"More than I can express." My hand settles against her waist as I grin in appreciation. She smells amazing too—it's that chocolate-caramel ChapStick I can still taste on my lips. "Mom will be here soon, so we should claim the better dessert crêpes. But we need to be quick."

She looks up at me in those big shades, a playful smile on her lips. "A good quickie always hits the spot."

I can't keep my mouth from falling open.

"You should see your face," she says, her smile turning wicked. "It's like something short-circuited in your brain."

"It did."

A series of bright flashes goes off, and I drop my cane.

"Pike! Let's get a nice smooch for the camera!"

Skylar clings to me. "What's happening?"

I lift a hand to shield my eyes from the next flash. It's the man from the cul-de-sac. A reporter? A fan?

The camera keeps clicking. "Looking forward to talking to you and Skylar!"

What? How did he find out about us? How does he know her *name*?

"Pike! Get me inside!"

I tuck Skylar under my shoulder and half run, half limp with her to the porch.

"Where are you going? It's Chris Blake from *Playbook Confidential*. I was promised an exclusive!"

He *is* a reporter. Shit!

After I shove Skylar inside, I finally address him. "By who?"

I have this gut-punching feeling I already know the answer.

Of course, Mom shows up ten minutes later. Of course, she's the one who brought the reporter here.

Now she sits at the kitchen table, acting innocent. Skylar's under the covers in my bed. I made her go rest because she wouldn't stop trembling.

And because I need to deal with my mother. Alone.

"Your stunt at the doctor's office caused a cascade of problems. A staff member recognized you and went to *Playbook Confidential*. Blake came to me for commentary about your relationship."

"So you offered him an exclusive?"

"It kept him from writing his own story. You were at a *neurology* office. We can't have people thinking you have brain damage."

"Who! Cares!"

"More people than you think."

"You should've come to me first!" I don't give a shit what they say about my brain. It's Skylar I'm worried about.

"Blake wanted to see for himself. Since it's the first time anyone's heard from you since rehab, it's important we show them you're doing well. Better than some sob story about pity sex in a supply closet after bad news at the doctor. Her words, not mine."

My stomach turns over. I can see why the tech would twist it that way. That's the only reason anyone would have sex with me now, right?

"There's got to be some HIPAA violation there."

"You weren't a patient, honey. She's free to say she walked in on you having sex."

"I wasn't having sex!"

"All Blake wants is one interview about your life post-accident. And he wants Skylar to be there too. Just give him a happy ending."

I glare at her, even though I know it's not all her fault. She's putting out my fires, like she always did as my manager. That wasn't my choice as a kid, but it was the only way she'd let me board professionally. With all the traveling and older influences, she wanted to be in charge. Until suddenly, she wasn't, and I was, and we got stuck in this strange tug-of-war I should've ended years ago.

"If Skylar's going to be with you, she'll have to accept that you're a person of public interest."

But Mom has made it all about "proving" I'm fine. It's not enough for her to see that I'm "happy" with a girlfriend. The whole world needs to know as well. She was probably thrilled when Blake came to her. It's the attention she thinks I need to land more gigs.

"Go stall Blake," I say. "Tell him I'll talk to him."

"And Skylar?"

"Do not say one more word about Skylar without me present, or I swear I won't even spend holidays with you."

Mom only smiles at my threat. "Look at you, so protective. I'm happy for you, Brandon."

I shut myself in the laundry room after she leaves and text Kal.

Help. Mom sold me and Skylar out to a reporter. I have to give an exclusive now.

Kal writes back immediately. **On what?**

My life. My relationship.

Dude. Your relationship isn't even real.

And how do I tell everyone that? Now?

My phone rings.

"Can you give them something else?" Kal asks.

"Like what?"

"Something to keep him out of her business and focused on yours? Could you do something scandalous? Hang on. I just got to Lennox's." His voice grows muffled as he talks to his future wife. "Sorry, my buddy's having a crisis. I need a few. Oh, got it." He comes back to our conversation. "Never mind, she's busy with something urgent."

"Kal. Focus."

"Can you break up with her publicly? Make it ugly?"

"That'll make Blake even more interested."

"What if you get with someone new immediately after? The press will want to know whoever you're sleeping with, like they used to."

The idea makes me physically sick. It's not just that I'd have to find someone who's interested in me *and* media attention. I don't want to sleep with more random women. I want to sleep with—

Oh.

Oh, no.

But it's more than physical. I'm into Skylar, and realizing it shocks me down to my core.

"I don't think that'll work," I say weakly.

"Other scandalous things besides sex…" Kal starts his car. "Rehab? Drug scandals are big with celebrities."

"No." The last thing I need is for the public—or my doctors—to think I'm abusing my meds. I will not give opioids more bad press.

"You could pay Skylar to do the exclusive with you."

My phone beeps. An unrecognizable number. I decline, but it beeps again. Same number.

"Kal, someone keeps calling, hang on."

"Hi, sweets, it's Noemi."

"Who?" I demand.

"Skylar's friend? Emy?"

I frown. "How did you get this number?"

"You gave it to me, pal. The same night you promised to protect my friend. I'd like to know what happened between then and now."

I sag against the dryer. "I swear I didn't have anything to do with this."

"Don't care. How are you fixing it?"

"I don't know."

"Why are you hiding out while Skylar is freaking out in your room?"

I look up suspiciously. Emy's probably getting a play-by-play from Skylar, who never gets off her phone.

"You're going to take care of my girl. That's what you signed up for when you recruited her as your fake girlfriend."

"I didn't recruit—"

"Fix it or I'll go to the paparazzi myself."

The hell she will. "What are you going to say? Skylar was also involved."

"I'll make something up. Analia will corroborate my story. You do not want to mess with me."

So. The sweet Italian girl on video isn't so sweet after all. I should threaten her back with lawyers I can afford and she probably can't, but I'm not like that. It doesn't help me out of this situation with Blake either.

In truth, I'm relieved Skylar has friends she can count on.

"I don't want to mess with anyone, especially Skylar. I *like* Skylar." More than I've allowed myself to admit.

"Go reassure her."

"I need to talk to the reporter first. Otherwise, he'll do whatever he wants. Do you and Analia want to come over? I have lots of food, and Skylar would probably appreciate a familiar face after all this chaos."

For once, Emy stays quiet.

"What?" I ask.

"We haven't met in person. Probably not the best time to make that introduction." Emy hangs up.

They haven't met? What?

It shouldn't change things, but it does. I've never had online friends, so it's hard for me to understand. But I know how relieved I was to find a safe space in the group. For Skylar, it's her *only* safe space. She's invested immeasurable time in that community and has built great relationships from it while still maintaining her privacy.

All that could blow up in her face if I make the wrong move here. What can I give Blake that'll make him leave Skylar alone? How can I break up with her believably? I can't think of anything except Kal's suggestions.

Unless.

There might be one way.

My heart sinks, but I need to get Skylar out of this mess. I'm the one who should deal with the consequences of my fame, not her.

I head to my room. "Skylar? Can I come in for a sec?"

"Okay." Her voice is small.

"Hi," I say quietly.

She sits in my king bed with the flannel covers pulled up to her chin, her expression full of anxiety. The window's open despite the cold, like she needs more air, so I lower my voice in case Blake can hear us.

"I'm going to talk to you about this, but I need to take care of the reporter first."

"You're going to take care of it?"

"Yes."

Relief floods her features, and I know I've made the right choice—even if I hate it.

"Can I get you some crêpes while you wait? I need to get rid of Mom, too, or we can't talk freely."

"I've lost my appetite."

I sit down on the bed and pull her into a hug. "I'm sorry." I want to tell her everything will be all right, but I'm not yet certain this will work.

She squeezes me back, leaning her head against my chest, and I'm tempted to pull her down onto the bed with me so we can shut out the rest of the world.

I let go reluctantly. "Give me a couple minutes."

"Could I borrow some of your clothes? I'm uncomfortable in my skirt."

Not the time to picture Skylar naked in my bed, but it happens. The last time she wore my clothes, she was in only my shirt and a thong. I manage to point her to my walk-in closet, then force my weary muscles into submission.

One foot after the other until I make it outside.

I plaster on my camera-ready smile and offer a handshake. "Mr. Blake, Brandon Pike. Sorry for the confusion. It's nice to meet you."

"Heard you were hooking up in a closet," Blake says with a laugh. He's not much older than me. The sort of guy who gels his hair into spikes.

"Yeah." I give him a cocky shrug. "You know how I am."

"I hear Skylar's your girlfriend."

I keep my smile easy. "I owe you an exclusive. Unfortunately, Laurie didn't run this by me first, and I have a busy schedule."

"I already have a draft typed up. Coupled with the photos, it's enough for our readership even without your comments. They're dying to know what you've been up to."

"You can print something now, but if you do, I won't give you the only interview I'll do in Whistler for the Shred Awards."

Mom's face betrays her shock, but luckily, she's not facing Blake. I hold my breath even as my stomach turns over. The longer I wait to talk to him, the more likely he'll print something without my input. The awards are two weeks away, but it's the biggest bargaining chip I have.

When he takes a while to consider it, I say, "Well, if you don't want my post-accident take…? I'll share my story elsewhere. Sorry you had to make the trip."

"No, it's no trouble," Blake says. "We'd love that exclusive."

"It's yours."

"Excellent." He pockets his recorder. "So, Skylar's going to Whistler with you?"

I keep smiling. "Of course. I'm excited to debut her to the world—at the right moment."

Blake chuckles like we're good buddies. "Between us, my girlfriend hates spontaneous photos too. But you know how it is. Part of the job. No hard feelings."

"None at all."

"We'll stage some great shots."

"Perfect. She'll love that."

I head back inside and wait for my mother in the kitchen. I'm itching to grab my journal and process every warring thought currently racing through my mind.

I grab the takeout receipt and start folding it. Once. Twice. Again and again. She walks in while I'm reducing it to a tiny, crumpled square.

I don't look at her.

"I'm so proud of you," she says. "And Whistler!"

At least one decision doesn't need to be overthought.

I take a deep breath and chuck the receipt in the trash.

"You're fired."

17

Skylar

I'm *excited to debut her to the world.*

An ache burgeons deep beneath my ribs. Pike said he wasn't going to Whistler. He said he wouldn't tell the media about me.

He *lied.*

I bury myself under his duvet, hating how it smells like him. Ten minutes ago, I loved being covered in his clean, manly scent. After that hug, I even fantasized about Pike joining me in bed.

I should have known better. I've never been able to rely on anyone in person—it's why I prefer my support group. I can't believe I thought Pike was different. That I could trust him.

But this entire relationship has been a lie from the start.

My stomach bubbles with nausea. I pretended to be his girlfriend so I wouldn't risk losing my group. Now he expects me to go to Whistler too?

A muffled version of his argument with Laurie drifts into the room. His mom interrupts him constantly, like mine does with me. Once she leaves, I sit up too quickly. My head swims, the way it always does when I lie flat too long.

"Sorry for the wait." Pike drags his ergo chair over to sit across from me. "Brought you something."

It's a strawberry crêpe with a dollop of whipped cream. Damn him for picking the one I would've chosen myself. He holds out the plate between us, along with one of two forks. The intimacy of sharing food makes my heart twinge.

I can't play nice anymore.

"Does it give you some kind of twisted satisfaction to keep blackmailing me? Have I not done everything you've asked?"

"What?" Hurt flickers over his face. "I'm not blackmailing you."

"What do you call this fake-dating thing?"

"An agreement…?"

"The only reason I agreed to this is because you threatened to ruin the one good thing I have. But pretending to be your girlfriend in front of a million people?" I point at the open window, like Blake's still standing out there. "I can't. I don't want my life blasted on the internet. I thought you knew that. So go ahead. Tell the admins I lied to your mom. I'm done."

Pike's jaw goes slack. "I'm not going to tell them. I never was."

"Then why did you tell me you would unless, and I quote, 'your performance is satisfactory'?"

Shame flashes in his smoky eyes. "I didn't know the group was that important to you."

"I *founded* it. It's the only thing that gets me through my shitty conditions."

"I mean—when I first met you—" He struggles for words. "I didn't realize you were so—that you kept to yourself like this. That you haven't even met your best friends."

I don't know how he found out, but his words unhinge something in my chest. "That's not weird. Online friendships are valid."

"I never said they weren't."

"My friendships are *real*, and I'd do anything for them. Including date *you*."

Pike shoves a hand into his hair. "I'm sorry. I did, initially—wrongfully—hold the group over you. I was afraid you'd flake. But after the snowstorm, I thought you were still doing this because we're friends."

I scoff even though his words cut like a razor. "You said I had to meet your mom *twice*."

"I see. Well." He makes a grand sweeping gesture toward the door. "Consider yourself off the hook."

"How? You told Blake I'd be in Whistler!"

He smiles sadly. "I lied to him so he'd get off my case. I'll show up with someone else. Everyone will forget about you, and you'll be out of the spotlight."

The air punches out of my lungs. "But...who?"

"Who cares? Someone I meet the night before. We'll do our thing, and I'll move on to the next one. That's what everyone expects of me. Hell, why don't I bring two women while I'm at it?"

I can't think of anything to say. I feel too small.

Pike was *protecting* me?

"Sorry I come off as that big of an asshole," he says. "If it's all the same to you, I'm going to go enjoy my crêpe."

He leaves without another word. The longer I sit there, the worse I feel. He told me the very *idea* of going to Whistler made him want to throw up. He's not only going to face the media, he's going back to where he had his accident—his old home—to face his friends and the passion he can no longer pursue, all to protect me.

I'm not that guy anymore. He's told me that many times. For some reason, it's important to him. Now he's willing to let everyone think he's still the same so I won't be in the spotlight?

Pike did a huge thing.

For me.

I run after him.

He's perched on the edge of a square ottoman in the den, elbows on his thighs.

"You're not an asshole," I say quietly. "That's exactly it. I got so upset because your words with Blake contradicted everything you've shown me about yourself. I got scared and assumed the worst of you. I'm really sorry."

He nods. "It's fine."

"Thank you for protecting me."

"It's no big deal."

But he's doing that thing again. Answering in clipped words. Not looking at me. Pretending he doesn't care.

It's how he is with his mom.

"It is a big deal," I insist. "Please don't pretend it's not. I know you don't want to go to Whistler."

"Better to get it over with."

"Pike." I lower myself to my knees. He finally looks at me, his intense eyes filled with something I don't recognize. "Why would you do all that for me?"

"I'm the one who's famous. It's not your job to be my buffer."

"True, and I appreciate that." I gently put my hands on his knees to keep his attention. "Fake dating you hasn't been that bad. I've enjoyed getting to know you. I like the man you've become."

"I care about you," he says gruffly. "It's been a while since I've been a decent friend to anyone, and I didn't want to mess this up." He reaches for me, covering my hands with his own, and a thrill rushes down my spine at the unexpected reciprocity. "I didn't want you getting hurt. But you did anyway."

His words hit hard. I don't want him hurting because of me either.

"I'm sorry I lashed out," I say.

He threads his fingers through mine and squeezes. "I'm sorry I didn't explain beforehand. It was intense, right?"

Intense. That's a good way to describe everything swirling inside me. And sitting here touching each other, knowing he's as decent as I thought, makes me want to touch him in other ways.

I force myself to my feet. "Do you have any more strawberry crêpes?"

In the kitchen, I watch his delectable mouth devour two crêpes while I finish my strawberries and whipped cream. We eat in contented silence until curiosity gets the best of me.

"What do you actually need to do in Whistler?" I ask.

"I'll go to the ceremony, do the interview, see my crew."

"Will there be paparazzi around your crew all the time?"

"Before big events, there's more media involvement. We're well known in snowboarding circles. Grace gets the most press these days."

Emy and Analia's **Pike!!** emails come to mind. "Grace Kwon, who won gold in women's halfpipe?"

"Yes." He beams at the mention of his friend, warming my heart. "We're not movie stars. Unless something juicy's going on, no one cares."

"But I thought your interview was a big deal."

"It is. For me. There will be curiosity from the community, especially since I'm the one who usually . . ."

"Had something juicy going on?" I tease.

"But their interest will fade once my story's wrapped up. How often do you hear reports on past Olympic medalists?"

"Not too often . . ."

"After this exclusive, they'll forget about me. I'll say I'm doing great, Blake will write something inspirational, report I'm still moving from woman to woman, and that'll be the end of it."

I put my spoon down, a knot pulling tight in my stomach. "And the woman you present as your girlfriend?"

His attention drifts to the window. "They'll comment on who she is, compare her to past flings, then never see us together again. That's why I'll pick someone eager for five minutes of fame."

"Huh. I imagined photos on red carpets, constant media attention, people following me at work. Blogs dedicated to us as a ship."

Pike laughs lightly. "I doubt it would be that extreme, but they would dig into your life. Post private things if they found anything juicy."

"And there's the ableism," I point out.

"Exactly," he says. "Maybe, if this were real…I don't know. It'd still be better to keep you from being exposed."

I chew on my crêpe, absorbing it all. Is Pike really *that* famous? I didn't know who he was. It's a niche sport. Who's really going to care?

The fans and snow bunnies, probably. His old friends. Other disabled people for sure.

It'll matter to them.

"I wonder if there's another way," I say. "Something that doesn't exploit your disability or hide it. We could ask our support group what they'd say if they were interviewed about living with a disability."

"Skylar, all I care about is getting through the weekend without losing my shit in front of everyone." He stands and carries his plate to the sink but doesn't wash it. He just braces both hands against the counter until, eventually, he drives out a harsh breath. "Lately I feel more like a museum exhibit than a person. My body on display for everyone to critique."

I hate seeing him like this. Being around people who don't understand this kind of grief is incredibly isolating. I remember how it felt to mourn my old life as I struggled to accept my new reality. After my diagnosis, my friends planned a trip to New York City. I wanted to be included, even though I'd been sick all year, and it hurt that hardly anyone made the effort unless I could go out with them and be active.

I went, but nobody mentioned my illness or asked how I was. They expected me to keep up with their plans, and there were no accommodations. When I spoke up about it, they said the whole group couldn't adjust for only one person. After several nights of crying myself to sleep while they partied, I lied and said something came up with my brother.

I went home. We never hung out again.

I don't want the same thing to happen to Pike. It was the worst trip of my life, and I didn't even have to give an interview about it.

Pike's sitting at the counter now, drinking orange juice, not looking at me. Not looking at anything.

Shit. I care about him too.

I sink onto the stool next to him. "So, um, out of curiosity. What if I actually went to Whistler?"

The glass trembles in his hand. "People will find out who you are. It'll be too much."

"You said it wouldn't be a big deal."

"Compared to other celebrities."

"But aside from the interview," I say, "it's mostly a vacation?"

"All-expenses-paid. First-class flight. Luxury hotel."

"Would there be a hot tub?"

"I mean." Pike's suddenly heated gaze flits over the length of my body. "There can be."

"I'm listening."

"You'd have to come to the awards show. Otherwise we can do our own thing. Whistler's gorgeous."

I haven't been on vacation since that trip to New York City. A luxury trip—even with strings attached—is likely a once-in-a-lifetime opportunity. And with this broody hot poet?

"That doesn't sound as awful as I imagined," I say cautiously.

"I don't know, Skylar. I'd make it worth your while, but I don't want you to get hurt."

My hands are trembling, too, so I fold them in my lap. This isn't a good idea. I don't want strangers knowing about me. Commenting on my life.

But I can't shake the feeling that Pike shouldn't do this alone. And maybe, if I'm honest with myself, the idea of doing the interview isn't as unappealing as it seemed when I thought he was forcing me into it. Platforms can be powerful.

"Could I mention IIH in the interview? Name the one research foundation we have?"

"You can say whatever you want, as long as you don't tell anyone we're pretending."

"There wouldn't be another woman—or two—if I came?" The thought of him with other women for a publicity stunt leaves a sour taste in my mouth.

The thought of him with other women, period.

"Only you."

"What about kissing?"

Pike's eyes drop to my mouth. He wets his lips, making my toes curl. I cannot be the only one feeling this vibe.

"What about it?"

"Would we need to kiss on camera?" I'm not sure I could do that in public. Pike's lips make me lose rational thought. Now, in private…

"No, but I'd appreciate some hand-holding." He looks at me, all hopeful, and I melt. "My crew probably wouldn't believe it otherwise. You know."

"Because you're a physical guy."

His neck turns adorably red. "I was pretty affectionate—playful kisses, having women on my lap."

My skin goes hot at the thought.

"But I know that's not your thing," he says quickly.

I blink. It's not?

"I don't have to be the same," he says. "Maybe it'd show I'm serious. Whatever works for you is good with me." He takes my hands. "And if you needed to bow out, you could."

"Okay," I say. "I'll think about it."

"Really?" Pike scoops me into his arms so quickly I'm pulled onto my feet. I relax in his embrace. I didn't realize how much I needed this hug, but Pike's arms are strong and hold me perfectly. They make me feel safe. "I don't know why you changed your mind," he says into my hair, "but thank you. Thank you."

"I need to see what happens with my pressure. If it gets worse, I can't fly."

"Just the fact you're considering it."

He kisses the top of my head, and in that moment, I know I'm making the right choice, even if it's scary. It's what I'd want a friend to do for me.

"Aw," Luis croons, and we jerk apart. Pike's roommate rolls into the kitchen in pajama pants and a faded Bills sweatshirt. He smirks as he ruffles his hair, pushing the dark brown waves out of his face. "Did you two make up?"

"Get out of here," Pike growls.

"But now that all the drama's over, I want my crêpes. All I've eaten for the last three days is Cyrus's sholezard."

I head to the fridge. Luis was so sweet earlier when I was freaking out. "Come eat. I want to hear all of Pike's dirty secrets."

Pike groans, but when I wink at him, he smiles like I'm his favorite person. Something buried deep inside tells me I'd like to be.

18

Pike

So. I'm a real genius, aren't I?

I've avoided snowboarding for almost two years, and now I'm standing in front of a whole fucking mountain. Technically, it's *two* mountains.

I turn my back to Whistler-Blackcomb. I need to chill out or Skylar won't enjoy herself.

"Here we are," I say as I guide her inside my former favorite bar. After a nap, Skylar insisted we do something "fun." If it were up to me, I'd still be at the hotel after the long flight and drive from Vancouver.

But Skylar was miserable on the plane ride with her pressure, so if she wants to go out, I'll do my best to keep up. She deserves a night to enjoy herself. And I should savor our time together while it lasts.

"My crew used to hit all the clubs," I explain, "but we migrated here when that scene got tired. It was a great place to unwind without forgetting our names the next morning."

"And whoever you hooked up with the night before?"

I hate that it's the first thing she thinks of, seeing me back in my old territory. But the band's twang drowns out my retort. I shudder. This is the only place I tolerate country music. Every other Friday, it's line dancing in the middle of the floor.

"If the music bothers your head—" I start.

Skylar pulls me into the crowd, giving me a perfect view of her gorgeous ass in that tight little skirt I love. Maybe going out is worth it after all.

She finds us a table away from the band so we can still hear each other. I squirm on the uncomfortable bar stool, unable to get my hips happy.

"Brandon *fucking* Pike? No way!"

Please no. Not on my first night back.

Someone slaps me on the back. *Ow.* But all my annoyance vanishes at the sight of a stocky Vietnamese man with gauged ears and a barbell through his nose.

"Ryan?"

The owner of the bar crushes me into a hug. "I can't believe it! How have you been?" Before I can answer, he notices Skylar. "And who is this fine lady?" He waggles his eyebrows.

I have the sudden urge to protect Skylar from my past. Ryan has witnessed many of my indiscretions here. I may hate country music, but women sure love line dancing after a long day of shredding.

"This is my girlfriend, Skylar. She's new to this scene."

"No way!" Ryan regards her with reverence. "Pike's a *legend* around here. Not just for snowboarding." He proceeds to tell her about a time I got shitfaced and danced on the bar. While stripping.

"Thanks, Ryan," I say, cringing. "Can I get a pint of whatever you're brewing and one of every appetizer?"

"Sure thing. On the house." He slaps my back again. "Brandon fucking Pike."

Skylar won't stop smirking. "You danced on tables like Magic Mike? That's the most adorable thing I've ever heard."

I grunt. *Adorable* wasn't the adjective used when that dance went viral the next morning.

When our food and drinks arrive, she watches me accept my beer.

"It was easier to order one than to explain why I don't drink anymore," I say.

Skylar selects the small Caesar salad bowl, then grabs a couple of celery sticks from the wings platter. "I do the same thing sometimes. Just to avoid standing out."

"Really? You seem like you've navigated the whole disability identity thing smoothly."

"Hardly. When I got sick, I had to compromise constantly, even if it was subconscious. I'd hide my needs because people made them seem like inconveniences. It's why I don't bother much with in-person friendships anymore."

"But the girls are disabled too," I say. "Wouldn't they get it?"

"Who's to say they'd want to meet in person? Let's talk about you. Can I see your old place later? It's huge, right?"

I reach for a fry that's been smothered in cheese curds. "It's a small chalet."

"That sounds cute, though."

"If two flights of circular stairs to get to the loft bedroom is cute, sure."

Her face falls. "I'm sorry. It must've been awful, not being able to go home after all that time in the hospital."

That was one of the hardest parts. In the midst of my pain, all I could think about was selling the chalet, but now I wonder if I should've handled it differently—maybe rented it out or made it more accessible and hired a nurse. I knew my friends would be busy with their lives, training, and traveling, and I wanted a familiar face during my recovery, so moving to Rochester to be with Mom seemed like the best choice at the time.

"I miss the people," I admit. I miss the view, too, but I don't want a daily reminder of what I've lost. I pour ketchup on my bison sliders but can't muster the appetite to eat. *Being here* is a reminder of what I've lost.

"What's the plan tomorrow?" Skylar asks. "Room service in bed all day?" Her fingers trail up my hand, and my imagination goes a little haywire.

Since she agreed to come to Whistler, the vibe has shifted between us. There's more trust. More playfulness. We chat online almost every night, and now I'm not the only one who reaches out first. She even looks at me differently. There's an undercurrent of tension whenever our eyes meet, a magnetic pull.

But it's only Friday, and I need to take things slow. My only aim this weekend is to gently nudge Skylar toward the possibility of something more between us. We'll have some time by ourselves, and with its picturesque landscapes and romantic ambiance, Whistler's a perfect backdrop to plant some ideas.

But if she makes a move? Hell if I'm putting on the brakes.

"We could totally do that," I say slowly.

She snorts. "I'm kidding, Pike."

Of course she is. I smile like we're in on the same joke until I notice Jax, Macken, and Grace heading straight for us.

I take Skylar's hand in mine and grip a little too tightly. "Things are about to get awkward. If you want to bail—"

Jax sidles up behind Skylar, holding a tube of Smarties.

A beefy arm wraps around my shoulder. "That's how it's going to be?" Macken's gruff voice sounds in my ear. "No message you're here already? No nothing?"

Skylar's eyes widen as she takes him in. Macken's a white-blond Norwegian built like a truck. A truck with tattoos all over his face.

I grin. "I had prettier faces to see than yours."

Macken's deep chortle nearly bursts my eardrum. "Oh yeah? This Skylar?" He puts me in a chokehold. "Jax says you're the woman who finally has our boy whipped."

Skylar's lips quirk up. "I am, in fact, Skylar. And you are?"

"He didn't tell you?"

"He did, but he also said you like to introduce yourself."

A beat. Then everyone's laughing and I'm shoving Macken away. I could kiss Skylar for saying that.

"Macken does like being the center of attention," Jax concedes. "I'm Jax, and this is Grace."

Skylar eagerly turns to Grace. "The other gold medalist."

Jax strides over with a roguish grin, his fair skin already flushed pink from the heat of the bar—or maybe from drink. Jax loves to pregame as much as he loves to party. "Didn't think you'd come," he says, pulling me into a hug.

It feels so normal to be around him again, like I haven't been gone for almost two years. Even his thick brown hair is mussed up as usual, making it seem like he just got off the slopes, but I'm betting he still styles it that way on purpose.

Macken pulls up a bar stool. "So, you're healin' and all that?" He jerks his chin at Skylar. "Can my man still fuck?"

She chokes. *Damn it, Macken.*

"Stop that." I smack him in the shoulder. "You're an asshole, you know that?"

Macken just looks at Skylar like, *Well?*

Eyes watering, Skylar nods. "Yep. Hard."

My turn to choke.

"I'll drink to that," Macken says. "I was afraid he'd be stuck in a wheelchair forever."

Skylar glances at me, cheeks pink, clearly expecting me to challenge him. I should clarify that I'm not *stuck* in my wheelchair—it helps me get around—and that his assumptions about sex and disability are as tired as they are outdated. Plus, my chair is now half-destroyed from the flight, and I spent most of the drive from Vancouver fighting with customer service.

Before I can reply, Jax orders shots. A couple fans approach us for pictures. Unfortunately, they recognize me.

Skylar's smile tightens when a woman approaches Jax, Macken, and me for a photo and drapes herself across our laps. I'm sandwiched between the guys, so I make sure my hands are up in plain sight.

When the picture's done, I shake my head. "Don't drag me into that anymore. Things are different."

"Yeah, things are different," Macken scoffs. "You're too good for us now. Barely even recognize you without your hair."

I shift uncomfortably. "Where are Brick and Luce?"

"Why? You only ignore half our crew?"

"Macken's just upset you didn't come to Mammoth," Jax says, massaging my shoulders. "Now that you're out of rehab, you could visit more."

I smile and nod, but why is it always on me to make the effort? None of them can come to Rochester for a weekend? But I already know why. My friends are like I used to be, seeking excitement wherever it is, not wasting time in boring towns with small hills.

My throat tightens, and I reach for my untouched beer.

Skylar takes it away. She leans across the table and pulls me to her by my shirt. Our lips lock, and then I'm catching air off a jump again, caught in a moment of weightless bliss. I told her to go with whatever PDA she's comfortable with, and if this is what she wants? Fuck if I'm complaining.

Wolf whistles go up around us, and Macken slaps me on the back again. I almost forgot what a dipshit he can be. I grab his wrist even as I keep kissing Skylar, wishing I could block out the bar and just focus on her. I know why she's kissing me, and I'm grateful, but every caress of her tongue pulls me deeper into something I can no longer ignore.

It can't all be in my head. It's too damn good.

A soft sound of pleasure pulls from her throat. *Fuck.* The things I could do to make her give me more of them. I reach for her face, willing to keep her close as long as she desires.

She drops one last kiss on the corner of my mouth. "You've got this," she whispers. "Relax."

It's nearly impossible with her lipstick lightly smudged from my own mouth. I probably look like someone whacked me upside the head.

Jax pockets his favorite chocolate candy and pulls Skylar to him. "Done eating? How about a dance?"

Skylar's mouth forms a small O as she takes in Pretty Boy Jax's hands on her waist. Mm-hmm. I've heard countless men and women wax poetic about his *startling green eyes and soft, sensual lips*. But does that mean I want Skylar looking at him like that? Hell no.

"I could dance," she says.

Not with him. I want Skylar to dance with *me*. I reach for my cane, but it's gone. Macken twirls it like a baton, dangerously close to smacking everyone in his vicinity.

I scowl. "Give me that."

"Brandon Pike is back," he drawls, throwing my cane in the air. It seems to move in slow motion, and my only thought is that it's going to strike Skylar in the face.

I jump for it, but the shaft smacks my knuckles, and the jolt sends a sharp pain through my hip as I stagger to catch my balance.

Gritting my teeth, I bend stiffly to grab the cane. "Never touch my cane again."

"I'm just having fun."

"I need that to walk."

"I was going to give it back, bro."

"Never. Touch. My cane. Again."

"Chill, Pike." Macken turns back to the crowd. "Who's buying me a drink?"

My fist stays clenched around the handle. Macken's always messed around, but this is different. In the hospital, he used to play with the bed controls, raising and lowering me and doing all sorts of annoying shit. But trying to get your friend to change his personality so he doesn't fuck up your recovery is harder than it sounds.

"Oh wow, you really *are* Brandon Pike!" A woman thrusts a napkin in my face, her number scrawled with hearts. "I cried when you had your accident!"

"Pike?" Grace draws my attention away from the fan.

I slide into the seat across from her. Grace is the glue that's always kept our crew together. As the only woman until Luce, she's put up with a lot. She's seen each of us in the buff a hundred times, purely by accident. She's fended off more snow bunnies than anyone ever should. Now she has four overprotective brothers for life.

Or three. Pretty sure I'm kicked out.

Grace's warm brown eyes meet mine, triggering a rush of nostalgia. Her glossy black hair falls past her shoulders now, and she's lost some of the roundness in her face. A knife twists deep in my gut. I've let too much time pass.

"Hey," I say, careful to keep my cane between my legs so it doesn't fall over. "How have you been?"

"Tired but good. My grandma just turned eighty, so we all went back to Korea for a huge birthday celebration. I'm still jet-lagged."

I smile fondly. I've met her parents multiple times, and her younger brother snowboards as well, but he's into slopestyle. "I'm so glad you could see everyone."

She exhales through her nose, shaking her head just a little before meeting my eyes. "Me too, but you and I aren't going to sit here and pretend like everything's fine, are we? You can leave that act for everyone else."

My throat dries up again. "Right."

"How come you don't reach out? I miss you."

I look down. "I haven't been in touch with anyone. Jax is the first person I've talked to recently."

"So we were good enough company in the hospital, but not out?"

One beer should be okay. Small sips over time don't interfere *too* much with my meds. I did that once when Dad visited after rehab.

But I spot Skylar doing a heel kick with Jax, her diamond septum piercing glinting as she tilts her head back with a delighted laugh. I won't be able to keep up with her if I get woozy.

"It's…complicated," I say. "Talking to you guys made me feel even more alone. No one understood what I was going through, and it reminded me of everything I lost. So I pulled back, and before I knew it, everyone else did too."

She places her hand over mine. "I know none of us can begin to imagine what you've been through, and I'm sorry we couldn't support you the way you needed. But we're a family. You're still part of it, even if you can't snowboard anymore." Grace glances at Macken and rolls her eyes. "Everyone feels the same, even if they have their own ways of showing it."

Words I didn't know I needed. It's always felt like all or nothing.

"I'm sorry I fell out of touch." I give her a quick squeeze, her palm tiny under mine. "I'll do better."

I need to have a similar conversation with Jax, but it'll be tougher. He visited a lot at first, but he kept insisting I'd get better—I had to push myself because it meant I'd return to snowboarding. At first, I believed him. But then the surgeries piled up. Jax couldn't accept it. The further I got from snowboarding, the more distant Jax became. Our calls were only ever about *the good old days*. How do you move a friendship forward when it only looks back?

I shake my head as he mimes something silly at Skylar. She laughs again and trips into his arms. Jax has been my best friend since I was seventeen. I should be honest with him.

"Why don't you ask Skylar to dance before you incinerate Jax with your eyes?" Grace says, a knowing smile on her lips.

That's not quite it, but I force out a laugh. "I can see Skylar anytime. I've ignored you long enough."

"You're here all weekend. I insist."

A new type of nervous energy hums through me as I head toward Skylar. I want to dance. Can I? I haven't tried since everything happened. But I want to hold her in my arms. I want to be the one making her smile. Even if I can only make it through one song, I want that.

I slide in behind her. One step, two step, shit, I'm-going-to-fall-over step. I laugh at myself as everyone rotates, and Skylar slides to my left. She grins at me, so I push through one more chorus, using my cane for balance.

I move between her and Jax. "Wanna dance, sweetheart?"

She gestures at her ears. "What?"

Ah, she's wearing earplugs.

"She can't hear shit," Jax explains, pushing her into my arms. "Hates noise or something?"

I put my mouth to her ear. "Wanna dance?"

She beams and brings me to the side of the crowd. As her hands wrap around my neck, pulling our bodies together, my chest expands uncontrollably. It feels like I'm flying twenty feet in the air again.

I haven't danced in two years, and even then, it was always with a purpose. A means to an end. Now I don't want the song to end.

Not when Skylar's looking at me like I'm her perfect man.

The banjo plays fast, but we move slowly, our rhythm isolating us from the rest of the bar. Her thighs brush against my knees as her fingers trail over the nape of my neck. The sensation draws my eyes shut, and I lean my forehead down against hers.

"I hope it's okay that I kissed you," Skylar whispers. "You seemed like you needed the distraction."

I'll take any touch she'll give me. "Whatever you're comfortable with is fine with me."

"Let's keep doing what feels natural."

I clasp a hand gently around her neck and pull her closer until her head leans against my shoulder.

Part of me resents my legs for not allowing me to do this whenever I want, but the other part loves them for bringing me closer to Skylar. If my life had stayed on the same path, I'd never have met her. I don't know how to reconcile that with the fact that I still long to snowboard with every fiber of my being.

Still, tonight, I'm grateful. For friends who haven't given up on me, and for this surprising woman in my arms.

Even for fucking country music.

19

Skylar

'm on a helicopter.

A scenario I'd only imagined in the event of an emergency medevac. But this is a private chopper, arranged by Pike's friends for backcountry snowboarding. Being dropped off on a remote part of the mountain with avalanche gear sounds risky, but since Pike's last helicopter ride *was* a medevac, I support his decision to join as a bystander.

As we soar over Blackcomb, I gradually adjust to the sensation, mesmerized by the vastness around us. The sky is a clear expanse of blue, the morning sun casting warmth on the pristine white landscape below. People become miniature. Soon, we're far removed from ski lifts and groomed trails.

Today, Pike looks every bit the hot snowboarder, clad in a thermal shirt tucked into sleek black snowboarding pants, and his short hair concealed beneath a beanie. Grace, Jax, Macken, and Luce, another member of Pike's crew, are all here.

They discuss snowboarding tricks while my headache intensifies from my tight headset. I have earplugs in to mitigate the chopper's noise, but it still triggers my IIH-induced hyperacusis. Their conversation, peppered with snowboarding jargon and different accents, sounds like a foreign language to me. I catch degrees of rotation and phrases ending with *out*: *stomp out, pretzel out, wash out*. I think.

"Pike." Jax leans over from my right, his sexy rasp catching my attention.

Emy thinks he's Pike's hottest crew member and wants me to get his number for her. I don't think he has anything on Pike, but he does have a jaw that could cut glass and striking green eyes framed by lush dark hair.

He raises a pierced eyebrow. "What's with the ski shop gig?"

"Yeah," Macken says. "Only people wanting discounts for equipment work at ski shops. The hell you need discounts for?"

"We can hook you up if you need anything," Grace offers.

"I tried getting other jobs, but without a degree, opportunities are limited. Phone interviews went well, but when I showed up in my wheelchair, they'd mysteriously ghost me."

"Yeah, right," Jax says. "That shit's illegal, isn't it? Even in the States?"

"And yet…" Pike trails off, likely thinking what I am. Not worth explaining how much people ignore the ADA and other anti-discrimination laws. People don't admit to denying you based on disability, but a lot of "mysterious" things happen once you reveal you need accommodations.

Another reason I'm grateful for my job. It's a means to an end: insurance, a paycheck, and stability.

"I got more callbacks when I didn't use my wheelchair," Pike continues, "and even more when I forced myself not to limp without my cane. Super-demoralizing experiment."

"But you're not staying at the ski shop forever." Why can't Macken drop it? Who cares where he works?

"You could start an organization," Grace suggests.

Oh, boy. I reach for Pike's hand, already resting on my knee. We're crammed so close together that every part of us touches from shoulder to toe. I intertwine my fingers with his and offer a reassuring squeeze. This can't be easy for him.

His gaze softens with acknowledgment—and something deeper. It mirrors the look he gave me yesterday while we danced. Seeing the care on his face stirs something tender in me. When Pike looks at me that way, it makes me believe we could be something more. Something real.

I wink at him before I dissolve into a gooey sap in front of his friends.

"It's a crying shame, what happened to Pike," Jax says. "He really could've been something."

Ugh. "He *is* something."

Everyone turns to me, surprised.

"There's more to life than snowboarding."

"No offense, Skylar, but you have no idea," Jax says. "Pike was a prodigy. It's hard to understand if you're not into the sport. To waste that talent?"

"He dedicated every moment of his predisabled life pursuing his passion. How is that wasting talent?"

"Skylar, it's okay," Pike starts.

"No, you got into an accident. That's not your fault. That's not *wasting* anything. Let's keep things in context here."

Macken barely conceals an eye roll. "We can't be sad for our friend? Okay, peach."

"You can, but it's been almost two years. Maybe start supporting him in what he can do instead of making him feel bad about what he can't?"

"Thanks, Skylar. It's okay," Pike says. "We're just reminiscing. I miss snowboarding."

"The good old days," Jax adds, but thankfully, they move on.

When everyone else removes their headsets and prepares to leave, Pike wraps his arm around me. "Thanks for sticking up for me. I'm fine, really."

Jax eyes us curiously, so I snuggle closer to Pike, fluttering my eyelashes adoringly. "I wish you'd stick up for yourself."

He gives me a playful nip on the neck, and even though it's pretend, goose bumps prickle my skin.

"Not the time," he murmurs, giving his crew a final wave.

I stretch out, watching them get going, then shriek as Grace soars off a cliff and disappears from view.

Pike stifles a laugh. "She's good, trust me."

Once they're out of sight, I turn back to him. There's sadness in his eyes.

"You've considered adaptive snowboarding, right?"

"Yeah," he says, "but the pain makes it difficult to stand for long, even with ski crutches. My knee also doesn't bend fully anymore, which is dangerous if I fall."

"Could you sit? Like some skiers?"

"I could, but it's not the same. I know it sounds whiny, but sitting feels like sledding to me."

"It's not whiny. Give yourself some credit."

He exhales deeply, as though allowing himself that luxury for the first time. "I know I should be grateful to be on the mountain at all, but imagine a marathon runner only doing the fifty-yard dash forever. Maybe I'll feel comfortable going down the mountain with adaptive equipment someday, but I wish I could still do my sport."

I brush my thumb slowly over the back of his hand, a quiet, steadying motion. A reminder that he doesn't have to push the sadness away. That it's allowed to exist.

"Before you ask about the Paralympics," he says, "I don't qualify. They're for specific disabilities. Anyway, we should go." He signals the pilot, once again surprising me with how fast he can flip off his emotions. "I have a surprise."

"There's more?"

"You don't want to stay on the helicopter all day, do you?"

After we land, we take the lift up to a cluster of wooden lodges back in the resort. I follow Pike across the packed snow as skiers and snowboarders zip by toward the runs. I ignore the way my ears have been plugged like I'm on a plane all weekend, a constant reminder my pressure's getting worse.

I need a nap. I'm not used to doing more than one thing per weekend, and that's usually going to Wegmans. Tonight, we'll be busy with the awards ceremony and after-party. But I want to see what Pike planned for us.

Closer to the mountain's edge, there's a cluster of people lying down.

On lounge chairs.

With blankets?

I tug on Pike's jacket. "Wait. Is that…?"

"Apparently this is the newest way to get some rest around here. Come on, I reserved us three hours."

He hands over a ticket, and a man with a coral beanie leads us to the last two chairs in the front row overlooking the mountain. There's no railing, just a drop. Skiers and boarders come and go (off the drop!). The chairs have plush cushions and the option to recline all the way down, and are so wide Pike and I could easily share one. I'm grateful for the sun umbrella too.

The host hands us a tablet. "What can I get you?"

We settle on burgers and hot chocolate. I breathe in the crisp air. The enormity of the mountain makes my problems seem small. If we stay here long enough, we might even catch the sunset.

Pike adjusts his sunglasses and focuses on me instead of the view. "Good? Comfortable?"

Everything about this feels romantic. But this is his home mountain. It's probably ordinary for him. "It's…kind of perfect?"

"I assumed this was for people afraid of skiing. But it's nice."

"And we'll get in less trouble lying around here together than in a hotel room." It slips out before I can stop it.

Pike's lip twitches.

"I have no filter," I say. "Ignore me."

His smile widens. "I know, and I won't."

A waiter brings our food. Pike slathers his curly fries in ketchup and devours his massive burger. I nibble on my kid-sized burger, pushing my bun and most of my fries onto Pike's plate. Dr. Wharton said I need to drop two pounds a week, which is bullshit, but I want that brain scan.

I've severely restricted my calories for weeks, yet I've only lost one pound. It's messing with me mentally, like every forced weight loss attempt. A few years into my diagnosis, I realized moderation and limiting sodium feels best for me, even if it doesn't change the scale.

Pike gets a partial chocolate mustache on his stubble.

"I'm digging this mountain man look," I say, unable to resist wiping at it with my thumb. "Even if you're not boarding, you could still wear this outfit sometimes."

His hand catches my wrist before I pull away. He sucks my thumb into his mouth, his tongue so soft it takes a second to register.

"Mmm," he murmurs. "Chocolate."

Heat rushes through me, but Pike resumes eating like that didn't just happen. The barest hint of a smirk graces his lips, and I'm left reeling and needy, my breath shuddering out in small pants. *Um. Sir? Was someone we know nearby?* I glance around but don't recognize anyone.

I go back to my hot chocolate and try not to think about lowering Pike's chair and climbing on top of him just to see what might happen.

He watches the skiers and boarders, his chest rising and falling in slow breaths, face void of emotion once more.

"I'm sorry you can't enjoy it," I say.

"I'm enjoying a beautiful view with a beautiful woman. What's there to be sorry about?"

It's the sweetest line. He's had a lot of those lately.

"It's okay to still like snowboarding."

Pike keeps his expression mild but stays silent.

"It doesn't have to be all-or-nothing. It's okay to cultivate new passions. It's okay to miss it and be upset sometimes that you don't have it anymore. It's okay to have moved on."

"The problem," he says quietly, "is that I haven't moved on at all."

"You never mention it, though."

"I can't change it. Why bring it up?"

"It's still a huge part of you." I think back to some of the snow metaphors in his poem. "It must be painful to be back here."

"I can't figure out how to merge my two lives."

"It's the same life, Pike."

There. He finally looks at me. "I thought you, of all people, would understand."

"I do. But sometimes it's a good reminder that even if it feels like a part of us died, we didn't."

"Even if we have to be grateful for scraps sometimes?"

"Especially then."

He's silent for a long time before he reclines to be level with me. "What happened when you first got sick?"

"It's not that interesting."

"Sure it is."

I remember when I shared this with my uncle, who promptly fell asleep on the couch within five minutes. It's hard to summarize how your entire life was derailed by chronic illness, and I don't want to bore Pike, who thinks I've figured out the whole "disability identity thing."

But he waits. "What happened?"

"Fine," I say with a sigh. "I started birth control pills. Did you know they can cause intracranial hypertension?"

"Skylar, I hadn't even heard of IIH until I met you."

"Within sixteen hours of taking the pill, I started getting

excruciating headaches. It was my first month at a marketing job. It felt like a chain was pulling me to the floor from the back of my head. Three days later, I started seeing double. I rushed to the ER, where they did an MRI. I stopped the pill, but nothing changed, so my doctors insisted it couldn't be that."

"Sure, because no drug can give you lasting side effects."

"Right? I've argued with Dr. Wharton countless times about that. He ignores the fact that I was perfectly fine the day before. He also overlooks new studies that suggest potential hormone issues related to IIH. It's always BMI, BMI, BMI. Anyway, weeks later, I saw an ophthalmologist who found papilledema and referred me to a specialist with better equipment to examine the optic nerves. But I'd already started falling behind on everything at work."

I fell behind on *life*.

"Long story short, the second ophthalmologist diagnosed me with 'likely' pseudotumor cerebri, but I needed a neurologist to write me a prescription for a lumbar puncture in order to confirm the diagnosis. But his buddy neurologist wasn't available for five months. I asked for a different referral. He refused. I remember crying in the reception because I couldn't get my vision to focus enough to do my job. But they called security on me for making a scene. Then I got fired because no doctor would sign off on any accommodations."

"Is this Dr. Wharton?" Pike cracks his knuckles. "No reason. Just wanna chat."

"Nope, just bad experiences all around." I massage my sore temples. "Eventually, I found a new ophthalmologist who sent me to a neuro-ophthalmologist. That's how I ended up with Dr. Wharton, where I had to repeat all the same tests. He finally ordered the LP and prescribed meds, and I've been stuck with him ever since."

"I despise that man," Pike says. "I know people talk about it in the group, but it was shocking to witness how he treated you. My doctors have always been helpful."

"You're a celebrity. And a white man, on top of that. The more marginalized you are, the worse you're treated in medicine, usually."

"Luis says that too."

"I may have finally found a new lead, though. My IIH group recommended this interventional neuroradiologist in Manhattan. No referral needed, just scans. I sent an old one before we left."

"Would going around insurance help? Can I pay for a consult?"

I swallow the lump in my throat. I don't think he means it with any strings. Most people, when there's help involved—financially or otherwise—expect some kind of repayment.

"That's really generous," I say, my voice full of emotion. "But I don't know. I'm not used to someone wanting to be part of this."

"Skylar," Pike says softly. He comes to sit on my chair and drops an arm around my shoulders. "Whatever happens, you can always call me. A year from now, whatever—I'll try to help if you ever need it, okay?"

I appreciate the offer as much as I appreciate his warmth. I lean into his strong chest and pull the blanket over us. "If I can get into a specialist without insurance, I might take you up on that. Thank you."

For a long time, we sit there watching the sun dip toward the snowcapped peaks, both of us eventually dozing off for some much-needed sleep. Before we leave, I make him take a picture with me for the girls.

And for me. I want to remember this moment for a long time.

20

Pike

Do my words sound slurred?" Skylar asks in the elevator.

"No?" I say.

"My brain-to-mouth thing isn't working right. I feel like I have to force everything off my tongue."

"Is your head worse?"

We rested this afternoon, but we've still done a lot. Luckily, tomorrow's a nothing day. Brunch with Jax for me, and a spa visit for Skylar before we fly back.

"The altitude changes aren't helping. But I'm also nervous. Are you sure I look okay?"

"'Okay'?" I echo in disbelief. "You're stunning."

She still regards me doubtfully. I get it. I'm acting confident, but my heart's knocking against my rib cage. We're about to be featured in a national magazine for a relationship that isn't real, and I'll have to talk about the one thing I'm always avoiding.

"I'm having a hard time not staring at this...this *thing*." I indicate her soft white shirt that isn't quite a shirt. It's got long sleeves and all, but it's skintight and has a cutout off the right shoulder. From there, it runs downward diagonally toward the smooth dip between her breasts, baring her left shoulder completely. I want to press my lips to that shoulder so badly.

"It's a bodysuit." She turns to the right. "This is my better side."

I have to pinch my leg right where it hurts over my bursa in order to force my attention away from how her hips pop in those high-waisted black pants. Her soft curls are straightened into light waves that fall halfway down her back. "All your sides are good."

"You're lying, but thanks."

"Do I need to get on my knees?" I lean closer, brushing a finger over her bare shoulder. A faint blush spreads across her skin. "They don't hurt that much today, sweetheart."

Our eyes lock for one potent beat. A spark of confidence blooms in my chest. Her bright red lips part, and I wait, mere seconds that seem to expand into hours. I promised myself I'd take things slow, but Skylar might make a liar out of me.

I inch closer.

The elevator opens.

Her lips meet my cheek in a barely there kiss. "You've got this," she says softly.

The only reason I'm able to leave the elevator is that she takes my hand.

I walk a little less steadily than usual, unable to get used to the handle on the elegant cane I'm using tonight. Mom got it for me along with three others after I graduated from using a walker. She was under the misguided assumption I'd care enough to "accessorize" with them. The only cane I've ever used is the black ergo one I purchased for myself, unless you count the time I strutted around in front of a mirror in a moment of boredom and mild pharmaceutical influence.

I was not accessorizing, for the record. I was trying to figure out if I could still have swagger with a cane. The verdict is yes. Yes, I can.

This cane may be a nod to fashion over function, but it matches the outfit Skylar picked out for me: a casual dark navy suit—"jacket unbuttoned, please"—a slim brown belt, and a white dress shirt open at the collar.

"You look good, obviously," she said earlier, "but I still wish you had to wear a tux tonight. I need to see this Magic Mike level of hotness I've heard so much about."

Now I'll have to find an excuse to wear a tux around her.

Blake's already at the bar, his recorder next to his wineglass. After we grab a table, he dives right in, asking the basics. Where I work, what I'm up to now, and anything about Skylar we'll reveal. She's smart with her answers but grudgingly admits she's a regional admissions counselor.

"How did you two meet?"

"A lot of things lined up." I give the same cover story. "We eventually started talking in the support group, and one thing led to another."

Blake pushes his glasses up his nose. "I've gotta say, that's not your usual style."

"Wasn't looking to settle down before." I beam at Skylar, meaning it.

Blake turns to her. "What's Brandon Pike like off camera?"

Her hazel eyes meet mine, and my pulse spikes. We didn't prepare for this question.

"He's really sweet," she says. "And…quiet, in a good way. He's thoughtful and generous and validating. He's kind even in situations when you'd expect him not to be. Those are qualities I've previously found rare in a man, if I'm honest."

I'm a little stunned. People usually talk about me in relation to my body—what it can do in the pipe, how sexy it is, how much it can please a woman. I don't remember the last time anyone said anything about my personality.

"One reason Pike and I get along so well is that we've both had our health change the course of our lives as adults, which nondisabled people can't fully grasp. We're able to understand each other on a deeper level, and that makes everything else in our relationship easier. It also doesn't hurt that he's gorgeous."

Blake chuckles. "I bet."

"Yup. Just one broody look from him has me melting."

"Broody, huh," I say, making sure Blake sees me wink.

Under the table, Skylar hasn't let go of my hand, and her knee bounces at my side. I put my leg out slowly, so she won't startle, until it rests against hers. She releases some of her nerves at the connection.

"He's such an attentive boyfriend," she says. "Truly, I couldn't ask for better."

Blake scribbles a note. "And what's your disability?"

Skylar eagerly talks about IIH, explaining its impact on her life, and the lack of treatment options.

"And what about you, Pike? Has your accident changed you?"

My stomach turns acidic at the question. But that's what people will be most interested in. Am I a sob story, or am I inspirational? I don't want to be either.

"I think pain changes everyone. For me, it was a quicker, sharper change than for those who develop chronic pain over time. I had to change my entire way of life the second I fell." I see Skylar's face soften at my words. "No pro athlete can continue at the same level forever. My body just wore out sooner than planned. But recovery's going well, so I can't complain."

"More positive than I expected, I'll admit. You don't miss snow-boarding?"

How is that even a question?

"I miss my crew. Being one with the mountain. The air and the adrenaline. Go big or go home, right? Well, I went big, and I also went home." I laugh to lighten the mood, and thankfully, Blake joins in. "But I'm lucky," I add as I catch Skylar's eye. "I've got a great trainer, a low-key job with flexible hours, and an amazing girlfriend. All in all, I'm excited to see where this new direction will take me."

Because hell if I have any idea where to go from here.

Skylar nods at me and picks up where I left off. "A lot of Pike's new lifestyle is only possible because of his wealth."

It's also because Luis has an accessible home, but I let Skylar talk about financial barriers to access and treatment. She discusses medical ableism and that it's worse for people who are multiply marginalized. I nod. Luis, who's Mexican American and disabled, has explained how medical racism compounds ableism, and it's a topic I still need to learn more about.

I love listening to Skylar talk. She's intelligent and direct, and she challenges my thinking, the way Luis does. I'm proud of her for using this opportunity to spread awareness. If her hand weren't trembling in mine, I'd never guess she was nervous.

"Let's grab some pictures outside," Blake says, closing his notebook but keeping the recorder on.

I sweep Skylar's long waves to the side and drop a quick kiss to her delicious neck. Her breath hitches. Sweet floral notes from her perfume waft over me, making me want to lick and linger. "You did amazing," I whisper. "Just a few more minutes, then we'll be out of here, I promise."

"Are you okay to walk?" Blake asks. "We could find a bench. Lose the cane?"

"I can stand for a few shots." I want my mobility aid in the photos. Normalizing them is important, especially for younger people.

Outside, Blake tells us to talk amongst ourselves and pretend he's not there. Snowflakes land in Skylar's hair and on her cute, freckled nose. I slide my hands around her soft waist and draw her close so Blake won't hear.

She drapes her arms around my neck. "You're quite the tease today."

"Oh?" I ask innocently, but I know exactly what I'm doing. "Do you want me to stop?"

"How about a kiss?" Blake calls.

"We don't have to," I reassure her.

"We're doing what feels natural. And this," she says, pushing up on her toes, "feels perfectly natural."

Her lips meet mine with a confidence that leaves me breathless. She kisses me more slowly than she did last night, but still just as passionately, like she's savoring every moment. I know I am. This kiss is deeper, more real, and somehow even better than before. With each slide of my tongue against hers, my body tightens everywhere. I know it's not supposed to mean anything, but how can a fake kiss be this good? I can't even remember if I've had *real* kisses this good. Right now, there's only Skylar, the warmth of her mouth, and her arms around my neck.

When we separate, I hold her face in my hands and fight the urge to invite her back to my room. For the first time in my life, I'm considering a relationship.

Later, I think. When we're back in Rochester. When I've had the chance to tell her how I feel.

I just want this night to be over.

To be alone with Skylar. To not have to put on a show anymore.

Throughout the awards dinner, she touches my leg, massages the nape of my neck, and sends me reassuring smiles. She notices when I'm too overwhelmed for words and redirects the conversation, usually by asking Grace something. Everyone's eager to get to know Skylar better, and with all her allure the focus shifts easily from me to her.

I want to thank Skylar properly for everything she's doing to help me get through this weekend. I hope the luxury spa package I got her is a good start, because my other ideas end with her moaning beneath me, and I'm not certain that's what she wants yet.

I try to focus on the awards. They're chosen by peers, so the ceremony is cozier and more meaningful. When it's almost over, Jax jogs to the stage and claims the mic.

"How's everyone doing tonight?" he drawls, only to get drowned out by applause. "The last award is new, but we hope to continue it. I'm honored to present the Legacy Award, meant to recognize someone who has contributed immensely to the sport over their career."

I clap along. It's a good addition.

"This inaugural award goes to someone who pioneered countless moves and paved the way for the next generation of riders. We haven't seen him around in a while, and it's my immense pleasure to welcome him back now. The Legacy Award goes to someone I have the honor of calling my best friend, the one and only, the inimitable…Brandon Pike!"

Thundering applause destroys my ears. I don't have time to react before a slideshow of me starts playing behind Jax. It's gut-wrenching, showing my best runs, snippets of interviews, and part of my speech after my first Olympic gold.

I watch myself in a daze. Morbidly, it reminds me of the Oscar remembrance reels of those who passed. It feels like death, like the me now is so separate from that me on the screen that I must be watching from the grave.

Just as quickly, it's over, and Jax is beckoning me to the stage. My table is on their feet hugging me. I'm hyperaware of everyone watching me limp to the stage and struggle up those steep stairs. Fucking hostile architecture. Had I known, I'd have brought my comfortable cane, not this elegant one with its silver engraving and awkward chrome-plated bulb handle.

By the time I reach Jax, my hands are shaking as much as my legs.

He pulls me in for a bear hug, and I take the Burton board off his hands. He realizes how awkward the award is at the same time I do; we've always given out boards and never thought twice about it.

"I guess I'm donating this," I say to a round of nervous laughter.

Pretty sure I black out after that, but later, Skylar says I thanked my crew, my mom, and even her.

I keep hoping time will make the sting of my accident less pronounced. It hasn't. Being here with everyone just makes the wound gape wider.

21

Skylar

The after-party is a lot like a music video. A massive, chaotic dance floor, bodies grinding on each other, a stage with a famous DJ, flashing lights, drinks passed around by decked-out waiters, and private booths for the famous.

So. Much. Alcohol.

I'm not sure how long I can stick this out. The flashing lights make me feel like I could have a seizure, and my earplugs barely dampen the bass vibrating my bones as we plow through the crowd.

I've lost count of how many people have approached Pike, stunned, to thank him for his contributions to snowboarding. I've spotted a few actors, a musician who judges a singing competition show, and endless beautiful people.

Pike slides a possessive hand to my hip as we make our way to his crew's reserved area, the warmth of his body keeping me steady. We survived the interview and awards show. After this party, it's over. The pretending. The fake dating. What'll be left of us tomorrow?

We reach his crew's booth, and they immediately order more drinks. Pike shrugs out of his suit jacket. He rolls up his sleeves, and I have to sit on my hands to keep from touching his veined forearms. I miss remission, when a little alcohol would give me some liquid courage when it came to men.

Jax throws back a shot. "Let's dance!"

I stay seated and glance at Pike.

"You go," he says quickly. "I'm gonna rest my legs."

He sits back, actually expecting me to leave him alone. I know I danced with Jax yesterday, but that was when Pike was talking to Grace.

"I want to stay with you."

"Aw," Jax says. "You take care of my boy, then. I'll see you two later." He struts away, high-fiving the guy dancing with Grace before disappearing into the crowd.

"Sorry." Pike plays with his cane. "My knees didn't hurt that much before, but after those stairs…"

"Don't apologize."

"I wish I could still dance, though. With you."

I'm surprised by the admission. And the dejection in his posture. He's been a cool cucumber all night, even though I know he's hurting—not just physically.

I would like to distract him. I'd like him to enjoy himself. And if I'm reading him right, I think I know what might do the trick. Even if it would normally require liquid courage first.

"Then let's dance," I say.

He grimaces. "I know I danced yesterday, but my legs—"

"I'm not questioning your abilities." I get up. "Come with me."

"I don't think—"

"Trust me," I say, extending my hand.

He takes it, albeit cautiously, and I lead him to a different area, further from the dance floor. It's a little quieter and more sensual, with silky, see-through curtains acting as separators, creating semiprivate lounge areas. Each space features plushy ottomans that probably serve a much different purpose from what I have in mind. I part the curtains to an empty section.

"You want to rest?" Pike asks.

"No, I want to dance."

"Here? Skylar, my legs."

I urge him onto a deep-purple ottoman, then lean down and plant my hands on his thighs. "You sit. I'll stand."

Not letting go, I find the beat to a Pitbull remix and sway my hips a little. I hold his gaze and watch comprehension—and intrigue—dawn in his intense eyes.

Before I got sick, I loved going out to dance with friends. When I give him a shoulder shimmy, Pike's megawatt smile bursts across his face, the first I've seen all evening.

I wink. "That's an advanced move, I know."

He laughs, quick and dirty, sending a thrill up my spine. I keep moving to the same rhythm and watch his eyes grow cloudier. He's trying hard not to stare at my chest, which, to be fair, I'm flaunting right in front of his face. I let go of his legs and slowly straighten, accentuating the roll of my hips.

There's been an ache deep in my core the whole night. He teased me all day. He kissed me like he owned every one of my heartbeats. Time to show him I'm not shy about what I want either.

I'm almost his height this way, so I treat him to a seductive pivot like I would on the dance floor, giving him a view I hope he enjoys. I glance over my shoulder and find his eyes pinned exactly where I want them. This time, his laugh is softer, but he doesn't even pretend to look away. His restraint is slipping, and I love being the reason.

I grind down toward his lap. Just as I brush against him, I pull back, moving in a slow arc. I work my way up, then turn around to face him. "Didn't I tell you to trust me?"

Pike's mouth parts. "You didn't tell me 'dancing' meant 'lap dancing.'"

"If this were a lap dance, you wouldn't be allowed to touch me."

The tortured look in his eyes is a reward I didn't know I was chasing all night. He scoots to the edge, his legs splaying wide, and pulls me between them with a commanding grip on my hips. I start to move again, my senses sharpened by the way we're now connected.

His body shifts beneath mine, following the rhythm. I'm acutely aware of him and how his hands hold me in place but also let me take the lead. His gaze never leaves me. There's something raw in the way he watches that makes my chest tighten.

I think he wants me as much as I want him.

The air between us grows charged with all the unspoken things I wish we'd say. I keep dancing, aware that people could be watching. A part of me is scared we'll end up online somewhere, but all I care about right now is the way Pike's fingers flex against me like he's barely holding himself back. The tension between us is stretched too tight, and I'm eager to see what it'll take to snap.

When the song ends, he doesn't let go. We stay there, moving together, until another song starts. And another. Every nerve in my body sings. His hands slide down but always stop too high, too gentlemanly. I need more.

I turn around. Press myself closer.

Pike captures my waist, drawing me flush against him until I sink down onto him fully. I lean back and close my eyes. His clean scent envelops me as he holds me tight.

This is what I wanted, but it's too much. Too consuming. I need more friction. I need his hands running over the length of my body while his teeth graze my skin.

I roll my hips experimentally. Feel what I'm doing to him. A low groan escapes his lips.

I reach over my shoulder and find the nape of his neck. "Pike."

His warm breath ghosts over my cheek. "Who's this show for, sweetheart?"

"Why, are you enjoying it?"

"I'm not the only one. These curtains don't leave much to the imagination, so unless you want everyone knowing how hard I am watching you..." Pike's mouth this close makes goose bumps spread over my skin. "Do you want to go somewhere more private?"

My heart hammers out of my chest. "Please."

Pike sets me back on my feet. My thighs shake from the workout I just got, and the sudden change in position shoots a bolt of pain down the back of my head as he tugs me back to the booth, his warm palm covering mine.

When we find the rest of the crew to say our goodbyes, Jax drapes an arm over Pike's shoulders, his breath riddled with vodka. "This is my best friend in the whole wide world. He can't leave again."

Pike tries to untangle himself for a good ten minutes, but eventually, we resign ourselves to Jax tagging along and head to the car. During the short ride, he rests his head on Pike's shoulder, reiterating how much he's missed him.

Jax is a cute drunk, all affection and no filter, and Pike's softness with him is sweet, though his timing could use some work. I take a moment to bask in the quiet and close my eyes. The invisible vise around my head tightens, and the pain sends a prickle of anxiety down my spine, an autopilot system meant to warn me about the implications of overdoing it. I hate how I can never enjoy myself without having to worry.

At the hotel, Pike slips the driver some cash. "Can you make sure he gets back to the club?"

"Noo," Jax slurs. "Let's get a drink for the good old days. Minibar!" He skips to the elevator.

"Er," Pike says, "I forgot we have separate rooms. Could you— would you mind coming back to mine with me?"

"We were going to end up together in a room anyway. Can I rest in your bed until he leaves?"

"In my bed?" he echoes. I shiver at the way his expression darkens, as if he's only just remembering why we're up here in the first place. "Yes. Yes, good. He'll leave soon."

In the elevator, Jax plays with an empty tube of chocolate candies. "One time, Macken dared us to board naked."

I smile to myself. "There seem to be a lot of stories about Pike naked."

"Remember when you got frostbite on your ass? Where was that again?"

Pike rubs the space between his eyes. "Davos."

Jax puts his arm around Pike as we reach our floor. "I miss you, man."

"I miss you, too, buddy, but I can't walk with you hanging on me." He indicates his cane.

"It's such a shame." Jax's raspy voice grows husky. "Isn't it a shame?"

"Yes, yes, it's all very sad." Pike swipes his key card. "Listen, I'm tired. I'll talk to you tomorrow, okay? You and I are having brunch."

"Oh, yeah!"

"So, we'll see each other tomorrow?"

"But. I need my wingman." Jax has a gorgeous, pouty smile, and if he were directing it at me, I'm not sure I'd be able to turn him away either.

"You haven't needed me as a wingman in a long time," Pike says.

I hide my laughter as Jax heads straight for the minibar. Pike snatches the liquor out of his hand.

"If you still want to drink, you and Macken can get another round at the party."

"Macken's bo-ring."

"I won't tell him you said that."

"If you hadn't had your accident…if it were the good old days, you'd still be here."

"Jax. I can't have this conversation with you again. Things are different, but—"

"I miss you, man."

"I miss you too," Pike says, and Jax starts the hug fest all over again.

I sit on the bed. Pike looks at me with sad eyes. Mouths, *Help*. If

I didn't know how much all of this upsets him, I wouldn't intervene. I'd simply lie here and watch these two hot men hug.

"Pike and I were looking forward to some alone time, Jax."

"Exactly," Pike says. "I'll see you tomorrow?"

With conviction, I think, but Pike still hasn't learned to stick up for himself. He just waits for Jax to leave. Which, of course, he doesn't.

"Pike." I lean back on my elbows seductively. "I need you."

His head whips up.

I beckon him with a finger.

Pike puts his fist to his mouth. "Jax," he says hoarsely, "get out of here, man."

"I've been thinking about this all day," I say. It's not even a lie. Lust has jammed any good sense I have left. "Don't keep me waiting any longer."

His eyes grow as glassy as Jax's even though Pike's had nothing to drink.

I'm the one intoxicating him. Me.

Pike extends his arm vaguely in Jax's direction, finds his face, and pushes. "Go."

I laugh to myself and flip onto my side for comfort. I steal all the pillows to give my brain a fighting chance against gravity, then pat the spot next to me.

Pike takes off his shoes and jacket. He slides in with the careful posture of someone trying to avoid pain. His crisp white shirt hugs his firm shoulders. I can't tear my eyes from the exposed skin underneath his undone collar. I want my mouth there. My lipstick.

"That was cute."

"Hmm?" Pike murmurs.

"Jax. He clearly loves you."

"Oh. Yeah." He clears his throat. "It's hard to concentrate when you're looking at me like that."

He doesn't move closer, though, clearly still determined to be a gentleman. Too bad I'm not much of a lady.

"Looking at you like what?"

"Like you want me for real," he says helplessly. "You've looked at me that way all night. And that dance…this vibe between us…I need to know if it's all in my head."

My heart melts. Brandon Pike is *nervous*.

I understand his hesitation. After all the faking, it's hard to believe we've reached this point. I scoot close enough to feel the heat radiating off his body, but not so close that we're touching. Stroking his face isn't something we've agreed is allowed outside of pretending.

So much of my life is pretend. Pretending I'm fine at work when I feel like passing out. Pretending I'm not upset when Dr. Wharton bullies me about my weight. Pretending I don't have pain around my parents. I'm always holding it together for the sake of people around me.

I don't have to pretend around Pike. He never judges me or tells me to try yoga, juicing, or meditation. He just lets me be real. I want to be real with him now too.

"It's not in your head," I say. "I do want you."

He gives a hard swallow, but his body remains tense, and I don't understand why he's not already kissing me.

I move back, but Pike reaches for me.

"Wait. I want—"

His words hang there, suspended between us. He shifts forward, and as our bodies slowly melt together, it's clear I wasn't reading him wrong. There's nothing fake about this attraction.

His fingers trace up my bodysuit until he's leaving shivers all along my exposed shoulder. "Are you sure?" He cups my cheek, his thumb smooth on my skin. "You want this? Me?"

My eyes fall shut because he feels so, so good against me. I curl my fists into his shirt. "More than I can articulate."

"Tell me again it's not fake."

"I don't think anything has felt more real."

"Me neither," he starts, but we run out of space between us before he can finish the words.

His mouth crashes onto mine like a wave, pulling me under with a force that knocks the breath out of my lungs. We've kissed before, but it's always been for show. This, all of this, is only for us.

And soon, there's only Pike. I drink in his sweet taste, breathe in his fresh scent, and sink into the warmth of his body. My fingers leave his shirt and dig into his short hair. An indulgent hum rolls through his chest. The sound ignites me.

I reach for his dress shirt. "Can I?"

He rucks it loose without hesitation and grips my jaw, the hold possessive as he kisses me. "Touch me, Skylar. I'm all yours."

A moan escapes me before I can stop it, but he swallows it with his own. I undo his buttons and relieve him of his shirt, then slip my hands under the soft white T-shirt beneath it.

He sucks in a breath, muscles tightening under my touch. "And you?" His voice is rough, almost a growl. "Do you want my hands on you?"

"Not just your hands."

"Fuck."

While I'm busy exploring the warm planes of his abs and the sexy dip of his hips, his fingertips run up my back, somehow managing to press us closer. But we're not close enough, not nearly enough for what I need. I entangle us further until my thigh is draped over his side.

He grabs my ass to hold me to him, a little rough. Yes. *This.* A whimper escapes me, and Pike breaks our kiss, leaving me panting.

"Is this okay? Your head. Your pain."

I drag his mouth back to mine. "Sometimes sex helps the pain."

I'm lightheaded already and have to talk to him about all that, but we'll get there.

There's a part of me that says I should ask about his pain, too, but another part remembers how annoyed he was when other women made him overthink things. We shouldn't overthink this.

Pike moves on top of me. His hips press me into the sheets perfectly, and I forget any questions. I can feel the ache between us, how long it's been since we've found relief. I doubt it'll take long for either of us to get there.

I slide my legs around his waist, locking him against me, and we groan together at the contact. But it's still not enough. Not yet. I tilt my hips up, and he grinds against a perfect, devastating spot that makes my thighs tremble around him.

He drags hot kisses over the tender skin at the hollow of my throat. I ignore the pain on the other side of my neck, at the base of my skull. What Pike's doing doesn't take it away, but it certainly draws my attention further south.

I focus on the contrast of rough stubble and soft lips on my shoulder. On the dominant hand kneading my ass and the tender one cradling my face. On the drag of Pike's tongue and the light scrape of his teeth.

I pull his T-shirt up, the fabric straining against his impressive biceps. "A little help, please."

He obliges, pulling it over his head in one swift motion, every muscle contracting as he does. The sight of him—broad and strong, a faint sheen of sweat already glistening on his skin—sends a sharp pang of want through me. My hands roam over his chest, tracing the hard ridges beneath the smooth heat of his body. His heartbeat is wild under my palms.

"What's your tattoo?" I trace the numerals with a finger.

"The two Olympics I won."

It's so simple. I rise to my knees and kiss my way up his stomach, watching his abs flex in response. He hisses softly through his teeth, the sound low and primal.

"Skylar," he breathes.

I grin, and with a gentle push, he's on his back and I'm on top. But instead of staying there, I work my way down. As I memorize his pecs and torso with my mouth, he runs his hands up my back, massaging my spine and shoulder blades. Every so often, he strokes my cheek.

I can't believe he ever worried about making it good. Everything with Pike is good. How can he not know? I need to make him understand. To show him.

I trace my tongue along the cut lines of his hips and reach for his belt, but he pins my hand to the bed.

"Not yet." His fingers thread through mine, giving me a reassuring squeeze, before he flips us over again. He stays raised on his veined forearms, keeping his weight off me. "We'll get there. I want to savor this."

I tug him down on top of me. I don't mind being squished. I need to feel him there.

"Savor it, then," I whisper.

I suck on his bottom lip until his eyes fall closed. I love seeing him like this, serene and enjoying himself. After all the attention Pike has given me this weekend, I want to give him attention now.

I work my hands lower, teasing his waistline, but I'll slow it down if that's what he wants. We can take our time learning each other. I sweep my fingers over his gorgeous ass and up the taut muscles of his back. If I'm honest with myself, this pace feels better for my head too.

He kisses me deeply, his hips beginning to move against mine. It draws a gasp from both of us as he hits exactly the right spot. I bite off a curse when he does it again.

"I want to put my mouth on you," he begs. "Touch you all night."

I'm only capable of a soft, needy groan. His lips find the slope of my shoulder while his hand slips beneath the edge of my bodysuit to release the clasp. He eases it down and lowers his mouth, his breath hot against my collarbone, before dipping even further, scattering kisses across the curve of my chest.

He lingers with his tongue, tracing the swell of my breast as though memorizing every inch. Deft fingers brush along the edges of my bra, then slip behind my back to undo it. His mouth closes around me, his tongue flicking lightly. I dig my heels into the mattress and arch up. A low grunt escapes him. He sucks gently, and the coarse drag of his stubble against my skin only makes me needier. I thread my fingers through his hair.

He pulls away with a soft growl, his eyes locking on to mine. "You're so beautiful, Skylar."

Something sharp flares in me at the intensity in his gaze. And then his kisses are no longer measured or soft. They're greedier, messier. My breath falters with each scorching stroke of his thumb, each tantalizing pull of his mouth. I knew it would be amazing with him, but he's turning me into nothing but sensation and desire.

He teases pleasure out of me while his other hand slides down my thigh, tracing a path to the button of my pants. Everything in me tightens when he pops it open.

He dips his head and kisses his way down my stomach until his lips brush the hem of my panties. I lift my hips to meet him, silently begging for more, and he smirks against the fabric. A single finger traces along the edge, dragging out the wait like he's enjoying every second of my desperation.

"You're trembling for me, sweetheart."

I inch my bodysuit down, just enough. "Don't tease."

He hums, smug, his mouth hovering over the waistband, letting his long exhales tickle my skin. "No?"

"Pike." I reach for him, a helpless attempt for more that only makes him smirk harder.

I run my thumb over his bottom lip, craving the slick heat of his mouth since he won't give it to me where I need it. He kisses the pad of my finger before sucking on it just like he did this afternoon. But this time, he doesn't pull away.

He tastes me, prolonging it, savoring the way I squirm beneath him, empty and aching. If he'd just put that skilled tongue elsewhere, I'd be done for.

"Please," I beg. The graze of his teeth makes my thighs clench. "Not tonight. I've wanted this for too long."

"Okay, sweetheart." He tugs at my pants, peeling them away. "I'll give you what you need." He places an open-mouthed kiss on the damp fabric still separating us, his throaty moan a low vibration I feel everywhere.

I press my face into the pillow, muffling the frayed cry that breaks free. Now that I'm getting what I want, it's almost too much.

"No," he says, "I want to hear what I do to you. Every last sound."

It's not a demand. It's a claim. A promise that he'll break me apart piece by piece. And I'm going to love every second of it.

A sudden bang rattles the door. Pike jolts up, covering me.

An unmistakable masculine voice, slightly muffled, calls out, "Pike? Are you still in there?"

He growls. "I'm going to murder him."

"Ignore him." I pepper his jawline with kisses.

More knocking. "Pike? We should go back to the party. Everyone's waiting."

Pike sighs into my shoulder. "I'll put him in a cab. Make sure he gets out of here."

A whine leaves my throat. The thought of stopping now sends an unexpected arrow straight through my heart.

"I know, sweetheart. I'm sorry."

Whenever he used to call me *sweetheart*, it would often come with impatience, but lately, it's always said with affection. Tonight, it's whispered tenderly. Like I really am one.

Like I'm *his*.

I wrap my legs around him. It's all that keeps me from saying it aloud. He rolls his hips again, a sweet torture that sends shocks through my entire body.

"Pike . . . you're not making a good case here."

I claim his broody mouth in a deep, desperate kiss. He grinds down more purposefully, and I rock back against him, the friction exquisite, and I think he's going to stay. I think he's going to give me everything that I need.

More banging.

"I know," he says again, nuzzling my nose. "But I don't want to think about anyone but you."

He lifts himself off me and fumbles for his T-shirt, cane, and coat. He looks so thoroughly kissed it threatens to burst my heart. There's a lipstick stain on his neck already, and satisfaction hums beneath my skin knowing I'm the one who put it there.

"Please," he says. "Stay exactly, exactly like this. I'll be right back."

Jax says, "You came!"

Pike growls something that sounds distinctly like, "Actually, I didn't, you little shit."

22

Skylar

I sit up with a long, sexually frustrated sigh, my body buzzing. I pull my bodysuit back up but leave my pants off. He'll like that, I think, when he finds me under the covers. I run my fingers through my hair and use the plastic-wrapped toothbrush on the sink.

I can't stop beaming as I text the girls. **Pike and I kissed!!! I'm in his room!**

Emy sends an Elmo fire GIF. **what r u doing talking to us, sweets? go do the mattress mambo.**

Is that what they call it in Italy? I tease. **There was a small hold up. I'm waiting for him to get back.**

ah, pharmacy run?

No, but thanks for the reminder.

I chew on my lip. I didn't bring condoms. Should I text Pike? He might be too wiped from today, anyway, by the time he gets back. We can still make each other feel good, though. I have so many new ideas for how to make this gorgeous broody poet unravel.

r u having a good time? Emy asks. **how'd the interview go?**

I'll fill you in tomorrow, but yes. We're both into each other! I drop a bunch of excited emojis.

***groans in singleness* have fun. u deserve it.**

I press my phone to my chest. I can still taste him on my lips, and we've barely even begun.

I slip back in bed, but the reclined position sharpens my pain. I grab a migraine abortive from my purse, even if it doesn't feel like migraine. It feels like my damn pressure, like things are getting worse instead of better.

I know I've done too much, brain, but give me this one night. Please just give me this one night.

There's a knock, and I half expect Jax.

"Sorry." Pike drops his wallet on the bedside table. "Should've done that earlier."

"He's your best friend. It's okay."

Pike sits on the edge of the bed. Finally. I reach out my arms, but he makes no move to join me. He's not even undressing.

"Skylar, listen…" he starts. "We need to talk."

"Do we?" I say weakly. I want to talk with our bodies instead.

He rubs his palms over his slacks. "I was thinking while waiting for Jax's ride…"

"Okay," I say, uncertain.

"About us. About everything."

My stomach drops. Does he regret kissing me?

He reaches for my hand, fingers intertwining with mine. "You make it near impossible to think straight, so I need a beat to make sure we're on the same page." He rubs the side of his neck, a nervous laugh leaving him. "God, why is this so fucking hard to say?"

It hits me what he's doing, and I want to crawl under the covers. I'm the one who told him to make sure the people he sleeps with are on the same page. Now he's trying to let me down gently.

"Don't worry," I say, forcing a laugh. "It's just a hookup."

His breath comes out in short bursts. "What?"

"We'll still be friends after." The words taste bitter on my tongue.

"Oh," he says. He's still holding my hand. "Great." But he doesn't say more. Doesn't kiss me.

The more we sit in silence, the more it stings.

"I get it." I give him a gentle squeeze, trying to convince us both. "I don't do relationships either. You don't have to worry about me falling in love with you."

"Right, of course." He grabs his cane and stands abruptly. "Listen, I've had such a good time, but I think we should stop here."

I pull the covers over me, feeling exposed. "What happened to 'I want to touch you all night'?"

"I do, but I just…" He looks down. "I don't want to complicate things more."

"A little late for that." I can't keep the hurt out of my voice.

"I don't do one-night stands anymore," he says. "Being here in Whistler must be bringing back bad habits. I'm sorry."

My face floods with unwelcome warmth. I know he doesn't want to have sex with *just anyone* anymore, but I didn't think I was *just anyone*.

"I think you're overthinking this like you said you do."

A muscle in his strong jaw tightens. "You don't get to analyze me because I told you one story. That's not what this is about. I'm different now."

"Don't worry. I'm not going to make you do something you'll regret." I scramble out of his bed, but I move too fast. My vision fills with black spots. The sudden darkness shocks me out of my feelings. I grasp for something, anything, and sit back on the mattress.

A sob works its way up my chest, and fuck, crying always makes my pressure worse. This keeps happening. It only lasts seconds, probably, but it feels like a lifetime.

The mattress dips. "No, please," he says, wiping away a traitorous tear. "That came out horribly wrong—"

"I'm not crying because of *you*. I can't *see*."

"Is that normal?"

"It usually comes back quicker. Can you get me some water?"

It's been a long day in changing altitude. I was also flat on my back with Pike. Sex can be tricky for me when my pressure is up, especially if I hold my breath too long. I was going to tell him, but we didn't even *have* sex.

By the time he returns, my vision's mostly back. But part of my peripheral vision is still missing, and I have four floaters instead of my usual two.

When I'm confident enough to stand, Pike hands me my pants. "Found them in the bathroom."

He gives me privacy as I slide into them, my cheeks burning.

"Let me walk you to your room," he says. "Make sure you're okay."

"I'm fine, really. I got extra meds for the flight tomorrow. I'll take one of them now."

"If you're sure." He sounds agonized. "Skylar, about what I said—"

"It's okay. We should've talked about our intentions first."

I don't even know what my intentions are. I don't do relationships, but I also didn't think this would be a one-time thing. With how we've gotten to know each other, I thought, maybe with time—

It doesn't matter.

I go back to my room. My head feels like a cinder block is crushing it, so I'm afraid to lie down. I grab my ice hat, turn on the hot tub, and sink in until my neck is heated, then message the girls to explain the situation.

I was lying there, totally exposed to him, and he just . . . didn't want me.

what the actual fuck, Emy says.

Is it possible he didn't want to sleep with you because he wants a relationship? Analia asks.

Why wouldn't he say that then?

and if he did?

He won't. And why does it have to be all-or-nothing?

When the hot tub water starts sending faint electrical currents into my fingertips, and the heat makes me even more lightheaded, I climb out. **I've gotta go. My pressure's so bad, I lost my vision temporarily.**

I sit by the window with my eyes closed. So what if Pike doesn't want to sleep with me?

I'll be fine. Everything's fine.

23

Pike

Everything's completely fucked.

Not sleeping with Skylar is one of the hardest things I've ever done. If I thought I had feelings for her before Whistler, thinking we'd get together that night only ramped everything up unbearably.

I should thank Skylar for interrupting me before I could pour out my sappy feelings. Still, I regret every word unsaid. Instead of telling her how much she means to me, I made her feel undesirable.

But sex with Skylar, knowing it'd only be a one-time thing? I'm not sure I'd recover.

She made it clear she doesn't do relationships. Why did I think she might change that for me? Just because we're attracted to each other doesn't mean she wants to date. I know this tune; I used to sing it all the time.

"Pike!" Ranielle's voice snaps me back to the present as a ball hits my chest. "You suck today."

I wobble on my right leg, catch it, rebalance, and hurl it back. Her sculpted brown arms receive it like a lobbed feather.

"Engage your core."

Easy for her to say with her enviable six-pack and stable SI joint. I lose balance on the next toss and stumble. Pain radiates up my back. "Shit!"

My phone buzzes again, and I steel myself. It's been three days since we got back, and I'm already dealing with paparazzi and countless interview requests. A few disability advocacy programs even reached out.

I mark most emails unread. I could barely think of what to say to Blake. How am I supposed to make a good impression when it really counts?

The article's reception has been mostly positive, but there's still shit. Comments like He's too young to be disabled and It's such a shame and He had so much potential. And then there's Poor guy can only get a disabled chick now.

Any commentary regarding Skylar makes me want to kick in some teeth. She texted saying it could be worse, and that she's mostly disappointed Blake left out everything she said about disability except that she has IIH.

We've barely spoken since. I've called her a few times to check on her, since she was sick the entire flight, and even texted a borderline-desperate **Can we talk about Whistler?** But she responded, **Sorry, I can't right now.** I keep hoping the next notification will be from her.

But it's just Mom with the latest article.

Olympic Medalist Forced to Work
Minimum-Wage Job Due to Disability

Next time, she writes, **focus on the job you *could* have. The three of us should prepare a strategy for the next reporter.**

I reply, **After what you did with Blake, your Skylar privileges are revoked.**

"Don't mind me," Ranielle says. "I'm good getting paid to do nothing."

"Sorry." I close the thread, but another text pops up immediately.

Great article, kiddo. Happy for you, finding someone to settle down with. How about a weekend in Vegas so I can meet her? Let's talk about that venture too.

I scowl. **Not a good time.**

"What's up, Pike?" Ranielle's tone is unusually soft.

"It's nothing."

She points to my PT table. "Then let's stretch."

I lie down, and she pulls my left leg toward her.

"Why'd you leave your favorite trainer out of the article? Do you know how many celebrities I could work with if you name-dropped?"

"If I name-drop, you'll leave me."

She laughs, but I make a mental note to hype her if I do another interview.

After a shower and nap, it's already past dinnertime. I microwave popcorn, divide it into two bowls, and head to the den, where Luis is glued to that reality show where people box their loved ones' exes. He started watching it when he got sick, probably as a distraction, the same way I watch game shows.

"Where's Skylar?" he asks.

I shrug. "Home."

"I thought everything went well."

"It did. Everything's great." Obviously can't admit I've fallen for her and then screwed up any chance of intimacy by failing to express my feelings, as usual. "How're you feeling?"

"My PEM's been bad lately, but I lined up a new investor for my start-up while you were gone. Maybe you should go on vacation more."

"You mean so you can have the house to yourself with Cyrus?"

He chucks a kernel of popcorn at me. "That too."

"Let me know if you need me to find a new place. I like living here, but if you want to move in with him, I get it."

I need to find a permanent place anyway, but I don't know where in the world I want to live. And, frankly, it's nice having company when I get home from work.

"Eventually, that's the plan," Luis says. "For now, I'm happy to have you pay up so I can save for that future."

"If I can help with any connections or introductions," I say, "please let me know. I don't know how much snowboarding overlaps with IT, but it's no problem."

"For sure. Thanks."

My phone rings.

"I read your article," Kal says as I head to the kitchen. "Why didn't you tell me Skylar is Skylar King, aka Lennox's friend?"

"What?" Skylar's last name isn't in the article. "I've never heard Skylar mention Lennox. Are you sure?"

A long sigh. "Analia?"

"Analia I've heard of."

"Pike."

"What?"

"Analia *is* Lennox."

"What…?"

"Are you serious right now? How can you not know this?"

"It's not like I've met her."

"I remember showing you pictures of her at your house."

That was middle school. We had pictures of *every* girl. "You always call her Lennox. Why?"

"Her full name's Analia Lennox."

I sit. Did I ever know her first name was Analia? When I was ten, maybe. "Hey! You *met* Skylar. If you're such good friends with Analia, wouldn't you recognize her?"

"I've never seen pictures of her. Lennox won't share much about her two online besties. Honestly, I'm relieved at least one of them isn't a sixty-year-old man."

I run a hand through my hair. "Has Analia said anything about me?"

My bigger concern: that she's said something to Skylar. I can only imagine Analia telling her about the time Kal and I met up while he was backpacking in Europe. We drank so much grappa we tried to scale an Italian national monument.

Kal lets out a low laugh. "She was worried. Thought you might be an asshole."

"Why?" What did Skylar say?

"It's not personal. She's just not a fan of my friend group and assumed you were part of it."

"What's wrong with your friend group?" And why isn't Analia part of it?

"It's a Lennox thing. Don't worry about it."

"Did you at least tell her I'm not an asshole?"

"Yeah, but she's being ridiculous. We generally avoid talking about my friends, but now she's mad because I didn't mention my friend was fake dating a girl named Skylar." I can practically hear his eye roll. "Somehow it's my fault I've met Skylar when she hasn't."

"Yeah, what's with that? Why haven't they met?"

"Lennox has always been an introvert. Her future husband's probably gonna be some online nerd."

You better get online, then. "What if the four of us went out for dinner?"

"Sure, if Lennox wants to."

My phone beeps. I glance at it and forget Kal is still talking. It's Skylar.

"Hey," I breathe.

"Pike? I'm sorry to call so late."

"Is everything okay?"

"Is there any way you could come over? I...I need help." Her weak voice sets off alarm bells.

"I'll be right there."

"I can't answer the door, but I'll tell my landlord you're coming. He's at the end of the row."

"Why? Are you hurt?"

"It's . . . embarrassing."

I don't care what it is. I'm already halfway out the door.

As I enter Skylar's town house, my heart pounds in my ears. The first floor is dark, and a horrible retching echoes through the quiet space. I speed up until I reach the stairs.

Shit. Stairs.

I heave myself up, wishing I hadn't done physical therapy earlier. When I finally make it to the top, it takes a moment to pinpoint the gut-wrenching whimpers.

I rap on her bathroom door.

"J-Just a sec. It's gross in here," she rasps. "Maybe it's better if you don't come in."

"I'm coming in anyway."

I'm still unprepared for the sight inside. Skylar lies curled on the floor, a white towel barely covering her. Her eyes resemble a vampire's, red and swollen. Snot streaks her face, and her wet hair is coated in puke. A trail of vomit and water stretches from the still-running shower to where she lies, halfway to the toilet, like she tried crawling there but couldn't make it.

"Fuck," I mutter.

A tear tracks down her dirty cheek. "I'm sorry."

I instantly regret my reaction. She thinks she's an inconvenience, someone I have to deal with, when it's the exact opposite. I want to be there for her, to make the hard moments easier if I can, or at least keep her from facing them alone.

"There's nothing to apologize for," I say. "What happened, sweet-heart? Are you hurt?"

"My ped is exploding with hain."

What?

She squeezes her eyes shut and clutches her head. *Oh.* Her *head* is exploding with *pain.*

"I was shaking a tower. Got dizzy. Had to sit down so I wouldn't fall." My mind scrambles to interpret her aphasia. "But I couldn't get up. Feel like...I'm in a submarine. Ears screaming. Eyes stabbing." She gasps. "Sorry."

"It's no problem. I've thrown up plenty, believe me." I remember how vulnerable I felt vomiting after my surgeries, and I wasn't even lying naked on a bathroom floor. I find more towels and cover her body and the mess.

"What do you need? What would be helpful?"

"In the linen loset. Blue. Emesis bag."

All too familiar with those hard-rimmed hospital bags, I grab two. She vomits again, but at least it's contained.

"Maybe we should go to the ER," I say.

"No!"

"I'll go with you."

"They hon't—*won't* help me."

"You're throwing up pretty badly." *And barely able to speak.* "You could get fluids. Nausea meds."

"They *won't* help me. I'm *not* going."

Her refusal sends unease down my spine. Did something happen to her at the ER?

"Do you want help getting to your room?" I ask.

"Not yet," she says weakly. "I'm covered in puke."

"I'll take care of it."

"Can you give me my nausea meds?"

After I locate her pill collection, I get to work cleaning, but all the bending is agony. I need a mop.

Which means going downstairs.

I miss Luis's no-stairs floor plan. Skylar's lack of railing makes it worse. Balancing a mop and bucket while pushing up with my cane results in too many wobbly steps before I give up and sit. I shove the supplies ahead of me, step by slow step.

When I moved into Mom's house, I had to crawl up and down like this to my room. That only lasted two weeks before I bought a temporary bed for the first floor and started looking for a new place.

After disinfecting, I force myself to sit behind Skylar. Now we'll both struggle to get back up. But it's the only way I can help.

I pull her head onto my lap. "I'm going to wash your hair, okay?"

I dip a washcloth into the shower and clean her matted strands the best I can. I smooth a thumb over her cheek when I'm done. "Good as new."

It's getting harder to hide my worry, though. She says these symptoms are common. She's made it this far without my help. But Skylar's dry heaving, already on her second emesis bag in less than an hour.

"Can I call Analia or Emy?" I ask. "I really think we should go to the ER, but I can't manage the stairs alone."

"Nooo. Don't make me." Fuck, she sounds so short of breath. "It's worse than Dr. Wharton."

An acidic taste fills my mouth. She'd rather lie in her own vomit than see a doctor.

"We need to get you off the floor. You're shaking."

I grip the toilet for help, my back splitting in half as I push up with one leg. In her room, I grab a chair, sweats, and a shirt.

I slip her feet into the sweatpants. Her legs are freshly shaved, and I have to resist running my hands up her smooth skin to soothe her. She takes over when I reach her thighs, and I turn around as she finishes dressing.

"I'm going to pull you up." I sit in the chair behind her. "You hold your bag. It's going to suck, but we can do this."

I hook my elbows under her armpits. She vomits, but I get her onto my lap. When I likely tear another hip labrum trying to stand, I realize I physically cannot do this. I'd have to drag her across the floor.

Tempted to hate my body, I scrub a hand over my mouth. Two years ago, I would've been able to carry her, no problem.

But I know it's not my fault. What happened today isn't Skylar's fault either.

Fuck all that noise. It's okay to ask for help.

I take out my phone.

"Way to hang up on me," Kal says.

"Listen," I say. "Are you sober?"

24

Skylar

I wake to burning light seeping through my eyelids. I pull the covers over my face, but my eyes still threaten to burst from their sockets. The pressure in my skull is unbearable. Sharp, deep nerve pain pierces my body.

But I'm not throwing up.

My tinnitus is a relentless Weedwacker in my ear, and it only heightens my anxiety. How did everything deteriorate so quickly? Even my hair hurts.

I need a lumbar puncture. I need a higher dosage of medication.

When I reach for my extra pillows to elevate my head, I hit a solid mass instead. It groans.

Pike.

Pike is in my bed.

Fragments of last night crash back. I threw up all over him. It was embarrassing enough before Kalle showed up. I don't remember if I threw up on him too.

Squinting, I see Pike snuggled on his side, a soft gray shirt clinging to his firm shoulders. His mouth is parted, but he doesn't snore.

I don't remember why he's in my bed.

"Are you awake?" I whisper.

His eyes stay closed. "I am now."

"Was the guest bed uncomfortable?"

He shifts a little, as if testing his limbs, then stretches out his legs.

His toes brush mine, sending a pleasant tingle rushing up my body. Forget that. After all this, there's no way he'd ever think of me sexually again.

"Dunno." His lashes flutter against his cheeks. "I didn't have enough spoons to make up the guest room, but I didn't feel comfortable leaving you alone. Sorry. I'll do that tonight."

"No, no…it's fine." Guilt twists my stomach. He overexerted himself helping me. "You don't have to be here."

"You don't want me here?"

"I'm sure you have better things to do."

"I don't, actually."

I press my eyes shut. "Liar."

"Will you please just let someone help you?"

"You're not just someone. You've helped more than anyone ever has. It's too much."

A gentle hand finds my shoulder. "When I moved back here, I said the same thing to my mom. She had to do everything for me. You know what she told me? Helping someone you care about shouldn't be transactional."

My heart pangs. "Your mom seems decent about some things."

"She is. But, Skylar, I've been here less than twenty-four hours. If that's your standard for *too much*, raise the bar."

A lump forms in my throat. It's less about my standard and more about what others have told me is too much.

"Do you need anything?" Pike asks. "Kal brought my wheelchair so I can roll you to the bathroom."

"Could you close the blinds?"

"Give me a sec." When "a sec" turns into ten minutes of stretching and groaning in pain, I feel worse. Eventually, he shuts the blinds, and I open my eyes to blissful dark. But I can't shake my guilt.

"I'm not trying to use you," I say.

"What?"

"Calling you only when I need help. I didn't call you back before because it hurts to talk. Physically."

"So don't talk."

"I mean in general. I've barely even chatted with the girls. I don't want to do anything when I'm in this much pain." But I also don't want to be alone with my thoughts. "I couldn't think of anyone else to call."

"I'm glad you called me. Really."

Me too, but I wish I had more people to call. I wish my family made me feel safe when I'm sick.

"I was caught off guard," I whisper. "In Whistler. When you stopped. I wasn't trying to get you to fall back on bad habits. But you also didn't have to make me feel like I was one of them."

"Skylar? We can talk about it, but not when you're hurting this much."

I nod miserably as another wave of nausea overtakes me. Besides my pain, I've thought of nothing but Pike since we returned from Whistler.

"I just can't believe this is happening again," I burst out. "I'm doing everything I'm *supposed* to be doing." Unwelcome tears cascade down my cheeks. I press my fingers into the grooves beneath my eyebrows to redirect some of the pressure. "It's all so unfair."

"Can I hold you?" Pike asks.

I slide back, succumbing to what's become a weakness: his arms. He draws me close to his chest and spoons me. It makes my head worse, but right now, I'd rather be comforted than comfortable.

"I'm sorry, sweetheart," he murmurs. "I wish I could make it better."

"You do," I insist. "You've been great."

As much as Pike's support means to me, I wish Analia and Emy were here too. I wish they weren't just online friends but people who could also stay with me while I go through this shit.

It's not that I doubt they'd come. But what if it's uncomfortable without the natural pauses that being online affords? What if they find something about me that's too overwhelming, the way everyone else always does?

"Do you want to tell me what happened at the ER?" he asks.

I tense, torn between wanting to shut down and knowing he deserves a straight answer. He's dealing with his own pain—pain he never talks about—but he's here anyway, holding me like my world hasn't fallen apart.

"I've never had a positive experience," I say. "Most doctors are clueless about IIH. Usually, they're just assholes. I always leave feeling traumatized and gaslit. They say there's no way my pressure's the issue—it must be a bad period or anxiety."

Most doctors just tell me it's all in my head.

Yeah. *Literally.*

Pike's thumb caresses the inside of my wrist, coaxing me to share more.

"That's the hardest part about invisible disabilities," I say. "Learning to exist with pain when no one acknowledges its existence. I've tried therapy to have less anxiety about it, but none of that matters unless I have a doctor who actually helps me."

Pike draws me closer, his arms tightening.

"I need a lumbar puncture," I say miserably. "I wote—*wrote* Dr. Wharton to prescribe one, but that appointment's not until next week. The ER will defer to his prescription. And he won't authorize an emergency LP."

Emergency LPs are notoriously traumatic. Scar tissue in my back and a fried nerve in my butt that took six months to heal are proof. I always request guided LPs with fluoroscopy now.

"I'm sorry I made you come to Whistler," Pike says.

"You didn't. And it's not your fault, so don't even go there."

"I'll admit I don't fully understand," he says. "You're taking your medication. Why won't your pressure regulate?"

I remind myself he doesn't doubt me. "It's called 'idiopathic' intracranial hypertension because it's brain pressure of unclear hause—*cause*. We know *some* underlying causes, but it can be more than one thing or something still completely unknown." I pause. Whenever I talk, the pain doubles in my head. "I'm constantly battling the pressure increasing. Just because one day it reacts well to medication, another day it might not."

"I hate this for you," he says quietly.

I reach back, sliding my hand along his arm until my fingers find his. I hold on tight.

"Do you want more meds? Something bland to eat?"

"Soon." Right now, I just want him to hold me a little longer. But I can't sit in this heaviness forever. Luckily, I know just the topic. "Can you believe we have friends in common?"

The girls and I screamed when Analia found out *Kal* is actually *Kalle*. Turns out the man never goes by his full name because everyone sucks at pronouncing it.

And now I've met him twice without really meeting him. Last night, Kalle apparently dragged Pike's *wheelchair* up the stairs, half carried me into bed, and brought me nausea remedies.

"It's funny how small the world is," Pike says.

"Is Kalle in love with Analia?"

"Ha. He's never outright said that, but the way he talks about her, it seems obvious. Why? She in love with him too?"

Analia's also never admitted it. When we push the topic, she withdraws. I'm tempted to share Pike's insight, but it could end badly. Their decades-long friendship might not survive unrequited feelings.

"Emy and I just ship them," I offer.

"What kind of Scandinavian is he?"

"Pike! Seriously?"

"Two things always come up with Kal. His heritage and his girl. Didn't realize he meant Analia the whole time, so yeah, I suck."

His girl. My heart.

"He's Swedish."

"Thanks," he says sheepishly. "Felt rude to ask when I should remember. Also, why doesn't Analia like his friends?"

I hesitate, but if Pike knows, Kalle must've mentioned it. I press my eyes shut against the unrelenting pressure. "I don't think she likes who he becomes with them."

"Huh. He's always been cool around me."

"That's good. It's nice you have disabled friends."

"Just Luis and Cyrus."

"And Kalle."

Pike pauses. "Kal's disabled? He's never said."

"Maybe it's mental health."

"I don't know him well enough to say. He's a childhood friend, but we've only seen each other a few times since I moved back. I've been terrible at keeping up with friendships."

"Never too late to reconnect." Kalle driving to Naples for Pike speaks volumes. But Pike remains silent, prompting me to moisten my parched lips. "We're okay, right? You and me?"

"Of course," he says. "And you're not a bad habit. You're probably the best thing that's happened to me in a long time. I don't want to risk our friendship by having a one-night stand." He sighs into my neck. "Speaking of. You rest. I'll make up the guest room. We can discuss it more once you're back to baseline."

He plants a soft kiss against my skin before releasing me.

25

Pike

Falconry or treasure hunting?" I ask Skylar.

"What."

"It's a quiz."

"Treasure hunting," Skylar says, adjusting her pillows so her head is more elevated despite her sideways position.

I resume rubbing her back. "Mountains or forests?"

"Mountains, especially after Whistler."

"Gnomes or trolls?"

She glances over her shoulder. "Is this a D&D quiz? Are you secretly a nerd?"

"It's from the support group's 'Bored AF' folder. Just pick one."

"Gnomes?"

"Same. Astrology or psychology?"

"Astrology all the way."

"Necromancy or—"

"No."

I grin. "What does your favorite lamp say about you?"

"That your privileges in my bed are about to be revoked."

"Lamps are touchy subjects. Noted. What kind of mushroom are you?"

"Brandon Pike."

My shoulders shake with smothered laughter. "Okay, real question. Dream vacation. Anywhere, doing anything. What would it be?"

She shifts closer, trying to get comfortable. I resist the urge to cuddle her again. I've taken off work this week to care for her until she gets her LP, and most of our time has been spent in bed. Sometimes, she wants space. Too much pain to communicate. Other times, we accidentally fall asleep together and wake up entwined, though it's usually me who migrated over from all my pain-induced position changes.

Today, I woke up with my face in her lap, knee over her legs. Skylar brushed her fingers through my hair and said she was glad I could rest. She didn't mind as long as I avoided her head.

It doesn't help with the whole trying-to-be-platonic thing. I keep picturing her sprawled out beneath me in Whistler, her hair fanned out on the pillow. Jax did me the biggest favor. I don't know what Skylar tastes like, how she feels clenched around me, or what her face looks like unhindered by bliss. If I did, I'm sure I'd accept any casual thing Skylar wanted just to have more of her.

"I'd go somewhere with Emy and Analia," she says. "A Spoonie vacation. Doesn't matter where. We'd relax without any pressure to sightsee or engage. Just rest and good company."

The more I know Skylar, the more I understand how close she is with them. They keep messaging me in the group to make sure I'm staying on top of things. Emy even directed me to the "Caregiver Resources" page for suggestions on making Skylar's life easier, not just physically, but also emotionally.

It's not that I doubt Skylar can handle this by herself, but she shouldn't have to. She's always there for her support group. It's time someone showed her the same kindness.

"Emy liked every single one of Jax's recent sponsor pics," I comment.

"You follow her?"

"She followed me."

"You're not even on social media."

"I don't post," I correct. "Doesn't mean—"

A loud *ding!* sounds, and I expect Skylar to reach for her phone. There's always a new reminder to take a med, check this email, drink more water, stretch her legs, call this doctor, plan a meal.

But it's the doorbell.

"Ignore it," Skylar mumbles.

Thank fuck. Her stairs are murdering me.

But it keeps ringing until I want to tear my eardrums out. When I finally fling the door open, lecture locked and loaded, I freeze. The older woman staring back with a stony expression looks unsettlingly familiar.

"You must be Brandon," she says, a smile morphing her stern features.

"Hello," I say suspiciously.

"I'm Skylar's mother, Jeanie."

Skylar's mother. That explains the similarities hidden among their differences. Mrs. King has the same nose, but without Skylar's piercing; the same fair complexion, though hers is lined with age and carries a warm tan, while Skylar's remains pale from her need to stay out of the sun; the same shape of her lips, but with less of Skylar's usual bright makeup.

She barges in, her pressed white slacks brushing against my sweats. Her heels click as she spins to face me like I'm the guest. "We didn't even know Skylar had a boyfriend."

"That's right," I say. "I'm the boyfriend."

We're supposed to be fake breaking up, but Skylar's been a shield between me and my mom, so why not return the favor?

"I was sorry to read about your accident," she says, moving toward the stairs. "Sky?"

A fierce rush of protectiveness surges through me. "She's sick."

"Yes, I know. Sky!"

"*Mom.*" Skylar mirrors her mother's expression from the door, but in pajamas and an oversized sweatshirt, she looks more exhausted than intimidating. "What are you doing here?"

"I brought dandelion tea. And I'm here to drive you to Devlin and Jennifer's dinner."

Ugh. Skylar already declined that invite.

"You can bring Brandon, of course."

"Thanks for the tea, but I said I wasn't going. I'm not feeling well."

"You're always unwell. Why miss out on family time?"

"I'm *especially* unwell. I won't be able to hide it."

Mrs. King pinches her nose. "If it's that bad, why don't you finally get a shunt?"

Skylar inhales and exhales like a damn yoga instructor. "I want to know if there are any underlying causes of my intracranial hypertension first. Like stenosis."

"Well, in the meantime, don't let pain control your relationships. Come say hi to Jasmine. They drove all the way up here."

I flinch. My mom's interference bothers me, but she'd never force me to go somewhere if I said no.

"Devlin can bring Jasmine here for once," Skylar says.

"Well, could you be more upbeat if he does? Jasmine's friend showed her your article. She googled IIH. She thinks you're dying!"

"That's what happens when they refuse to tell her what's going on." Skylar raises tired eyebrows at me. "Jen doesn't want me being real with her. All that negativity is 'bad for children.'"

What the fuck?

Mrs. King glances sidelong at me. "Would you excuse us?"

"Why?" Skylar asks. "Afraid someone might disagree with your ableist opinions?"

"Skylar loves using that word," Mrs. King says to me. "Is it ableist to want my daughter to live her best life? Is it ableist to love someone so much you don't want them to be sick unnecessarily?" She regards me as though I'll validate her.

I cross my arms and stay silent.

"Her father and I have been imploring Skylar to get a shunt. It redirects cerebrospinal fluid out of the brain," she explains. What's with these King women, thinking a boyfriend wouldn't know? "The solution is there, but she won't take it. I even set up a consult with a neurosurgeon. Brandon, she didn't show."

"A shunt isn't a cure-all!" Skylar says. "I don't want multiple brain surgeries if it's not necessary. You can become shunt dependent."

I finally find my voice. "Maybe rethink your definition of love, because it sounds conditional to me."

Mrs. King's pleasant smile returns, but her eyes tighten at the corners. "Things are more complicated with chronic health issues."

"Mrs. King. I have chronic health issues."

"But you're managing wonderfully! Traveling, working with a trainer, going from wheelchair to walking. You understand."

Is that what she got from my article? Damn.

"Skylar's a charismatic woman with lots of potential," she continues. "If you care about her, you also need to care about her emotional well-being. Dwelling on illness when there's a *solution* isn't healthy."

"Skylar knows her body best. She's doing an excellent job managing a horrible condition." There's more I want to say, but I open the door. "Thanks for dropping by."

I wait. Staring her down until she finally huffs and leaves.

"Skylar?"

A nurse in blue scrubs pokes her head into the waiting room.

Skylar's grip on my hand tightens. "That's me."

According to Skylar, this LP will serve two purposes: to figure out her current cerebrospinal fluid pressure, and to temporarily drain some of it. Sadly, her pressure will go right back up over the next forty-eight hours.

She looks like she might faint, so I help her to her feet. But when I pass her to the nurse, Skylar won't let go.

"You're coming, right?"

I'm hit with a sudden rush of relief. She still wants me by her side in public.

Our physicality has increased so much this week. We touch each other playfully all the time now. If we're in bed together, we're connected. I keep trying to remind myself that it's because she needs comfort.

I tell myself I'll dial things back, stop touching her, stop talking to her at night until I fall asleep. I'll get over her. But I think I'm falling in love with her instead.

After she changes into a gown, we enter a large room, and my stomach drops into my feet. I've had seven surgeries since my accident, and the smell of chlorhexidine makes nausea swirl around my gut.

Skylar climbs onto the table without waiting for instructions. "On my left side. I know." She curls up, legs toward her knees. "Pike, come here."

I stand in front of her. The nurse unties her gown from behind, and Skylar stares up at me, her hazel eyes cloudy. Unsure what to do with my free hand, I stroke her cheek as the nurse preps her back.

The radiologist explains the procedure. I don't have time to process before he begins numbing her back with lidocaine.

Skylar hisses with each shot. "It's like being stung by bees."

"This is the worst part," the radiologist says. "There should only be pressure next."

"*Should* is different from reality." Skylar's face is as white as a sheet.

What the fuck? Where are the drugs for pain control? The radiologist preps the next syringe. I start sweating. It's fucking *five inches* long. From my angle, it doesn't look like there are five inches from her back through her stomach. The room gets woozy as I imagine it puncturing through her belly button.

Her fists clench into tight balls. "Tell me something, Pike. Distract me."

My mouth feels stuffed with soggy paper as I watch the needle go in. A long tear spills down Skylar's cheek.

"This boy wrote me," I blurt. "Aiden. He's in middle school and uses a cane. He gets bullied because of it."

Skylar flinches so badly she almost lifts off the table. "Ow! *Fuck.*"

"I need you to stay absolutely still," the radiologist says.

"You're not in. It feels like you're electrocuting me."

I try to remember my story. "I was thinking of writing him back. Sending some swag."

There's a squishy noise. I can't help it; I look. Something's squirting out of Skylar's back. It takes everything in me not to puke all over everyone.

"I'm in position now. Extend your legs slowly," the radiologist says.

With the fucking needle still all the way jammed in her spinal cord, Skylar straightens her legs.

"How…?" I can't get the words out. "Are you…okay, sweetheart?"

"It's uncomfortable," she says. "Like something's tugging inside my back."

"Opening pressure is thirty," the radiologist says.

"I *knew* it," she says. "An opening pressure above twenty-five is indicative of IIH. Meds should be lowering it more, so I'll need a higher dose."

"Is that…?" I sputter at the clear, gooey mess on the table. "Is that cerebrospinal fluid?"

"You've really needed an LP," the radiologist says. "We'll drain you down to a ten."

"Twelve," Skylar insists. "Any lower, I'll get a low-pressure headache."

"Take a deep breath."

Instead of breathing, Skylar says, "You should write him." It takes me a second to realize she's talking to me.

I rush to say, "I could do a school visit. I've never done anything like that before, only visits to snowboarding camps. I don't know what I would talk about or if anyone would even want me there. But I want to show those little bastards that having a cane isn't weird."

"Take the needle out," Skylar says through gritted teeth.

Seriously. Why is it still in her back? The fuck is he doing?

I keep stroking Skylar's cheek. "Would that backfire because I can't snowboard anymore, so I have nothing to show for myself?" And why do the opinions of middle schoolers matter to me?

"You have a lot to show for yourself." She bares her teeth. "Stop selling yourself short."

"I don't want to be the pity story that makes them appreciate their life more."

"Did you learn nothing else from snowboarding? *Fuuuck*," she says again, but not because of me. "You gained no skills besides flipping in the air? How about perseverance? Innovation? Discipline? Dedication to a passion? Do those qualities just disappear because you're no longer in a halfpipe?"

I almost back away in shame. My worth has always been tied to what I produce.

"And…done." The radiologist withdraws the needle. "I'll send your sample to the lab."

I sag against the table. Skylar's whole body starts shaking, and the nurse covers her with a blanket. "Stay still. We'll bring you a bed."

"Why does she need a bed?" I ask. "Is something wrong?"

"She needs to lie flat for an hour so the hole seals. There's always a risk of a spinal leak."

Great.

I follow them to the recovery area, an open space separated only by beige curtains around each bed. I'm relieved to see a chair. I've been standing for twenty-five minutes, and I'm not okay.

"Does your head feel better?" I ask.

"I need…quiet," she mumbles. "My back feels bludgeoned. And my butt is fried. Again."

"Fried?" I ask weakly.

"He botched it. Hit a nerve. I don't have normal sensation in my leg." She reaches for my hand, and I gladly take it. The feel of her pulse loosens the knot in my chest. "Thanks for staying with me."

Emy texts, **don't let her tell u she doesn't need help. she'll be lying flat once she's home. how's she going to get water? food? entertainment?**

Emy's obviously playing matchmaker, which is good with me. Excellent, actually. Sign me the fuck up for that.

Her friends wouldn't push if they didn't think there was a chance. I know the attraction's there, but this time I won't assume she wants more than sex. Not yet. I need to work up the courage to talk to her first.

I told her I don't want to complicate things between us, but if our time together this week has convinced me of anything, it's that I don't want to settle for excuses and hide my real intentions anymore.

Maybe she doesn't want a relationship, and maybe she never will, but I haven't given her a reason to consider one with me. I haven't told her how I feel.

Now's not the right time, but once things are less urgent with her health, I need to speak up. I need to show her I'd treat her like a queen if we got together.

For now, I'm totally worn out from going back and forth to Skylar's all week. And those damn stairs.

"Skylar," I say. "Will you please stay at my place tonight?"

26

Skylar

I drop my recruitment brochures into my roller suitcase with relief. This never-ending day is a wrap. My arms shake as I take down the life-size South Carolina University flyer. I'm struggling despite the increase in meds—or maybe because of them.

Picking up my life after two weeks off is a nightmare. But I gave what I had at this fair: my time. I doubt I convinced anyone to apply, but at least I didn't take more PTO.

My suitcase drags behind me like an anchor as I slosh down the walkway in the drizzle. My only goal is to make it to the parking lot, rest on a bench, and then gather strength to reach my car.

I'm behind on everything, even my support group. I was overdue to host movie night but had to pass it off to Adiba when I couldn't stay focused on the concurrent chat. I haven't talked to Emy or Analia much either. I was with Pike for the last week after my LP, but even when he went to work, I couldn't muster up the energy to look at screens.

In my car, I scroll for nearby hotels. There's no way I'll be able to drive the hour and a half back to Rochester.

A few notifications pop up that make me peek into my chat with the girls.

how's ur first day of unemployment going? Emy asks.

I treated myself to thirty-dollar vegan, gluten-free cake, Analia says. **Not sure what else to do after getting fired for taking too many bathroom breaks. **Already in pajamas and ready to curl up with a good book.**

Wait, what? Analia got fired?

I scroll up until I find more details from the conversation yesterday.

I've had to leave in the middle of sessions, Analia wrote, **so I saw it coming.**

By the time I scroll back down, there are fifty new messages. It's hard to keep up with everything because of the mildly blurry vision I'm still experiencing.

Emy says, **we can buddy-read something! after spending all day at the hospital yesterday, i'm not leaving my bed either.**

The hospital? I feel off-balance when I learn that she and Analia messaged the whole time she was there. I know my pain's really at fault, but would I have checked on them more if Pike hadn't been around? They've been there for me all along, and now it feels like I've let them down.

Just catching up on everything, I say, adding hugging emojis. **I'm so, so sorry! Please text me in the future about this kind of stuff if I'm not on.**

SKYLAR! HULLO! Emy says. **how r u?**

First day back at work, I write. **Wharton upped my dosage so my ears are ringing, my face is tingling, my brain fog and fatigue are off the charts, and I'm still short of breath. Oh! Part of my back tooth crumbled, too. Sorry I haven't been on much. I miss you.**

We miss you too! Have your eyes been hurting too much for screens or were you with Pike? Analia asks. **He said you slept at his house?**

Yup, I stayed at Pike's until yesterday.

R U SERIOUS!? Emy writes.

My cheeks flush with happy warmth. I was there a week, and I've never felt more cared for. Pike is kind of wonderful, in a quiet strength way that sneaks up on you. I'm chaotic about everything, and he's calm skies after a storm.

I went home sometimes! But his house is more accessible without stairs.

Emy sends so many exclamation points, I swear they reach Pike all the way in Perinton. **so he stayed in bed with u for two weeks?**

No! Once we moved to his house, he went back to work.

but u slept next to each other?

We did, but I'm strangely nervous sharing that part. It'll seem like we're sleeping together, which Pike doesn't want. It's beyond confusing. I often thought things would head in that direction when we cuddled, but maybe that was just the intense lust talking. My body responds to him like his presence commands it.

His roommate would find it suspicious if we didn't, I say. **We talked a *lot*. He ordered food because neither of us had the spoons. When I was up for it, we did easy things like board games with Luis and Cyrus, who are super adorable.**

And then we stayed up talking in bed every night. It was cute to watch him fight sleep but keep nodding off until he finally succumbed.

Analia sends a thinking face. **And you still don't think he likes you?**

right! Emy says. **no straight man brings u to his HOME to take care of u if he's not in love with u. no! man!**

Well, I mean, Kalle totally would, Analia says.

I resist the urge to mention this is further proof he's probably in love with her. That line of thinking would also suggest that Pike could be falling for me. It's crossed my mind.

Maybe I've been single too long to tell the difference between friends and lovers anymore. I don't understand why we keep waking up attached to each other. He's the big spoon, and I'm helpless to his ministrations. Which, since he doesn't want to go further, range from him running his fingers up my arms to holding me so tenderly I feel like I'm wrapped in a cloud.

It's innocent, but that makes it worse. It feels like dating, like romance. But wouldn't he want more touching if he's caught feelings? Is he just trying to make me feel cared for and has no idea what he's doing?

Whatever this is, I write, **I don't want to mess it up. Pike's so sweet and surprising. I love men who aren't afraid to be soft with you at the right time.**

and he took care of u for two weeks, Emy says. **omg** ♥♥♥.

Right, I say. **I just want to make him smile and give him a bunch of orgasms.**

Analia sends blushing emojis while Emy sends her usual eggplants.

Wish I could chat more, but my eyes are still little shits, I say, then log off, but a call from Devlin makes me pause.

"Sky." My brother's gravelly rumble greets me. "How's your head?"

"Not that great," I say. "Sorry I missed your visit. How's everyone?"

"Good. Everyone's good." It sounds like he's scratching his thick beard. Devlin has red hair like me, but Jasmine got Jen's blond.

"So I was talking to Mom," he says, sounding uncomfortable. And immediately, I am too. "She's really worried about you. So am I, but I'm not a mediator. Can't you just get over it?"

"What exactly am I getting over this time?"

"Your boyfriend kicked her out of your apartment. Is this Brandon dude living with you?" Devlin has never been a protective older brother, but there's a hint of something in his voice I can't place.

"No. He was helping me through a health crisis. Mom would know that if she was involved in my life."

"She's involved in your life." He sighs. "I know Mom has her issues. Just make peace and move on."

And this is the other reason I don't talk to my brother a lot. Rather than try to see it from my perspective, he just wants everyone to get along.

"Sounds good," I say, because I know I won't change his mind.

"Another thing. Got some news."

"Yeah?"

"Jen's pregnant."

"Oh." I grip my phone a little tighter and force enthusiasm into my voice. "That's great. How far along is she?"

"Thirteen weeks."

"Congratulations. Has Jen had a lot of morning sickness?"

"Nope. Just a little nausea a couple times a week but it's mostly passed. She didn't have to miss any work."

"Lucky her." I have to miss work for nausea, and I'm not even growing something beautiful inside me. There's no ultrasound, no name to pick out—just lost hours, a job that doesn't wait, and a body that won't cooperate.

"Hey, I've gotta run, so..." I let it hang there, knowing he'll be just as glad to get off the phone.

"All right. Take care, Sky."

"You too."

I sit in my car for a long time, mind numb, watching the parking lot empty. Jen and Devlin have been trying for a second child for two years now. The news still hits me like a freight train.

For the most part, I've made peace with my illness, but sometimes envy creeps up on me. Time moves forward when you're sick, but not in the same way. I still feel twenty-one, a time capsule frozen at the age I got sick. News of babies always reminds me how much time has truly passed. My uneventful birthday, usually spent curled up in bed, always reminds me.

By the time I reach the hotel, I don't have energy to shower, and my dizziness and weakness remain after three hours of resting. Before I can chicken out, I call Pike. I miss him.

My stomach flutters when he answers with video. He's shirtless again, back to his regular routine now that I'm not there. His hair has grown out a little since I met him, and it's even more attractive than his former brush cut.

"I'm about to fall asleep," he says.

"Sorry. I forgot how early you go to bed."

He turns onto his side. It's like we're back in bed together, so close I can feel the heat radiating off his skin. The desire to reach out and touch him through the phone is so strong I put my hands under the covers.

"Tell me about your day," he says.

"It was long and full of jocks. Nothing interesting."

"So, tell me about something else."

I close my eyes. "Like what?"

"How about something from your past? You don't say much about it."

"That's because while you were touring the world and becoming one of the coolest athletes ever, I was going to college, getting sick, and trying to stay alive."

"Correction. I am *the* coolest athlete ever."

I squint through one eye. He's smirking. I love this playful side he usually keeps contained.

"See! We should talk about you."

"Eh. You can read about me anytime." His face grows serious. "Skylar? You've had boyfriends, right?"

"Yes?"

"You mentioned they didn't care about your health?"

Did I say that? My memory's always shot when my pressure is high. I've probably said lots of incoherent things to him.

"What is it you want to know?"

"What happened with your last boyfriend?"

"Owen? We broke up two years ago and I haven't been in a relationship since then. By choice."

Pike whistles under his breath. "Why'd you break up?"

"You don't want to know."

"I really do."

All right. He asked for it. "I broke up with him after he said our relationship would never be completely fulfilling because I wouldn't let him go bare. According to him, that was the ultimate culmination of good sex. Of a good relationship."

"Oh." Pike clears his throat. "Uh…yeah. I guess some people like that. But…not…you?" He refuses to meet my eyes. "Or…he wouldn't test?"

I almost laugh at his discomfort, but it's weird to discuss it out loud. Why do I need to feel ashamed, though? If he does any digging, he could find my posts about this in our support group.

"I got IIH after starting birth control pills, remember? I can't use *any* hormone-based birth control. Owen was offended on a deep level that I wouldn't get a copper IUD for him." At Pike's blank expression, I add, "That one doesn't use hormones. But I did have it, once, and it gave me other side effects, so it didn't work for me. It's gross I have to put my body at risk while he refuses to wrap it up."

"Well…" he says weakly. He probably hasn't considered a scenario like this before. Most guys assume women will handle birth control eventually. "I'm glad you dumped Owen."

"I should've broken up with him sooner. We had other irreconcilable differences."

"Are they as graphic as the last one?" He laughs at the face I make. "Kidding. You do need to be on the same page about that kind of stuff, and it's shitty he didn't care how it affected your health. Any other boyfriends?"

"You're curious tonight."

He waits, his dark lashes fanning his cheeks like he has all the time in the world.

"There were two others since I got sick," I say. "None as serious as

Owen. I realized it's easier to keep things light, you know? Keep it sexy, be done with it. That way, I can decide what I feel up for. No one's annoyed or disappointed."

"Disappointed." His brown eyes fill with understanding. "Like your mom?"

"Like everyone. Most friends don't stick around when you get sick, and it's even worse with men in relationships." How can I break this down? "Men, for the most part, run from relationships when a woman gets sick. They're too selfish. Maybe not in bed, some of them," I concede. "That's a statistical fact, before you get offended."

"Not offended."

"Most men who promise 'in sickness and in health' don't have any idea what that actually means. They imagine their wife getting sick at, like, sixty. They don't sign up for illness to ruin their honeymoon or prevent them from having kids."

"Is that it? You can't have kids?"

I scoff even though my heart pinches. "It's not *it*. I can have kids if I can be off meds long enough to not harm the baby." And as long as my pressure doesn't rise exponentially during pregnancy, which can happen. "I don't know if I should have kids, though."

I shouldn't think it, but I do. If Pike has developed feelings, this could make him disqualify me as someone he could have a future with. Might as well rip off the bandage.

"Among other things, Owen implied I'd be a bad mother. And . . . I don't know, maybe he had a point."

"Owen sounds like an asshole. Why would he have a point?"

"I don't know if I could take care of a child. How will I handle a wailing newborn when I can barely stand someone talking too loud? How can I take care of a child when I need to spend so much time in a dark room? How can I keep up with a child when some days I can't stand without growing faint? I've probably internalized all of this because of eugenics, but I'm also scared. I don't see my experience reflected much in society, so it's hard to picture making it work."

"What if you have someone else to help out?" Pike asks. "Like if you find the right person to be the second parent?"

"The right person." I shake my head sadly. "How can you know someone's the right person? How do you know you'll feel the same way in ten years when your wife is in and out of the hospital every few months or unable to have kids or you're not getting as much sex as you thought you would?" I hold up a hand. "Rhetorical. But when you're sick, you have to know how your partner will respond to those scenarios. It's too draining to invest in someone else like that when you barely have enough energy for yourself. I know you get that with your pain."

He stays quiet, and the weight of his gaze urges me to keep sharing.

"Sometimes I think about this big future I envisioned. Not with Owen, necessarily. But I did think my life would go a certain way. I want a family. But when I look in the group…"

"All you see are the horror stories," Pike finishes.

"There are good stories too. There are resources for disabled parents."

"But you also hear about the men who leave. I've seen it, and I've only been in the group a couple months."

I've seen much more than that. I've seen disabled women abused, CPS called on them for simply being deemed "unfit," and ex-husbands who take their kids away because the courts usually side with the nondisabled parent.

"And you've experienced them leaving firsthand," Pike says softly.

"I told you, I dumped Owen." But my eyes sting.

"My dad left my mom long before he physically walked away. She knew he was cheating on her. He mentally checked out, from me as well, and it broke my heart. Mom and I bonded a lot over him. She was always easy to talk to." He sighs. "You know, before."

"Sorry. I don't know why I'm getting so emotional." I wipe my face. "Devlin told me Jen is pregnant again, and it's bringing up a lot of feelings I've tried to repress about spending most of my twenties sick, and what that means for my future."

"This kind of stuff is why I journal. It's hard to talk about." His expression pinches. "I've had sad thoughts about kids too."

"Yeah?"

"No one expects to compete past a certain age. But I still expected to be on the slopes. I thought I'd teach my kids to snowboard. Never thought I'd be the dad who sits in the lodge."

"Hey. You sold me on the whole lodge thing in Whistler."

He shifts onto his back. This isn't a date, but it feels like one. Most days with Pike feel like dates, no matter what we're doing. He has a way of making even the mundane brighter.

"I hope I didn't minimize your feelings about being a mom," he says. "Losing snowboarding isn't the same."

"We can both mourn the things we've lost. It's not a competition."

His eyes search me. "You deserve to be with someone who loves you for more than your ability to perform at a certain level."

I know that now. But reconciling what I deserve with reality is another story. "Do you believe that too?" I ask.

"I live with Luis. He tells me every day."

"Good."

"Also? Owen is a piece of shit. Just wear a condom? My guy…"

I grin and flip onto my side, only to find Pike staring at me with unexpected tenderness.

"I wish I was there. Next to you."

My heart does all sorts of weird things. "I'll be fine, don't worry."

"It's been strange not having you in my bed. Not having you around, period."

"I'm sure you don't miss my noise machine," I joke, but Pike breezes past it.

"I'd take it if it meant you were here."

We lie there staring at each other. For too long. But the silence isn't uncomfortable. None of this intensity is.

"I wish you were here too," I finally confess.

"What would you do if I were?"

A hot flame licks down my spine. Not the response I was expecting. Especially not in that suddenly husky voice.

I swallow. "Would you still be shirtless?"

"Depends if you are."

His words shoot straight between my legs. "Don't tease me, Pike."

"I'm not."

"You're . . . you're not?"

He wets his lips. "That scenario is all I can think about lately. Whistler is all I can think about."

"But . . . you said—"

"I've said a lot of things I regret. When you're back in Rochester for more than a night, I intend to rectify that."

Oh my God?? *Rectify* suddenly takes on a host of new meanings when Pike says it like that.

But what would that mean for us, if we made things physical? Much as I want him, I'm not sure I'd be satisfied with only physical stuff anymore. We've gotten to know each other so much better since Whistler. We talk every day.

"It might be a few weeks before I get that kind of break."

"I can wait," he says. "I don't want to, but you're worth it."

27

Skylar

The night of my birthday, I step out of the hotel in slim black pants and an emerald-green crop top, pulling my long, open jacket closer around me. Normally, it's just pantsuits and pajamas on work trips, but Pike insisted on taking me out tonight. He's arriving in Ithaca in two minutes, according to his texts. My fingers find the silver chain around my neck, and I thumb it gently as I wait.

A limo glides into the hotel loop, and I move aside. But when the chauffeur opens the back seat, the tip of a black cane appears, followed by polished black dress shoes and sharply pressed pants.

I inhale sharply.

It's Pike. Wearing a *tuxedo.*

"Happy birthday, Skylar." He smiles like he just won Olympic gold.

"You got a limo!?" I can't stop staring. "And you're…in a tux!"

"What do you think? Magic Mike hot?"

I approach cautiously, like his attractiveness might light me on fire. My mouth parts as I run my fingers over his lapels. "Hotter."

"You haven't even seen the best part." He retrieves a black-and-white umbrella from the limo. It has a cartoon of three snowboarders in a chairlift with the inscription BOARD MEETING.

I burst into laughter, increasing my head pain, but it might be the first time I've truly laughed since my LP. I'm too delighted by everything to care—the umbrella, the limo, the tux—and by him, always surprising me with his thoughtfulness.

Pike's smile turns up to full voltage. "Seeing you laugh makes this entire trip worth it. How's your pain? Still up for dinner?"

"I left work early and rested for three hours. I'm underdressed, though."

"No, you look beautiful as always. The tux is merely for your enjoyment."

I step into the limo, still dazed. There's room for eight with leather seats and an impressive beverage bar.

"Hi." Pike sinks into the plush seat next to me. "How was your day?"

"Ending on an interesting note."

More interesting is Pike's arm easing around me.

"Can I lean on you a little more?" I ask. "Right now I have to twist a bit, and my back's not loving it."

"Of course. Today is for you." He moves over, unbuttons his jacket, then slowly shrugs out of it and loosens his bow tie. The temperature rises twenty degrees. He splays out his long legs and pats the space between them. "Come here."

I scoot over until my back aligns with his chest. The pain in my lumbar area eases as soon as I stretch out my legs.

His hand drops to my hip. "Good?"

"Perfect."

His phone buzzes against my thigh, and he grimaces. "Sorry, my mom's been calling all day about the surprise. She can't grasp the concept of *evening*."

"You haven't told her we fake broke up yet?"

"Have you told *your* mom?"

Fair point.

"I picked her up," he says, putting Laurie on speaker. "Everything is fine, Mother."

Her squeal is earsplitting. "Of course it is! How could Skylar not love it?"

"If you knew what was going to happen, why continue calling?"

"Let me enjoy this, Brandon! First Whistler, now Ithaca? I knew once you had something else to focus on, all those bad thoughts would disappear."

The spark leaves his voice. "I'm glad you're happy," he says before hanging up. He fiddles with his cuff links. "Sometimes it feels like all I've done is solidify her ableist viewpoint."

I blow out my cheeks. "Will you eventually tell her the truth?"

"That would defeat the entire purpose."

"Not about us. About how you struggle sometimes. With everything."

He pauses. "I don't know how."

"There may not be an easy way. I hope you can figure out what role you want her to play in your life, though."

"Well," he says, "first I need to tell you what role I'd like to play in yours."

I glance over my shoulder. He's staring down at me with unbridled affection.

"Is this it, then?" My voice comes out rushed. "For the fake dating. Your image. It's about as good as it'll get in terms of publicity, so..."

"Yes, I promise it's all over. The fake dating, at least. But all of this today, Skylar, it's not—"

The chauffeur opens the door. We're at the restaurant.

"—fake," he finishes, quieter, but with his mouth by my ear, I hear it.

He tells the driver to leave us.

"Are you sure you didn't rent a limo to convince me to keep fake dating?" I tease. "Because it's kind of working."

"Now there's an idea. Whenever I need you, I'll show up to cart you around."

"You're shameless. You just want me to help you keep up appearances."

"No," he says softly. "I just want you. Full stop."

I go still. "Pike?"

"I was going to wait till dinner, but…" He straightens up. "In Whistler, I fucked up. I was trying to admit I wanted us to date when we got back to Rochester, but when you said it was a one-time thing and you'd never fall in love with me, I played it off as not wanting to overcomplicate things." He strokes my hip, a soft, steady pressure. "But that complication is me. My own feelings getting involved. I'm really into you, Skylar, and not just physically."

"You are?" It's the only coherent response I can form.

He lets out a low laugh. "I see a *Buy Two Get Two* coupon for Wahlburgers and think about surprising you with lunch. When Luis and Cyrus play a board game, I want to invite you over for a rematch. When I see anything related to head pain, I think about IIH and ways I could help make things more tolerable. When the forecast says low seventies, I think about ice cream by the canal with you, just because you said that's your most tolerable temperature range."

"You remember that?" I ask, more than a little stunned.

"It's a detail about you. Of course I remember."

I feel a surge of something unnamable, too overwhelming to put into words. I suspected he caught feelings, but I didn't expect him to say anything. Not this soon. Or this directly. Why does he have to get confrontational now, with the only thing I don't know how to talk about?

"We saw each other so much after Whistler," he says. "I thought I'd be relieved for space once your fairs started. Instead, I just miss you. I know you don't normally do relationships, but Skylar, I don't either. We've got something here, and I think it's worth seeing how it could grow. It could be easy between us, if we let it happen. And I'd be good to you. That's the one thing I can promise. I'd be so good to you, sweetheart."

I'm totally speechless. My limbs are all sorts of shaky. Pike's telling me he wants more.

In a limo.

In a *tux*.

The only thing more appealing than Pike in a tuxedo would be Pike stripping *out* of his tuxedo. That could be a reality now. All I have to do is tell him I want him too.

The thought of his mouth moving forward just an inch and connecting with mine sends a surge of electricity through me. I can already taste the fireworks that would ignite if our lips were to meet. My stomach twists with anticipation.

But this is going to change everything. Every nerve ending in my body is on high alert from his confession. What if this shift in our dynamic ruins everything between us?

"I'm guessing you still feel the same as you did before," he says, unable to hide his disappointment. "I wasn't sure if this vibe between us was just sexual tension or if you were into me too. But at least now you know. It's not fake on my end. It hasn't been for a long time."

"No! I…I care. For you. It's not fake for me anymore either. I need time to…to think. I…" *I don't think I've ever felt this way about anyone. I don't want to mess it up.*

"Yeah?" He releases his breath in a rush. "Okay. Yeah." He hugs me with his whole body, and I relax. "You may not be ready for more yet, and that's okay. I've waited this long to find someone who makes me feel the way you do. I can wait a little longer if you need time."

Dinner passes in a beautiful blur. We get a romantic, candlelit table with a view of the gorges. There's deep conversation. Laughter. Pike surprises me with a necklace that matches my septum piercing. He assures me the diamonds are modest, urging me not to feel pressured to accept it, but he saw it and thought of me.

"You do deserve diamonds," he says, and I flush from head to toe. "Analia and Emy thought so too."

Pike's confession lingers at the center of my mind. He wants a relationship. There's so much I need to discuss, so much I need to confess, too, but this moment he's crafted is too perfect. I just want to savor it.

Because he's right. It does feel easy. It feels natural.

We head back to the hotel together. He booked his own room to avoid another drive tonight, and it's taking all my self-control not to suggest he cancel and stay in mine. The last thing I want to do is toy with his feelings. They're important.

In the elevator, I try to wrangle all my screaming thoughts into something resembling coherence, but a new notification blinks onto my phone.

Still up for tonight?

Shit. I totally forgot about Marcus. I hastily reply, **Sorry, no**, and shove my phone back into my purse, but Pike's already seen it.

"Who's Marcus?"

"Just someone I sometimes meet up with," I explain awkwardly.

"'Meet up with' . . ."

"Hook up with," I clarify, my cheeks burning. "I forgot to cancel."

"I see." Pike jabs the elevator button with his cane. "If you were planning on being with someone else tonight, I guess I have my answer."

"That's not fair. My birthday was approaching, and I didn't know you were coming here when I first messaged him. Once you told me, he slipped my mind."

Pike keeps his eyes on the floor.

"It's just sex," I say. "It doesn't matter."

"Who you're sleeping with matters to me."

"Hey. I don't have feelings for him. Not like that."

I reach for Pike's hand, and we stand there, connected but still too far apart, and I know I should follow up with something like *I have feelings for* you. The unspoken words choke the air around us, and before I can gather the nerve, Pike lets go.

"It's none of my business. I'm sorry for overstepping."

The elevator dings, and he hurries out. I catch up with him in front of my door.

"Pike…"

"Please don't," he interrupts, soft but gruff. "I want to be in your life no matter what, but it needs to be without all this touching. I'm having trouble separating what's real and not, and you know my feelings." He grips the back of his neck. "Let's call it a night, yeah? Talk more after we've rested. When you're ready." He steps away with a nod. "Good night, Skylar. Happy birthday."

My head pounds along with my heart. If he hadn't pulled away so quickly, would I have managed to tell him how I felt in the elevator? Could I have walked away if he didn't?

I check my phone. No one's online. Just messages asking how the surprise is going.

Anyone available? I write.

No response.

Damn it.

I shouldn't have mentioned Marcus. He's a math teacher at the charter school, and we usually grab drinks when I'm here—or, honestly, skip the drinks entirely. Twice a year, max. But I told him I'd be in Ithaca before I even went to Whistler.

It's my birthday. I didn't want to spend it alone. Pike and I aren't even together. He only admitted that he wants more tonight.

I try to put myself in his shoes. If Pike had met up with another woman tonight, would I be upset? He'd have every right, thinking I'm trying to let him down gently. But that's not it at all.

I swipe my key card but can't bring myself to go inside. The lock shuts again, three blinking red dots.

I can't leave it like this.

"Pike!" I run down the hallway. Pound on his door. "Pike!"

"What's wrong?"

I gape at him, out of breath. "You're…"

Half naked.

Shirtless.

Too beautiful.

"What?" He peers into the empty hallway. "What happened?"

"I need to talk to you."

"Maybe we should talk tomorrow."

"It can't wait. Please."

He studies me, eyes serious and sad, then pushes the door open wider and walks back inside. His back muscles contract, and my knees go weak. How does he always manage to look this good?

He sits on the bed. "So, talk."

"It's… What you said earlier…" I spin toward the door. "I can't focus when you're not wearing a shirt. It's muddling my thoughts."

There's a sigh, then some rustling. "Shirt's on."

But when I face him again, it's only closed with two buttons in the middle. "How is this better than being shirtless? You're on a *bed*."

"I'm tired, Skylar."

I gesture toward the armchair where he left his tuxedo jacket.

"Too deep," he says, but gets up and limps into the bathroom.

I follow hesitantly, digging my palms into my eyes. I need a moment of respite from my pressure so I can think clearly.

Pike sits on the wooden bench inside the accessible shower and leans forward, elbows on his knees. With his tux shirt still mostly unbuttoned, he looks like a model for accessibility.

"Skylar," he says, his voice strained. "What do you need?"

I tremble. "You."

He flexes his hand, and I exhale another pent-up breath.

"I need *you*."

<h1 style="text-align:center">28</h1>

Skylar

I close my eyes, giving myself ten seconds for this spell to break. Ten seconds to convince myself it's just physical. But I've known it's so much more than that for a while.

"You're such a good man, Pike. I love talking to you on the phone, spending time with you in person, waking up next to you—even going to appointments with you. I love our friendship and our conversations. But I want more than that," I say, trying to calm my racing heart. "I want to make that gorgeous face smile and remind you what happiness feels like. I want to see how you look when you're completely blissed out. I want to touch you and taste you and make you moan. I want to feel you for days."

Pike's pupils blow wide. Amid my nerves, there's also…longing. A deep, unquenchable longing that's heightened to a breaking point.

"But that's not all I want," I continue. "I want coffee in bed, dinners together, visits like this while I'm on the road if you're up for it. And I want texting at night, even if you go to bed at nine. I can adjust. You'll just wake up to a bunch of messages the next day."

Pike laughs, but it's hoarse. His voice is low and intense when he replies. "In Whistler, you said I didn't have to worry about you falling in love."

"I thought you were implying it was a one-night stand, so I beat you to it. I didn't know what to expect afterward, but I was hurt when you stopped, even though you had every right. I said I wouldn't fall in love to keep you from freaking out. But the truth is, I could fall in love with you. And that terrifies me."

"What are you scared of?"

"Fucking it up," I whisper.

His gaze softens. "You couldn't."

"I've never had a good relationship. I'm scared if we put a label on it, it'll stop."

"What will?"

"The good stuff. We could lose what we've built."

I could lose you.

"Come here," he says, gesturing to his lap. "I can't stand right now, but I can't bear not holding you."

I make my way to him on the bench, my body still trembling from my admission. I take a seat on his left thigh, the one that wasn't injured, worried that I'll hurt him with all my weight. But he draws me fully into his lap and slides his arms around my waist so I'm sitting sideways, the way I did when we first kissed in his wheelchair, my thighs resting across his lap and my legs dangling off the side.

"I love your arms," I admit, curling into him more. He smells so good. I run a finger across the tempting skin below his rolled-up sleeve. "Not just your arms. Everything about you. I feel safe when you hold me."

He lifts my chin, his smoky gaze heavy, but beneath it, there's something achingly gentle. "I want to know all the things you hide from everyone else. I'm all in, Skylar." He traces my lower lip with his soft thumb. A shock of pleasure courses through me. "I want to give this a shot."

"I like what we have," I whisper. "If we were together, really together, it could be even better, right?"

"It could be amazing."

"Can we see how it goes? One day at a time?" It's all I know how to offer.

"One day at a time sounds perfect."

He brushes his lips against mine, just breathing me in, barely touching. The soft press of his mouth becomes a gentle torment, drawing out every drop of repressed tension until I think I'll burst if we don't kiss for real.

I lean in, winding my arms around his neck to pull him closer. His mouth curves, catching my bottom lip between his teeth. It's a whisper of a kiss, all restraint and patience, except for his hold tightening just above my hips, betraying how much he wants to lose control. He pulls back a fraction, long enough for me to feel the space between us, then finally claims my mouth.

He kisses me so well I feel it between my legs, and I go soft against him. He tastes like birthday cake and apologies and desire.

Pike's hands shake. Just a little. Just enough for me to feel it where his fingertips brand my skin. But the second my lips part beneath his, he's gone, sinking into the kiss like he's drowning in it.

A low, insistent pull starts somewhere I can't ignore, but there's something else too. Something deeper. For the first time, there's no hesitation. No second-guessing. I didn't realize how much I needed that. This kiss feels different. Important.

He whispers one word against the hollow of my throat. "Stay."

I abandoned any other plan the moment I knocked on his door.

I remove my jacket. Since I made him put on his shirt, it's only fair that I take it back off. Undoing those two damn buttons, I attempt to climb onto the bench, but the slatted wood jabs my kneecap. He bands an arm around my waist, dragging me up his lap until my back is against his chest and I'm facing the shower.

He moves my hair aside and kisses my jaw. "You and me," he says, "are going to be just fine. We'll make our own rules." His thick fingers spread over the back of my neck and sink into the soft waves at my nape.

"Don't tug too hard," I murmur, tensing slightly. Owen hated when I set boundaries because of pain, saying it ruined the spontaneity. But Pike is different, ten times the man Owen ever was, and he simply places a kiss on my sensitive hairline.

"Good. Tell me all those details."

He massages my scalp gently, asking what I like until I fully relax. His lips barely graze my ear with each word, but I'm already fantasizing about them running all over my body.

"Pike?" I say. "I noticed your profile picture before you posted your poem." It feels like falling, admitting that, but Pike's grip around me is strong.

"Yeah?" Intrigue creeps into his husky voice.

"You know you're attractive. You've heard it all before."

"Not from you. I'm always wondering what you're thinking and feeling, what's going on in that beautiful brain of yours."

"My squished brain," I mumble, distracted. His mouth hovers near my neck, but his hand in my hair keeps me from closing the distance.

"It's beautiful," he insists. "Do you still want to touch and taste me?" His voice grows rough. "Feel me for days?"

My pulse quickens. "Desperately."

"And do you want me to do those things to you?"

It's hard to concentrate with his sculpted chest against my back, his stubble on my cheek, and his mouth so close to where I want it. "More than anything."

"My breath alone just made you break out in goose bumps, sweetheart. Imagine what my fingers will do. What my tongue will do."

He nips at my pulse point. I shift in his lap, trying to ease the ache inside me, and his arm tightens around my stomach.

"I've fantasized about making you feel good." The tip of his tongue traces the outer shell of my ear. "Getting you out of your head so you don't have to only think about your pain. You tell me if you want to stop or change anything."

"Don't stop," I beg.

He skims kisses up my neck. "I won't." Muscles ripple against my back as he slips a hand under my crop top. He traces a slow path along the hem, nudging it higher. "You could never mess this up. You know how I know?"

My head falls back. I'm drunk on the drag of his lips across my skin.

"You're incredible," he says, moving the fabric out of his way completely. "Smart. Driven. Generous. Stubborn and sexy as hell. And everything I want."

His thumb glides along my jaw, angling my head back up. The flecks of gold in his eyes turn molten. "And I'm obsessed with this sassy mouth."

He kisses me roughly and cups my breasts. His growl of approval spills into my mouth, and I clutch his thigh, my body pulling tight under every flick and squeeze.

"Pike…"

"I know." He takes my earlobe between his teeth, sucking and nibbling just right. "I feel it too."

"I need you."

"How much?"

I shiver. "So much I'd drop to my knees right here in the shower."

"Soon," he promises. "You'll have all of me soon." He pops the button on my pants and lowers the zipper. "No interruptions this time."

I gasp as the pads of his fingers brush over me with teasingly slow circles that set my skin on fire. His presence consumes me completely.

I love being trapped in his strong arms, left with no choice but to receive whatever he's giving me. He takes his time, touching me leisurely like he could do this forever.

"Please." I squirm in his lap, desperate for more. More friction, more pressure—*more.*

"So impatient," he murmurs. But he doesn't waver, just keeps working me over at the same agonizing pace. Each measured stroke toys with the edge of my control. "I think I like you like this," he says. "Worked up. Needy. Just waiting for me to push you further."

As if to prove his point, he gives my nipple a firm tug between his fingers, the sharp pull sending a zing straight down to my core. I slide my hand down and grip him over his pants, squeezing just enough to make him feel it. His movements momentarily falter. A tortured groan slips from his mouth.

"Skylar," he warns, but he's so hard already, so ready for me, that I can't *not* touch him.

This man is mine now, only mine, and the thought of what's still to come makes a dizzy flash of color burst behind my eyes. I tighten my grip, wanting to see how much I can push him.

That's when Pike finally picks up the pace. He hooks his ankles around mine and spreads me wide for better access, giving me exactly what I need. I press my face into his neck to stifle my moans, but he tilts my chin up to take my mouth in a blistering kiss. My mind goes hazy. Every nerve ending zeroes in on where he's touching me. His heady, wintery scent surrounds me as I spiral higher, higher, climbing toward something vast and uncontrollable, until it peaks with wrenching intensity.

I shatter in his arms, raw and undone. He works me through every last wave with sweet, filthy affirmations until I collapse against him, my body weightless as I come down from the high. A glorious current pulses beneath my skin.

"I could get used to you like this," he murmurs, voice honeyed. "Wrecked and resting right where you belong."

Fuck, I am so gone for him.

"Mind if we move to the bed?" he asks after a while. "My back hurts, and you craning your neck can't be good for your head either."

But when we attempt to stand, neither of us wants to pull away. He moves with me, and we go slow, mouths fused together. Our hands grow clumsy. My top and pants fall to the floor.

When the backs of his knees collide with the mattress, I hesitate. "I don't want to hurt you."

He sits at the foot of the bed and pulls me between his legs. "We're not going to do anything that hurts me. Or you."

I move over him, my knees settling around his hips. He cups my ass and molds me to him. Our kisses turn sloppy, lips missing their marks, but neither of us cares as long as we're connected. I explore the curve of his jaw and lose myself in his sculpted shoulders and chest. Soon he's bare beneath me save for his boxer briefs, his mouth hot and open over my breasts.

I'm desperate for him. I press closer, my nails biting into his shoulders, and roll my hips until he's surging up to meet me.

"*Fuck.*" He forces the word out through clenched teeth, his grip tightening.

My body thrums with a deep ache I can no longer ignore. I slide off him, down to the floor and onto my knees. A trail of hair disappears under the waistband of his boxers, where he's straining against the fabric. My mouth waters as I reach for him.

Pike's next inhale is sharp, his exhale unsteady, but he tugs me back up. "It's your birthday, Skylar, not mine."

"But you've already…" I trail off at the hunger in his eyes.

"Every time I woke up with my head in your lap, I died a little knowing I couldn't strip off your clothes and have breakfast in bed."

My chest flushes with excitement. "But it's been a long day. Your knees must hurt."

"They do," he says. "But my mouth doesn't. Get on the bed, sweetheart. Now."

29

Skylar

Pike's rarely bossy with me, and fuck, it's such a turn-on. I crawl backward. He follows, eyes glazed with want, drinking in the sight of me laid out before him. The bed dips under his weight, and his hands find me the moment he's close enough to touch.

I feel the press of his fingertips as they continue upward, watch his lids grow heavier with every inch they climb. Slowly, his palms shift inward, skimming over skin already alive with sensation.

When he reaches my panties, the breath leaves my lungs, and Pike actually smirks. Holy shit. He loves seeing my reactions, and that gorgeous, assured face guarantees I'm about to have a lot of them. But when he pulls them all the way off, he looks at me like he's the one who gets to unwrap presents tonight.

"Goddess divine," he says, and my heart may actually explode.

He drags his face up my thighs, inhaling deeply, the coarse texture of his scruff electrifying my skin. His mouth finds my center in a long, luxurious lick that leaves me panting his name.

"One taste and I'm fucking done for." He lets out a quiet, stunned laugh, like he can't believe this is happening to him. "Yeah, I live here now. This is my new home."

I slide my fingers through his hair, tugging lightly. His eyes flutter shut, savoring the touch as much as the taste of me.

"I'm yours, Pike. Take what you need."

"I don't think you realize what you're doing to me." He rolls onto his back. "Get up here."

I hesitate when I realize his intent. "Are you sure?"

"Can't articulate the depth to which I've fantasized about burying my face between these thick, luscious thighs."

I'm lightheaded already, so I'm more than okay staying upright. But he teased me earlier, and now it's my turn. Heat courses through my veins as I pause to straddle his hips, then grind down against the hard press of him beneath me. The most incredible moan leaves his lips, and now I'm the one smirking.

I have him. Completely. I shift with more intention, just to drag out another ragged sound. His fingers flex on my thighs like he's barely holding on.

I'm not holding on either. Not even a little. I'm ready to skip the rest of foreplay and strip off the last barrier between us.

Until Pike lifts me up over his face.

I grip the headboard and hover, but he says, "Happy to die like this, Skylar," and pulls me all the way down.

I almost faint from pleasure.

He's—

It's—

"You...do that again," I gasp, already nearing incoherency.

I've always felt self-conscious in this position, but Pike makes me feel desired, even *needed*. He grips my ass like it was made for him and brings me down a little more, guiding me into the rhythm he wants.

"Let me feel all of you," he says. "I've never wanted anyone the way I want you."

Heat licks up my spine, pooling low, spreading through me into something unstoppable. It's a powerful feeling knowing he's enjoy-ing himself, too, that we can do this without causing him more pain.

He groans, the vibration ripping through my body, and I feel it everywhere. A broken sound tears from my throat as my legs shake, and I go taut, my fingers tangling in his hair.

"You like that, don't you?" he says.

"Your mouth, Pike. Oh fuck, your mouth."

He hums against me, smug, then sucks harder. My thighs tremble and my breath comes in sharp, uneven pants. I can't stop it. I don't want to stop it.

He flicks his tongue just right, and I cry out.

"Oh my God, I—I can't, it's too good." Every stroke pulls me under again, drowning me in it.

My head tips back. It's not enough. Nothing is enough. My body is caught between trying to escape the unbearable pleasure and grinding down, chasing more, needing more.

His fingers slip inside me.

"Yes! Right there." The words break from me, frantic, as pleasure claws higher, sharper, and I swear I nearly collapse.

His approving growl rolls through me as his hold tightens, helping me ride his face. There's no up, no down, just his mouth, his fingers, and the fire he's building inside me. His stubble scrapes my skin, a perfect contrast to the devastating pressure of his tongue.

I dissolve into heat and hunger. My pulse pounds thick and insistent, every nerve strung tight, body primed for the next lick, the next touch. It's like he knows every part of me. What I need, how I need it.

I open my mouth in a silent plea.

"Let go for me," he says.

He curls his fingers just right, and I jolt, a wrecked sob breaking from my lips. His tongue flattens against me, and it's too much. It's everything.

"I can't— Pike, I'm gonna—" The tension inside me snaps so fast I almost scream. My entire body clenches, and I finally fall apart, but still, he doesn't stop, doesn't let up, pulling every last tremor from my body, devouring every bit of my pleasure until I'm nothing but a whimpering, trembling mess in his hands.

He gently lifts me off him and lowers me onto my back.

My body melts into the mattress, boneless and oversensitive. His hand smoothing up my stomach is the only thing keeping me tethered to reality.

"That was the best orgasm of my life."

"I'm not finished with you," he says, a low chuckle slipping past his lips, because he knows exactly what he's done to me.

"I'll need two to four business days to recover first."

Another quick laugh, now tinged with something dark. "There's no rush. I'll take my time until you're begging me not to." He kisses his way down my legs again, soothing and sweet, massaging each foot. "In fact, we should probably stay in this bed forever," he murmurs, "just to be safe."

I close my eyes and smile, still buzzing all over. My pulsatile tinnitus thrashes in my ears, matching the frantic rhythm of my heart. My IIH has unwelcome opinions about this position, but I push those thoughts aside, focusing only on the press of his lips as they work their way back up my body.

"I could be good with staying in this bed forever."

"Perfect," he says, trailing his mouth over the curve of my stomach. "Let me give you head, not headaches."

I laugh and reach for him, needing more of his delicious weight. He lowers himself down and brushes a sweaty curl off my face. When we kiss again, it's a perfect mix of sweet and wonderfully dirty. We make out for what feels like hours, hands wandering, fingertips tracing skin like we're mapping new territory, until our breaths grow heavier and Pike's sounds melt into mine.

When he shucks his boxers, I stare.

"No way."

He has a *piercing*.

Of course he has a piercing.

This is Brandon fucking Pike.

A smug smile tilts his mouth. "I promise you'll like it."

I do like piercings, as evidenced by the one in my nose, but it's nothing compared to the barbell through his head.

"It was a dare," he says, "but I realized—" He shudders as I wrap my hand around him. "Realized it made the experience better for everyone involved."

Anticipation makes the ache between my legs unbearable. I drop my face into the crook of his shoulder as I stroke him from base to tip, desperate to get him inside me.

"Do you have condoms?"

"Of course," he says. "You'll never have to ask."

Unexpected tears prick my eyes.

"Hey." He thumbs them away. "Just tell me what you need."

"I need *you*," I say, then move so I'm on top. Small black stars dot my vision for a second, but the throb in my skull lessens a fraction. "When I'm flaring, gravity is my friend."

He rubs my thighs, his mouth parting as his gaze moves to my chest. "Apparently, mine as well."

"Sometimes I black out when things get intense. Before it goes to your ego, let me tell you: That's all me."

He chuckles, but just as quickly, his brow creases. "Wait, what?"

"It doesn't always happen, but it can, with my pressure. Usually, I just get lightheaded. Don't hold back because you're afraid to hurt me."

"We don't have to—"

I put a finger to his lips. "I want to."

"Anything else?"

"Don't dangle my head upside down off the bed."

His abrupt laugh vibrates my body. "Tall demands."

"What about you? What bothers you?"

"I don't think you could do anything to bother me," he says earnestly.

"Stuff bothers me, and I haven't even had major surgeries. There are a million ways to do this."

"A million sounds like a good start."

He sits up, pulling me more firmly into his lap. With nothing left between us, it becomes difficult to concentrate as our bodies press together. I'm sure he can feel my erratic heartbeat, but his arms around me are steady. His quiet strength pours gasoline over the fire kindling inside me.

"Standing up for too long," he says. "I just can't have sex that way anymore."

"A million ways," I remind him. "I couldn't care less if that's one of them."

He kisses me again, sweet at first, but it grows with hunger until the world blurs into insignificance.

He grabs a condom. I push him gently onto his back and lower myself over him, inch by breathtaking inch, until all that remains is sharp-edged bliss. I gasp, my senses pushed into overload.

"Skylar," Pike grits out, holding me still. "Just—stay like this for a second. You feel unreal."

I brace my hands on his chest and give him a moment. The stretch is exquisite. He's so deep inside me his piercing rubs against places I didn't even know existed.

He reaches between us, his thumb working soft, steady magic that turns me liquid until we're both ready to move. Another tortured sigh escapes him when I rock my hips forward. I do it again, and again, until we find the perfect rhythm.

I love learning what he likes. I memorize the bitten-off noises that leave his mouth, the way he drives up into me, how he relishes every desperate sound I let out. His words are full of praise and adoration, but his eyes flicker with a possessive gleam. And his hands. God, those hands. Each touch is more filthy than the next, only intensifying the all-consuming way he fills me.

"Fuck, look at you." He tilts my hips back, watching us move together. "So damn gorgeous, the way you take me."

Pleasure zips up my spine, an unrelenting inferno. It's terrifying how much I want this—how much I want him. But that noise fades away with every slide of skin against skin. I've spent so much time fighting this, trying to control something that was clearly inevitable. Now, all I can think is how grateful I am that neither of us gave up.

When my muscles begin to shake, he takes over, wrapping me in his arms before gently flipping us. "I've got you," he murmurs, kissing my temple.

He props my head up with pillows, making sure I'm comfortable, before taking me in long, unhurried strokes. It's slower, more intimate. My man likes to kiss while he fucks.

"That's it," he breathes, dragging his lips along my jaw. "Just feel me everywhere."

I surrender to him, my body no longer my own as he learns me in real time, adjusting to every reaction. When he finds the perfect angle, he drives into me harder. I struggle to kiss him back, too overcome by the emotions welling up inside me.

"Never gonna get enough of this," Pike says. He cups my face, and I think if I died right now, I'd have no regrets.

He's unraveling every fear I've ever had, one by one. Every kiss, every deliberate snap of his hips, feels like a promise, the start of something I've been waiting for my entire life. I can't believe we've made it here, how every messy, unexpected step led us to this moment. There's no more pretending, no more walls between us, just me and him.

I didn't expect him to feel like home, but here we are, and I can't imagine ever wanting to be anywhere else.

"More," I beg. "I'm getting closer."

He lifts my legs over one shoulder, getting deeper and making me feel a million times fuller. I clench around him, that piercing driving me to ecstasy, and another low moan works from his throat. I want him to feel this, too, as completely and endlessly as I do.

"Don't stop, Pike." My stomach coils tighter. "I need it, need you—"

His thrusts increase until I can do nothing but feel. White-hot pleasure floods my senses. I fist the sheets, my vision fading. He slips a hand between my legs again.

"Eyes on me, sweetheart."

I meet his heated stare and nearly come undone at the bliss written across his face. Half-lidded and lost in euphoria, he can barely keep his eyes open either.

"I want all of you," he says roughly. "All of you is mine."

It's his words that tip me over the edge again. Knowing he wants me for more than this, even on the bad days, is everything.

"I'm yours, Pike. Only yours."

"Skylar." His voice catches on my name, like he's trying to hold back, but his control shatters as he gives in. The rhythm of his hips falters, his body tensing before a ragged, broken shout escapes him. We come together, the world narrowing to only us.

He releases my trembling legs and relaxes on top of me, breathless and sweaty but happy beyond a doubt. *I did that*, I think. We did that. Brandon Pike is happy because of us.

"I don't even have words for that," I say, then laugh because it's so good. When he aims another blissed-out smile at me, I know I'll remember this moment forever.

We kiss as we return to reality, deep, languid kisses interspersed with savoring breaths and whispered affection, neither of us willing to part. Eventually, he curls up with me, our legs stacked and our foreheads pressed together.

I run my fingers through his matted hair. "Were you able to disconnect?" He said he always gets stuck in his head.

"Didn't want to. I've never wanted to be more present." He rubs my back. "Can I get you anything? How's your head?"

A band of pressure has tightened around it, and my vision is still speckled with black, but I'm grateful I can still focus on Pike's addictive scent and the warmth of his arms.

"Can you squeeze my head? That sometimes helps."

I show him how to gently press his large palms on the sides of my head. I'm sure it's different from what he expected, but he squeezes while nuzzling into my neck. Sleep begins to tug at our spent bodies.

"I need to grab my ice from my room," I say. "Plus meds and things I need to sleep. But, Pike?"

"Yeah, sweetheart?"

"I want to wake up together tomorrow."

"Of course." He sweeps a thumb over my swollen lips, kisses the tip of my nose. "I want you in my bed today, tomorrow, and as many days as you'll give me. This is different."

My heart threatens to burst out of my chest.

"For me too."

30

Pike

After sleeping in, we have a slow morning in bed together. We splurge on shitty budget-hotel room service so we can take our meds, putting it on Skylar's work tab even though I'm happy to cover it. Once we're slightly more coherent, my girlfriend pays me back for yesterday by wearing my boxers and tuxedo shirt, only one button closed, no bra.

After I have a second breakfast, Skylar goes down on me in the shower, and I know I'll never look at an accessible bench the same way again.

Now I'm lying with my head on her soft stomach while she brainstorms support group events. My oxy has kicked in, sending a cooling sensation over the burn in my firing nerves. She leans against a stack of pillows, her ice hat covering half her face. Her fingers keep stroking my hair, and every once in a while, I pluck them up to kiss each tip. Each time, she smiles like she has a secret.

"We should do a virtual game show night," she says. "You could be the announcer."

I crack an eye open. "Me?"

"You'd be a natural with that sexy voice."

I give her a low rumble just to see her lips twitch up again. She's so fucking cute. "I wanna play."

"Of course! But if you could read any comments, that'll help my eyes."

"Anything you need."

She beams at me. "Perfect."

I turn on my side and wrap my arms around her waist. "With you, yeah, it will be."

There's a lot of good sex, and then there's too much good sex. I think I finally understand where that line is, and I've blown right past it. My glutes are spasming and my back feels like it's broken.

I wish I could work up the nerve to tell Skylar. She's open with me when she's not in the mood because of her pain, so I'm not sure why I can't admit when my body's too sore. Instead, I'm trying to lean into the natural breaks while she's traveling for fair season.

I'm still having trouble managing spoons. Not just with sex. I'm staying out late, sacrificing sleep, constantly driving to her place, climbing too many stairs, and overexerting myself. I'm slogging my way through work, relying on my wheelchair more often, and some-times I even skip PT knowing I'll need to ice instead of hanging out with Skylar afterward.

I should find a better balance, but I don't want to lose any time with Skylar. Being with her makes me feel like things are good again. Like good is *possible*. It's been too long since I've felt that way.

Tonight, she paces around the kitchen talking on the phone while I wipe down the counter after dinner. Even doing everyday stuff together feels like an overdue exhale when I'm with her.

I finally pinpointed the right emotion. *Happy*. It's a word that hasn't graced the pages of my journal since I started writing. Now, when I do write, there's less about the past, and more about the now, even if it doesn't erase all the bad.

I don't want my pain to overshadow what's happening between us if Skylar's happy too. It's already taken enough from me.

Skylar hangs up the phone. I put down my rag and seriously

consider hiring a cook and a cleaner. Every movement lately is agony. Maybe I should invest in a bathtub while I'm at it. That could be sexy but also soothing for aftercare. It's too bad Skylar can't do saunas…

She throws up her hands. "Mom's mad we're not going to Long Island with them, even though I already explained it's too much for me right now."

"Hey," I say. "Come here."

She joins me where I'm perched on a stool and slides between my legs. I hug her.

"Sorry she continues to disregard your health. Proud of you for sticking up for yourself."

"They could all come here if they want to meet you properly. We've been together officially for a month, and my dad won't even feign interest in you unless I drive six freaking hours. He's too busy planning fishing trips with Devlin."

My ability to remain upbeat dissipates. She never mentions her dad. Mrs. King always shows up alone, reminding me too much of my own mother.

"Have I told you much about my dad?" I ask.

"Just that he left."

I sigh, rubbing a hand over my jaw. I need to get better at sharing. It's hard to talk about, but I want to give myself to her as wholly as she gives herself to me.

"Mom and I traveled for competitions. We'd go away the whole week, and he'd promise to come to my events on weekends. He'd rarely show, but I'd always scan the spectators anyway. Early on, he'd make excuses. He was on the slopes himself and popped in for my run. I just didn't see him, he claimed. Even when I went pro, I still hoped he might show up. Surprise me. But he only ever came to the competitions with substantial prize money. Then, with me high off my win, he'd ask for a share. He'd tell me how hard it was to see me, how he missed me and wished I lived closer. How a little bit of money could help him afford this extra expense."

Skylar strokes my cheek. "I'm so sorry."

"I finally accepted that he only came when he needed something. He has a gambling problem."

"He's an addict?"

I nod. "When I had my accident, he only came to the hospital once. *Once.* When he showed up the day I wheeled out of rehab, I was done with him. He still has the audacity to ask for money."

"You don't deserve that." She kisses me softly.

All the tension in my shoulders releases. I take her face in my hands before she can pull back. I feel every caress of her tongue, every tiny thing she communicates. I realize now that I missed this type of real connection when I was on mindless hookup autopilot.

Skylar's lips find the curve of my jaw. "I have some news."

"Does it involve your mouth?"

"My brain."

I pull back. "What is it?"

"I got an appointment with a neurointerventional radiologist, Dr. Richardson."

"When?"

"June second. It's to redo a lumbar puncture and get my imaging, but then the follow-up is with him on June tenth. Could you drive me on the first?"

"Of course. I'm sorry you have to get another tap, though."

Something buzzes against my inner thigh. Skylar's phone.

"Not another article," I say.

Yesterday we were included in a think piece on inspirational love stories. I know Skylar hates it, which kills me. I assured her it would die down by now.

"No." There's a worried slant to her eyebrows. "Emy's trying so hard to get an hEDS diagnosis, but her doctors keep blowing her off."

The fuck is wrong with all these doctors?

"What if we went to the appointments with her?" I haven't been helpful with Dr. Wharton, but maybe it'll work for Emy.

"Her family goes with her." Skylar worries her lower lip. "And we haven't met in person. Remember?"

"Would meeting them be so bad?"

"No, you don't get it. I want to meet them, but I tend to mess everything up. I don't want to risk messing up these friendships too."

I frown, but I've learned not to push her about this. She didn't want me to set up a double date with Kal and Analia, either, unless Analia suggested it.

A lot of people have left her. I think she's afraid they'll leave her too.

"Would you prefer if I didn't stay over tonight so you can talk to them? Figure out a new strategy for Emy?"

"Would that be okay? We don't usually talk till later, so you and I still have more time."

"Of course. I'll stay another hour, then."

She runs her fingernails down my thighs. "There's a lot we can accomplish in an hour."

Hazy pleasure snakes through me. "Indeed."

She nibbles on my ear, and I'm already half-hard by the time her mouth finds its way back to mine. "You're not too exhausted?"

I'm grateful she's asking, but I want to celebrate her news and not worry about the heavy for a bit. "Not if we take it easy." I slip the corner of her sweater down and kiss the smooth line of her throat. "Besides, I haven't had dessert."

"I can't be horizontal right now, though. My head."

"Do you want to stop?" I ask.

I don't want her to have pain, either, but it's hard sometimes to tell what will help. There was one scary moment when Skylar did black out. I got her ice and water until she recovered. Other times she says sex lessens the pain.

"No," she says, "but I need to stay upright."

"No complaints from me." Skylar on top is my favorite position.

"Ugh, I hate my body right now."

"Unacceptable." I nip the pulse point on her neck. "Your body's a work of art." I swirl my tongue until I pull out that little gasp of hers, the one I'd do anything for.

Next time. I'll tell her next time.

I suck on her tender skin. She straddles my thigh to get closer, and a small shift in my position sends a pinch to my hips. Fuck.

I consider asking to stop, but she reaches a hand between us, and my eyes roll back into my head. Relocating will kill my mood, so I do a quick mental calculation. With my back to consider, there are logistical issues with going at it in a kitchen, but it's a challenge I'm more than willing to accept.

"Here," I say, "get up on the countertop."

Skylar's forehead pinches with concern.

"No worries." I've told her I have hard limits, like standing up. It's never been an issue. I don't need to make my pain one now. But this chair is out of the picture if I don't want her doing all the work.

She climbs up hesitantly. I pull on her legs until her exquisite ass reaches the edge of the counter.

"Pike, what are you—"

"Shh." I undo the buttons on her jeans and tug until she lifts up. A scrap of lace that skims her ample curves sends all my blood rushing south. Why would I ever say no to this? She's everything I want.

When her jeans hit the floor, I kiss my way up the freckles and stretch marks on the inside of her thighs. Every part of her is a masterpiece, and I want her to know it. I spread her wide, and fuck, she's already drenched.

"Look at you," I grit out, my voice nothing but gravel. Every inch of me is tense, throbbing, fighting against the confines of my jeans. "So damn pretty."

She tries to shift beneath me, but I hold her still and watch the way she squirms, already restless, already needy.

I love this too. I can still take care of her without increasing my pain.

Slowly, I nudge the lace aside, making sure she feels every second of it. My breath hovers just close enough to make her beg.

She reaches for me, fingers raking into my hair, trying to pull me to her. Trying to set the pace. "Pike, please."

I smirk, keeping her exactly where I want her—open, waiting, *mine*.

"Relax, sweetheart. Let me ruin you properly."

31

Skylar

T hat's it," Pike says with a happy moan. "Don't stop."

I rub the Voltaren gel more vigorously into the left side of his spine and drop a kiss on his shoulder blade. "It's tough, touching your beautiful back, but it's a sacrifice I'm willing to make."

"I would've asked you to be my girlfriend sooner if I knew you'd get all these hard-to-reach spots."

We're having a slow morning before work. Watching *The Price Is Right* on my sectional is soothing my soul.

After I apply a lidocaine patch to his right back dimple, I unwrap my legs from his waist and get up to wash my hands. My phone pings with another article. I can't help but read the headline aloud as I return to the living room.

" 'Trouble in the Bedroom for Snow Playboy?' "

I laugh at the snow playboy part, but Pike scowls.

"Fuck them," he mutters.

My grin fades. "What's wrong?" He's usually—almost annoyingly—unfazed by anything they write.

"Boo-hoo, Brandon Pike is disabled. Boo-hoo, Brandon Pike can't walk. Boo-hoo, can Brandon Pike still fuck?" His expression darkens. "They wish they were hitting this."

His cockiness catches me off guard. Pike's amazing in bed, the kind of generous lover every woman dreams of finding, but he's always humble about it.

"I'm sure it's trash," I say, reading the subtitle.

Does Brandon Pike's Girlfriend Have Too Many Issues for Him to Handle—Even in Bed?

My heart thumps in my chest. It's like someone's uncovered my deepest insecurities. Pike's been great about all the complaints Owen had, but it's hard to let go of the residual worry I carry with me from that relationship.

The accompanying picture is from the Shred Awards. Pike's laughing with Grace, his hand brushing her wrist, while I sit in the background looking murderous. I recognize my resting pain face, but to everyone else, I must seem like a jealous bitch.

As I read, my pulsatile tinnitus whooshes to an alarming level. My own words, some of which are from over three years ago, leap off the screen.

Skylar King: How do I tell my new boyfriend that orgasming sometimes hurts my head? He doesn't know I have health problems yet.

Skylar King: My hair came out in a clump when my boyfriend tugged on it during sex. Despite explaining it's from my meds, he was super grossed out.

Skylar King: I know, right? How do I tell a guy I sometimes get a headache from farting?

Skylar King: It feels like a pickaxe is cutting out my eyeballs, so I asked my boyfriend if we could skip a party. He said it's boring to stay in all the time and that I'm using pain as an excuse not to meet his friends.

It's all Owen. My sex life. My health.

But everything's framed to make it seem like I'm complaining about Pike. It goes on and on.

Until I get to the next set of screenshots.

Skylar King: The National Association for College Recruiters has this ableist rule that recruiters must stand during fairs. What the actual fuck is wrong with them?

Skylar King: Sometimes I hate my mom. I feel like I'm trapped in a borderline-abusive caregiver situation even though I don't live with her.

Skylar King: I think I'm becoming allergic to underwear. Has anyone else experienced this?

Skylar King: Has anyone else essentially blacklisted all nondisabled people from their lives? If not, how do you stand being around them?

Skylar King: TMI alert. My kidney stones are so bad I've lost bladder control, to the point where I've had to sneak out of work fairs early.

My knees give out.

"Whoa." Pike catches me before I hit the floor and gets me on the couch. "What happened? Your head?"

I point wordlessly at my phone. He sits down and pulls my legs over his thighs, massaging my feet while he reads. "This is so unserious," he says. "Grace and I never…" He trails off, and soon there's only sharp intakes of breath that seem to go on forever.

I want to rip my phone away so he won't see all the embarrassing questions I asked. Every intimate detail I shared. All my problems.

"This is from our group?"

I figured Pike had internet-stalked me like I did him, but I used to post daily. It's a lot to catch up with. Someone clearly went through all my posts to find the most humiliating ones.

"They're not about you," I say quickly.

"Obviously," he says. "I'd be thrilled if you never wore underwear again." But as he keeps reading further, his jaw tightens, and his eyes darken with anger. "They leaked my posts too. Fuck, now everyone knows I take opioids. Hey! They posted my poem!" The indignation in his voice makes me sit up. " 'Commentators believed Pike to be suicidal, including his own mother. Is it possible his girlfriend's problems are too much for him?' " His fists clench. "I can't believe they posted it."

"That's what you're concerned about? People are going to *love* your poem."

"Well, I resent them outing my mental health issues."

His comment stops my anger short. It's the first time Pike has ever truly acknowledged out loud that he struggles with mental wellness. He always skirts over the topic.

"That's not fair of them," I agree. "But they're only speculating about your mental health. They're twisting *my* words to make it seem like I'm the reason for your poem. Like I'm the one making you depressed!"

"You're right. At least my poem doesn't mention bodily functions."

"If you laugh right now—"

"I'm not laughing. I'm going to call my lawyers and have them file a takedown notice. Then I'm going to sue this magazine for violating our privacy."

"How long does that take?"

"I'm not sure. I've never done it before."

I take his hands, finding we're both shaking. His lips brush my cheeks, nose, and forehead, lingering at my mouth before we pull each other into a long hug.

"I'm so sorry," he murmurs. "This is why I didn't think we should go public."

"I didn't realize they'd leak our support group chats! Oh, fuck. I need to talk to the other admins immediately. Someone fake is in our group!"

"Or someone sold us out."

"You have to make a statement. Tell them support groups are for venting. You're allowed to be negative and *get support*."

"Commenting on it publicly will only fan the flames. If we leave it alone, no one will care in ten minutes." He gets to his feet.

"People *will* care." I scramble up after him. "I'm not a hot athlete. I'm the one who'll suffer from all of this."

"I have to go." He tugs on his shirt and shoes faster than I've ever seen. "I'll call my lawyers on the way to work."

"But what about a statement?"

A muscle jumps in his jaw. "It's not a good idea."

"But—"

"It'll make it worse, Skylar. Trust me."

He gives me another kiss, grabs his wide-brimmed baseball cap from my key rack, and leaves without another word.

32

Pike

Brandon?" Mom sounds worried as Ollie whines in the background. "The article's awful. We should talk about how to approach this."

My knuckles turn white against the spinner knob. "That's all you have to say for yourself?"

"What?"

"I expected better from you."

She pauses. "You think I did this?"

"Didn't you?"

"I would never," she stammers. "This is bad for your image."

I struggle to keep my voice calm. "You've pushed me to do publicity stunts since my accident. Even when you first met Skylar, the only time I've ever brought a girl home, you couldn't let it go."

"I don't want you to miss out on opportunities."

"How much money did you get?"

"Brandon, it wasn't me."

But no one else makes sense. "The rest of us in the group actually *have* chronic pain. We wouldn't do that to each other." I snap my fingers. "You had my tablet. Do you have my support group password?"

"Why would I?"

"Skylar removed you from the group. Did you log in with my tablet to get the screenshots? Did you only pretend to like Skylar, thinking I'd tire of her, but when things got serious, you did this so I wouldn't date another disabled person?"

"I like Skylar," she whispers. "I didn't leak the information."

I can't with her. Not anymore. "It's really time for you to get a life. You were so preoccupied with my career that you never did anything for yourself. I knew it. Dad knew it."

I feel like shit the moment I say it.

"This isn't like you." She can't restrain her sob.

I fight down my instinct to comfort her, to change my words so she'll feel better. This level of betrayal is too great. "No, this is exactly like me. You just don't have any idea who I am anymore."

I hang up, then give my lawyers hell. I don't tell them I think it was Mom. I can't sue my own mother.

My phone rings.

"Lennox passed me your latest article," Kal says. "You okay, Pike?"

"I'm fine."

"Saw your poem. Good stuff."

"I'm not talking to you about poetry."

"Well, just a heads-up, the girls are pretty upset. Emy's out for blood."

"This isn't my fault," I growl.

"Pike. Do you think Skylar's posts would've leaked if you weren't famous? You brought her into the spotlight with you."

I hang up on him too. It's not my fault. I'm 99.9 percent sure it's Mom's fault, even if that 0.1 percent uncertainty makes me sick with nausea. Even if she didn't leak the information, I had to fake a relationship because of her. She tried to call the cops on me. Who the hell does that to their grown child?

When I get to work, I can't bring myself to leave the car. I sit in the parking lot for over an hour, my legs refusing to move, and not because of pain. If I feel this shitty, I can't even imagine how Skylar feels.

Called the lawyers, I text. **How are you doing?**

My phone vibrates, but it's not Skylar.

Maria Hammond has sent you a message.

Maria? I click the notification hesitantly.

Hi, Pike. It's been a pleasure having you contribute to our group. Unfortunately, following this morning's exposé, several members feel unsafe sharing. Whoever did this may continue to take screenshots related to you and Skylar. The admins have spoken, and the four of us agree we must remove you both from the group so members feel safe again. Please know we don't blame you. I wish you all the best.

I stare at my phone in horror. We're removed from the group? Skylar only agreed to help me in the first place because she thought I'd mess things up with her group. And now I have.

My anger flares again. Mom ruined everything.

But Kal's voice echoes in my head. *Do you think Skylar's posts would've leaked if you weren't famous?*

And then Skylar's. *I'm the one who'll suffer from all of this.*

They blasted all her personal health details online—things she told me in confidence, things I didn't even know. I video call, but she doesn't answer. I try again.

Pick up, Skylar. Please, please pick up.

Each unanswered call further hollows out my chest. It *is* my fault. Her most vulnerable thoughts blasted on the internet because of her association with me. And now she's lost her group.

I yank out my journal as my eyes prick, unable to stop the bad thoughts. The first time we met Mom, we got into an accident while I was driving. Skylar had a horrible flare because I couldn't get her home safely. I couldn't help her with Dr. Wharton. I forced her into the spotlight. I took her to Whistler and her pressure got worse. I told her the news would stop caring about us.

I'm the worst boyfriend ever. It's all I can write. Skylar deserves the world, and I've just shattered hers.

I tear out the wet page and crumple it. It's a good thing Skylar didn't answer. She doesn't need to see me like this.

She's right; I got off easy with speculation about my mental health. I hate it, but it's still just speculation. Meanwhile, Skylar's entire health history is all over the internet.

I'm so sorry I had to leave, I text. **I'll be back after work. Everything's going to be okay.** I add a bunch of hugging emojis.

I'm already taking care of things with the lawyers. Now, I just need to be strong for her. To hold it together.

I need to be steady. Stable.

That's the only way we're going to get through this without both of us spiraling.

33

Skylar

We'll still talk! Analia says. **We always have our private chat. But half the things we talk about are based on stuff in the group.** As I type, my hands shake. **I'm going to miss out on everything.**

We'll fill you in! ♥ Besides, you have Pike. You're not online every night anymore anyway. ♥

I hate the hearts she sends. She's trying to make me feel better, but I don't like missing out every time I'm with Pike either. And now I've wasted the past two days since the article came out freaking out about what everyone is writing about me.

My conversation with the admins broke me. I saw the messages we received. People are afraid their vents will be made public. Even if their background comments aren't of interest to the press, are they fodder for trolls? Employers?

My employer was interested. I'm on probation now. They'll review my contract once the school year ends. They were already annoyed I took so much sick leave, and now my boss made me take the week off to avoid drawing more attention.

The takedown notice didn't help. The website removed the article, but the damage was done. People posted, blogged, and took screenshots. Someone created a subreddit. They debate which issue Pike should dump me for. (Top contenders? Not giving him enough sex and "being a whiny bitch.")

But it's even more worrying to know one of my doctors could learn what I wrote about *them*. What if Dr. Richardson reads the article and drops me before I even see him? What if Dr. Wharton learns how much I bashed him? He could drop me too. Then I'd have no access to my meds or treatment again.

I wish I hadn't used my full name, I say. **Analia, you were on to something.**

***blush* I have to be careful because I talk about my vagina.**

Emy sends a hug. **i have to go but we'll msg tonight.**

Thank you. I need to be present more than ever now, before Analia and Emy get used to me not being around.

I push away the cold-sweat panic that keeps strangling me, and try to think *proactive*. I could rejoin my group with a fake name, but if I do that, am I any better than whoever did this? I could spend more time in my IIH support group. They're all lovely and helpful, but it's just a Q&A board. No live discussions, no group streaming nights or activities. I could message an admin to organize an event, but with twenty-three thousand members, could I pull it off?

My phone rings, and I grimace. Mom. I've avoided her calls, but if I don't answer soon, she'll come over. We'll have to do this in person.

I pick up.

"Skylar Rebecca King."

I wait.

"I've never been more humiliated in my life."

And there it is.

"My friends have been calling nonstop, thinking I'm a bad mother! That our family is completely dysfunctional!" She continues yelling. I hold the phone away and head to the kitchen, hesitantly putting it back to my ear when I can't hear her anymore.

"I'm sorry," I say. I have to smooth this over. "I know that's hurtful to hear. But I feel like you're centering yourself when—"

"Centering myself! The things I do for you. Pay for. Help you with!"

"You're right. I'm sorry." I hang up and busy myself making tea before I burst into tears.

"Honey, I'm ho-ome."

I shriek.

"Skylar? Are you okay?" Pike rushes into the kitchen with takeout bags as I flop against the countertop.

"Your creepy singsong voice scared me! I thought someone online found my address."

"Sorry, shit." He kisses my temple. "Just me."

I normally melt at his adoring smile, but I want him to be mad like me. But Pike doesn't get mad. He's always fine. Always great. He's told me a million times that this'll blow over. If we ignore it, it'll go away.

"What are you doing here?" It comes out harsher than I intended. He often stops by to bring me dinner, but I wasn't expecting him tonight, and I'm not myself right now. I gesture at my laptop, though I've just been moping. "I'm supposed to get started on work prep for next week."

He holds up two white bags. "I got us Tahou's. Want a Junior Plate?" At my expression, he laughs. "All right. Someone's hungry. Regular plate for you. But I'm not sharing the hots."

"I can't eat any of that." I point to my head.

"What about the patty or fries? You had both in Whistler."

"I was on vacation. Treating myself. Garbage Plates have more sodium than my brain can handle daily."

"Is your pressure up again?"

"It's always up. That's the point." I wince as soon as I've said it. "Sorry. Just got off a bad call with my mom."

"No problem." He takes out the aluminum containers, the

mouthwatering scent of home fries and hot sauce wafting over me. "Have you talked to Emy and Analia today?"

My chest tightens unbearably. "Barely."

"I won't stay long, then." He wolfs down his white hots and attacks the macaroni salad. "You can chat all night."

"It's not the same without the group. I keep clicking on the icon instinctively and then remember I can't see what everyone's posting."

"Maybe you can meet up with them in person now."

"It's not that simple! If they want to meet me, too, why don't they ever suggest it?"

"Maybe they're thinking the same thing."

"Well, I don't want to be the reason my friendships get awkward." It could mess up our dynamic, but I don't know how to explain that to Pike, who doesn't have online friends. The thought gnaws at me, but so does something else. I pivot to the elephant in the room. "Why won't you make a public statement?"

I wish I weren't looking at him. Then I wouldn't see the grimace that twists his lips.

"It's going to make it worse."

"What about a quick post on social media?"

He puts down his fork. "I'm trying to protect you. Engaging with this kind of thing just gives people more to talk about. It's already embarrassing enough, and I don't want it to blow up more. Trust me when I say it's better to move on with our lives and ignore them."

My nausea from earlier returns. *Embarrassing.* Right. He's not the one with his deepest insecurities plastered across the internet for strangers to dissect, and he's certainly not the one whose life has been turned into a spectacle.

The stool squeaks as Pike gets up. His arms ease around me from behind. "This will pass."

I swivel to face him. "Why doesn't all this *bother* you?"

"Of course it bothers me."

"Then why won't you admit that?"

"I don't need random people online to validate my feelings." He doesn't say it, but it feels implied. He's not *me*.

"Not all of us have the luxury of an in-person support system."

The amber specks in his gaze catch the light as his expression softens. "I get that. I don't have anyone besides you either."

"Have you even tried?" I place a hand on his chest, feeling his steady heartbeat, hoping it'll calm me. "You have a supportive roommate who keeps inviting you to meet his disabled friends, and a childhood friend who'll drive an hour out of his way to pick you up. And your mom. She's made a lot of mistakes and has even more to learn, but maybe she could be capable of it if you talked to her earnestly. She seems interested in your life. Your health."

"My *mom*," he scoffs. "Please don't make assumptions about my relationships."

"Is it an assumption to say you're not open with anyone?"

Hurt flashes across his face. "I'm open with you."

"Are you? Because that stuff online? That's one hundred percent me. I'm open about everything. You've seen me at my absolute worst. Throwing up naked on the bathroom floor. Meanwhile you coast along with whatever as long as you can keep up your happy image."

"How am I coasting along? I went after those bastards!"

"Yeah, in *private*." I cross my arms. "But in public, you're receiving condolences for a so-called 'crazy' girlfriend. You'd rather let that slide than admit you have depressive thoughts."

His lips flatten into a line. "I thought you, of all people, would understand. Your mom's ableist too."

"The difference between my mom and yours is that I've told my mom multiple times that what she says hurts me, and she doesn't change. You haven't even *tried* having that conversation."

"I shouldn't have to out myself to anyone."

"No, Pike, you shouldn't. But you should ask yourself why you had to pretend to be in a relationship to avoid being honest with your mom. Because if you don't want to keep feeling ambushed by her, you'll eventually have to say something."

"*You* were the one who pretended to be my girlfriend. *You* messaged my mom."

"Sure," I say. "Blame everything on me. The whole world already does."

"That's not what I meant." He grabs his cane, and for a second, I think he's going to leave.

"Wait, Pike—"

"You want me to be more open? I can do that. I'm not okay about a lot of things, Skylar. This relationship came out of nowhere. I have zero energy anymore. I'm entirely spooned out all the time. My pain has increased tenfold," he says, and it feels like a slap in the face.

I wanted him to be upset, but I didn't expect it to be about us.

"I barely sleep. I skip PT so we can hang out together because your stairs kill me. Even without the media attention, it's been a lot to juggle." He pushes a hand through his hair, fingers gripping briefly, before dragging it down his face. "I didn't know this would all be so much work. Please cut me some slack for trying to stay positive amidst all that. I'm just so fucking *tired*."

"Oh," I whisper as something inside me breaks. "I didn't know it's been so bad for you. I wish you would've said something sooner."

Because this is exactly why I didn't want to be in a relationship in the first place.

"Skylar." He looks up at the ceiling with clear exasperation. "That came out wrong."

"It's okay. We only promised to take this one day at a time. In the end, this is all probably too much for me as well."

"Wait." A note of desperation leaks into his voice. "What are you saying?"

I push to my feet. What *am* I saying? "It's clearly not working."

I run into the living room so he won't see me cry. His cane clunks erratically as he rushes after me, and I choke back another sob. He has pain walking, and I just made him rush.

Our relationship causes him pain.

His arm snags around my waist, gentle but firm. Pulling me back toward his large body until I'm pressed completely against him. He always knows exactly how to touch me. Pike's presence alone can calm me down.

But not now. Not when he's just admitted how bad things are for him.

"I said the wrong thing," he murmurs into my hair. "I'm sorry."

"You said what you were really thinking. I'm sorry you didn't feel safe saying it sooner."

"No! Argh." He tilts my chin up. "Look at me, please."

But it hurts even more to see the misery on Pike's face. I wish more than anything that I could take it away and rewind the last few minutes.

"I know you feel like everything's spiraling out of control," he says. "It'll feel that way for a while, but it'll be okay. You don't have to be in control all the time." He thumbs away a tear. "I've got you."

I sniff. "But you *don't.*"

Pike's face shutters, but how can I let him be there for me when I'm the reason he's miserable?

"Skylar, please don't do this. Relationships are new to me, so I have a steep learning curve. I know I don't do everything right, but I'm working on it." His voice breaks, sending an arrow straight through my chest. "I'll get there if you just give me a chance."

His words are a tiny stitch in the gaping hole that is my heart. They're sweet, but they can't undo what he admitted. I don't want to be the reason he's spooned out. I want him to be happy. Truly happy, not just pretending to be.

"I'm sorry," I choke out. "It's better if it ends here."

He'll understand eventually. Everyone's rooting for us to break up anyway.

"I guess I was hoping you'd tell me I'm at least doing *something* right."

"It's not that," I say. "I...I can't give up my friends for you."

"I would never ask you to."

"All the time we spent together made me miss out on time with them. I already lost my group. If I don't change my priorities, I'm going to lose them as well."

"I said I'd leave early so you could talk to them, but okay." He lets go of me. Backs away. "You do you, sweetheart."

"I will."

"Great."

My heart splits in two.

He turns on his way out. "An observation. You judge me for not sharing everything, but it's easier for you when you never have to face your friends in person. Well, let me tell you something. It's scarier to be open with people you see every day. Even more so to depend on them. But you know that already, don't you? You're just as afraid as I am."

"I stay in control of things so they can't wreck me," I call after him, then crumple in on myself.

Like this just did.

34

Skylar

The music is obnoxiously loud.

But the DJ is amazing, and it's been way too long since I danced all night. I grind against a guy whose hand's been on my hip for three songs. I barely remember what he looks like—my eyes are shut to block out the strobe lights. He was cute. Whatever.

We're tangled in a sweaty mess of bodies in downtown Rochester's newest club. After two Blue Hawaiians, I feel like I'm back in college, before I got sick, when I had in-person friends.

It's been so long since I drank that my body's all tingly. For once, it's probably not the meds. I feel better when I don't drink, but since I feel like shit no matter what, why not enjoy the escape a buzz provides on a Saturday night?

It's been a week since my screenshots leaked, and I've started getting hate mail at work. Turns out some of Pike's fanboys didn't like the boundaries I put up when it came to sex. They think I'm denying one of the greatest athletes ever.

It doesn't matter that those posts weren't even about Pike. One email said I should be grateful someone's willing to fuck my "disgusting, broken body." Another described graphic ways to "stop my whining." And then there are the creepy men with fetishes for disabled women.

I forward every email to Pike.

It's our only contact since we broke up. After receiving the first email, I threw up in the bathroom, then sent him a screenshot to see if his lawyers can pursue any legal action.

Pike said he'd take care of it and to be in touch if I needed help with restraining orders. He also offered his legal team to me personally, even saying they could talk to my employer if needed. Luckily, it hasn't come to that. Yet.

I've stared at my phone all week, hoping Pike's name will pop up for any other reason. I can't stop thinking about him leaving. About how exhausted he was because of our relationship.

I miss him so much it physically hurts. I keep rolling over at night expecting him to be there. Needing his arms around me.

This is why I don't get attached. The more you rely on someone, the more your life stops being your own.

I drown out all those thoughts now. I'm having a great time dancing, and I'm going home with this guy tonight. That'll show everyone. I'm not damaged. I can be easygoing and fun. I can still perform abledness.

Except the music is *really* fucking loud. My head is pounding. The strobe lights burn behind my eyelids. And this guy's grip is really, really tight.

I jerk my thumb in the direction of the bar. He orders us shots, and I accept because it's what healthy women do. They flirt and laugh and don't explain that their head always feels like an overfilled water balloon.

I used to pretend, and I can do it again.

I smile at my companion. I don't remember his name. Zach, maybe. Nice arms. Decent smile. He won't remember my name tomorrow either.

"Why don't we get out of here?" I ask.

His green eyes light up, but maybe that's just the strobes. "My place or yours?"

"Yours."

I sway as I stand. Not sure if it's the alcohol or my head. He takes my hand, and I recoil a little. It's warm and big like Pike's hand. Smoother, though. I follow him out of the club, letting him handle the brunt of the crowd.

Outside, the air is too chilly for this late in May. I rub my arms as he calls for a ride.

"Chilly?" he asks, his body encircling me as he leans us against the wall.

My heart races, but not in a good way. I don't want to stand here holding each other like we're a couple. I just need to get out of here. Then I can feel good again. I can.

"Car's a minute away." Zach angles my chin up and leans down. But as his lips near mine, all I can think of is Pike. The alcohol hums through my veins, dulling the ache, but not enough to keep the wrongness from creeping in.

"No." I turn my head. Push him away. "I don't want this."

I want a kiss that takes up space in my chest and leaves an imprint on my skin. Pike has ruined me for anything less. Why did I think I could go back to how it was before? Why did I believe I could want anyone else?

"Hey," someone says. "Everything okay over here?"

I barely register Zach letting go and another man placing a hand on my shoulder.

"Is this guy bothering you?" he asks.

"No." I brace myself against the wall. "I'm fine."

"You don't look fine."

"Leave me alone!"

His hand leaves my shoulder. "Skylar, it's Kal." He snaps his fingers at Zach. "You. Go away."

Confusion creeps in through my head pain. The guy next to me is indeed blond and blue-eyed, but he's not in sweats holding a sponge for Analia. This look-alike is slimmer in person, wears trendy ripped jeans with a black button-up, and has an unlit joint between his fingers.

"Kalle?" I look around for Analia, but when I only spot a group of guys, I burst into tears.

"It's *Kahl-leh*," he murmurs as I sob into his shirt. "Not *Kahlee*. Oh, never mind." He gestures to his friends. "You guys go ahead."

"Ooh, Kahl-leh," one guy says with an exaggerated accent.

Kalle flips him off and then takes out his phone.

"N-No. Don't tell Pike. Please don't tell Pike."

A pause. "Is there someone else I can call? Lennox—*Analia*?"

I shake my head. I'll talk to her and Emy when I get home. Kalle pockets his joint and steers me toward the sidewalk. If it were any other man, I'd be freaked out. But I get in the Uber with him when it arrives. If Analia and Pike trust him, then I will too.

Another sob escapes, but Kalle stays quiet. He just lets me cry. The minutes stretch like hours until we reach my street. He finally glances over when the car slows.

"So…is it safe to say you and Pike broke up?"

"Analia didn't tell you?"

"There have been…hints."

"And…Pike?" Saying his name stings. "He didn't mention anything?"

"Haven't talked to him since the article came out. I didn't even know he liked writing."

"He keeps to himself."

"Yeah." Kalle tucks his hands into his pockets. "He was always quiet, even as a kid. And now, with the accident…it's a lot of changes. I'm sure it's hard."

I nod.

"Let me walk you to your door."

"It's okay. Thank you."

"I insist." He shoots me a quick wink. "Don't want Lennox telling me I wasn't a gentleman when she finds out about this later, do I?"

I study him as he strolls beside me. It's the first time we've met that I've been able to focus on him. He's more serious than the pictures I've seen of him, but it'd be weird if he were all smiles right now.

"I wonder," he says as we reach my door, "if there might not be a way to reconcile? Whatever Pike might've said, I'm sure he didn't mean it. I know quite a few dipshits. He's not one of them."

"No, he's not." I fumble with my key, and Kal helps, my motor skills off from the mix of medication and alcohol.

Another tear threatens to fall, but I blink it back. I don't know why I ever thought I could fake being okay. I can't escape my problems because I can never escape myself. No matter where I go, my body—and my pain—will always follow.

"Ah. It's not him, then. It's you, and all that?"

"Yes," I say. "Everything I build gets broken."

35

Pike

The door to my room opens.

"Kal's here," Luis says.

"Go away." I keep my face buried in my pillow, but when neither of them leaves, I eventually force myself to roll over. My lower back screams. I needed ice hours ago, but I couldn't bring myself to get out of bed.

Kal lets out a low whistle. "Dude, you have ink all over your face."

"At least it's not a dick drawing," Luis offers.

I self-consciously rub at my cheek as Kal snorts.

"Your hands are covered too."

"Thanks, genius. I've been writing."

"No shit." Kal picks up one of the many discarded journal pages that litter my room. "'Dear Skylar,'" he reads in a mock-lovey voice. I jerk up as fast as my battered body can manage. But it's not fast enough. "Håll om mig! Jag saknar dig!"

"What?" Luis asks as I rip the paper out of Kal's hands. "What does that mean?"

Kal rolls his eyes. "It's Swedish for 'this is an intervention.'"

But it's just a crumpled-up paper with a few lines. Nothing important I actually wrote to her. "I don't need an intervention."

"He hasn't left his room," Luis says, the traitor. "He even canceled physical therapy."

I growl at my roommate. "Do you not run low on spoons as well? I feel like crap."

"Put some clothes on," Kal says briskly. "And meet us outside in ten. We're going out."

I glance down at my boxers. "I'm not—"

"Make it twenty. You need a shower."

I want a beer. More than I've wanted one in two years. And as Kal orders one, I want to be a nosy asshole and ask what his disability is and completely disregard any form of privacy. Whatever it is, he can still drink, and I'm jealous as fuck.

"A Coke," I say flatly, then busy myself with picking out a flatbread pizza. Everything at this microbrewery has mushrooms and kale and goat cheese. Why.

I settle on sweet potato fries.

After our food arrives, Kal leans back in his chair. "Talk," he commands.

He's such a bossy fucker tonight. But under his unwavering gaze, I feel like the pathetic, closed-up person Skylar made me out to be.

I stare at my plate. "Everyone hates Skylar. And it's all my fault."

"It's not," Luis says.

"Kal even said it was."

"Aw, come on." Kal pushes his long hair back. "I just wanted you to take *some* responsibility."

"Skylar's getting hate mail. You have any idea how disgusting people are?" I crush my napkin in my fist. "She forwards me her emails. I can't stop thinking about all the graphic things they wrote."

Luis grimaces. "Understandable. Have you talked to her about anything other than the emails?"

"No." I stab an unappealing orange fry into some nondairy mayo concoction *thing*. Misery washes over me. Skylar would love all this health food. "She said the relationship wasn't working. And maybe she was right."

"At least Skylar ended your drought with women," Kal says. "Plenty of fish in the sea."

Luis raises a skeptical eyebrow over his bacon and butternut squash pizza. "That doesn't matter if Pike's still into Skylar."

"I'm not," I say quickly. "I just feel guilty over the pain I've caused her."

"Great." Kal pulls out his phone. "I know the manager at Sensation. Let me give him a call. I can usually get a booth."

"That new club? I don't feel like going."

"You didn't feel like showering either. That was still good for you. It'll be good for you to meet other women."

"I'm *not* going."

"Why not?"

"I'm not the same person anymore."

"I agree." Kal takes a long pull of his beer. "You're not happy anymore."

"You try breaking most of your body, asshole."

"My point is, you're going to be living in that body for the rest of your life, so you might want to figure out how to be okay with that."

Luis tugs on the brim of his Red Wings baseball cap. "Pike can grieve his situation. His entire life changed in a heartbeat, and he's done a damn good job trying to adjust."

"Thank you," I say.

"But I agree you might want to figure out how to be okay. I read your poem. Seems like a good start."

My neck grows warm. "It's something my therapist suggested." Which I never thought my friends would know.

"Sounds like a good therapist." Luis doesn't seem like he's teasing.

"It helps me get all the noise out of my head," I admit. "Do… either of you go to therapy?"

"Nope," Kal says.

Figures. Kal never has any problems.

"Every Thursday," Luis says, like it's no big deal.

"What Pike needs right now is a different kind of therapy." Kal makes a crude gesture, and my fists curl below the table.

"I don't want to hear any more asinine comments from you about my sex life."

"Come on. Prove to yourself that you can still have a good time without this woman."

"She's not just some woman! She's incredible, and I'd have a better time taking her to a doctor's appointment than hooking up with twenty women at your boring-ass club." I glare at him, but Kal grins like a little shit.

"Thought you were over her."

"I am."

He smacks me in the shoulder. "Quit lying."

"Ow, what the fuck? It doesn't matter whether I'm over her or not. She ended it. It's done."

Kal's eyes narrow. "Why don't you stop bullshitting and finally tell us what happened?"

"She broke up with me. I don't really know what happened. I've filled up my notebook trying to figure it out." I pause. Why can I write so much but never seem to find the right words when I need them most? "She wanted me to make this statement. Something publicly denouncing the article."

"Why didn't you?" Luis asks.

"Because I know what I'm doing with the press. If I fed them anything, it would escalate."

He frowns. "It's already escalated for Skylar, though. If saying something will make her more comfortable, why not do it?"

It sounds simple when he says it like that. "Water under the bridge now."

That's all I feel like saying, but a nagging feeling in the pit of my stomach says I'm supposed to be opening up more. I inhale my Coke, take a deep breath, and do something I haven't done with anyone but Skylar recently.

I share.

I run through it all, including our last argument. I'm on another round of orange fries by the time I'm done.

"So, as you can see," I finish, "I never should have said anything was bothering me. It all went downhill from there."

Luis holds up his hands. "I feel like I'm missing something. You said you listed things that upset you?"

"Yeah." Shame crawls down my spine. "At first, I was trying to be strong for her. Positive. But that pissed her off. She accused me of not being open, so I listed a bunch of things that upset me."

"About how much the leak bothered you?"

"No." I swallow. "About the relationship."

Luis becomes the personification of a question mark GIF. "You were unhappy with Skylar?"

"No. Not her," I explain. "But, like…the stress of it all."

I tell them how overwhelmed I've been since we started dating, and how the article only made things worse. I skip any talk of sex. I didn't even tell Skylar about that.

Kal nurses his beer. "No wonder she was upset."

"I know," I say. "It had all built up and I shouldn't have exploded like that."

The right thing would've been to tell her I was having trouble balancing everything from the beginning. That's on me. Not her.

"No, man," Kal says. "The problem isn't the relationship. It's you not stating your needs."

I scowl. "All that cuddling with Analia make you a psychologist?"

"Why, want a session?"

Luis clears his throat. "Cyrus and I both have disabilities. You think we don't need to communicate about our competing access needs?"

"That's different."

"How?"

I squirm. I can't think of a reason. "I was planning on telling her. But I let my pain slide because I enjoyed being with her too much. She was the best part of my day."

"Did you tell her that?" Luis asks.

I deflate. I didn't. I just threw my problems in her face.

"I know I said the wrong things. And I was trying to be *too* positive, which is what she doesn't like about her mom, and I didn't realize that quickly enough. But maybe she could, I don't know, cut me some slack? I'm working on communicating more effectively. I'm trying."

"Pike." Luis pulls out his phone. "I don't want to risk pushing it after my last crash, so I have to go soon, but you need to see this." He passes the phone to Kal. "Can you read the top two comments aloud?"

"Why can't you?"

"I don't like repeating stuff like that, even if they're not my words."

"'Bitch is a nightmare,'" Kal reads. "'No wonder he wants to kill himself.'" My body goes rigid. It's that fucking subreddit. "Next comment: 'Someone better take away his opioids. I'd OD if I was saddled with a freak like—'"

I rip the phone out of his hand. "I don't need to hear that shit."

"I don't either," Luis says. "But have you noticed the trend? People think Skylar's the reason you're depressed."

"I know," I growl.

"You don't agree with them, right?"

"Of course not."

"She knows you don't agree?"

I scoff. "Of course."

Luis goes quiet. "Are you sure? You told her that specifically?"

I went into damage control mode the second I saw the article. I can think of a hundred things I did to show her that, but did I say it? Specifically?

"I thought suing those bastards made it obvious."

Luis pockets his phone. "To Skylar, it probably feels like the entire world thinks she's not good enough for you. That she's the reason you're unhappy. And then you dumped all your pent-up frustration on her?"

Kal whistles as I absorb Luis's words.

"She thinks I agree?"

Luis lifts his hands. "From where I'm sitting. Maybe."

But she can't think that. I've told her I want to know all of her. I expressed my frustration about the article as soon as I read it.

Except.

Every time she brought it up, I focused on other things. I said everything would pass, which, looking back, could've come across as me dismissing her concerns. *Why doesn't all this* bother *you?*

My fries threaten to come back up. Does she think I'm embarrassed to make a statement because deep down, I believe she's too much, just like everyone else does?

The way Owen likely does?

The way her mother probably does, too?

"Oh, fuck."

My phone vibrates, but it's my dad again. He's been calling me all week.

"Not her," I mutter.

"Any reason it would be?" Luis asks.

"She has this important appointment. I was going to drive her because she needs another spinal tap."

"You should definitely drive her."

"I already asked if she still wanted me to. She said no."

Quick, simple: **No.** No *how are you*. No *thanks for offering*. Just no.

"Surprise her," Luis insists. "Be reliable. Show up anyway."

"I don't know." I want to be there for her. But I also know taking her doesn't fix anything between us.

"Pike, in all seriousness…" Kal rubs his forehead. "You should surprise her and show up. Consider it a grand gesture." His sudden change in tone puts me on high alert.

"What do you know? What did Analia say?"

He stays quiet, though, and only fiddles with the label on his bottle.

I doubt my presence would be welcome. The last thing Skylar needs when she's in pain is to talk about heavy things. I don't even know, after everything, if she'd believe I'm sincere.

But Kal wouldn't encourage me to go if Analia was telling him there's no hope.

"I need advice," I say.

They lean forward, but I need to talk to someone who knows Skylar. I could message Emy and Analia, but this needs a more delicate approach.

"Kal, do you think you could get Analia on the phone for five minutes to hear me out?"

His blue eyes narrow. "Are you going to get me in trouble with her?"

"How would I do that?"

"I can think of a dozen things you could say to make me look like I'm the douchebag enabling your bad ideas."

"Texting her could enable me to run my own intervention when it comes to you and *Lennox*."

"Empty threats," Kal said. "Unfounded. Uncalled-for."

But he's already dialing.

36

Skylar

On the day of my imaging for Dr. Richardson, I rush around, cramming things in my backpack and answering last-minute emails.

I've had three LPs in the last six months, and my back isn't ready for another. My right butt cheek still hurts, and my heel shocks me a couple times a day. But this will hopefully be the last one for a while. Dr. Richardson agreed to a telehealth appointment once he's reviewed my scans and won't make me travel down to Manhattan for another LP.

Mom sends me a message, probably annoyed I'm not already outside. I'm sure the only reason she agreed to drive is so she could yell at me more about the article. Constant invalidation is the last thing I need today, but I can't maneuver between campuses on my own after my procedure.

You should've said Brandon was driving you so I didn't take PTO, she writes.

What? **No, he's not. That's why I need you to drive me.**

He said he was on his way to pick you up.

My pulse skyrockets. I can't deal with my feelings for Pike while I'm already anxious about getting another five-inch needle in my back. **I still need you to drive me. Please tell me you're already in your car.**

I'm at the mall. Text Brandon.

I let out a small scream in my empty living room. It had to be Kalle. That blond bastard told Pike about the club! My tinnitus whooshes unbearably, and I squeeze my ears to stifle the sound, but muffling environmental noise only submerges me in my own screechy head.

The doorbell rings. I don't even have time to text the girls. Why is he here when I told him not to come? Is this his attempt at reconciliation? Could he have regrets?

I'll tell him I don't want to talk about our breakup. I need to make it to my appointment. That's the most important thing right now.

I catch a glimpse of myself in the hallway mirror. Yikes. My hair is piled on top of my head in a frizzy bun born of necessity. Without makeup, the bags under my eyes are a deep, bruised purple, stark against my ashen skin.

I steel my gaze as I throw open the door, but my emotions scramble again immediately.

Because outside my door isn't a hot, disabled ex-snowboarder. It's two women: one tall and skinny, with purple-streaked bangs framing her jawline as they sweep from her inverted bob; the other sits on a rollator and has long raven hair and an all-knowing smirk.

It takes me several heartbeats to process what's happening. In my mind, the girls always look exactly like their profile photos. Not like real human beings here in front of me.

"Hi," Emy says. Her wide grin shows off the cute gap in her front teeth. "We're here to take you to your appointment."

"Pike called Analia," she says. "Personally, I think he should've called me, since we'd communicated before. Analia gets nervous talking to men."

Analia blushes, looking at her sandal-clad feet. "Pike said he didn't want you to have to go with your mom, but he didn't think he was the appropriate person to drive you."

"I'm sorry," I say quickly. "I told him we hadn't met. This is probably such an inconvenience."

"Oh, stop." Emy puts a hand on her hip. "It was a collaborative effort."

"It was?"

"It's high time we met already."

Analia nods. She must be at least five foot ten—I had no idea. "Pike didn't want to force us to meet if we weren't ready."

My heart thrums with nervous, happy anticipation. *Are* we ready?

"We all thought you'd appreciate us being here." Analia keeps her gaze down, her cheeks pink. She's always said she's "autistic and shy," but shyness doesn't present the same way online.

"I appreciate it more than you know," I say. "But why didn't you tell me you were coming?"

She finally looks up, her soft green eyes apologetic. "Pike said you'd say it was inconvenient for us."

"Which is exactly what she did say." Emy can't hide her pointed grin. "Looks like someone understands you better than you think, sweets. Now, are we going to this appointment or not?"

"You're really driving me?" I ask, still unable to believe it. "It's going to take hours."

"No one should be alone when they're sick. We understand that better than anyone."

"And then, if you want," Analia adds, "we'll sleep over so we can take care of you. We won't be offended if that's too much for you."

A lump forms in my throat. "I've been scared we'll mess up our dynamic if we move things offline."

Emy makes an exasperated Italian gesture, pinching her fingers together. "Our friendship is only going to get more epic now."

"I'm a little nervous too," Analia admits. "I'm really awkward in real life."

Emy squishes us to her sides. "I'm so glad Pike had the sense to call. This is way overdue. We talk *every* day. We're going to be just fine."

My eyes spill over, and I hug them tightly. "Thanks for being here. It means the world."

37

Skylar

"That was terrible," Analia says with a shudder. The car jolts as she hangs a right.

I clutch my back in agony. After today's LP, the physician's assistant only allowed fifteen minutes to lie flat, instead of the usual hour to prevent a cerebrospinal fluid leak. I need to reach a different health campus quickly, before my pressure builds up again, in order to make the CT venogram on time and have my veins properly checked.

The last time I had a CSF leak, I needed my own blood injected back into my spine to seal it. Every pothole makes me sweat at the thought of another blood patch.

When we pull up to the hospital, Analia's knuckles turn white. "This is the same building where I get my bladder instillations. My stomach knots up every time I turn this corner."

I put a hand on her shoulder, knowing that dread before an appointment, those familiar streets leading to your personal medical hell.

Analia gets me a wheelchair. "I have to stop in the bathroom as soon as possible."

I hope her interstitial cystitis isn't flaring too much today when she can't be at home. "We can stop now."

"No, I'll hold it until we get there." She pushes me down the many corridors despite my protests. We go slow so Emy can keep up with her rollator.

At radiology, Emy checks me in. My pain is so intense I can barely stay lucid.

"I need to lie down," I gasp.

Emy looks expectantly at the admin. "She needs a bed."

"Once it's her turn, she'll have one."

"She needs one now. She just had a spinal tap."

"She can have a seat in the waiting room. The chairs are soft."

Emy mutters irritably in Italian. Analia pushes me to a corner and excuses herself. I can't keep my head up. The low-pressure headache and post-LP back pain have the room spinning.

I crawl onto the floor and use my sweatshirt as a pillow.

Emy perches cross-legged on her rollator. "I went out with this guy on Tuesday."

My head swims. "Yeah?"

"Shh. You rest. I'll talk."

Emy talks nonstop. I love seeing her online personality come alive right in front of me. She talks with her hands more than I expected, all emotion, and the funny way she describes her night with a Brazilian man she met online makes me laugh despite my pain. She's a shark with men, but her increased pain has kept her from going out lately.

"He already wants more," she says, reading me one of his texts. "But I don't know. Everything gets complicated if you meet a guy a second time. Ginevra tends to turn men off."

It takes me a second to remember Ginevra is her rollator. Emy names all her mobility aids.

"You didn't tell him about your pain?"

"I was having a good day when we met," she says. "I figured, better to wait and see if it goes anywhere. Now he might question if I'm truly disabled since it wasn't visible before."

"Tell him before a second date, then."

Analia's long skirt swishes as she joins me on the floor, one hand clutching her lower stomach. The patchwork fabric is stitched from vintage scarves, and she's paired it with a worn-in tee, the neckline stretched just enough to slip off one shoulder. She's told us she favors flowy fabric when she's in pain, as it makes her feel less constricted. I wish we were meeting in one of our homes instead, where we could each curl up in our preferred pain positions with heat and ice packs and no outside stimulation.

"I can't believe they haven't taken you back yet," she says.

"What do you guys do while you're waiting for appointments?" I ask.

"Talk to my mom," Emy says. "She always takes me."

"Lucky," Analia and I say at the same time.

I turn to her. "Kalle doesn't go with you?"

She fiddles with the mixed metal bangles on her left wrist. "To appointments about my vagina? He'd black out."

Emy's lips tilt into a devilish smirk. "From what you've told us, it sounds like he's quite comfortable with vaginas."

Analia turns into a tomato.

"If I'm not at fairs, I'll go with you," I say, and Analia looks at me gratefully. "I play game show apps while waiting. Pike likes game shows too. Did I mention that? He used to watch them at rehab."

"Sounds like you have a lot in common." Emy raises a suggestive eyebrow.

"You need more in common than *The Price Is Right*."

"Hmm," Analia murmurs, but she changes the subject before I can say anything else.

"So," Emy says.

She and Analia sit at my desk eating homemade Florentine bean soup, the sharp scent of sage filling the room. I lie flat on my stomach in bed with an ice pack on my back—the same position I've been in since we got home twenty-four hours ago.

"We've avoided the topic long enough. I refuse to leave before we talk about Pike."

A different kind of headache creeps in, unrelated to the low-pressure one from my LP. They only know the basics of the breakup. Every time I try to bring up Pike, I close up.

Maybe he was right. I'm also afraid to be open in person.

But these are my best friends. They get me. And even more, they came here to be with me because they love me. I want to be real with them.

I force myself to recount everything in detail. My heart is raw and beaten by the end.

"But after Whistler," Analia says, "he basically moved in when you were sick." She tucks a strand of her hair behind her ear again, her fingers often finding ways to stay occupied. "Why would he suddenly think you're too much now?"

"It could've added up over time."

"He could've paid for a cooking and cleaning service if he was tired of helping you," Analia says, even if I wish it weren't so logical.

I adjust my ice pack. Logical or not, it doesn't matter anymore. "It's over either way."

"He seemed concerned when he called me," she adds.

"He feels guilty. He's a good guy."

"Interesting." Emy scrapes her bowl with a slice of baguette. "He's a good guy, he takes care of you when you're sick, he's breathtakingly gorgeous, he's rich, and he can relate to your pain. What's the problem again, sweets?"

"My employer knows my *bathroom* habits. My mom knows how much I can't stand her. I got kicked out of the group I created. And Pike let me take the fall with the paparazzi. He should've said something."

"Honestly, what was he supposed to say? 'Please stop invading our privacy'? Doesn't every celebrity want that? Has it ever stopped anyone? He's *suing* them."

"I can't really explain it. But it feels like Pike will only stand up for us when he doesn't risk losing face. I think he was afraid of the blowback."

"That's valid. Honestly, for both of you." Analia climbs into bed beside me and curls on her side with the heated electric blanket she brought with her. "We just want to make sure you're leaving him for the right reasons."

"You didn't see the look on his face when he said he was so fucking *tired*. I don't want him worse off because of me."

"It's not because of you," Emy says sharply.

"It still hurts. I thought he was different. Maybe even, you know, the one. I know it's not always easy, but I don't want to convince someone I'm worth being with."

Emy grimaces but joins us on the bed. "We're here if you want to talk more."

Analia nods. "And we don't think you're too much at all."

38

Pike

I connect my Bluetooth in my car. The ache in my sternum intensifies when I see my phone still has zero notifications.

Skylar hasn't reached out except for a quick **Thank you for Emy and Analia**.

Since acknowledging her text, I've picked up my phone a hundred times this week, desperate to know more. I keep typing, **How did your LP go?**

I always delete it. I'd follow it up with: **You've never been the problem. I hate that I made you feel like you were. I want to be with you.** But I'm not telling her that in a text message.

I had a better idea. It involved a lot of prep and a long talk with Jax because I needed all the help I could get. Then there were all the interviews for a publicist. I finally picked one, and if she can spin this in a positive light, I'll keep her on retainer.

Now I'm thinking all of this is too much. Maybe Skylar doesn't want to hear from me.

As I head toward Naples, I press the contact I've been avoiding all week.

Dad answers on the first ring. "Hey, kiddo."

"Dad. You've called me a dozen times. What do you want?"

"Is that how you speak to your old man?"

"What do you want?"

"Brandon, there's something I need to tell you."

Here we go.

"So, I spoke with your mother last week—"

"You don't get to talk to me about Mom. You left her. You left us."

"Are you ever going to forgive me for that?"

I go silent. *Are you ever going to make amends?*

"Right," he says, sounding too much like me when I don't know what to say. "I guess it's for the best you already hate me. After this, you'll never want to speak to me again."

My chest tightens. "How much money do you need?"

"I did something awful." There's a choked sound.

"Are you *crying*?"

I've never seen or heard him cry. Didn't matter how much *I* cried when he left or when I begged him to come back. Now he's upset about whatever thing he needs me to bail him out of again. Fucking figures.

"It was me," he whispers. "A reporter approached me after your exclusive. They wanted more information on Skylar. I-I didn't think it'd get this out of hand."

My grip on the hand brake falters as if I've been hit.

"I needed a few bucks for rent." His voice breaks. "I'm really sorry they smeared your girlfriend. Your mother said she was lovely."

I feel like I'm floating above my body. "You leaked those screenshots?"

"I only told them the name of the group. I never thought they'd post what you wrote. Brandon, I'm sorry."

Of course he wouldn't think that. He never thinks of anyone but himself.

My dad once again chose money over me.

"How did you know the group name?" I demand.

"That night you posted your poem, your mother called me, wondering if I'd heard from you. If I thought you'd been acting strange lately. Hell if I know what you're up to, so I signed up for the group." A ringing fills my ears, drowning out everything around me. "It sounds rough, son, chronic pain. I'm learning a lot. I'm sorry you're depressed."

Is no one safe from their parents in this fucking group? If I were still with Skylar, we'd be having words about those rules.

I hang up, and have to pull to the side of the road.

Mom opens the door.

Ollie runs out, so I scoop her up. "Hey, Olls." She licks my wrist, her tail thumping against my chest. "Sorry I haven't been around. I missed you."

Mom huffs and goes back inside.

I was about to tell her I missed her too. This is the longest we've gone without speaking, and I've made things worse by blaming her for everything and then ignoring her. Son of the Year right here.

I follow her out to the backyard deck. There's a local wine, unopened truffles, and a complex puzzle laid out on the table in front of her hammock.

"Mom..."

"I'm busy enjoying my afternoon, Brandon."

"I'm here to apologize. I shouldn't have said what I did—any of it. The truth is, I wasn't just angry about the article. I was upset with you for other reasons. If you could let me explain, I'd appreciate it."

Mom considers me but doesn't relent.

"I'm flying to New York City on a red-eye and want to make things right before I go."

"What are you doing there?"

"If you let me explain, I'll tell you."

Her eyebrows soften a fraction. "Let me tell my friend to stop by later."

What friend? As she makes the call, I reconsider the truffles and wine. From the way she blushes as she speaks, I'm guessing her friend is a man. A conversation for another day.

She brings out blueberry scones, a sign she's cooling off. She sits in her hammock while I give my legs a rest on the lounger. Ollie's snout nudges my knee, so I lift her into my lap.

"I talked to Dad," I say, but Mom looks unsurprised. "Why didn't you tell me it was him?"

"I only found out after. And you weren't speaking to me, so what was there to say?"

"I'm sorry. Really." I glance down at Ollie, absently running my hand through her fur, then meet Mom's eyes again. "I didn't want to believe you were capable of that, but after what happened with Blake, it made sense. I was wrong to yell at you."

She considers my words while pouring herself some wine. "I'm sorry I didn't consult you about going public with Skylar. I was trying to help, even if I know you don't need me anymore."

"I've always needed you, both personally and professionally. I wouldn't have achieved anything pre- or post-career without your unwavering support and sacrifices. But you have to stop meddling in my life." My chest grows tight. "Tell me honestly. What were you thinking, joining my support group? How did you even find out about it?"

"You were logged in on your tablet one day," she says, fiddling with the cloth napkin in her lap. "I took a picture of the group name. Then I turned on notifications for when you posted. I wanted to know what you needed support for."

"You should've asked me first."

"You would've said no."

"And? That's a boundary you don't get to cross."

"I'm sorry," she says softly. "Even sorrier I called your father."

I grab another scone and break off a corner. "I didn't know you two still kept in touch."

"When you share a child, it's hard to never speak again."

"Yeah, but...you called him that night. I'd never call Dad if I was upset about something."

She sets her wine down too hard. It sloshes but doesn't spill. Her fingers knot in her lap. "It's hard to think about what your son would rationally do if he's about to hurt himself."

I ignore the blood rushing in my ears. This is why I'm here.

"I've never been suicidal. You can't assume how I'm feeling by reading some vent I wrote, especially in a support group meant to be a safe place." I hold up a hand. "Unless it's *actually* a suicide note. If Skylar hadn't stepped in, you could've gotten me put in the emergency psych ward."

She pretended to be my girlfriend so I wouldn't get hurt. It seemed absolutely batshit at the time, but now? It's an honor she wasted her time on me. Have I ever even told her how grateful I am?

Probably not. When I met Skylar, I just wanted to get it over with. If I could redo that lunch now, I'd appreciate every moment. I'd tell her from the start that she already had me then, I just didn't see it. Her swagger. The long curls. Her ability to surprise me. The no-bullshit way she said she'd pepper spray my ass.

I want a redo. No faking. I want to stand up for her the way she stood up for me from day one.

"You weren't opening up to me," Mom says. "I just want you to be okay."

"I didn't feel comfortable opening up. You do things that make me not want to talk to you."

Her shoulders slump. "What are those things?"

"Like the incident with the poem! If I'm open about how I feel, you think I'm going to hurt myself. Like disability is some death sentence. And for it not to be, you need me to inspire people. You make me feel like if I'm not okay, you can't be. You can't put that kind of responsibility on me."

"*Are* you okay?"

"Hardly. This whole paparazzi thing cost me the only romantic relationship that's ever mattered to me."

Her eyes widen.

"Yeah, Skylar broke up with me." I tilt my head back and stare at the sky for a moment, blinking hard. "I don't even blame her. She has enough on her plate without internet trolls."

"But that'll calm down. Didn't you tell her? They won't care after a while."

At least we agree on something. But that's what I'm comfortable with, and Skylar's comfort matters more on this. I should've realized that sooner.

"I don't want to talk about that." I inhale another gulp of much-needed air. "Despite everything, I'm better than I've been in a long time. Being with Skylar helped me start to examine my internalized ableism and, along with it, some of the depression."

I think my depression comes from PTSD I haven't dealt with related to my accident, and all the grief there I struggle to process, but Mom already looks scared at the word *depression*.

"Yes," I say, "*depression*. Mine makes me numb. I ignore my sadness and grief, force apathy, and zombie through life. I tell myself I don't care, but really, I'm afraid to. It hurts to care."

Great. Now Mom's crying. My chest churns with that familiar feeling of wanting to adjust what I'm saying to avoid upsetting her, but I can't anymore.

"You *are* depressed."

I focus on a crack in the deck wood instead of her face. "And there's nothing wrong with that. I'm allowed to process my feelings in a journal and share with a support group. You took that safe space away when you threatened to call the cops."

"I'm so sorry." She comes over and puts a hand on my shoulder. "I know I messed up. I don't know how to fix it."

"Please educate yourself for the future. Talk to a therapist yourself, if you need to."

"I promise I won't make any more assumptions."

"Or give me health advice."

"I—"

"And stop telling me what to do with my job."

"But—"

"No buts. I wanted to stay connected with snowboarding. Do retired football players never watch a game again?"

She shakes her head. Truthfully, I also wanted to force myself out of the house so I wouldn't lie around overthinking, and at least this job was something I knew.

"My worth isn't tied to snowboarding," I say. "That's one thing I'm confident about now, even if it took me time to get there. You need to let go of my worth being tied to a job as well."

"I'm having a hard time with that," she admits. "The job part. But of course I believe you have value without snowboarding. You're a wonderful man with so much to offer, no matter what's going on with your body."

Mom has never said that before, and I didn't know I needed to hear it from her.

I stand to hug her. Her arms tighten around me without hesitation.

"There will be bad moments," I say. "Please trust that I'll be okay despite them. Let me experience whatever I'm going through without having to be fake around you."

Mom's breath is shaky against my neck. "I'll do better."

We still have to talk about how I said she needed to get a life. I handled that horribly. I also need to let her know I'm not going to keep paying her a salary indefinitely either.

For now, I've opened the lines of communication. It's a small thing, but it feels like I've dug myself out of an avalanche.

I hope Mom will take it seriously. I think she will. I think Skylar was right about her.

Ollie lets out a little huff and settles next to us, tail flicking against the wooden deck.

Mom pulls away, her gaze turning sharp. "Now, about you and Skylar—"

"What did I say about meddling?"

"Not meddling! Just wondering."

Well, at least she didn't figure out the relationship started out fake. Some things I'm taking to the grave.

"How do you feel about her now that you've had time apart?" she asks.

"More than words can cover."

My mind drifts to my journal, to the pages I've written. Skylar hasn't just made life bearable. She's made it better—fuller, brighter, like the world shifted back into color the day I met her.

"Skylar reminded me that life doesn't just have to be about survival," I say, no longer afraid to admit it out loud. "She makes plotlines exist beyond the pain."

Mom studies me. "So you'll fight for her?"

I give her a wary look. "Well, for starters, that's why I'm flying to New York City."

39

Skylar

By the time I'm done with my telehealth appointment with Dr. Richardson, my hands are shaking. They always shake when I leave a doctor's office, but it's usually because I feel awful about myself.

This doctor treated me with respect. Listened to me. Answered my questions. Didn't bring up my weight. He also gave me answers. For the first time in five years, answers.

I hurry outside. I'm late to meet the girls for lunch. I knew I'd need support after today's appointment regardless of the outcome, but I never thought we'd be celebrating.

Happy tears spill down my cheeks. I'm so overwhelmed. And there's someone I need to tell before Emy and Analia.

I haven't spoken about anything of substance with Pike since we broke up, but surely medical news is different. One short phone call won't scream, *I miss you so much it hurts.*

I dial his number.

It rings once. Twice. Three—

"Hello?"

My heart stops. I almost forget to breathe.

"Skylar?" His voice is low, deep, and so familiar it makes my stomach twist. "Are you okay?"

"I—uh, yeah." My voice is small, not at all what I intended. "Yeah, I'm fine. Hi."

There's a beat of silence. Neither of us seems to know how to fill it.

"Hi," he repeats, a little softer. I can hear the uncertainty in his voice. "What's going on?"

"I, um . . ." My mouth goes dry. Hearing his voice again sends an ache straight through me. But I swallow that down. "I wanted to thank you for encouraging me and the girls to meet. They were who I needed at the time, and I'm glad you were able to see that. So, thank you."

"Of course. I'm glad it worked out."

"I also have some news. I had my appointment with Dr. Richardson today."

I'm met with another beat of silence. I wish I could tell him this in person and feel the reassuring weight of his arms around me.

"And?" he prompts gently.

"And . . . I was right. I do have stenosis—narrowing of the veins that drain the cerebrospinal fluid from my brain into my bloodstream. And it's severe."

"That's . . . wow. Skylar, that's huge. I mean—" He pauses. "Not that it's good that it's severe, but I'm glad you finally have answers."

"Me too." My voice cracks slightly. "What's more exciting is the stenosis likely isn't caused by my pressure. When they did my LP, they drained my CSF beforehand to see if my veins opened up again or not. They didn't, so Dr. Richardson thinks it's from damage inside the veins—arachnoid granulations."

He's quiet again, and I can almost picture him processing the information. Pike's never one to react impulsively. He thinks things through, tries to see all the angles.

"What does that mean for you?" he finally asks.

"It means if I get stented, it might stop the intracranial hypertension." Saying all this out loud makes it feel even more real.

"That's incredible news."

The tightness in my chest eases just hearing the support in his voice. But the part of me that misses him, that longs for more than just his support as a friend, aches even more. I try to shake it off.

"Thanks, Pike. It's a lot to process. I'm hopeful, but brain surgery is—well, brain surgery, you know?"

"I know," he says softly. "But you don't have to figure it all out today. You've got time to think about it, right?"

I nod, even though he can't see me. "Yeah. I do."

There's another silence, but this time, it's heavier. I can feel the weight of what's not being said between us hanging in the air. We're both avoiding it, and maybe that's for the best. But it's hard not to feel it.

"How," I start, and have to clear my throat. "How are you?"

"I'm actually in New York City with Jax and Grace," Pike says after a moment, and there's scattered chatter behind him.

The idea of him being away—especially with them—takes me by surprise. Are they just catching up, or is there something more? Mostly, I wonder if he can be himself around them now after their conversations in Whistler, or if he's still faking being okay.

"Can I call you when I have more time?" he asks.

"Oh, sorry. I didn't mean to hold you up."

"No, I'm so glad you called. I really want to hear more—if you want to talk, I mean."

"I'd like that," I say, my heart skipping a beat. "I'd like that a lot."

"I should have some time on Friday."

"Friday works."

"Friday it is. And, Skylar?" he says. "You've got this. Whatever you decide."

"Thanks, Pike." I should hang up, but there's one more thing I desperately need to say. "Please don't think you always do the wrong thing, because it's not true. I'm sorry I let you believe that. You do so many things right."

"Skylar…"

"Okay," I whisper. "That's it. Talk to you soon."

We hang up, and I stare at my phone, a mix of emotions swirling inside me. Friday can't come soon enough. But for now, it's enough to know that he's still there, that he still cares.

With a deep breath, I head toward the bagel shop to meet the girls. There's so much to think about. While my mom will see no reason not to get the surgery, Emy and Analia understand that every treatment comes with risks that need to be weighed against the potential benefits.

I can see the trolls laughing at me now. If they thought I was too much before, imagine what they'd say if they heard the words *brain surgery*. Or does this finally put me in another category—the pity category, where they no longer mock your health condition but still despair for your loved ones who put up with it?

I don't want to be in that category either. I just want someone to love me for me.

I start my car.

I love me for me.

And I'll be okay. Somehow.

I find another number on my phone, one that always makes my stomach churn whenever I call it. I attach my Bluetooth and start driving.

The admin takes me off hold when I'm halfway to Bruegger's.

"Hello?" I say. "I'd like to leave a message for Dr. Wharton. Yes, I'm a patient."

I rattle off my name and birth date.

"I see you're due to schedule your two-month follow-up," the admin chirps.

"No, I don't want an appointment. I'd like to leave a message. That referral Dr. Wharton denied me for a CTV? Said I just needed to lose weight to cure my condition? Well, I got the scan. It turns out I have ninety percent bilateral venous sinus stenosis, which is likely causing my intracranial hypertension. My weight has nothing to do with it. In fact, I've had the same narrowing in my veins since Dr. Wharton first did initial scans on me several years ago. He didn't even note that on the report. Please let him know he's fat-shaming and gaslighting his patients. And, also, that I'll be reporting him to the board. Thank you, have a nice day."

40

Skylar

Over a sesame bagel with herbed cream cheese, I tell the girls about stenting. "I've already gone down the medical rabbit hole of cerebral autoregulation and cerebral venous outflow disorders," I say. "There are many success stories with stenting. The possibility of improving my quality of life, even a little, is worth considering. But some people don't get better."

"Rude," Emy says. "I was gunning for the miracle cure."

"Some people do well for a few years before experiencing high-pressure symptoms again," I say, "suggesting compression might not be the only issue. There could be other procedures still down the road. Dr. Richardson said it'll take up to a year to judge results."

"Okay," Analia says. "What else?"

"If the procedure doesn't work, that's one thing, but I'm not a fan of the risks: seizures, strokes, blood clots, hematomas, and brain bleeds. I'd need to be on blood thinners and aspirin long term. Some people develop another vein narrowing after the stent is placed. There's also the risk of persistent head pain from the stent irritating the dura." I look down at my plate, wishing I had easy answers. "And someone in my IIH group died during her procedure, even though it's rare. She was only thirty-five."

"I remember you mentioning that," Analia says. "That's awful. When do you have to decide by?"

"I could get surgery whenever I want, wait list pending, because my stenosis is so severe. I just have to figure out if the risk of not doing it is worse than the risk of the procedure, especially since I've gone into remission before."

After we make a pros and cons list, Analia summarizes, "Here are your choices. One, you get surgery this summer when you're off work, leaving time to recuperate. You won't need sick leave, and hopefully, by next summer, you'll no longer have high pressure."

I blow out a breath. "That's so soon. I'm already on probation. What if I'm not recovered enough by recruitment season?"

Emy counters, "What if they don't renew your contract? You wouldn't have insurance to get the procedure done."

Unease slithers down my spine, but Analia taps her notebook. "Option two is to stick with meds. We know they work for you, but we don't know if surgery will. The longer you wait, the more research there'll be. Downside: no pain control, lots of side effects."

"Definitely fed up with the devil's Tic Tacs," I say.

"But it's the least invasive," Emy says, "and you might go into remission again."

"The meds aren't good to take forever, though. I've already had four kidney stones, they're giving me mouth sores, and I keep getting deep muscle aches—though that could be from IIH. My ringing tinnitus is getting louder because the drug is ototoxic, which can lead to hearing loss, among other long-term effects I'd prefer to avoid."

But it's easier to stop taking a pill if something goes wrong. Unlike a shunt, you can't take a stent back out.

Analia circles option three. "Then you stay on meds for now, but if your symptoms get worse, or side effects increase, you opt for surgery."

Emy sips from her iced tea. "But what if you go blind? Isn't that common?"

"Vision loss can be reversible with surgery if caught in time. As long as I keep up with my eye exams, I should be okay. Dr. Richardson is referring me to a new neuro-ophthalmologist. In my IIH group, many people regained much of their vision within a few months after the surgery, if not all of it."

"All right, then." Emy leans back in her seat. "We wait. See how it goes."

I smile at the *we*. I still can't believe they're sitting here with me. "If I knew there'd be no complications, I'd have surgery tomorrow. I wish fixing one thing didn't open you up to a dozen new problems."

Analia's soft green eyes meet mine. "If you feel you need it, it's okay to take that risk. You don't have to justify it to anyone. And if you're not ready and want to research more or consult other doctors, that's okay too."

"Thank you," I say, my throat growing thick with emotion. "Both of you." I open a memo on my phone. "If you have the spoons, I have one more thing I wanted to discuss."

Analia, especially, looks a bit worn out. She said she might need more space than Emy or me because she's not used to talking a lot in person except with Kalle. She also gets easily overwhelmed from sensory overload.

Emy perks up. "Ooh, did Pike already call you back?"

"No, this is about something different. It's about me not wanting to go back to *only* online friendship."

"I thought we already decided that wasn't happening," Emy says.

"No, that's not what I mean. I had given up on this before— meeting in person, going to dinners, wearing actual clothes that aren't pajamas outside of work. I was fine by myself, as long as I had you two online. Sitting in bed talking to you is probably my favorite activity." I grab their hands across the table. "But having you at my appointment was everything. Having you at my house was everything, even if it was overwhelming to have people there the whole time."

Pike was a big part of this shift too. Our time together made me realize that being around someone in person didn't have to only be emotionally draining. It could be affirming, fun, and even fulfilling. He gave me hope that someday someone would actually choose to be with me, no matter my health.

The truth is, I thought *Pike* might be that someone. But that person would stick up for us as a couple. And I'm not sure if Pike can stand up for himself, let alone us.

"I want to create something for people like me and Analia who don't have supportive families. What the three of us have grown into is unique, but maybe it shouldn't be. I think I want to start a type of care network."

"Like mutual aid?" Emy asks.

"Kind of an offshoot, on a smaller scale, but a bit more like a support group that doesn't only focus on sharing feelings. I want to explore, with other disabled women, how we can support each other in daily tasks. All of us will inevitably have different strengths and different needs. Maybe sometimes it won't work because we'll all be out of spoons, and of course, we'll still talk online. But maybe by getting to know each other, we'll find people in our networks who can fill a need. Like a ride to the hospital. Or picking up groceries. It doesn't need to be labor-intensive help. There's emotional support. Researching. Sharing knowledge. I don't want any of us to feel alone."

"Would it be people from the online support group?" Emy asks.

"I haven't figured out all the details yet. Do you think others would be interested? Would you?"

Analia hesitates. "I'm not sure. I like the idea, but I also like my life the way it is. I'm not a huge fan of change. This"—she gestures at us—"is a big step for me. I'd need time to adjust to another group."

"I like it," Emy says. "But I like being around people."

Analia rests her chin on her fists. "I noticed. Why do you spend so much time online, then?"

She scoffs. "Because of you two dorks, obviously."

"Aww," I tease, but my heart is full.

After we say goodbye, I'm dying to collapse in bed. But there's something else I need to do before I chicken out. Now that I've met Analia and Emy, things can change. I know they'll be there for me in person if I need it. I'll get this care network going too. While I'm building these relationships, it's time to sever another.

When I get to my parents' house, I remain on the front stoop until they join me. Then I take a deep breath.

"I've been tiptoeing around your feelings for five years," I say. "Forcing me to be positive all the time is for your benefit, not mine. I know you're uncomfortable with illness, but that's not my problem. Do some research. Join a support group. Get to know other disabled people."

Mom opens her mouth, but I cut her off.

"It's not my fault I got sick. I'm no longer going to let you treat me like it is. It hurts me every time you speak over me and make me feel unworthy because I haven't gotten a shunt. It's a major, life-changing surgery. Yes, it's helped a lot of IIHers. It's currently not the right option for me. I don't want to hear another word about how I should handle my condition."

Tears streak my cheeks, but it's from relief. I'm no longer trapped with them as my sole support.

"I know my body best," I say. "Not you. So, choose. Either you let me be open about my life—pain included—or I walk away. Either you love me unconditionally, or you get nothing."

Mom's red-faced by the time I'm finished, but I leave before she can say anything. This declaration is long overdue, and I'm completely out of spoons.

"Skylar!" she calls after me.

I don't look back. I'm serious. Even if it hurts, I'm done. If they want back in my life, it's up to them. Letting them make me feel less than worthy hurts more.

And I deserve better.

41

Skylar

By Friday night, I'm desperate for Pike to call already. I had to wake up early this morning for craniosacral therapy, and now, I'm already in bed at eight with my ice hat and kale chips, trying to de-stress.

I'm having annoying dreams about Pike, I admit.

Emy sends expectant "I'm listening" eyes. **sex dreams?**

Future dreams. Like we're old and married. I wake up yearning because it's not real. But how can I change that if he won't call me?

Analia sends a hug. **He said he was away.**

But it's Friday. He said he'd call Friday.

It's not a good sign, she admits. **Maybe his ego's hurt. Kalle said Pike never wanted to break up.**

Oh well, I say quickly. **I've got you two. ♥ What are you up to tonight?**

i actually gotta go, Emy writes. **my brother is making me go to water street to see some rock band he follows on youtube (kill me).**

Kalle's coming over, Analia says. **Sorry! But I'll be on later depending on when he leaves.**

That's okay. I'm relieved they can't see my disappointment. **Have fun, both of you!**

Let us know if Pike calls! Analia says.

They log off. Emy will likely be out late, and Kalle usually occupies big chunks of Analia's time. I'm not jealous. I'm not.

But as I lie in bed trying to entertain myself by making a care network task list, it's hard not to feel like something's missing. Both of my best friends have other things going on in their lives—other people to connect with.

It's me who doesn't have anyone else.

It didn't bother me before, because there wasn't anyone I *wanted* to connect with offline. Good people in my life have been rare. But now that I've been with Pike, I know there are other people besides the girls. One other person, specifically. I don't want just anyone.

I want *him*.

I dial his number. I don't need to wait for him to pluck up the courage to call. I come up with a list of things to say as it rings. *I want to meet up. I need to explain. I may have reacted too hastily. Can we give this another chance? I miss you.*

But he doesn't answer. I hang up before I can embarrass myself with a voicemail.

In the middle of a teary spoonful of cookies and cream, my phone vibrates. Pike!

But it's just a text. **Hey Skylar, sorry I haven't called yet. Could you please put on NBC at 11:30 tonight? Or if that's too late, could you stream tomorrow?**

Eleven thirty on NBC? That's a late-night talk show. **Why? Are you going to be on TV?**

I'm being vague on purpose. I promise it'll all make sense if you watch.

I put down my spoon. **Okay, I'll watch.**

Thanks, Skylar. Talk soon. 🖤🖤

I stare at the hearts he sent, then press the group call button for Analia and Emy.

"I know you're both busy, but something just happened." I fill them in, hope blooming with every word. "What do you think he's doing?"

Analia squeals. "Kalle said there was something he wanted me to watch on TV. It's probably Pike!"

"It can't just be about his career, right?"

"I mean," Analia says, "maybe a change in his career."

Emy says something muffled, probably to her brother, then comes back. "I'm so mad I'm missing this. Send me updates, though. I'm excited to see what he says!"

"Hang on, let me ask Kalle," Analia says. "Is Pike being on TV a good thing?"

Kalle makes an exasperated noise in the background. "I obviously can't say anything."

"But should Skylar *watch*?"

"Wait, are you on the phone with her? Stop trying to trap me, woman!"

There's a muffled screech and a thud. Scuffling ensues, and when Analia returns, she's breathless. "I'll text you again when Pike is on!"

"Is he—"

She's already hung up.

I putter around my apartment for the next three hours, unable to accomplish anything. Five minutes before eleven thirty, the TV's on and I'm vibrating with nervous energy. I'm usually horizontal by now, so I sprawl across my sectional with my ice hat.

The announcer says, "Making his first television appearance in two years, Olympic gold medalist Brandon Pike!" A picture of Pike soaring through the air with his snowboard fills the screen, and I melt into the cushions.

Johnny Clapton's cold open feels endless. After the first commercial break, I sit up when they announce Pike's name. He makes his way out with his black cane, wearing designer jeans and a black zip-up hoodie with RIDE stamped across the front. He adjusts his gray flat-brim beanie before giving the audience a wave.

They are *not* playing "Fight Song" right now, Analia texts.

"Pike!" Johnny exclaims. "We haven't seen you in forever."

"It's good to be back." He leans his cane against his chair. "How's everyone doing tonight?"

The audience cheers.

"New haircut, I see," Johnny comments.

Pike takes off his beanie and runs a hand over his hair with a wink, making the audience scream. Confidence radiates off him in a way I've only ever seen in his videos. Would I have gone through with our arrangement if he'd been this cocky when we first met? He's intimidatingly hot.

"So, how are you doing?"

"I'm doing good." Pike shifts, giving an almost imperceptible jerk of his right foot, but I catch it.

"Liar," I say under my breath. He does that when his sciatica's bothering him.

"The last time we talked was before your accident. Walk me through that moment when you knew you were going to crash."

I recoil at a picture of Pike sprawled out in the superpipe, his body bent at unnatural angles.

"It didn't hit me that I was going to crash until it happened. Sometimes you feel it when you take off, like you didn't hit the angle right or rotate enough. But I'd had a solid run, and things were going well."

"I remember watching it. You were so unlucky with your legs."

"I was lucky my pelvis took the brunt of it. If I'd hit my head harder, my brain probably wouldn't have recovered."

Johnny gestures at Pike's cane. "How's recovery going?"

"I was in the hospital a long time, then in a private rehab center learning to walk again. Now, I'm happy if I can walk without pain for even a minute. But I'm working with an amazing trainer who specializes in rehabilitation and fitness for disabled athletes." He makes finger guns at the camera. "Shout out to Ranielle Thompson."

A picture of Pike weightlifting in his wheelchair with a fit Black woman in her early thirties fills the screen. I smile. I haven't met Ranielle, but she sent me exercises for my back after Pike told her about my LP nerve damage.

"Do you think you'll be able to snowboard again?" Johnny asks.

"It's unlikely I'll be returning to the sport. The accident left me permanently disabled with chronic pain, mostly in my back and lower extremities."

"I'm so sorry, man. What's that like?"

Pike looks at the audience. "Anybody got chronic pain? It's a bitch, right?" Everyone laughs, including Johnny. "It's a lot to adjust to. Being disabled presents challenges that nondisabled people don't necessarily face."

"What kind of challenges?"

"Ever tried using a public bathroom with a wheelchair? Why is the toilet paper a mile away from the seat in the accessible stall? Why is there a blue wheelchair symbol in front of one sink, but that sink is identical to the others?"

Johnny laughs again, but so does Pike.

"No, but seriously, accessibility's a huge issue." He gestures at the entrance from which he came. "This set wouldn't be accessible for me if I was using my chair today."

"Don't call the ADA on us now," Johnny jokes.

Pike coughs into his hand. "I can't, Johnny, because the ADA is a law."

I snort as the camera zooms in on Johnny's face, which will likely be a meme by tomorrow.

"Anyway," Pike says, "pain can be tough if it's part of your disability, like it is for me. But the hardest part is how society treats you. How it expects you to perform as a disabled person. That's what I'm learning anyway."

"Perform how?"

"Well, you saw all the crap that got posted about my ex-girlfriend, Skylar, right?"

Johnny falters, and my heart hiccups in my chest.

Oh no, oh no.

This is my doing. I wanted him to make a statement. To stick up for us.

"You mean those chat room posts?" Johnny asks, clearly surprised Pike brought it up.

"Yeah, the screenshots from our support group."

"Wait. *Ex*-girlfriend? You and Skylar broke up?"

To my surprise, there are *aww*s from the audience.

"Thank you." Pike gestures at them. "I'm sad about it too."

The picture of Pike and me kissing in Whistler appears on-screen behind them as Johnny leans forward.

"What happened? You seemed so happy."

"Those screenshots happened," Pike says, "which brings me back to performing. Everyone was excited we were together until some jerk decided to break into our group and leak intimate details about Skylar's health. Who does that? Who actually thinks that's okay?"

Johnny cringes. "Yeah. It was bad."

"The thing is, nondisabled people don't want to hear what it's like to be disabled. The truth is somehow too difficult. Too uncomfortable. You should see some of the responses to Skylar's private posts. People are rude as fuck." He covers his mouth as Johnny winces. "Oops. Well, they're rude anyway. But it illustrates my point. A lot of us have to modulate what we say around nondisabled people because we get the same reactions." He ticks off on his fingers. "You're too negative. You complain too much. You focus too much on your body. You're too much to handle."

The last one stings. I've tried not to look at more comments, but I haven't forgotten how unworthy of Pike everyone deemed me. Still, nothing stung more than Pike's face when he said our relationship was so much work.

"A lot of us get those comments from family and friends already," Pike continues. "Even from strangers on the street. If you don't meet their exact expectation of a disabled person, the judgment rains down. Look at what happened to Skylar. She was considered an acceptable match as long as she performed correctly. Then people had the audacity to say Skylar wasn't good enough for me because of health details that made them uncomfortable."

"People like to gossip. You know how it goes with anything viral."

"This is different. It's like posting someone's medical records. Beyond the invasion of privacy, the whole thing is actually bizarre to me. As if some health details could disqualify her from being good for me? The only difference between Skylar and me is that no one's leaked all *my* health details." Pike scowls into the camera. "Shame on all of you who responded cruelly. Do you think you'll never have a disability? You think you're invincible? I thought I was. Look at me now."

Johnny clears his throat and shuffles his papers. This show is usually lighthearted. I'm so proud of Pike for making him uncomfortable.

Pike drapes an ankle over his knee to open his hip in a subtle stretch. "What people don't get is that none of what Skylar wrote would ever turn me off. I've been with her when she's gotten a spinal tap, seen her in unbearable pain, and held her hair back while she puked. All of that's just part of being intimate with someone." He shifts his legs again. "If you're only interested in a woman when her health is perfect, maybe you should consider that you're actually trash."

The audience cheers. They actually *cheer.*

"And if you're with a partner who acts like you're a burden because of your health, I hope you can get out of that relationship safely."

Ahhh, I write to Analia. Watching him has turned me into a pile of noodles, and I need something to ground myself. Pike isn't just condemning what they did to me, he's calling out *everyone* who pulls this bullshit.

Johnny says, "That's big relationship advice from someone who avoided relationships not too long ago."

"Right." Pike smiles like he has a secret. "I've become a one-woman kind of man. And that woman, for me, is Skylar."

I'M SCREAMING, Analia texts, but I'm too engrossed to reply.

"What are you doing, then, breaking up with her?" Johnny asks.

I clutch my pillow harder.

"Believe me, if it were up to me, I'd be with Skylar right now. But as much as I try, I'm not always the best boyfriend. Still learning the territory there."

Pike is—was—an amazing boyfriend. I'm so mad at myself for making him believe otherwise.

"After those screenshots leaked, I don't think I did a good job of supporting Skylar. I might've given the impression I agreed with some of those commentators. Like being with Skylar is hard work. But that's just me failing to express my feelings. I'm better with words when I write. I get less flustered."

Another chorus of *aww*s goes around the studio, and Pike's neck turns red.

"I've kind of been avoiding her since we broke up—"

"Pike!" Johnny scolds.

"I know, I know. I suck." He holds up a hand, and I half laugh, half cry. "I've been writing a lot to come up with the perfect words. But there aren't any. I filled a whole notebook trying."

He reaches behind his chair and pulls out his reading glasses and a small Moleskine notebook. He licks his thumb to flip the pages, and damn, if that isn't the hottest thing he's ever done.

"Do we get to hear more of your poetry?"

Pike raises an eyebrow over his glasses. "No way, man. That's private. At least, it should be. When my poem was leaked, I was ashamed. Because everything in that poem was real, and the Brandon Pike I presented to the world was the performance. The truth is, chronic pain can be really lonely. It's easier to pretend everything's fine than to admit you have to reshape your entire sense of self. And that you have no idea where to begin."

"That does sound hard," Johnny says.

"I'm trying to learn how to be more honest about my feelings and to speak up when things bother me." He looks straight at the camera. "Having difficult conversations and such."

I gasp, then cover my mouth as if he can hear me. Did he talk to his mom? His friends?

"This notebook is full of my thoughts since we broke up." He flips more pages, like he's trying to find a specific one. "I'm going to give it to Skylar so she can understand how much she means to me."

"Shut up!" I yell at the screen. I get to read more Brandon Pike poetry? I pick up my phone because I can't contain my feelings anymore.

There's another message from Analia. **KALLE IS SCREAMING TOO.**

Johnny is eating this up. "You can't just pull out that notebook like a sexy librarian and expect us to not even hear a stanza. Come on, Pike."

Pike chuckles, but it's nervous. *Come on* indeed! Johnny is right, and not just about Pike looking like a sexy librarian—definitely a look we're going to re-create the next time I see him. There's no way he pulled that notebook out without planning to share something.

"I suppose there's this one line I keep writing again and again." He bends the notebook flat, then flips it over and holds it up.

I squint even though the camera zooms in. There, repeated over and over, are seven simple words:

I'm in love with you, Skylar King.

The audience swoons as much as I do.

Pike said he loves me. On national television.

Pike said he loves me on national television.

"Skylar!" Johnny says, and I jump. "Take the poor man back."

"Screw everyone who thinks Skylar's hard to love." Pike closes the notebook. "She's hard *not* to love. I know because I've tried not to love her since we split up. Not working out real well for me."

My eyes well up. Me neither.

"All right, lover boy, last question before we run out of time. I'm sure everyone's curious what you're up to next, besides wooing Skylar King?"

When the audience finishes shrieking, Pike says, "I'd like to take a new professional direction. Use some of the non-snow-related skills I learned while boarding." He looks at the camera again, like he can see me. "People keep expecting me to start a disability-specific organization, but I'd rather partner with an existing one. I have a lot of privilege compared to most disabled people, and I'd like to use that privilege to lift up more marginalized voices who are already doing the work. I'm still learning a lot, but if you think I could be of use to your cause, please get in touch."

"I'm sure *a lot* of organizations will want to work with you." Johnny shakes Pike's hand. "We wish you and Skylar all the best. Folks, let's give it up one more time for Brandon Pike!"

42

Skylar

I call Pike as soon as the interview ends, but it goes to voicemail.

"Hi," I say, my voice wavering. "I loved the interview. It meant so much. Can we get together as soon as you're back? I'll keep my phone on." I start to hang up, then add, "I miss you, Pike. Every second."

The next morning, I wake to a text.

Just got off the plane. Forgive me for not calling sooner—I wanted to surprise you but should've reassured you. I want to see you too, but I meant what I said about the journal. It's yours.

I grin, still amused by Pike's em dash use. **I'm excited. Let me know when you stop by.**

You mean you haven't found your package yet?

I've never run so fast. Outside my door, I find a brown bag with a single red rose sticking out. Inside, there's a T-shirt with Johnny Clapton's cartoon face and a little black notebook.

The one that says he loves me.

Found it! I text. **I'm sad I missed you. I really need to talk to you.**

We'll have plenty of time to talk afterward. It's important you read it first.

I send him sweating emojis.

It's nothing bad, he says, **but honest. And maybe a little intense. I want you to know me, Skylar. For real.**

I hold the Moleskine to my chest. **This is really personal, and it's not what I meant by being open. I don't want you to feel like I'm sitting in on your therapy sessions.**

Those journals are staying private. He sends a wink. **This one I wrote for you.**

I want him to come over and read his words to me after we've properly made up all day. But it's important to him, so I'll do it.

Give me a call tomorrow if you're done, he says.

I make myself a cup of tea. Hours pass before I eventually get up to stretch my neck, which feels like a rusted hinge. I'm too enraptured by Pike's writing to stay away from the journal for long.

It's not just love poems. There are scribbled thoughts and letters addressed to me. Some nostalgic about things we did together, like when we first confessed our feelings or our trip to Whistler. Others surprising, like his impressions during the fake-dating phase of our relationship. And some are so erotic I blush at the way they're detailed on the page.

My heart hurts when he admits he wasn't overwhelmed by me, but by trying to balance everything at once. He needs to figure out how to manage his energy so he can enjoy our time together without pushing himself too much. I understand the battle against burnout and wish he had confided in me sooner. I always want him to feel comfortable telling me when he needs rest.

I'm initially hesitant to tarnish the journal with my clumsy scrawl, but he asks a lot of questions. Makes great points. I scribble notes in blue ink over his black. Sometimes, I simply draw hearts or highlight beautiful phrases. When he gets down on himself, I leave supportive thoughts. I'm no writer, but I hope it's encouraging.

He says he's kept his old snowboard in a dusty bag in his garage, unsure of what to do with it since his accident. He might want to keep it, after all. Hang it up somewhere he can see it instead. A way to honor everything he accomplished in that phase of his life.

Among the pages are lists outlining hopes, fears, and ideas for things to do if we got back together. He can see us buying a house. Sharing a life together. I don't know if we're ready to live together yet. We have a lot to figure out, especially when it comes to letting go of our old hurts and voicing our needs.

But Pike's main point is what matters. He sees a future with me. I want one with him as well.

When I reach the last page, it's early afternoon, and my eyes are wet.

You told me you always mess things up, he writes. *I think you're wrong. I think the people you relied on left you. I could see that the first day we met.*

I wipe my face on my sleeve.

I don't care about any of those things in the screenshots. My life has only gotten better since I met you. Don't push me away because you're scared. I'm scared too, but I'm not going anywhere. If you want me, I'm here. I love you, Skylar.

I know Pike said to call him tomorrow, but I can't sit here by myself after reading all that.

Safe to say Pike doesn't think I'm too much, I write the girls.

sweets, that boy wrote u a fucking book. if anyone's too much, it's him.

I grab my keys. I'm not waiting anymore.

It's hot when I arrive at Pike's house, another humid, ninety-degree day. I park at the end of the driveway near a late-blooming lilac tree. As soon as I step out, my curls start to frizz and swell, a few strands already sticking to my neck. A car door slams behind me.

"Skylar! Hey, Skylar!"

I shield my eyes as camera flashes go off, making my heart somersault.

"Are you and Pike getting back together?"

Two reporters stand in the cul-de-sac, one with a camera, the other with video equipment. A third man steps out of a white truck.

"Did you read his journal?"

"What did he write?"

I back away slowly, careful not to show my unease. At least I look cute. My favorite color-blocked dress from last season still fits, its braided halter straps flattering my chest and arms. I manage a shaky smile.

They want the conclusion to Pike's story. To our story. I shouldn't engage with them; they almost destroyed us.

But I won't let them.

I head up the ramp. They call after me, and I can't resist. Just as I reach the door, I pull out Pike's notebook. I hold it up for them to see, let them have their photo, and ring the doorbell.

43

Pike

The doorbell rings again, and I groan. My back aches from assembling a hammock with Luis, and my femur has opinions on all this humidity.

"I'll get it this time," Luis offers.

"Nope. Not your problem."

My glutes fire with pain as I head inside. Three reporters have already stopped by. One even followed me to Skylar's this morning. I had to circle a random block three times until a red light cut them off.

My new publicist says they'll go away if I humor them. She issued a statement: I dropped off the journal, and we'll update them with any news.

I throw open the door, but it's not a reporter.

"Skylar?" I say, startled.

She's here. Hugging my journal to her chest. Her freckled shoulders are bare, save for the tiny straps of her sundress, the fabric cinched at her waist before flaring over her tempting hips. Black shades sweep her red curls off her face, and today her hazel eyes are bluer as they drift down to my bare torso, lingering on my V-cuts.

"Brandon," she murmurs, her cheeks flushing. "You're…"

"Shirtless?" I offer.

"Stop smirking."

I grin. "Am I?" I love her looking at me like I'm a cool drink on this hot day.

"You're also sweaty."

"Just installed a hammock."

She blinks twice, registering my words, then manages to tear her hungry gaze from my torso. "You're also about to be half naked in whatever tabloid's camped out." She jerks a thumb over her shoulder.

The reporters. Shit.

I pull Skylar inside, moving too quickly in my rush to shield us. She ends up trapped between me and the door, with only the thin fabric of her dress separating us. My hands beg to be all over those beautiful curves.

But Skylar surprises me.

She hugs me. Tight. Her scent floods my senses. Salted-caramel chocolate. Skylar. Happiness.

"Hi, sweetheart," I murmur, burying my face in her hair.

"Hi," she breathes into my neck. "I missed you so much."

She steps back, and I wish I didn't already have to let her go. I shouldn't have let her go in the first place.

"Will the reporters stay until I leave?" she asks.

"Probably. It's the aftermath of my interview. But unless I go on to compete in another sport, this shouldn't be the norm once they get a conclusion for their stories." I stroke her cheek, loving the way her eyes flutter shut and her breathing steadies.

"I hope not."

"I can still say something to them. Whatever you want." I won't let this be like last time. I'll do what's good for both of us, not just what makes me comfortable. "But my publicist already tried pacifying them."

"Your publicist?"

"Got one ahead of the show. She's making sure we come out of this looking good. That's why I hired her."

"She can't control what people write."

"No, but she can defend us better than I can. She can manage anything you're uncomfortable with. I made sure of it."

Her pretty eyes open again to meet mine. "You did that for me?"

"I'd do anything for you."

Her face glows with a blush of pink. "I'm starting to realize that." She places a hand on my bare chest, sending a jolt to my heart.

I lean in, but she brings the journal up between us. "You're already done?" I ask.

"The moment I got your message, I cleared my day. Brandon... this is the most beautiful gift anyone has ever given me."

I would've settled for any assurance I didn't freak her out. But *beautiful*? If I had better knees, I'd do a backflip off Luis's kitchen table.

"That's the second time you've used my first name."

"Is that okay? It's how you signed your letters. After reading all that, it feels more...you."

"Hell yeah, it's okay. I love my name on your lips."

She beams, and my insides do more happy flips. I want to spend my days earning that smile, knowing I'm the one who put it on her face.

"But we do need to talk." She steps away.

I smooth a palm over my mouth. Talking is good, albeit terrifying. While she says hi to Luis, I duck back inside to towel off and look for a clean shirt to go with my cargo shorts. I settle on the fitted gray T-shirt Skylar borrowed the first time she was in my bed. I grab my cane, which I'm trying to use less around the house, but I've overdone it this week already.

I turn on the ceiling fan as Luis shuts the glass door behind him. "Is it too warm?"

"The breeze and shade are nice." Skylar perches on the edge of the hammock, letting her legs dangle toward me. Her dress rides up, revealing more of her smooth skin. I want to sob when she adjusts it back down.

"You wanted to talk?" I ask as I pull up a chair.

She reaches into her purse. My journal lands in her lap, and for a fleeting moment, I am irrationally jealous of stationery.

"I made some notes," she says.

"So, there are things to discuss?"

The future plans might've been too intense. I want to move in with Skylar, sure, but not *today*. Then there's that one dirty fantasy—either hot or crossing a line. I'm hoping I know Skylar well enough that she'll think the former.

"About living together, yes. But not about being together."

My heart thuds back to life. "No?"

She wrings her hands. "I'm sorry for ending things. It wasn't just the article backlash. I didn't want anyone thinking I was too much for them again."

"Skylar, sweetheart, I can't get *enough* of you."

"I understand that now. I also used Emy and Analia as an excuse because I was upset about the support group and worried about losing the people who've made me feel valued. But you've always made me feel valued."

I cup her face, needing to touch her because my words are failing me again.

"I'm sorry for making you doubt *your* worth," she says. "You mean more to me than I can express. While I love my girls, I also love you."

My breath catches. "You love me?"

"I love you. Very much."

She loves me. I press a kiss to her forehead, relief flooding me.

"You've always been good for me," she says. "I was scared and fell back on old fears. Thank you for seeing through them." She tilts my chin up. "I'm not afraid anymore. If you want me, I'm here."

She's quoting my words back to me.

"Of course I want you," I say. "I will always want you."

"I know I can be difficult. I'm not used to having someone around so much. But I can learn."

I run my hands over her smooth knees. "I'm learning too."

"I never want you to think I don't love you because I need space sometimes due to pain," Skylar says.

"Me neither."

Her hands cover mine, and I realize how much I've needed this reassurance. It's not just me who struggles with burnout. And talking things out, being open, it's not as hard as I thought with the right person.

"But you have to tell me when you're hurting," she says. "Even if we can't fix it, I want to know. You have to tell me what you're really thinking. No bullshit. You can't just say you're happy and great."

"What I'm really thinking is that I am, actually, happier and greater than I've been in a long time, knowing you love me too."

She beams, her smile too pretty for this world, then brushes her fingers through my hair. "I'm sorry you didn't feel safe telling me what was bothering you."

"It wasn't you. It was me. Sounds cliché, but I was scared that admitting my limitations would slow us down and bring back all the sadness I didn't want to feel." It's still difficult to admit that. "But you've had to slow down many times—"

"Every day, Brandon."

"Right. That's never bothered me."

"So why would it bother me?"

"No, you're right."

"And about the sex—"

I take a steadying breath.

"I'm not with you just for orgasms. That's a perk, of course, but I'm with you because of who you are and how you make me feel. Intimacy isn't just sex."

I gently grasp her fingers, the touch anchoring me. "I think I'm still trying to figure out who I am without my old body, and what that means for everything else. That's why I wanted you to read my journal. It'll help me be more open."

"I want your body exactly the way it is, but I also want your mind and heart. *You.*" She passes me the notebook. "My other thoughts aren't as important."

"Skylar." I slide a hand around her neck until my forehead presses to hers, then inhale her sweet scent. "All your thoughts are important. Even the ones you think might scare me off. They won't. I'm in this for the long haul."

"Me too," she says, and I brush my lips against hers until I pull a little sound of impatience from her throat.

I dig my hands into all that thick red hair and capture her mouth with mine. The raw throb deep in my chest fades for the first time in weeks. My body aches, but in a good way. The way it only does around Skylar.

Her tongue meets mine, warm and wanting, while her fingers grasp at my T-shirt, a silent plea. I trail my hands down her beautiful curves and bring her closer, the hammock easily allowing her to hook her legs around my back. She arches into me, a gasp leaving her lips.

I groan with pleasure. I need more of those breathy sounds she makes when she feels good.

She slips her hands under my shirt, nails lightly dragging over my skin. "I would also like to discuss page fifty-seven of your journal."

"What page was that?"

"It involved you, me, and a snowed-in cabin in the Alps."

I break our kiss, but the lusty flush of her cheeks pulls me right back to her mouth. I can't let her go. I'm too obsessed. She's mine. She loves me.

"If it has an outdoor hot tub," she says against my mouth, "I'm down."

Did I not mention the hot tub in my fantasy? What kind of brute am I?

"I think we can negotiate that."

"Brandon," she begs. "Get up here."

I nip at her lips once more before placing her down in the hammock, a vivid image already unfolding in my mind.

But my hips crunch as I get in, and I realize this might not be as easy as I imagined. No matter how hard I try, I can't lie on my side without irritating my bursa. When I move onto my stomach, the rope digs into my kneecaps.

After cursing up a storm—and nearly toppling out—I sprawl onto my back in defeat.

Skylar thinks my predicament is hilarious. But when she tries to move over me herself, she can't gain purchase on this infernal rope either. We sway back and forth, clinging to each other for dear life until we're both doubled over in laughter.

Ah, that laugh. I've missed it.

"Oh my God," she gasps. "All this rocking is giving me motion sickness. Can we nap instead and resume this after dinner?"

"It's a date." I stroke her cheek and close my eyes. "Just wanna be close to you."

She settles on her side and drapes a leg over me, dropping her head to my chest, and damn if I don't love this too.

Epilogue
Skylar

Six Months Later

"Come back to bed," Brandon calls.

"You're going to make me late." I emerge from the closet in faded jeans and a heart-print long-sleeved crew neck sweater. "What do you think?"

His gaze darkens as his eyes roam over me. "I think you're too pretty to be standing all the way over there."

"Seriously, what do you think?" I fiddle with the diamond necklace he got me for my birthday. "I need to look like a cute host who's not trying too hard."

He props himself up on his elbow in bed, drawing my attention to his awe-inspiring torso, where lipstick smudges are still visible on his abs in a trail I know leads further down below the sheets. "Since when do you worry about picking the wrong outfit?"

"Since I'm having people over at my house for the first time in, like, ever. I need to be approachable. You thought I was scary when we met."

"Intimidating, sweetheart. Not scary."

"Same thing."

He rakes a hand through his rumpled hair. His liquid eyes stay on me, still hungry, and the heat behind them curls through me. "You were intimidating because you were effortlessly gorgeous on a day when you had excruciating pain. Now, get back in here."

"Brandon Tyler Pike. The outfit!"

"I'll need to inspect it more closely to give an objective opinion." He tugs on his boxers and gets out of bed. "Let's see."

He cocks his head to the side, then spins me away from him. Before I can turn around, my back is pressed to his muscled chest. His hands run up my thighs.

"Looks good here," he murmurs, greedy fingers sliding to my waist. "Amazing here." He sucks on my earlobe. Shivers race down my spine. "It looks especially good up here."

My body moves against him involuntarily. "Brandon…"

"The outfit is perfect. But it would look even better off you."

I bite my lip to keep from smiling. "You are *insatiable*."

"I haven't seen you in a week. We should make a rule: The day after a work trip, you're solely mine."

"That only works if you want to spend all day in bed."

"Is that even a question?"

"Sleeping *only*. That's all I did yesterday." And all I'll do tomorrow. This week has wiped me out.

"You know I'd be happy only sleeping with you. If you can't keep your hands off me, well, I can hardly be held accountable." He spins me around and cups my cheek. "How are you feeling right now?"

I skim my finger from his chest to his navel. "Insatiable."

He growls and pushes me down on the bed. I sigh contentedly as he cages me between his arms. If I could, I'd stay here all night with him.

But considering how often I cancel plans due to health, I should take advantage of the fact that I *don't* need to cancel tonight. After months of talking online, a few of us from the care network are finally meeting in person. We're discussing how we can support each other during the holidays. I'm planning on hosting a virtual event too.

Except on New Year's. That's the anniversary of when Brandon and I met. He's taking me on a trip to Switzerland.

He moves my sweater off my shoulder, trailing kisses over my skin. My eyes close in contentment. I can't imagine ever getting tired of this.

He's home.

When the urge to have him again grows too strong, I murmur, "I really have to go. I can't be in bed with you when they arrive."

"Okay." He smacks my butt playfully. "Get your cute ass downstairs."

In the kitchen, I grab paper plates and cups. No way I'm doing dishes tonight. The food I pre-ordered—a variety to accommodate dietary needs—is still in the fridge, and I hope it goes with whatever Emy's mom made for the main course.

I put on my ice hat. My head's started bothering me more in the last few weeks, and all signs point to elevated intracranial pressure. There was no papilledema in my recent eye exam, but I scheduled a cerebral venogram with manometry for January before work starts up again. Brandon and I are going to New York City, where Dr. Richardson will snake a catheter into my brain and measure the pressure gradients inside my veins. This will confirm, officially, whether I can get a stent. Sometimes, I found out, the pressure inside the veins doesn't match the presumed severity on the CTV. I need to cover all my bases before proceeding.

"Well." Brandon shuffles into the kitchen, his thick hair sticking up in the front. He's keeping it trimmed at about an inch or two max, and it suits him. "My legs feel like burnt Jell-O."

I wince. "Too much?"

"A little."

"Do you need anything? Ice? Ibuprofen?"

We talked to Ranielle about positions, and she worked out modifications for both of us, but sometimes we still overdo it, especially when we get caught up in the moment. Like today, when we haven't seen each other in a week.

"I'll be okay." He pecks me on the nose.

Since he doesn't pretend to be fine anymore when he's not, I'm mildly reassured. He'll tell me if he needs anything. I love us even more for it. We can trust each other completely with our bodies. Intimacy is what we decide it is, at our own pace, in whatever way makes us both feel good.

"We can take it easy tomorrow," I say. "Cuddle. Maybe watch that new celebrity trivia show."

"Don't you need to rest your eyes?"

"I don't need to keep them open to beat you."

His smile turns smug. "We'll see about that."

"We will," I say, matching his smile. "I'm dying to find out if you're still as good while I'm on my knees in front of you."

The cockiness slips off his face, and he groans, low and needy. I can't stop my evil chuckle, even if I go hot all over again just thinking about my man moaning for me.

But I have to level the playing field somehow. I swear he studies trivia facts in secret just to show me up. It does work in my favor whenever we go to pub trivia nights with Emy, Analia, Kalle, Luis, and Cyrus (or play online if not all of us are up for it). Whoever's on Brandon's team *dominates*.

The doorbell rings, and I let out a small shriek. "You're still here! What am I going to do?"

"Should I hide in the closet?"

"We said no significant others. And you're famous! Some of them are shy."

No paparazzi have followed us in three months. It did die down, like he said it would. Brandon only comes up in the news now when he's helping with a big-name disability fundraiser or doing commentary for a snowboarding competition.

But his notoriety—and my leaked chats—initially made people nervous. I had to explain what his dad did and how he's now in rehab. I don't want Brandon's presence today to make anyone worry about privacy.

"I'm so proud of you." Brandon gathers me in his arms, his cane resting against my back. "You made all this happen."

When we open the door, thankfully, it's just Emy and Analia.

"Hi, Pike," they chorus, then exchange a knowing look with each other.

He inclines his head. "Ladies."

I give him a playful shove. "Get out of here."

"I'm going, I'm going." He gives me one last kiss. "Love you. Don't forget to check out those links I sent you."

"I will," I say. "I love you too. Have fun at Game Night."

After he leaves, Emy raises a suggestive eyebrow. "What kind of links?"

"Not the kind you're thinking about." I might as well tell them. "We talked to a Realtor last week."

"Shut up! You're buying a house?" Emy starts squealing.

"Not exactly. The Realtor said there aren't many accessible houses on the market."

"Wouldn't you have to bid right away, then?" Analia asks.

I shake my head and realize I'm still wearing my ice hat. I smooth down my static curls. "He wants to build a house with the right accommodations. Once we have a clearer sense of what's ideal, we'll think about the next step." I burst into a giddy smile. "But I can't wait for that step!"

I think Brandon will eventually want to move out of Rochester, but for now we're happy having our friends and his family nearby.

"We might rent something in the meantime," I say, "but I'm okay with waiting while we figure out what works best for us. I know Brandon's the person I want to spend the rest of my life with."

There's no deadline when you're with the right person. Whatever my future holds, he'll be in it.

Emy and Analia envelop me in a big hug. I love these women so much. Like Emy predicted, our friendship has only gotten stronger since we started meeting in person alongside our online chats.

A knock sounds at the door.

"Are we ready?" I whisper.

Analia sucks in a deep breath. "Freaking out a little."

Emy takes our hands. "It's going to be great. Trust me."

I straighten my shoulders and open the door.

"Hi," I say. "I'm Skylar."

Acknowledgments

Thank you so much for picking up this book and spending time with these characters. It still feels unreal that it's now out in the world, as it's taken six years for it to go from an idea to a published novel! Along the way, so many people have helped shape it into what it is today.

Like Pike and Skylar, when I became disabled, I had so much to learn about ableism, disability justice, and community. I owe a deep gratitude to disabled elders and advocates such as, but not limited to, Alice Wong, Imani Barbarin, Dawn Gibson, Leah Lakshmi Piepzna-Samarasinha, and Atinuke Abayomi-Paul for always speaking out, sharing knowledge, hosting events, and taking the time to educate so many of us on their own time. I'm also grateful to the disability community online for being a welcoming space, fostering conversations that challenged and deepened my perspective of disability representation in media, and connecting me with others who truly understood. Thank you also to Christine Miserandino for the Spoon Theory, which has given so many people a way to articulate their experience of energy and fatigue.

Niki, thank you for reading and critiquing every single one of my books. When I decided to take a break from the massive 250k novel you were helping me edit to pivot into writing romance, you excitedly brainstormed countless ideas about the *IAIYH* universe with me and read so many different iterations of each one as I figured out this world. (And all my other ones—at this point, I'm not sure

I know how to write a book without you anymore!) Thank you for your friendship.

Sam Farkas, thank you for liking my book during #DVPit, falling in love with Skylar, Pike, and the girls, and giving my career as an author a chance. Your guidance and belief in my writing made this possible—it's hard to believe we finally made it to this point!

My publishing team at Grand Central: Rachael Kelly, I'm grateful to you for recognizing the potential in this book and bringing it on board. And to Jacqueline Young, for taking the reins and guiding it through multiple rounds of revision. I truly appreciate both of your time, effort, and enthusiasm in bringing this book from manuscript to final version. Thank you to Mari C. Okuda, Angelina Krahn, Emily Baker, and Taylor Navis for paying attention to all the small details in order to make the inside of this book so pretty. And to Elizabeth McConaughy-Oliver and Liz Connor for such a lovely cover!

Lish, you were my first online writing friend, and I doubt I would have started writing original stories without your cheerleading. Thanks for sliding into my DMs and demanding I start a Tumblr and AO3.

To everyone who read my fics over a decade ago now, know that I still cherish every kudos, comment, and piece of fan art. Thank you for telling me I had a skill worth putting out there and for supporting me when I said I wanted to switch to original fiction.

Lea, thank you for years of writing friendship, critiques, international Starmix exchanges, and for creating the most beautiful fan art a writer could ever wish for. (Yes, you are a delight!)

Heartfelt thanks to everyone who read this novel, or parts of it, over the last six years and offered invaluable feedback and encouragement, as well as suffered through many long voice messages about it: Aparna Ramen, Niki Amin, Alisha Hillam, Jessica Corra, Katy J. Schroeder, Jennifer Dupuis, Janel Gagnon, Anakarina Vorbeck,

Lillie Lainoff, M. Stevenson, and Elissa Grossell Dickey. *It's All in Your Head* would not be what it is today without your input.

Stacey Parshall Jensen, Aparna Ramen, Sonora Reyes, and Niki Amin, thank you for your thoughtful insights on representation and intersectionality.

Natasha Hanover, Jeni Chappelle, and Heather Kamins, thank you for giving query critiques and feedback on early pages, and to everyone who amplified my pitches during #DVPit and #PitMad—you helped this book find its way!

Lillie, thank you for all your Spoonie writing support and friendship over the years, and for believing early on that *IAIYH* was "the one." It was!

Jen and Katy J., your support through the editing process was unmatched, and I can't express how much I appreciate your willingness to look at so many reworked lines and tweaked paragraphs. I can't wait for your books to be out in the world, and for our eventual Spoonie writing retreats.

There are so many writerly groups that have shaped my journey to becoming an author. Stana, Janelle, Roh, Sarah, Jen, Janine, and the rest of the Arenap writers, thanks for listening to me drone on about so many of my novels and always encouraging me to keep writing. Thank you to the Submission Slog Comrades, Yappers Club, the Covid Cautious Creatives, the Disabled Romance Authors, and the 2026 Debut Group for so many helpful conversations, insights, and support. You've made all of this so much easier, and definitely more enjoyable. And to the MSS, thank you for your friendship through sprinting, querying, and more. You were the first people to hear a snippet of this book, and your excitement made me believe my story was something worth continuing. I still crack up when I think about your responses to Pike's commentary about Skylar and the banana.

I'm very thankful to my parents for instilling in me a deep love of winter sports from the age of two, when they first took me out on the slopes. Though that era ended with my own disability, many of those memories are what made me want to write Pike. Dad, thank you for being excited about my books before they even existed. When I sent out an email about my very first novel idea, you were the only one who responded—complete with a list going through all my points, and "by the way, I also had a dream about your book, so here are another five pages of ideas." I didn't end up using most of them, but it made me feel like this might not be a total waste of time. Mom, you drove me to pick up every single library hold as a kid, allowing me to cultivate a deep passion for books that I would carry throughout my life. Thank you for letting me read whatever I wanted, even if you secretly phoned the library to ensure all those Babysitters Club books didn't actually contain something "weird."

I'm thankful for Dragon Speech Recognition, which let me keep writing when my hands stopped functioning and my eyes made staring at a screen impossible. Our relationship is very much enemies-to-lovers-to-enemies, depending on the day, but I'm holding out for a third-act comeback. Until then, its approach to homophones remains a mystery (or, as it insists, "Mr. E"). All jokes aside, I'm grateful to everyone who has created tools that make writing more accessible, for the writing communities, events, and bookshops that keep disabled people in mind, and the spaces that still make sure high-risk folks like me can be included.

Janel, Kerstin, Tiffany, Tara, Hayley, and everyone in my IIH support groups, thank you for making life a little less hard. Your excitement and encouragement when I shared that I had written two books with IIH representation meant the world.

Thank you to my husband, who was excited about the idea of me becoming an author from the start. Through a decade of trying to get published, you've always believed in me and encouraged me to keep writing, and never minded when I had to interrupt a conversation, movie, or car ride to scribble down an urgent book idea. Penso che ora finalmente sia il momento per te di leggerlo.

Finally, to the Spoonies who shared how much this book made them feel seen and who told me this novel needed to be out in the world: I probably would've given up without your support. Thank you for showing me there's an audience for this type of story. This book is for you.

Visit **GCPClubCar.com** to sign up for the GCP Club Car newsletter, featuring exclusive promotions, info on other Club Car titles, and more.

Reading Group Guide

Discussion Questions

1. This novel blends popular romance tropes—fake dating, only one bed, secret celebrity, injured athlete, reformed rake, hurt/comfort, and more—with disability representation. What are some of your favorite romance tropes? Are there other common romance tropes you'd like to see explored through the lens of chronic illness, pain, mental health, or other disabilities?

2. Skylar's friends from her support group eventually become her found family, stepping in when her biological family doesn't. How did her friendship with Emy and Analia affect the novel's themes of love, support, and belonging? Why do you think the found family trope often resonates deeply with many readers?

3. Pike's snowboarding career is loosely inspired by the early career of legendary professional snowboarder Shaun White. Were you familiar with professional snowboarding or Olympic halfpipe events prior to reading? Have you ever had a passion or skill that shaped such a big part of your identity? Did any aspects of Pike's experience surprise you?

4. How does the novel reflect the real-life struggles of chronically ill and disabled people navigating the healthcare system? In what ways does it explore biases related to perceived gender, body size, and privilege in medical treatment?

5. Why do you think the author decided to alternate perspectives between Skylar and Pike? What do you think the

book might have lost if we saw the book only from Skylar's perspective? Or only from Pike's?

6. After his injury, Pike privately struggles with how to communicate his physical and emotional limits, especially given his past image of athleticism and physicality. How does Pike's internal conflict reflect societal pressures about masculinity and virility, particularly in media? What does Pike's hesitation about vulnerability say about broader cultural attitudes toward men expressing physical or emotional challenges?

7. What were your perceptions about online friendships before reading this book? Did the story change anything about your perspective? Have you personally experienced meaningful connections online, perhaps through support groups, reading groups, or long-distance friendships?

8. Skylar and Pike share moments of deep emotional and physical intimacy throughout the book. How does the book challenge common ideas about intimacy? What do you think makes intimacy feel truly authentic?

9. Pike and Skylar both experience friendships changing or fading after major life events. Have you ever experienced a friendship that shifted due to major changes in your life? How did it affect your understanding of connection and support?

10. Skylar and Pike discuss a lot of stereotypes about disabled people. Have you seen any of those stereotypes represented in media? Which books or shows have authentic representation that you enjoyed?

11. Skylar and Pike each hesitate to reveal parts of themselves as they get to know each other. How does their gradual openness with each other shape their relationship? Have

you ever felt the need to hide or downplay parts of yourself due to fear of rejection, misunderstanding, or judgment?

12. Pike's interview humorously highlights accessibility issues, such as badly designed bathrooms. Did this novel make you think differently about the challenges disabled people face navigating public spaces or social interactions? How could greater awareness of these everyday barriers positively affect relationships and community building?

Sabina Nordqvist

Sabina Nordqvist began writing as a way to distract herself from chronic pain and illness, and before long, she couldn't stop creating imaginary worlds and swoony book boyfriends. When not immersed in her latest project, she's likely doing physical therapy, reading, or searching for answers to her latest mystery symptom. A polyglot with three nationalities, she's spent many years abroad and loves nerding out over intercultural communication and the languages she's picked up along the way. IT'S ALL IN YOUR HEAD is her debut novel.

Get updates and stay in touch:
    www.nordqvistbooks.com
    Instagram @nordqvistbooks
    BlueSky @nordqvistbooks
    Threads @nordqvistbooks
    X @sabinanordqvist